D1393212

KING OF RUIN

SOULLESS EMPIRE BOOK 1

SASHA LEONE
JADE ROWE

Copyright © 2022 by Sasha Leone & Jade Rowe

All rights reserved.

No part of this book may be reproduced in any form or by any electronic or mechanical means, including information storage and retrieval systems, without written permission from the author, except for the use of brief quotations in a book review.

1

"This is a bad idea," I mutter, as if it's not clear enough already. "I should have just stayed home..."

Yet here I am, standing in a seedy alley, waiting to be let into a club I've never heard of when I should be literally anywhere else.

Ahead, my friends crowd and giggle around the bouncer. I get a sinking feeling in my gut. They meant well by inviting me out tonight—this is supposed to help me loosen up after a disastrous week—but they don't know the whole truth.

How could they?

"Come on, Nat, lighten up!"

"Ow!" I yelp, stumbling when my best friend Yelena yanks me forward by the arm. "I'm not going in there!"

"Yes, you are," she fires back. "This is the last night we'll all be together for weeks. Maybe even months. So suck it up, buttercup. You've been working like a dog for too long. It's time to let that pretty hair down and party."

"How long has it been since you took a night off, Natalya?" my other friend Emily asks.

"Yeah," our friend Julia joins in. "Weeks? Months??"

"Not long enough."

"Oh, hush."

I try to roll my eyes in pretend annoyance, but Yelena won't take no for an answer. She tows me over to the giant bouncer standing outside the club door.

"This place looks like a dump," I mumble, wrinkling my nose at the dingy alley. "Listen, I have to work tomorrow. Can't we just—"

"No, we can't *just*," Yelena interrupts. "Now quit complaining and don't let appearances deceive you. Club Silo247 is the biggest, most elite club in town."

"I doubt that." The building in front of us looks more like a burned-out homeless shelter than anything else—and I should know, I've seen my fair share of shelters.

Shit, I quietly sigh, cranking my neck.

Overhead, the glamourous Chicago skyline glimmers; its tall, dark, sleek buildings reach up to the black sky. Just once, I'd like to be in one of those rooms on the top floors looking down on all this grime instead of up from it.

"Here you are."

Beside me, Yelena hands the bouncer a crumpled scrap of paper fished from the bottom of her designer handbag. He nods, then starts turning a variety of heavy-duty locks.

Each click is like a light punch to the gut. There's no going back now. Not unless I turn and run. But when I look down at my heels, I remember how that's not really an option. These old things would snap in a second. There will be no running tonight. I'm trapped.

"Damn it," I mumble, staring over at my friends. Their outfits put mine to shame. I bet I could run for miles in Julia's getup.

And don't get me started on Yelena—as always, she's dressed to the nines, wrapped in one of her own couture creations. Despite her shining elegance, she hardly seems bothered by the filthy alleyway.

Emily, meanwhile, actually looks excited by it all. With a tight little smile, she shrugs her shoulders at me and nods towards the door.

I purse my lips.

She was right. I never get a night off. In theory, this should be fun for all of us. But I'm already uncomfortable, and it's not just because of the dingy alleyway or mean-looking bouncer.

For starters, I'm completely underdressed—not that I had much of a choice. This plain black minidress and these old black shoes are all I own. If this place actually lives up to the hype, then I'll stand out like a sore thumb.

Hell, just standing next to Yelena makes me feel like a beggar in a potato sack. Though, to be fair, I can't imagine anyone inside will be able to hold a candle to the sheer sequined dress that's just barely hanging off her elegant shoulders. Sure, I could hover closer to Emily and Julia, but even they make me look frumpy by comparison.

And that's just the beginning of my issues. There's also the matter of how I'm going to afford anything. Places like this don't hand out free drinks. And if I'm not drinking, what am I doing?

You should be studying or working, a little voice scolds from the back of my mind. *Not out spending money you don't have.*

It's true. I have enough trouble keeping a roof over my head and not passing out at work from lack of food. So, I'll ask myself one more time. Why am I here again?

You know exactly why, that same voice replies. *It's the same reason your friends brought you here in the first place. And it's how you'll get all your drinks paid for. You just don't want to admit it to yourself because you think you're so independent... but how is that working out for you?*

Before I can bite back at my sassy subconscious, the bouncer swings the door aside. A heavy clunk echoes through the alley and deep into my belly. Without a care in the world, Yelena shoots the beefy brute one of her movie-star smiles and slips inside. Emily and Julia follow close behind. I look over my shoulder at the empty alleyway and give in.

"This is a bad idea," I repeat, scurrying in after them all.

An instant later, some motion-activated LED lights blink on over our heads, bathing us in a downpour of tiny strobe lights. I stay glued to Julia's back, half-blind, as we start climbing a narrow concrete stairwell. "Does anyone agree?" I sarcastically ask. But a thumping bass already envelops the walls. Nobody hears me. "... Guess not."

Closing my eyes, I try to picture a page from my "Understanding Architecture" textbook. I come up blank and a knot tightens in my chest. Even with all the studying I've done over the past six months, I feel too exhausted to remember anything. And with the entrance exam this summer, that means trouble... and more restless nights.

The knot deepens.

"Let's go!"

I open my eyes again as Yelena's rally cry pierces the thumping bass. Emily's hands fly up into the sky. Julia twirls. I meet them at the top of the stairs and stop.

Alright, maybe Yelena wasn't lying after all.

The club is *bumping*.

"Come on," Julia says, blindly reaching behind her back to grab my hand. She misses, but I tap at the back of her palm and urge her forward.

"Go ahead," I insist, transfixed by the scene. "I'll catch up."

It's hard to tell whether she hears me or not. Either way, Julia quickly melts into the electric crowd. Emily follows close behind.

A flash of energy tingles through me.

Ahead, loud techno music rocks the walls and vibrates through the floor. Colored spotlights wheel all over the dance floor. Over to the side, a throng of people stand five deep around a giant square-shaped bar. A flurry of bartenders rotate behind the counter trying to serve everyone at once.

The music grips my guts and a lightning bolt of adrenaline races through my veins. The knot in my chest loosens.

Maybe going out wasn't such a bad idea, after all. Hell, this might be exactly what I needed. The music and the sight of so many people dancing and having fun gives me a sudden surge of hope.

I want to go out there and have fun too. I deserve that much, right?

Suddenly, Julia steps out of the swirling mass of bodies. She's already dancing, and we only briefly meet eyes before she vanishes again. Still, her hand reaches out through the hazy air and beckons me forward.

My heart rattles with excitement. It begs to feel alive again.

"Fuck it."

Before I can take my first step forward, though, I feel a hand on my shoulder. It's surprising enough to make me jump, but when I look over, I just see Yelena bobbing her head.

"Don't worry so much!" she yells, leaning into my ear to make herself heard over the noise. "I'll pay for you."

My jaw drops. "Really?"

She shoots me a wild grin. "Yep! You need to let loose, girl. I know things haven't been so easy for you these last few months, but everyone's leaving town tomorrow and we won't be able to party like this until I get back from Milan. Hopefully, I'll come home richer than I could have ever dreamed. Then I can really *treat* you." I blush, but she only grabs my hand and leads me forward. "Now come on! This place will do for now. You have my official permission to enjoy yourself."

Instinct makes me hesitant to let my guard down, but in the end, I can't help but laugh and let Yelena pull me onto the floor. "Yes, Sir, Colonel Drill Sergeant, Sir!"

I snap a fake military salute and she laughs too. "Now drop and give me twenty, Private!"

The music grows louder as we venture into the pulsing crowd. I let the beat carry me. Yelena's smile reaches from ear to ear. I can feel mine stretch too.

Before I know it, we're at the bar. Somehow, Julia and Emily are already there. Emily is yelling orders to the bartender. He places a tray on the counter and starts pouring vodka into a dozen shot glasses.

Before I can ask who they're all for, Emily slides the tray over to Julia, Yelena and me.

"Don't think about it!" she shouts. "Just drink."

She doesn't have to tell me twice. Not anymore. Like old pros, we clank our glasses down then toss them back. A second shot quickly follows. Then we turn our attention to the dance floor.

That's when Yelena hooks her elbow around my neck. "What do you think?" Her voice is filled with a contagious buzz. It's hard not to follow as she points up above the dance floor. "Look at the giant gas mask hanging from the ceiling. They really took the whole nuclear-bunker theme to the next level, huh?"

"It's cool," I admit, my gaze wandering from the gas mask to the secluded mezzanine behind it. "I like it."

Something inside of me twitches. An odd sensation follows the sight of the dark balcony. Compared to the rest of the club, it's so still. So quiet. Part of me wishes I was there instead.

Leaning forward, I feel compelled to get a better look. But it's hard to see anything as the gas mask swings back and forth like a giant pendulum.

Still, for a split second, I swear I recognize a broad silhouette standing deep within the shadows. Before I can focus on it, though, Yelena twirls me around.

"Maybe you'll find yourself a rich sugar daddy while you're here," Emily teases.

I shake my head and return to the moment.

"As if," I snort.

"You could use one." Julia arches one of her penciled eyebrows at my plain black dress and shoots me a mischievous grin. "Maybe he'll buy you some new clothes too."

"Go easy on my girl," Yelena laughs. "I've been trying to hook her up with one of my designs for months, but she's too stubborn. Calls it charity. Well, I call it fashion, baby."

Yelena twirls and I can't help but admire her. She's right. I won't take one of her dresses, not until I can afford one on my own. If I did, then I wouldn't be me anymore. I'd just be cosplaying as someone else. One day, though...

"Better take her up on the offer before Milan poaches her from us," Emily says. "Then we'll never see her again."

"I'm not going anywhere," Yelena smiles. "And if I am, you're all coming with me, *capeesh*?"

"I'll drink to that," Julia says, turning back to the bar. "Another round for us!"

All four of us laugh. Still, when I look toward the dance floor, I can't help but measure myself against everyone else. Unsurprisingly, every girl here is decked out in the most breathtaking outfits. Hell, some even threaten to rival Yelena's original design.

The men, on the other hand, are far more subdued, but I still spot several diamond-encrusted watches in the throng. I would bet good money that most of these suits cost more than my monthly rent.

As expected, I'm the most understated person here.

My insecurity returns as my gaze lingers on some of the men. I'm not interested in a sugar daddy—even if it would be nice to have some extra spending money now and then... or really any money at all left after I exhaust my paychecks on necessities—but why would any of them choose me with all the other options here?

They wouldn't, and that fact both saddens and relaxes me.

I try to hide my inner conflict from my friends as they chat and giggle next to me. There's one thing I'm good at. Keeping secrets. They don't even know the full extent of my financial woes, and I'm not about to let them in on my shameful little secret.

Telling them about my broken laptop was enough. They know I had to dip into my savings to fix it. They just don't know that my savings are now non-existent. And they never will.

Twisting back to the bar, I grab another shot and down it, no chaser. Then I force a smile and try to listen in on the conversation my friends are having. The music is loud, but I can hear bits and pieces.

"Him..."

"... No, wait... him!"

God, are they already trying to find someone to set me up with? I'm not ready. Another shot doesn't fix my confidence issues, but the bitterness does help wake me up a bit more.

That's when I feel it. My phone. It buzzes violently in my bag.

"Shit," I groan, taking it out. "Not again!"

"What's up?" Yelena asks, sliding over to my side.

"My phone is almost out of juice," I sulk.

"Why didn't you charge it up before you came?" Emily asks.

I pretend not to hear. They don't need to know how I've gotten in the habit of charging my phone and laptop at work so I don't have to use power at home.

I hold out the phone to Yelena. "You have a portable charger in your bag, right? Could you plug it in?"

With a decisive nod, she pulls out a slim power bank and plugs my phone into it. Then she shoves everything back into her bag.

"All good?" she asks.

"Yeah, thank you."

"My pleasure. Now, you behave. I need to visit the little girl's room."

"Me too!" Emily joins in. "I'll go with you."

Those two disappear as Julia tries to wave down a bartender. I'm about to join her when someone bumps into me from behind. I stumble before catching myself on the counter.

"Hey, watch out," I mumble, turning around.

I'm greeted by a small group of guys. They stand too close for comfort. I blink in confusion as the nearest one shoots me a grin and juts his chin out in a suggestive gesture. "Hi there... Wanna dance?"

He doesn't wait for an answer. Before I can even open my mouth, he grabs my hand and tries to pull me toward the dance floor. Out of the corner of my eye, I notice his friends smirking and nudging him on. A few of them give me the same sly grin. It immediately rubs me the wrong way.

"No, thank you," I call back. "Sorry."

To my surprise, the guy doesn't push it. "Fine," he shrugs, laughing as he releases my hand and turns back to his friends. "Have it your way."

I barely have any time to bask in the relief. A second later, one of his buddies breaks away from their group to come stumbling toward me. "Hey, I know that guy's a loser. But I'm not," he drunkenly slurs. "So how about you give me a dance instead, huh? I have a Lamborghini outside. I'll take you for a ride after. Sound like a fair trade?"

I blush before finding my footing. "I'm not interested in trades," I say, ready for some banter. But he doesn't seem interested in talking. His sloppy gaze wanders up and down my body before he twists his lips.

"Your loss." With that, he spins around and waddles back to

his group. They take off, and I turn around, more confused than anything.

"What the hell was that all about?" I ask no one in particular. Only one answer comes from the back of my mind: *they thought you looked easy.*

Shit.

Just like that, my insecurities return with a vengeance. I retreat against the bar, feeling more and more claustrophobic.

Then, all of a sudden, something shifts.

A hot streak seems to pierce through the heavy air. My chest thumps. My skin pebbles. I turn around looking for the source.

But before I can figure that out, something else grabs my attention. A commotion up ahead. People stand aside as a drunk guy stumbles down the bar, only stopping to hit on every last girl he comes across.

The heat vanishes. I snap back to reality. My skin crawls and I look around for backup. But Julia has disappeared. Where the hell did she go?

It doesn't matter. I'm on my own.

I'm just about to make a run for it when the dude looks up and spots me. Our eyes meet and a stone drops in my gut. He must sense my fear, because he makes a beeline for my position.

"Shit."

My heels wobble as I make a move for the relative safety of the dance floor. I don't get far before the guy darts in front of me, blocking my path.

"Hey there, baby," he stammers, briefly glancing over his shoulder. "Where ya going? Dance floor? Well, I can dance. Don't you want to dance with ol' Mikey? Or are you like all these other *bitches.*"

His yellow teeth snap shut at that last word and a chill skates down my spine. Still, I've dealt with assholes like this before, and I know all the tricks. I just need to put some distance between him and me. Unfortunately, the club only seems to become more packed as I try to inch my way from the bar.

"I'm sorry, but I already have a dancing partner," I say, scanning the club in a desperate attempt to find my friends. But they're nowhere to be found.

So, instead, I try to sidestep ol' Mikey, but he cuts in front of me a second time. "Hold up, baby. Didn't you hear me? Don't run off so fast. We were just getting to know each other."

"Sorry," I tell him, trying to keep my cool. "I have a boyfriend. No offense, but...."

"A boyfriend," he scoffs. "I don't see any boyfriend."

"He isn't—"

"He isn't what?" Mike lashes out. Raising both his arms so that the drink in his hand spills down his wrist, he looks right and left. "He can't be much of a boyfriend if he leaves you alone like this... or are you lying?" He glares down, daring me to respond. When I don't, he takes a step closer, his voice lowering. "Come. Dance. I'll show you what a real man is made of."

He stinks of booze. His shirt is stained. His sleeve ripped. My hackles start to rise. This dick is trouble. I'm not looking for trouble and I'm definitely not a fighter, but I've always done what I've had to do to survive...

Without warning, Mikey lunges forward and grabs me. He hooks one arm behind my back and pins me against his body. Then, he shoves his prick into my crotch and grinds me through my dress.

"You'd like some of this, wouldn't you?" he snarls. "Come on. You don't have a boyfriend, *bitch*. You just need to loosen the fuck up."

"Get off me!" I yell, shoving him away with all my strength. But he barely budges.

"And who's going to make me?" he says, swaying back into my personal space. "Your fake boyfriend?"

"He's not fake," I hiss, lying through my teeth.

The bastard takes a step back and his slimy grin vanishes. "Where is he, then? *Who* is he?"

Without thinking clearly, I cast a panicked glance across the dance floor, desperately searching for a guy, any guy I can point to as my non-existent boyfriend. But all the guys in sight are busy dancing, drinking, joking with their friends, or getting close to other girls. No one's looking our way. No one cares that I'm in trouble.

Shit. Where are my friends when I need them?

The situation is starting to feel helpless when, all of a sudden, that strange feeling returns, stronger than before. The hot streak piercing through the heavy air.

It... it feels like someone is watching me.

My gaze immediately rips up, racing in a panic until it lands on the mezzanine that hangs over the dance floor. Colored lights have started to glow above it. They shine down onto a huge solitary figure standing at the railing.

The man towers above everyone else. A dark energy radiates from his broad silhouette. Then, suddenly, the colored lights vanish, leaving him behind. But even in the shadows, I can sense his immense presence.

A moment later, the lights return, and I catch a glimpse of his face. Even from this distance, I can see the striking glint in his strong green eyes. He's staring at me.

For a split-second, I'm lost to everything but him. Silence envelops the club. The people disappear. I gaze back at the stranger, trapped in his tempting pull.

My heart thumps. My stomach tightens.

Then, without warning, he lifts his hand and folds his fingers toward me.

The gesture is clear.

He wants me to come to him.

A rush of adrenaline sears through my chest.

"You stupid lying bitch! You don't have any boyfriend."

Just like that, I'm startled out of my trance. I remember ol' Mikey. I remember my problems. My loneliness.

A snarl curves my lips.

"He's right there!" I snap, pointing up at the man on the mezzanine. "And he's calling me. Gotta go."

With a burst of energy, I duck under Mikey's outstretched arm and break into the crowd. He reaches for me, but I manage to slap his hand away and keep going.

"You bitch!" he shouts, his voice quickly fading. "You made me spill my drink! I swear..."

But that asshole is already a thing of the past. All my mind can concentrate on are those piercing green eyes... and that subtle but irresistible command.

Come.

Am I really going to listen?

2

ANDREI

Through the tempered glass, they all look like disfigured monsters. Twisted, corrupted, shapeless.

I rotate the decanter in my hand and the whiskey sloshes sideways, drowning the demons that mingle before me. If I wanted to kill these men, it would be as easy as that. The tilt of my hand. The clenching of my jaw. A thought barely uttered.

Sometimes I wonder why I don't just wipe them all out and get it over with.

Then I remember.

It would be too easy.

And I need a fucking challenge.

"Fuck," I grumble, reclining back in my chair. The decanter hits the table. I replace it with my refilled Glencairn glass, swirling it in my fingertips as I carelessly listen to the conversation flowing around the dining hall.

From my throne at the head of the huge table, it all just sounds like thoughtless chatter. We might as well be on the dance floor downstairs, trying to talk among all the club-goers who came to Silo247 for a mindless good time.

But that's never been my scene. And outside of this private lounge and my office behind it, the club is useless to me.

Almost as useless as most of these men.

Bringing the glass to my lips, I let my gaze travel over the table. My distinguished guests stretch out all the way to the other side of the room, eating my food, drinking my booze, breathing my air.

For the most part, they fill me with a simmering disgust. Leeches. But there are two people in this room who I respect. And they're the only things keeping me sane right now.

The first of them sits directly behind me, watching my back with undying loyalty.

Without turning around, I can sense his sympathetic anger. Valentin Constanov, my second-in-command. He seethes over my shoulder, each breath like a low growl.

If I decided to massacre the room, he'd be the first to jump in—but only after making it a competition to see who could get the most kills.

Then, there's Ilya Rykov. My guest of honor. He may be new to this Bratva, but he's done more for me since arriving in Chicago than almost anyone else here. The man is a twisted genius. A cybersecurity expert. And one dark motherfucker.

He'll fit in well... as long as he stays on his toes.

These other fuckers, though...

They think they can get by on ass-kissing alone. I see them side-eyeing me, silently pleading for my approval. They won't get it at a dinner party, and it's pathetic that they even think they could. Everyone here should know better. They're from the same violent world as me. But where I rose up the ranks to strangle fate by the throat, they're still waiting for handouts.

It's pathetic. My reign has been too good for them. They've gotten comfortable.

I've gotten bored.

"Excuse me, Pakhan, but I must go—"

I hardly even flinch as one of the men from my South Bronx branch gets up from his seat—Ivan, I think his name is. The fool must be drunk because he immediately starts making his way toward me.

Before he can get anywhere close to my throne, though, Valentin springs into action.

"What the hell do you think you're doing?" my second-in-command barks, grabbing the fool by his shoulders.

The room goes silent, but the pounding bass leaking through the walls muffles the rest of the exchange. Valentin yells in the guy's ear. I catch something about proper protocol.

When the guy doesn't back down, Dima—Valentin's personal enforcer—gets up too. The two men block off his path. I gently place my glass on the table and stand up.

"What's the problem here," I ask, stepping between my two guards.

"No problem, Pakhan," Ivan cows, practically bowing before me. "I just wanted to say my farewells and got a little eager. For that, I apologize. I meant no disrespect."

Valentin steams next to me. I can tell he wants to use this as an excuse to break some skulls, but I know better. No matter how bored I am, there's no point in making an enemy out of an ally.

"Apology accepted," I nod. Lifting my hand, I allow Ivan to take it. He holds onto me with shaking fingers and dips so low his knees nearly hit the ground. "Now go."

The second I pull my hand back, Valentin steps between us. He whispers something in Dima's ear and the enforcer stiffens. I sit back down and watch as Ivan finally allows himself to be escorted away, his legs wobbly with fear and shame. With a tense silence still gripping the room, Dima leads him out the door.

Valentin returns to my side and casts a stern warning glance around the table. No one moves until Dima returns. Still, the tension remains until I take a long sip of my whiskey.

Only then does the table relax. Conversation returns. These things happen. If anything, everyone here is glad that I have so much restraint. The last Pakhan didn't, and it's why I had to overthrow him.

Another sip of whiskey makes me sink deeper into my seat. Now even Valentin can tell that I'm bored out of my mind. Standing up from his seat, he snaps his fingers at two servers waiting by the edge of the table.

They nod and eagerly make their way to the front of the lounge, disappearing behind two swinging doors. A second later, those same doors burst back open and a flood of scantily-clad models strut in.

With painted smiles, they spread around the table. My greedy guests light up. Just like that, the attention is taken off of me. Not a single man here can resist these kinds of treats. The chatter builds. Girls are waved over, hollered at, pulled onto laps. Kisses are shared. The tone in the room changes for the better.

But that doesn't mean I'm interested.

Not even when a few of the bolder girls head directly for my throne. Everyone here knows who I am, including them, and two actually manage to slip past the crowd until they're close enough to touch my shadow. Unsurprisingly, Valentin doesn't try to stop *them*. The cocksucker.

"Polina and Yana," Valentin whispers, leaning into my ear.

"We've met before," I remind him. "I know their names."

"My mistake, Pakhan."

The two girls flank my chair. "It's so good to see you again, Pakhan..." Yana smiles. But the second she slips her hands inside my jacket, I stand up and step aside.

"Tonight isn't about me," I warn them. "Do your jobs. Entertain the guests."

They should know better by now. I've had my fill of easy girls. The problem is, my world is filled to the brim with easy girls. They flock to me the same way these other sheep do. I'm sick of it. Just like I'm sick of everyone in this room.

"We'd rather entertain you," Polina flutters her lashes.

"Do. Your. Job," I growl, perhaps a little too loudly.

Silence falls over the lounge as I turn to leave, but the conversation restarts the second I walk out the door. None of those idiots can resist a beautiful girl.

Neither could I... until they became just another thing to collect. That's what happens when you reach the top. There's nowhere to go anymore... nowhere but down...

With a bullish huff, I turn down the corridor. What the hell is wrong with me? I used to starve for parties. For sex. But now that I have all the money in the world and access to any girl I could ever want, it all seems so inconsequential. So useless. So goddamn infuriating.

I want something more. I *need* something more. And it's not just because I'm getting old enough to marry, or that I'm starting to think about my legacy and how to pass this whole conquered empire down. It's the isolation. I used to have a band of brothers I'd kill for, fight for, die for.

Now, all I have is a kingdom, and I sure as hell wouldn't die for it. Shit, I might not even be able to bring myself to marry for it. And that's more infuriating than it is sad, because I'm trapped by the inevitability of it all.

In the end, the only way my hard work will pay off is if I have an heir to carry it all on, and I can't have an heir unless I marry.

It's a problem I haven't been able to figure my way out of. Maybe that's where all of this rage stems from. I'm too rich to enjoy the company of anyone, and too powerful to be at the mercy of anything; yet here I am, slowly being crushed under the weight of tradition.

Lost in my thoughts, I wander over to the stairwell. Part of me almost wants to go down to the club floor and pretend to check up on the place—anything to keep me busy. But I already know everything will be fine. It always is. My empire runs smoothly. That's how I designed it.

Now, I'm starting to regret that.

Perhaps it's time I do something reckless.

The idea swirls around my head as I step out onto the mezzanine overlooking the dance floor. Below, the young and the rich are having their mindless fun. It's almost enviable. But the longer I look, the less I want anything to do with them.

Behind all their bright clothes and glittering jewelry is the same emptiness that haunts me. I glare at them with disdain. Every last one of them is the same...

Then, my gaze falls on something that doesn't quite fit. My focus narrows. Among all the designer suits and high-fashion dresses is a little slip of washed-out black. The modest dress is wrapped around a petite body and split in half by a drape of golden hair.

Something kicks in my chest. My brow raises. My lips curl.

The criminal in me is immediately suspicious. The girl's body language sits in stark contrast to everyone else's. She isn't carefree. She isn't mindless. Those shining blue eyes dart back and forth, filled with a million conflicted thoughts.

A spy?

Without thinking, I lean forward, eager for a closer look. She looks uncomfortable... and shockingly innocent. My suspicion melts. Intrigue grips my entire body.

To my surprise, I feel a small smile relax my curled lips.

"You don't belong here, little deer..."

Resting my elbow on the railing, I watch as she goes through the motions.

It quickly becomes clear that she's not alone. A group of friends surround her, but unlike her, they clearly belong in a place like this. They sway with a familiar, flashy mindlessness, covered in their designer brands.

I observe as they order a round of drinks, knock back a few shots, and then scatter.

My little deer stays in place, though. And I can't help but study her.

That's a Russian girl, I tell myself. The chiseled cheekbones and soft pale skin make it undeniable. But she's not bone-thin for the same reason everyone else here is. She's starving. I know the look well... and the feeling.

How long has it been since I've been that hungry?

My empty chest starts to rumble. I cock my head to the side and sink into the strange admiration I find in this curious little stranger. She reminds me of a happier, more desperate time.

But that's not all she inspires in me. Something far less pure spikes my blood as I look closer. It's not just that she's uncomfortable or that she's filled with countless conflicting thoughts, it's that none of those thoughts seem to be about this place; about trying to fit in.

She isn't trying as hard as the other girls. In fact, she isn't trying at all. Those crystal blue eyes keep racing around like she's looking for an escape hatch. She doesn't want to be here. She doesn't want to be part of this world.

Hell, she might not even want me.

The thought is exhilarating.

"Hmmm," I rumble. "A challenge..."

For the first time in a long time, I feel like going down into that throng of people and pulling one out. For a brief moment, I'm the man I was before all the power.

I'm hungry. *Starving.*

The things I would do to that tiny frame, I think, licking my lips. *But would she let me?*

I love that I don't know the answer to that question.

"Look my way, little deer," I whisper. "Come to me."

Before she can follow my silent command, though, I spot trouble heading her way.

"Don't you fucking dare," I hiss, pushing myself off my elbows.

My fingers clench into fists as a familiar goon starts pushing his way down the bar.

Mike Spolanski.

The drunk has a history of causing small-time trouble at this club. The only reason we keep letting him back in is because it makes for easy blackmail. His dad owns half the buildings downtown, and by now, we get about half of the rent paid to those buildings.

But if he does anything to my mysterious little deer, he won't be able to buy himself out of the trouble I bring down on him.

Grabbing back onto the railing, I squeeze until my knuckles turn white. I'm already prepared to run down when Mike stumbles up to my Russian beauty. Of course he does. He can smell blood in the water. He thinks she's weak.

"Well, are you?"

Somehow, I stop myself from racing downstairs. Instead, I suppress the urge to protect, and I lean back down on the railing to observe.

Something tells me this girl is stronger than she looks. I *want* her to be stronger than she looks. So, I give her a chance to prove it.

Still, my teeth grind back and forth as Mike tries to talk to her. No matter how strongly she shakes her head, that dipshit won't take the hint. Then, he grabs her. I tense up, but force myself to stay put.

To my delight, she shoves him off and looks wildly around.

Suddenly, those beautiful blue eyes find mine.

Just like that, the rest of the club vanishes. My gut tightens. She practically sparkles in a spotlight all of her own.

Part of me expects her to grin or smirk or flirt the way another girl might. But there's no sign she knows who I am.

How fucking delicious.

My heart thrills at that thought. I swallow and bite down on my lip.

She doesn't know who I am.

... I'll have to change that.

Slowly, the club pulses back around me, but I stay laser-focused on the girl who's captured my attention. With a new fire burning inside of me, I lift my hand and do what a god does when he wants something.

I tell it to come to me.

My fingers curl as I beckon her.

Time freezes. For a split second, I'm not sure if she'll follow my order. It's such a novel doubt that the entire world suddenly feels new.

All I can do is watch with anticipation as a cloud crosses her pointed little face.

Oh, the fun I could have with you.

Then, the spell is broken. That bastard Mike distracts her and she looks back down at him. I'm nearly ready to write her off when she points up at me.

With a sneer that makes my cold heart jump, she ducks around Mike and rushes into the crowd. Without a second thought, I push myself off the railing and head for the stairs.

It doesn't matter if she's coming to me.

I'm going to get her.

3

NATALYA

The stairs rise up into an impenetrable darkness. They look too tall to climb; too steep to conquer.

... Or maybe I'm just out of breath from running through that crowd.

Shit. I work so much I should be in better shape than this.

My pounding chest clenches as I stare up into the unknown. All I can picture are those stunning green eyes... and that strong hand beckoning me forward. There's a thrilling warmth attached to the proposition that's taken over my entire body.

Who was that man?

Something deep inside me needs to find out. At the very least, I need to get away from that creep he saved me from.

After a deep, choppy breath, I make move for the stairway. But before my foot can even hit the first step, someone grabs my elbow.

I'm yanked back towards the dance floor and right into a sweaty chest.

"Don't you walk away from me, bitch!" Mikey shrieks, whirling me around so I get good a whiff of his wretched breath. Waving an empty glass in my face, he gets nice and close. "Look what you fucking did. You made me spill my drink. Now you're gonna replace it before I...."

Out of nowhere, a massive, muscular hand snatches Mikey's wrist. His fingers are torn from my elbow and twisted backward with such force that his arm nearly wrenches out of its socket.

A yelp of pain cuts through the busy air. Mikey is jerked toward me. I just barely manage to spin out of the way in time to avoid being bowled over.

That's when I see the man who summoned me.

With a jaw clenched so tightly I can see each and every muscle, he snaps Mikey's arm at the elbow, stopping just before it can break in half.

"You're making a nuisance of yourself again, Mike," booms a voice so deep it rivals the rattling bass. Two hard emerald eyes narrow into deadly slits as the mysterious stranger steps out of the darkness and snarls through gritted teeth. "Do you have a problem with this young lady?"

"Aarrgh!" Mike howls. "Who the—"

Without a second thought or wasted movement, the man slams the glass in Mikey's hand against the steel band of his wristwatch. The glass shatters into a million pieces. Before anyone can move, my violent savior lunges forward and presses the razor shard to Mike's throat.

"You know, Mike," the guy practically whispers, his voice filled with murderous intent, "I'm getting really, really sick of telling you to behave yourself in this club. In fact, I think tonight will be the very last time I ever tell you. Is that clear? Am I speaking clearly enough for your tiny, swollen brain to understand?"

Mike whimpers as the sharp edge of broken glass digs into his neck. A bead of shiny blood bubbles around the edge and trickles down to his collar.

"I asked you a question," the man snarls. "Do you understand what I just said?"

Mike nods fast. His terrified, desperate eyes dart around the dance floor in search of help.

But when I turn to look over my shoulder, I find a scene frozen in time. No one is moving. All anyone can do is stare. The club has gone dead quiet, except for the music thumping as loud as ever.

"Now, I want you to apologize to this pretty lady. Can you do that for me?"

"... Yes," Mike chokes.

"Go on."

"I... I'm sorry..."

"That was pathetic."

"I... I'm really sorry... really..."

The stranger presses the broken glass deeper into Mike's throat. "Now, tell her what a nice man I am. Tell her that she should come upstairs and have a drink with me. Tell her that's the only way I won't slit your throat right here and now."

Blood rushes into my ears as Mike clumsily stumbles through his lines. I hardly hear him, but it doesn't matter. I already heard the stranger.

"Good enough," the stranger grumbles. Then he looks at me. "What do you think? Should I slit his throat anyway or should we head upstairs for a drink instead?"

"I, uh..."

The answer is obvious, but the words won't come out.

Suddenly, two more powerfully built men appear down the stairs. They press right up against the stranger's back, their sharp eyes zeroing in on Mikey's petrified face.

"Of course, we could always do both, one after the other..."

"Please..." Mikey garbles.

The stranger leans down over his hostage's trembling

shoulder. "Your fate is in her hands," he states, matter-of-factly. "I'll do whatever she says. No matter what—"

"Don't kill him!" I manage to blurt out.

A glint of disappointment flashes behind those arresting green eyes. The stranger's jaw flexes. My heart stops beating.

Finally, he throws Mike off him.

A wave of relief crashes over me. But that relief doesn't last long.

The drunkard lets out a cowardly yelp as he falls to the floor, clutching at his wrist and then at his neck. With zero sense, he stares up at the stranger, mouth agape. "Haven't I given you enough already?" he chokes, tears streaming down his red cheeks

The stranger doesn't respond. He only glares. The silence becomes so thick it's nearly unbearable. Then, finally, and without another word, Mikey picks himself off the floor and stumbles into the crowd.

"Get out of my way!" he cries, disappearing into the shocked throng of onlookers.

By this point, even the music has been turned down. It's so quiet that I can hear one of the men whisper into my stranger's ear. He turns his back on me and says, "Throw him out and tell Vadi never to let that piece of shit on my property again. Mike is banned from all our other establishments too. I don't care who his fucking father is or how much money we make off him."

"You got it, Pakhan," the other guy replies. Then he and the stranger bump their forearms against each other.

I stare at them, completely lost.

Somewhere behind me, Mikey yells. A commotion breaks out. The two men behind my stranger share a glance. When the man from the mezzanine nods, they lift their chins and brush past me.

I can hear them grab Mikey in the crowd. He curses and

then starts begging for mercy as his voice shrinks into the distance.

But I'm already over that. All I can focus on right now is the broad, powerful back planted in front of me.

Without any hurry, the handsome stranger turns around again to face me.

"My apologies," he calmly says, wiping his bloody thumb against his pant leg. "That man won't bother you again."

Before I can thank him, he lifts his massive hand to my neck. With surprisingly tender fingers he tilts my jaw, exposing my throat. I gulp, too shocked to move.

"I..."

"Don't worry, it's not your blood," he almost sighs, brushing the back of his finger across my skin. A tingle of searing-hot electricity crosses through me. My eyelids flutter, blurring the world before focusing in on his hand.

He pulls his fingers back and I see the new smidge of blood on his thumb. Just like before, he wipes it off across his pants, right next to his smear of blood, but not before staring at it for a brief moment.

"Are you hurt?" he asks.

I gasp to get my voice working. "No... I... he... Thank you. I was just..."

"You were just on your way upstairs," he says, thick lips tightening into a heart-gripping smile. "Shall we?"

Taking a short step aside, he offers me his hand. But when I'm still too frozen to take it, he places an open palm on the small of my back and leads me forward.

"This way, darling."

The heat of his touch makes my knees weak. At this point, I'm not sure I could make it up these stairs alone, even if I wanted to.

And after what I just saw, I definitely shouldn't want to.

This is crazy, right?

No matter how undeniably handsome this man is, he nearly just killed someone in front of me. So why are my feet suddenly moving so comfortably alongside his? Why do I fight back the instinct that says run? Why do I let him lead me up into the darkness?

Why does he feel more like a protective blanket than a murderous maniac?

I struggle for answers as he whisks me from the crowd. The music starts to grow louder again, and I can hear the voices return to the dance floor as everyone starts to gossip about what they just witnessed.

All eyes are on us as we make our way up the stairs. I can feel them. But they don't bother me. Every other gaze pales in comparison to the rich green shine glowing over my shoulder. The stranger's strong, confident hand falls from the small of my back and brushes against my knuckles. Another warm shiver washes through my body. My toes curl and I reach to grab the railing.

Instead, I find the stranger's arm.

"That's a good girl."

"Excuse me?" I ask, still in a daze and not sure I heard him right.

Slipping out of my grip, he takes my fingers in a gentle embrace and rotates in front of me. "You're shaking," he notes, squeezing my palm.

A wonderful heat seeps into my core. If I wasn't shivering before, I definitely am now. It's embarrassing. We stop at the top of the stairs and I blush.

"I'm... I'm okay," I stumble. "I'm just... I'm just shaken up, I guess. Nothing like that has ever happened to me before."

That's a lie. I've been accosted more times than I can count. That's just how life goes when you grow up in foster homes. And it only gets worse when they push you out onto the streets. I've seen some of the worst humanity has to offer.

But no one has ever stood up for me like that before. It's nearly enough to make me forget about the danger and the violence... or at least overlook it.

"No?" the man asks, tilting his head to one side. A subtle amusement takes over his gruff face. "You handled him very well for someone with no experience."

My chin dips and I shake my head. "It wasn't enough. It never is. If you hadn't shown up..."

"Just doing my job," he smirks, tipping his brow. "The only question now is how I'll repay you for the grave injustice you've faced at my club. Or would you rather sue me?"

His smirk deepens and a pair of deep dimples are revealed.

I jolt upright, butterflies racing through my stomach. "*Your* club?"

He shrugs. "One of them."

I gulp.

That makes sense. It explains why no one tried to stop him downstairs. It also explains the two bodyguards who escorted ol' Mikey away.

My gaze drops from the stranger's face, washing down his expensive suit to the blood stains on his pants.

Something shifts inside of me.

This man is too much for me. I can't handle him or this. A small knot tightens in my gut, dragging down the butterflies.

I look over my shoulder, down from the mezzanine. From up here, everyone looks so small and insignificant—just like they would if I was on the top floor of one of those elegant skyscrapers downtown...

My heart stirs... then clenches.

I don't belong here.

"Look, I really appreciate your help, Pakhan, but you don't need to repay me. Really, I should get back to my—"

Before I can finish, he raises his eyebrows and tilts his head the other way. "What did you just call me?"

"I... uh... what do you mean?"

"You called me Pakhan. Why?"

"Isn't that your name? Your friend downstairs called you Pakhan..."

To my complete surprise, his sly smirk suddenly bursts into a boisterous laugh. For a split-second, the whole deadly, intimidating, brutal façade shatters before my very eyes. The mischievous sparkling in his emerald green eyes becomes almost boyish. He looks like a completely different guy. My fear melts slightly, replaced by another shock of embarrassment.

"My name is not Pakhan," he chuckles wiping his curled thumb against his lips. Slowly, his face stiffens again, but I swear I can still see that glint. "It's Andrei—Andrei Zherdev. And you are?"

He picks up my hand and presses it between both of his. Another tidal wave of heat rushes up my arm. The sensation floods into my core and untangles any remaining knots.

His whole enormous presence makes my head swim. I forget about the blood and the violence. I'm engulfed by his tender grip. I let myself sink into his touch.

"I'm Natalya..." I break off before revealing my last name. Even against all his distracting beauty, a voice in the back of my head reminds me to be careful.

This man is clearly powerful... and very dangerous. How much should I really be telling him?

"It's delightful to meet you, Natalya," he says, a mature tint replacing his boyish charm. "Welcome to my world. Let me get you a drink. On the house, of course."

He waves to the side and my heart starts thumping. At the back of the mezzanine is a door. The thick heavy wood is painted all black, except for the gold handle, which practically glows above a dark, ornate keyhole.

A gulp slithers down my throat.

It looks like a gate to another world. A world I'm not sure I want to enter. A world that's not so easy to escape...

Suddenly, I'm being gently pulled forward. The mysterious door grows larger. I want to lurch away, but I don't dare let go of Andrei's hand. It doesn't feel safe to be here alone. Plus, my knees are too weak. I'd fall. And despite my fear of what's behind that dark entrance, what's even more terrifying is the thought of embarrassing myself in front of this man again.

Hold it together, Natalya, I tell myself. *Let him lead the way. After all, this is why you came out tonight, isn't it?*

No...

Liar.

We reach the door and I swear I see scratch marks carved deep into the black wood. In fact, it seems to be covered in subtle scars, including splotches of dark red...

Before I can investigate too closely, though, the heavy door groans open.

"Ladies first," Andrei nods. His charm remains, but something more sinister has entered the fray. And I don't know if it's real or just a figment of my imagination.

"I... I shouldn't..."

My heart is in my throat.

"Isn't that the point of coming to a club," he counters. "To do things we shouldn't?"

It takes all of my willpower to keep from hyperventilating. This is too stressful. He's too hot and way too forward. What am I getting myself into?

"What's in there?" I swallow.

"I'll show you."

He takes the first step, but when I don't follow, those captivating green eyes study me with a blazing curiosity.

"What are we going to do?" I naively ask.

With his back pressed against the open door, Andrei leans down until his lips are mere inches away from my ear.

"Whatever we want."

Just like that, my knees give out. But Andrei is ready. He catches me under the elbow and holds me up.

"Are you sure you're alright?" he questions.

"Yes," I mumble, willing myself to focus. But his hands are back on me, and a searing pressure has taken over my core. It's all I can focus on. It needs to be satisfied. "I'm fine."

I shake away all the concerning signs and focus on the truth at the heart of the matter.

This is what I came out for tonight. I *need* this. Just one good thing—even if it's wrapped in a navy fleet's worth of red flags. I've had it way too hard for way too long. It's about time I indulge in something hard and long that can actually make me feel good... not that I would know exactly how good something like that can feel...

"You're more than just fine," Andrei says. "But I didn't mean it like that. Are you drunk?"

"No," I huff. Shaking my head, I straighten my back. "I'm not that much of a lightweight."

Andrei's green eyes scour my body. "You look pretty light to me."

"That's what happens when you don't have enough money to—" I cut myself off. *No, don't reveal too much. No one wants to hear your sob story, especially not a man like this. Let the night take you where it wants. Let him take you. Leave fear outside. Let some fucking fun in for once. This man protected you. Show him how grateful you are.* "Sorry, I..."

"No, keep going," Andrei insists.

But that's the last thing I want to do. So instead, I decide to test him, no matter how foolish that sounds.

"Why are you checking to see how much I weigh anyway?" I divert, treading into dangerous waters. "Are you trying to pick me up?'

That makes him laugh. But this laugh isn't mischievous. There's something far more... carnal about it.

"I thought that was obvious."

"I..." I'm not sure how to respond to that. This is really happening. "Are you being figurative or literal?" I hear myself ask.

"You mean about picking you up?" he asks, clearly amused.

"Yes."

"Let's say it's both," turning his head, he looks down the dimly lit hall stretching out behind the doorway. "If I literally picked you up right now, would you kick and scream?"

"I... I don't know what I'd do."

"Because it's never happened to you before?"

I was not ready to be called out like that. There's no ill intent in Andrei's accusation, but my lack of experience has always been a sore spot.

"I've been carried by plenty of guys," I naively declare.

"Oh, now you're making me jealous on purpose."

He takes a step forward and instinct makes me duck under his arm. Still, a very loud part of me is still fighting to just give in.

This is what tonight was supposed to be about, wasn't it? Some fun with a rich guy. It's just my luck that he's so stunning I can't think straight.

"I... I can walk," I try to recover, not wanting him to think I'm entirely uninterested. This wouldn't be the worst way to lose my v-card—not that I'm particularly precious about it. I've just never met someone decent enough to make me consider it.

But is Andrei decent? It's hard to say, and impossible to judge fairly. All I can do is step aside and stare as he steps by me, his massive frame shifting the air as he strolls into the darkness.

"Well, then follow me, little deer," he says, glancing over his shoulder so that I can see the sparkle in his deep green eyes.

Lifting his hand, he snaps his fingers. The lights turn on

and a soft warm glow fills the hallway. He doesn't wait for me. I have to hurry to catch up.

Shit. I must have lost my mind.

Struggling to clear my throat, I waddle up to his side, basking in the cool scent of his arctic cologne. "If your name isn't Pakhan, why did you answer to it?" I ask, filling the tense silence.

"It's a title." He cocks his head and eyes me suspiciously. "You really don't know what it means?"

"No. Why would I?"

Andrei shifts his jaw and looks straights ahead. "It's a Russian mafia title. I'm a Bratva boss—the *top* Bratva boss. It's a name that indicates respect, kind of like how the Italians call their top boss 'godfather' or whatever."

I stare at the muscles clenching on the side of his face.

Bratva? Mafia?

My heart does a little twirl then drops into oblivion.

No, thank you.

I've dealt with enough crime for one lifetime. When you live on the streets, you get to know all sorts of lowlifes. Scumbags like ol' Mikey who think they can do whatever they want just because society doesn't give a shit about me or them.

A gust of anger blows through me. I've always hated criminals. They've made my life so much harder than it has to be, and it's already been tough enough on its own.

I look over my shoulder just as the heavy black door groans shut behind us. It's too far to reach anyway—that is, unless this *mafia boss* is willing to let me go.

Shit.

Shit. Shit. Shit.

This is just my luck.

"I should probably—"

"In here." Andrei takes my hand, and I turn back around just as he opens another door.

"Woah..." I gape, stopping in my tracks. "Where... where are we?"

"My office."

"It's massive."

But massive is an understatement. The new room is set into the corner of the building, and it's even bigger than the dance floor downstairs.

"An office fit for a boss," Andrei notes.

"A *mafia* boss."

"A *Bratva* boss," he casually corrects. "Would you like that drink?"

I follow Andrei with my eyes as he strolls over to a giant oak desk. It's the centerpiece of the majestic layout, but it's not even the most impressive piece of furniture here. Neither is the regal leather chair behind it, the several deep couches, coffee tables, or private bar tucked into the far corner.

No. What really catches my attention is the bookshelf. It covers the entirety of the back wall and reaches all the way up to the extra-high ceilings. Even more intriguing, though, is the ornament-covered panel that fills the space directly behind the grand leather chair.

Gold leaves adorn the dark wood, framing a gilded crest with a fearsome-looking black viper on it. The snake slithers between the eye sockets of a gold skull, whose jaw is opened wide... as if locked in a scream. At the center, tucked between the cracked teeth, is the same ornate keyhole on the door outside.

A chill rustles through the vast room. My hands start to shake.

"Natalya." Andrei's voice snaps through my daze. "Do you want a drink? Here, at least have some water. You look pale."

"I... I always look like this," I say, my throat so dry it creaks.

"It's the Russian struggle," Andrei jokes, approaching me with a tall glass.

"I... uh... thank you." I take the glass and gulp the water

down in one sip. God, I was thirstier than I thought. "Wait, how did you know I was Russian?"

"It's written all over you face."

Before I can wipe the lingering water from my lips, Andrei cups my jaw. For some reason, all of my fear and doubt sinks into that massive palm of his. My eyes close as he traces a line down my cheek with his thumb.

Then, his grip tightens and I'm shocked back awake.

"How is it that a Russian girl like you doesn't know anything about the Bratva?"

Holding onto my empty glass by the fingertips, I try to take a step back, but Andrei doesn't let me go.

A whole new level of fear pulses through me.

"I... uh... I didn't grow up in the... what do you call it..."

"The Russian community?"

"Yes. Thank you."

"Why not?"

I cough and a bit of water trickles down my chin. Andrei releases my jaw to wipe it away with the back of his fingers.

"My... my mother died when I was young and my father abandoned me not long after that," I explain, coughing again as I stumble backward. "I've been on my own ever since. In and out of foster care, then in and out of..." I stop myself again. I can't tell him too much.

This man is even more dangerous than I thought. And it's not just because of who he is.

It's what he does to me.

I already miss the warmth of his demanding hand on my tiny jaw.

He could crush me... and the thought alone is enough to make my toes curl with more than just fear. Half of me wants to run away. The other half wants to run directly into him.

He could protect me from the evils of this world... or be my worst nightmare.

What am I willing to risk to find out?

"That's too bad," Andrei muses. When he steps forward, I flinch. But he only reaches down and takes my glass.

"I should probably get back downstairs," I whisper meekly. "I really appreciate you helping me and everything..."

"Those girls you came with," Andrei interrupts. "Who are they?"

He turns and places the glass on his desk.

I startle to high alert. "They... what? Why?"

"They don't seem like your type," he says. "That blonde girl... the one in the sequins..."

"Oh," I mutter, shoulders slumping. "Her."

Suddenly, this all makes sense. Andrei isn't interested in me. I'm being used to get to my prettier friend.

It wouldn't be the first time.

Shit. Suddenly, I'm not nearly as afraid as I should be. Hell, I'd even go so far as to say I'm a little fucking pissed off.

No one's ever stood up for me like Andrei did downstairs. Then, he made me feel special—if not scared-as-hell too—by pulling me up here, like I was the only girl in the world. And for what? To get Yelena's number?

"Why are you here with her? With any of them?" Andrei asks.

But I'm done with him and this.

"They're my friends," I say, shaking my head. "Look, I gotta go. I shouldn't be here."

"Fine," he nods. "Look I'm not insulting them. I'm just saying you're out of their league."

I stop dead in my tracks and spin around. "You're joking, right? Look, if you want me to introduce you to her, just say so. I'm sure she would love to meet a guy like you."

He arches an eyebrow my way. "What do you mean, a guy like me?"

I wave up and down in front of him. "Rich. Successful.

Influential. Dangerous."

He smirks. "Dangerous—me?"

I flush with shame and anger and regret. He's playing with me. But I'm not some little doll. I can walk out of here on my own. "Thanks for the drink. I'll see you later."

I turn around to leave, but I hardly have time to blink before he's suddenly standing right in front of me. "No. Don't leave, little deer," he says, almost like it's an order. "I'm not interested in your friend. I'm interested in you."

"Don't fuck with me, okay? I've had enough..."

Before I can duck under his arm, he catches my face between his palms and slams his lips against mine. It happens so fast I don't process it right away. By the time I do, he pulls back.

"Was that enough to convince you?"

I go to respond, but when I try to open my mouth, I can't. The taste of his lips still lingers on mine, tingling like a thin sheet of electricity. My heart is pounding. My stomach flutters uncontrollably.

"... What is going on?" I finally manage to mumble. Lifting a finger to my temple, I try to regroup. But Andrei doesn't give me a second to think.

"I'm proving myself to you." He moves in again, but much more slowly this time. "And I don't need to prove myself to anyone—not anymore." His massive presence wraps around me.

"So why me?"

"Because I want you to be worthy."

His hand slips up the back of my skull, and he holds me in place, lips inches from mine.

"Worthy of what?"

"Me."

A gasp rips from my lungs. Andrei's lips hover over my skin

as he pulls my head aside and exposes my throat. The heat of his breath nearly makes me sob.

I want him. I want him so fucking badly.

But I'm scared.

"Tell me to stop and I'll stop, angel," he growls. "You can walk out that door and never see me again. But is that what you really want?"

My answer comes without a second thought. I'm so lost in a haze of heavy lust that it could suffocate me and I wouldn't care.

"... No."

"That's a good girl."

4

NATALYA

My head is pulled back into position and Andrei's lips slip onto mine.

They're a perfect fit. So perfect that I can't help but do the single dumbest thing I've ever done in my life.

I kiss him back.

I know shouldn't, but I can't stop. I don't want to stop. He glides his fingers into my hair and my whole being melts in his grasp.

His mouth tastes incredible. His desire is so overwhelming that I can't stand it. I try to push back, but I can't match his power. My body explodes. I can't breathe. His tongue slithers into my mouth. I'm under his control.

"Oh!" A soft yelp rips from my throat when Andrei's big hand glides down my spine to clamp around my ass. He eats that yelp... and the moans that follow.

He picks me up and I gasp a little louder. But he only kisses me harder.

"Do you like that, angel?" he growls, picking me up. "How I hold you? How I devour you? How I want you?"

A high-pitched wine is all I can manage in response. I go limp. But that's not what Andrei wants.

"No. Don't hold back on me."

With a deep grunt, he starts to carry me through the office. It's like I barely weigh anything at all. Still, I wrap my legs around his waist and hold on for dear life until we crash into a wall. But we don't stay there for long. After a flurry of hot and heavy kisses, he turns around and whisks me across the office floor until we hit the next wall.

"Andrei," I gasp, running my hands through his hair as he thrusts into me.

I feel his hard bulge growing against my begging body. It makes my eyes roll into the back of my head.

"You can still tell me to stop," Andrei heaves, prying his lips from mine.

Those emerald green eyes blaze, covering me in a deep fire that lifts my hair on edge.

"Don't," I rasp, chest collapsing against the helplessness of my desire.

This is so wrong... but it feels so fucking good... and I deserve to feel good... for once.

That's it.

There will be *no* more dissent about it.

At least, that's what I tell myself as Andrei's strong fingers dig into my ass. Without mercy, he pries my cheeks apart. The fire grows. The pressure in my core is reaching critical levels. It needs to be satisfied.

For once in my fucking life, *I* need to be satisfied.

"Andrei!" I cry out again, just as the back of my legs ram into the edge of his desk. "Careful... please..."

"Hmm, I'm sorry, angel," he snarls. "But I will not be careful. That's not how I fuck."

"Fuck?"

The question is too quiet to be heard over the rustling of his jacket as he leaves me on the desk to undress.

"Stay put," he orders.

All I can do is obey. I'm too stunned to do anything else.

The immensity of what's about to happen isn't lost on me. But it doesn't matter how scared I am. My body is screaming to be devoured. I want to be swallowed whole.

Andrei's jacket hits the floor and the top three buttons of his white dress shirt burst from their seams. I get my first glimpse of his powerful chest... and the dark tattoos that cover it.

My breath hitches as he rolls up his sleeves, revealing thick, veiny forearms drenched in even more black tattoos. I swallow. My chest pushes towards him.

I'm no longer in control—not that I ever was. I've been hypnotized. Seduced. Caught. Call it what you want to call it, it doesn't matter. This is happening. I want it to happen.

I *need* it to happen.

When Andrei snatches another kiss, his teeth nip my lip and I yelp, half in pain and half in ecstasy. No one has ever kissed me like this. No one has ever turned me on like this. It's absolutely insane.

And completely irresistible.

I kiss him back as he props one mighty arm next to me on the desk and uses his other to undo his belt. It hisses and snaps as it's torn from around his waist and recklessly thrown to the floor.

"Oh my god..."

That's all I can say when I get my first glimpse of the mound pushing up on his zipper. It's massive.

It's too big.

I start to have second thoughts. There's no way I can handle that. Not for my first time.

I'm about to say something when Andrei grabs the back of my head again and steals another taste of my mouth. He crushes his lips against mine and drags his fingers down my throat, over my collarbone, and to my breast.

When he palms my tit, it feels like my entire being is curled up in his hand.

"Do you think you can handle me, angel?"

I whimper, desperate to say the one thing that makes sense. *No.* But instead, all I can squeak out is, "I'm not an angel."

It's the sad truth. Despite my sexual innocence, I've been through too much to be considered pure.

"No. You are," Andrei snarls, softly pinching my nipple through the thin material of my dress. "And that's perfect. Because I'm going to burn those wings right off, and you're going to fall into my kingdom."

"Your kingdom?"

"I'm the devil, baby. Welcome to hell. I think you're going to like it here. In fact, I'll make sure you do…"

His hand falls onto my knee and he shoves my dress up my thighs, exposing my panties. *Thank god they're black*, is all I can think. Otherwise, he'd see how wet I already am… as if he can't feel how hard my nipples are.

"What are you going to do to me?" I rasp, shivering with excitement as Andrei's thick fingers run up my waist, sneaking beneath the string of my panties to trace my hip bone.

"Like I said, little deer… Whatever I want."

Twisting his wrist, he pulls. My panties snap, and he carelessly throws them away. My last line of protection disappears into the darkness. Andrei spreads my legs apart.

"Wait!" I quiver, grabbing his hulking forearm. He's so thick that my tiny fingers barely make it halfway around.

For a split second, I feel him fight back against my resistance. Then, to my surprise, he halts his merciless advance.

"What is it?" he asks, panting like a beast. His strong face is flexed like one powerful muscle. All his focus is on fucking me.

But I don't know if I can handle that. He might destroy me.

"I'm... I... I don't want to get hurt," I quietly plead. My chest is still pushed out towards him. My soaking pussy is still exposed. I want him. It's clear as day. But I need to set this boundary... if just for my own safety.

"I can be gentle," he says, teeth sinking into his lip. "And I can be kind. But I think you'd prefer it if I'm not."

His words bleed with a monstrous sincerity. Clearly, he's more experienced than I could ever dream of being. But can he control himself enough to keep me from falling apart? Am I willing to take the risk?

Andrei shifts his feet and his pants slip to the ground. Black briefs barely contain his muscular thighs and eye-popping bulge.

My mouth waters. My eyelashes flutter.

I want what's behind those briefs so badly. It's an instinct I can't fight against. My lip drops. My mouth opens.

"I... I think I'd prefer it if you were..." I breathe. "Please... be gentle with me."

Tilting his head to the side, Andrei looks at me like I'm a puzzle he can't quite figure out.

"You are a mystery, little deer," he whispers, his scrunched face softening as a mischievous grin forms on his lips. "I can't even imagine what you taste like."

Kicking aside his pants, he sways into me until his covered bulge is practically touching my bare pussy. The heat sends a shockwave through my entire body.

Reaching around my back, he runs a finger down my spine to the folded hem of my dress.

"I'm sure you've tasted plenty of girls before," I meekly note.

"None like you. No... You. Are. Special." Leaning down, he whispers into my ear. "I will be gentle this time, angel. But you will learn how to take ALL of me. Understand?"

His hot breath swirls around in my ear, lifting my chin as he pulls at my dress.

"Yes," I mindlessly gasp, hardly taking note of his specific language.

This time.

Still, it rings like a foreboding note in the back of my mind as the powerful Bratva boss rolls my dress up until just above my hip bones.

"Then we have a deal."

With both hands, he grabs me by the ass and drags me to the edge of the desk.

"Look up at the ceiling if you want," he says, descending to his knees. "But don't you dare pray to any god. Me and him don't get along."

"I..."

Andrei grazes his teeth against the inside of my thigh and my entire body clenches. I gasp, but when he kisses the small bite mark better, my stomach billows with greedy desire.

"More," I hear myself whisper. Then Andrei's tongue comes out and my meek voice explodes. I scream as he paints a wet line directly to my soaking clit. "Oh my god!"

The cry rips from my throat and my neck snaps back. My hands are immediately in Andrei's short black hair, nails digging into every strand they can grab hold of.

"No. Say my fucking name," he growls, in between slurps of my soaking pussy.

"Andrei..." I putter.

"That's better."

His tongue circles my clit, starting slow, but with so much withheld energy that I can already feel the intensity to come. My legs spread further apart.

This is the first time anyone has ever tasted me here. It feels better than I could have imagined. Like I'm being tugged from side to side under the waves of a sizzling sea. Andrei is the ocean. His tongue, the waves. His power is unbelievable. Careless almost. But there's something so natural about it all. He circles my swollen nub faster and faster until I feel his scalp under my nails.

The world disappears. My stomach convulses. My chest pounds.

I cry out so loud I'm deaf to it.

It's the first orgasm someone else has ever given me. And it reaches a peak so high I'm breathless as I pant back down to earth.

But Andrei isn't done with me yet.

"You have at least one more in you," he says, kissing the inside of my thigh. "I demand you give it to me."

Standing up, he grabs the edge of my dress that's just barely crumpled over my tits. In one swift movement, he rids my body of it. Then, without pause, he tips me back, kissing my neck while flicking my bra clasp with expert fingers. When he trails his fingers over my shoulders to pull off my last line of defense, I nearly start to sob.

It feels like I've been plunged into a wet fire. I can hardly take it. And this is him being gentle...

"You're even sweeter than I expected," Andrei rasps, licking his glistening lips. "But my tongue isn't what needs to taste you most."

I gulp.

"What is?"

"Let me show you."

The back of his fingers brush against my flushed cheeks as he glares at me with those heart-throbbing green eyes. All I can do is stare back as his knuckles sweep down my throat to my tits.

He takes my hard nipple between two fingers and gently pinches.

I writhe and moan and he plants his other hand on my thigh, holding me in place as he twists and plays with me.

"You really are something," he says, eyelids dropping halfway over his eyes. "Oh, the fun I'll have..."

I'm quickly overwhelmed by the attention to my nipples. Sometimes, they're almost more sensitive than my clit. This feels like one of those times.

"... What did you want to show me?" I croak.

"Ah, there it is," he smiles. "That naughty curiosity. I knew I could eat it out of you. Here, angel. My gift to you."

Releasing my nipple, he slides both thumbs beneath the band of his stretched briefs. Then, without further ceremony, he disrobes.

My jaw drops to the fucking floor.

His cock breaks free, springing to life in all of its thick, veiny glory.

At first, I'm so blinded by a deep instinct to shove it between my lips, that I don't even consider if it will fit. But when that thought finally comes, my breath turns lighter.

"It... it's huge..." I whisper.

"You can handle it," Andrei quickly assures me. Slipping his hand back around my neck, he palms my skull. "I believe in you, little deer."

His free hand digs into the unbuttoned collar of his shirt. With hardly any effort, he rips it from his body, revealing a canvas of unbelievable muscle... nearly every inch of which is covered if dark, gothic tattoos.

His chest heaves as he draws closer. My back arches. The girthy head of his rock-hard cock touches my soaking pussy lips.

"I can't... it won't fit..."

His grip around the back of my neck tightens.

"Do you want it to fit?"

I nod. There's no hesitation. I'm lost in the moment, but even from the back of all this thick haze, my brain won't stop shouting at me to be realistic.

No. Fuck reality. It's fucked me for too long. Give some good fantasy dick. I want to drown in it. That's what brought me this far, after all.

"So full of surprises," Andrei grins, increasing the pressure of his cock against my lips. "But I promise you this, little deer. I will figure you out."

I grab his forearm.

He breaks the threshold.

"Yes..." The gasp rips from my throat just as one rumbles from his.

Our groans mix in a chorus of deep bass and heavenly soprano. He stretches me out more with every inch. My legs spread, then start to retract, thighs squeezing around his muscular hips.

"How are you so tight?" Andrei moans, his voice warbling as his fingers tremble around the back of my head.

"I'm..." I almost let it slip. But my innocence is the last thing I want to bring up right now. Andrei is burning it away. I say good riddance. "I'm sorry."

"No, angel," he chuckles. "This is a gift. *You* are a fucking gift."

With that, Andrei smashes his lips against mine. A searing pain rips through me as he thrusts his cock all the way in. His hard pelvis smacks against my writhing stomach. The pain is joined by a mind-numbing ecstasy and a life-altering relief.

"You feel so good," I choke, a hot tear running down my cheek.

Andrei bites into my lower lip and pulls.

"This is just the start," he growls, pulling his cock back, but not out.

"Please..." I squeak. "Please."

"Please what, angel?" His voice breaks. "Tell me what you want. Do you want me to fuck you? Hard or gentle?"

"I don't care," I surrender. "Just fuck me."

"As you wish."

He pounds into me and I almost split in two. Somehow, my body stays put. My mind, though, is torn asunder. Pieces of burning lust scatter from my core, melting into an agonizing euphoria that's so addicting I try to push back into it.

My hips start to sway mindlessly. Andrei's thick cock bends from side to side. It hurts too much to bear, but the thought of being without it is so much worse.

"I will give you the world," Andrei roars. "But only if you beg for it."

Easing back just an inch, he impales me again. Then again and again, all as I cry that word he seems so desperate for.

"Please... Andrei." I claw at his shoulders trying to pull him in. My thighs tremble with desire.

"Say my name again," he whispers. "Come on. Be a good girl. Do as I say. Beg."

"Andrei..." I rasp, beyond delirious. "Andrei... please... fuck me. I need you. I need you... please!"

My cries turn to sobs.

All the stress of the past few months evaporates in a terrible bliss. I'm plunged beneath waves of fire. Andrei growls in such deep, matchless satisfaction that I half believe he feels the same way.

My eyelashes flutter shut. I sink into it all. But Andrei will not let me drift too far from him.

"Eyes open, angel," he grunts, pulling at my hair. "You are going to look at me while I make you cum."

Those hard green eyes sharpen. His thrusts quicken. His cock swells.

I force my eyes back open. His lips are right there. I kiss them. Compared to the heat tearing through me down below, his mouth is a cool relief. Our lips lock as his body pounds inside mine. My juices gush down his cock and seep under my ass. I must be leaving a stain on his desk, but neither of us cares.

He strokes deep and steady in a carnal rhythm. I continue to mindlessly ride him back, despite the pain. My muscles match his tempo, contracting down his shaft. The pleasure is intense. I don't know what I was expecting from my first time, but it definitely wasn't this.

It feels like we're a perfect fit, even if I could split at the seams at any moment.

"Fuck..." I whimper.

This is incredible. Mind-numbing. Chest-pounding.

I'm lost in his body. He's lost in mine.

I hardly notice when he increases his speed. My breath comes quicker and shorter. Blasts of ecstasy threaten to rupture my mind. I hear myself screaming, but I can't stop kissing him.

Tearing off my mouth, Andrei stares deep into my eyes and continues to slam down into me. I stare back, shrouded in a state of shock. Our uninterrupted gaze only ends when he leans down and nudges his forehead against mine.

"You belong to me now," he hisses between gritted teeth. "Do you understand?"

I just scream in response. I can't form words. His cock is so damn hard I can't stand it. He pounds my thighs apart and my juices flood down my ass. I can't stop it.

"Listen closely, little deer," he snarls. "You're going to cum all over my cock. And then you're going to do it again. And again, and again..."

His voice spirals me into insanity. I never want to stop hearing that voice whispering filthy commands into my ears. I want to give him everything he wants. My body, my mind, my soul. I want him to own it all. I want him to own me.

But first and foremost, I want to cum for him.

"Now, angel. Cum for me now. Shed those pretty white wings. Soak them in cum. Cover my cock. Drown me. I want to feel you burst. Don't make me wait one second longer."

I scream again and I feel myself falling into a bottomless

chasm that I'll never be able to crawl out of...

Andrei drives in even harder. He starts yelling something, commanding me, but I can't hear him over my screams. I only know I have to do this. My whole life depends on this moment.

I go to scream one last time, but his kiss muffles the sound.

Then, I spin out of control. Whimpers mix with sobbing cries. They all echo in my mind as my body convulses in such a massive climax that I'm not sure I'll survive it.

Out of the deafening chaos, I hear Andrei roaring in my ear. "That's a good girl... Such a fucking good girl..."

For a moment, I linger in no-man's-land, unable to form a thought.

Then, very gradually, I swim back to reality... only to feel Andrei's cock rip out of me. The sudden emptiness is quickly replaced by a new type of thrill when his hot cum flashes over my tingling thighs and belly.

The juice feels alive. It sinks into my skin, staining my soul, marking me... mixing in with the blood that trails down my legs.

Blood.

The fantasy is shattered. Reality comes rushing back.

But when I look up, all I see are Andrei's eyes. His emerald green glare tells me everything I need to know.

He's not done with me yet.

Not by a long shot.

5

ANDREI

"You're a liar," I tell her, pulling on my shirt as I study the flushed little vixen with all the curiosity in the world.

She's perched on the edge of the desk, shamefully slinking her bra back on. Her pretty blue eyes have been avoiding mine since we finished, but now they snap up at me, wide and wild with fear.

"What? How?" she gulps.

But a smile creeps onto my lips when I see the subtle signs of a snarl on hers.

This girl is a fighter.

And she's mine.

"Those eyes of yours," I nod, turning my jaw. "They scream innocence. But that mouth does the dirtiest tricks."

"I..." Her bra clasps into place and she jumps off the desk. But she's too weak for such quick movements, and I have to step forward and grab her just to keep her from falling. "... My head," she whispers.

"Looks like I fucked a migraine into you," I note. "Here, let me get you something to help with that."

I place her back onto the desk, but before I can take more than two steps, she reaches out and grabs my wrist.

My smile grows wider.

She's afraid of me, but there's also something more going on inside that pretty little head. That's rare. Usually, the girls I bang are as vacuous as they are insatiable. But Natalya looks like she'd break if I tried to push her any further. So, why is she holding me so tightly?

"No," she says, so quietly I barely hear. "I... I should go..."

There's another twist. It makes me tilt my head and my lips clamp shut.

If only I could slip inside of her again and figure out what she's thinking. Learn how she operates. Then maybe I could get her to tell me what she's clearly too afraid to say. I could break down that fear and make her worship me. I could make her do whatever I want.

Actually, that's exactly what I'm going to do.

Fuck. She's perfect.

Natalya presents such a perfect blank slate. She doesn't come pre-programmed with a bunch of ideas about what I can do for her and how much money I can give her. She doesn't even want to be in the same room with me, even though we just shared the most mind-blowing sex.

I want to keep her for myself. I want to corrupt her and taste her sweet essence every day. But that fantasy is already in jeopardy. Something is wrong. It's written all over her face. She won't even look at me.

If she were any other girl, I would be relieved. I don't want another lovesick stalker. But it's not the same with her. I'm the one who's in danger of becoming obsessed. And I know exactly why.

She's the challenge I've been craving. And it's a completely different challenge than I was expecting. A far more delicate challenge. A harder challenge.

I'm going to shape her into my bride.

The thought nearly makes me shiver with excitement. It's a feeling I haven't experienced in forever. Somehow, though, this little deer has inspired it in me.

But if I'm not careful, she'll break. And I can't have that.

"At least let me get you something for the blood," I tell her.

"The blood..." she whispers as if just remembering it.

It's not the first time I've made a girl bleed. When you're as big as I am, it happens. But usually, I let them clean themselves up. With Natalya, though... shit, I want to kneel down and gently wipe her down myself.

"It's nothing serious," I assure her.

Still, her hand falls from my wrist. Before it can get too far, though, I take her fingers and pull them to my lips. The back of her palm is dewy and hot. The taste of her skin is divine.

I think about all that I have in store for her. And what that means for me.

I won't be able to consolidate power over the city without an heir. As it is, the other crime families in town are constantly angling for me to marry one of their daughters, but I don't want them. I want this girl.

Well, I want her if she is what I hope she is. And there's only one way to find that out.

Reaching down, I pick up my discarded suit jacket and reach into the breast pocket. "How about something else to calm your nerves?" I ask, pulling out my cigarette case.

I don't smoke, not anymore, but I've found it a valuable tactic in calming a room. Yet when I pop it open and hold it out to Natalya, she just glances up at me and shakes her head.

"No, thank you. I... I'm not nervous... just... in shock."

The second I let go of her hand, she stumbles over to pick up her dress and torn panties.

"I can get you another kind if you don't like these," I say, watching her with keen interest.

"I don't smoke," she says, more sternly this time. "I never liked the smell."

I bite down on my tongue. There's another difference between her and every other girl I've ever met. Usually, the thinner the girl, the more she smokes. To them, the numbing agent of nicotine is a way to keep them from getting hungry. But Natalya must not need that outside influence. Is it because she has more self-discipline than other girls or just better genetics?

I try to study her body for signs of an answer. But she quickly slips that old black dress on, and a small wave of disappointment crashes through me. I already miss the pale, tender skin of her petite frame. The pink mounds of her perfect breasts. The gap where her wondrous pussy is tucked so temptingly.

Lifting my brow, I snap the case shut and put it back in my pocket. Then, I button my shirt and pull on my jacket, but I can't stop watching her. Her small, perfect body enchants me.

My mind keeps flipping from one scenario to another. I think of everything I want to do to her. It's too much. I'm not used to getting overwhelmed. Men like me don't survive long if we do. But right now, I'm drowning in fantasy.

Natalya turns her back on me and straightens her dress. I can't help myself. I ease up behind her, and when I press against her from behind, my cock swells again. I cram my bulge into her ass and bend her over the desk. Then I slip my arms around her waist and talk directly into her ear. "Don't get dressed yet, angel. I need more of you."

She gasps and tries to turn around. But the tension running through her body makes me even more ravenous. Fuck, she makes me so hard. I pin her in place.

The torn panties slip from her fingers and flutter under the desk.

"Haven't I fallen far enough for you?" she asks.

I remember what I told her before we fucked.

"Wouldn't you like to see how much further I can drag you down?"

"I..." she struggles for moment before I feel her pause. Curious, I lean over her body and follow her eyes.

"What is it, little deer?"

"The cabinet," she gulps, staring up at the viper and skull crest that cuts through the middle of my wall-to-wall bookcase.

"What about it?"

"I... What's in there?"

I can see her staring at the scars on the black wood, the marks carved into the gold, the dark red stains covering the corners. The deep blackness in the keyhole. The silent scream of the viper-impaled skull. If only she knew what that thing has been through; what *I've* been through.

No. She can't handle that. Not yet.

So, I brush her off. "Wouldn't you like to know."

"I'm not sure I would." Her gaze drops and I can feel the tension of fear returning to her warm body.

It's another twist. She's denying herself. Again, I wonder if it's discipline or something else. "You're too strong to give into that fear," I assure her. "You want to know what's in there. And I want to tell you."

"But you won't," she guesses correctly.

"No. I'll show you... once you've earned it."

I glide my hands down Natalya's side until I get to her hips. She sighs, and when she strains again, her ass crushes my cock. In response, I grab her wrist and place her hand down flat on my desk.

She doesn't fight it. Instead, she moans, arches her back, and shoves her ass into me. "Fucking hell," I grumble. She is so fucking perfect. "You really are a good girl. Now bend over for me. Take what I give you, little deer. We can uncover all of our dirty secrets together."

"Little deer..." she whispers. "Why do you keep calling me that?"

"Because you've wandered into my dark forest on those long, unsure legs," I tell her, looking down at her irresistible thighs. "But don't worry, I'll steady them... and protect you from all the other wolves. All you have to do is stay close."

"*Other* wolves?" she gulps.

I pull my hand around her waist and she rotates her pelvis to draw me in. When she turns and meets my eyes, her face smolders with so much heat I'm nearly driven feral.

"That's right. The night is filled with them. But you've been claimed by the biggest and most savage of them all. So this time, you can close your eyes. I'll take care of you."

A silent gasp sticks in her throat when I squeeze her tight.

"Why are you doing this to me?" she asks, clearly hating how turned on she is.

"Because I want to. Because *you* want me to... or am I mistaken?"

"I don't know what I want anymore."

"Then do as I say. Close your eyes and let your body take over."

"My body is lost."

With a savage snarl, I hook my fingers under her dress and pull it up again.

"Don't worry, I've found it."

Her intoxicating smell hits me in the nostrils and my eyelids flutter. I want to tear her apart and put her back together. Then do it all over again. Forever.

"Just for tonight," Natalya whispers.

"What was that, little deer?" I ask, filled to the brim with curiosity.

"I said, just for tonight. I'll be your little whore. I'll let you do whatever you want to me. But only for tonight. I... I want to give in. But I need to know I can go back."

"Go back to what?"

"To being myself."

"This is you," I grumble, running my hand through her soft hair.

"No. It's not. But it *is* fun," she quietly admits. "I could use a little bit of fun…"

Just like that, it hits me.

Natalya is using me. But not like I thought. She never does anything expected.

To her, I'm not some all-powerful underworld king. I'm not some tit to suckle at, some god to worship, some mark to con.

I'm a hard body and an eager dick. An experiment for a naïve, sheltered young girl.

This little minx.

"I'll give you more than a little," I say, ready to throw my caution to the wind. But then I feel Natalya's body ease… and hear a small giggle float up from her lips.

Another fucking twist.

This girl is driving me wild.

With a vicious grunt, I yank my belt free and drop my pants to my knees. But just as my cock touches her velvet pussy, someone knocks on my office door.

I nearly explode with rage.

Who dares interrupt me?

A deep voice calls from out in the hall. "You in there, Pakhan?"

It's Dima.

Natalya rockets off the desk and spins around, her pretty eyes as huge as dinner plates.

To my surprise, the shocked look on her face snaps me out of my fit. An unexpectedly playful energy sparks between us. "Quick!" I whisper, stepping in front of her. "Get under the desk."

She snatches her dress and ducks out of sight. I don't have

time to put my pants back on, so I just kick them under the desk and sit down in my chair to make sure Dima doesn't see.

"Come in!" I yell as soon as Natalya is out of sight.

The door clicks open and Dima strides in. "I'm sorry, Pakhan. I wouldn't bother you if it wasn't an emergency."

My playfulness is immediately contained.

"What's the emergency?"

Dima approaches the desk and I straighten my posture. In this line of work, emergencies are almost always a matter of life and death. Playtime is over. It's time to get serious.

But Natalya doesn't get the message.

"Valentin is out of control," Dima starts. But I hardly hear him. Because the second he opens his mouth, so does Natalya... right around my fucking cock.

From under the desk, I feel her satin lips engulf my half-hard shaft. Her tongue flattens as she struggles to take me. My fingers dig into the arms on my leather chair and I forcefully suppress a grunt. Luckily, the sound of the crunching leather is loud enough to cover up the sound of Natalya choking on my erection as it reaches full mast.

"What has he done this time? I growl, gritting my teeth in a desperate attempt to remain in control of my senses.

But Natalya is quickly winning out.

This. Little. Fucking. Minx.

She's sucking me off under the table, right in front of one of my men.

"Well, we threw that jackass Mike out, just like you said," Dima explains. "But he started mouthing off to Valentin and Valentin just fucking lost it. He started beating the guy up and now he won't stop. None of the other guys want to interfere because... well, because he's Valentin. He usually only listens to his blood-brother. Can you talk to him?"

Natalya's delicate hands tiptoe up my thighs and her hair brushes the inside of my legs. My nails dig deeper into the leather. My thighs clench. I probably look furious, but in reality, I'm just barely holding myself together.

She feels fucking amazing.

"Fuck."

I feel my cock hit the back of Natalya's tiny throat. But that's too much for the vixen-in-training, and when she pulls out, I have to pound my fist down on the desk to cover up the sound of her coughing.

"I'm so sorry, Pakhan," Dima says again, falling for the act. "You're the only one who can control him. I'm worried he might kill the idiot."

Before he can finish, Natalya has already gone back to work. Her tongue ripples along the underside of my shaft and she lashes mind-blowing licks around my balls with every stroke.

I want to collapse and groan in agony. Fuck. No one has ever sucked my cock this good. Reaching under the desk with one hand, I grab a tuft of Nataly's hair and feel my way back into her dripping mouth. A light gasp is all that escapes her lips before I re-fill them with my cock.

I feel her gag, but I don't release her. Not yet.

This is what you get, little deer.

Two can play at this game.

"All right," I tell Dima, my voice shaking. "Go keep an eye on him and I'll be down in a second."

"Yes, Pakhan."

When Dima nods and turns his back on us, I finally give Natalya the chance to breathe. Still, I let out a loud round of coughs to cover up her desperate gasps for air.

Then, to my absolute shock, she immediately goes back to finish the job.

I cover my face with my hands and heave a heavy sigh. It's all I can do to smother another groan of desperate ecstasy.

That stops Dima at the door.

"Are you alright, Pakhan?" he asks, confused by my reaction.

"Yes," I growl into my palms. "Go!"

But Dima doesn't immediately leave, and for a moment, I just sit there with my face buried in my hands, secretly getting my cock sucked by an innocent dove as he watches, trying everything known to man to compose myself. But I can hardly sit still.

It's like Natalya can sense how restless I am. Without any provocation, she scoots in even closer. Her fingers flex on my thighs in a gripping movement before she threads them through my pubic hair.

She sucks me quicker in long, luscious strokes. She's really getting into it. I would give my right arm to grab her by the hair again and use that filthy fucking mouth right, but I can't move. I'm at her mercy.

"It's an emergency," Dima carefully reminds me, finally stepping out into the hallway. "Mike was already in pretty bad shape when I came up here."

"I heard you. I'm on my way. Just give me a minute."

"Yes, Pakhan."

He finally leaves and I collapse in my chair. I grab the arms and my last nerve snaps now that I can really appreciate what Natalya's doing to me.

She gulps me in greedy mouthfuls and her hot, deadly tongue brings me to the edge of cumming all over again. She sucks me like she's desperate to find out how I taste. It's irresistible. I just want to sit here and let her keep sucking me forever, but Natalya has other ideas.

Without warning, she glides off me. "Shouldn't you go downstairs and deal with Mike?"

The fucking tease.

I pry my eyes open and stare down at her pointed little face looking up from between my thighs. She kneels under my desk and rests her hands on my leg. My pre-cum dribbles down her chin.

My cold, dead heart twists. I don't want to go anywhere. But slowly, the reality of what Dima said dawns on me.

Shit. I trust Valentin with my life, but he's got to learn how to control his fucking anger. I won't always be there to save him from himself. But I am tonight. And I can't just sit here while he beats some rich asshole to death on our property. That's bad news for everyone, including me. Unfortunately, Dima is right. I'm the only one who can stop him. Everyone else is too afraid.

I need to go.

Still, I stare down at Natalya for a second longer, cupping her chin and running my thumb across her moist lips. Her saliva mingles with my pre-cum.

She is perfect.

"Stay here," I order.

Natalya rakes her teeth across her lip and then licks them. A mischievous flame flickers behind her pure blue eyes.

"You're leaving?"

"It's not up for discussion."

I start to stand.

"How long will you be?" she asks, letting me go.

"Not long."

Reaching down, I offer my hand. She takes it and I lift her onto my chair. It's far too big for her tiny body, and she sinks into the leather like a stone into black water. Yet it somehow suits her.

She looks good on my throne. Maybe I'll get her a matching one.

"So, have I earned it yet?"

Twirling the chair around, she stares off at the gold-encrusted cabinet at the center of my bookshelf. It's like she can sense what's behind it.

No, little deer. You have no idea what that holds, I think. *And you're definitely not ready for it. I'm not fooled by your little sneak attack. You're still far too innocent for the secrets I keep.*

"That depends on how well you listen," I say, taking my turn to tease her.

"Is it locked?" she asks.

Bending down, I pick up my pants and slip them on. Then I reach around the chair and grab a handful of Natalya's hair. Pulling, I expose her neck and kiss her lips. She tastes like me.

"Everything in here is locked up nice and tight," I tell her. "And if you do anything too naughty, I'll lock you up too."

I release her and zip up.

"Fine," she sighs.

Fucking Valentin.

"I'll be back."

Cursing everything, I arrange my clothes and pray that I can get rid of this hard-on before I go downstairs. When I get to the door, I look back over my shoulder. But Natalya is hidden behind the tall black backrest. She's still staring at the crest on that cabinet.

"Don't go anywhere," I repeat.

The door clicks shut behind me and I shake my head clear.

Fuck. It feels like I was lost in my own little world for a while there. How wonderfully rare.

Leaving that behind, I run down the stairs at a fast clip. The sooner I get this over with, the sooner I can get back to what really matters. I can't wait to get my hands on Natalya again.

I march through the club and break out on the street next to Vadi the bouncer. He stays at his station, but I can see the problem from here. Ten of my enforcers stand around watching as Valentin pounds Mike into the pavement.

Mike isn't moving anymore. Still, Valentin straddles his chest, swinging wild punches at his head. Mike's skull whips back and forth with every blow.

I shove my way through the crowd and grab Valentin by the

collar. I rip him off and almost lose my grip on him when he starts to thrash. For a second, he tries to fight me. "You son of a bitch! Get the fuck off me! I'll kill...."

I yank him by the shirt and shake him hard. "Wake the fuck up! It's me!"

He jerks right and left for a second before I finally get through to him. "Pakhan..."

"You've done enough, soldier. Are you trying to kill him or what?"

Valentin glances down at Mike and back at me. "Pakhan..."

"Is that the only word you know any more? Yeah. It's me. Come on. Pull your head out of your ass. I didn't tell you to kill the guy. Are you trying to bring the cops down here?"

He gulps and goes limp in my hand. I shake him one more time and finally let go of his shirt. He looks away and tries to straighten himself out.

I turn to the other guys standing around and point down at Mike's lifeless body. "One of you take this piece of shit to the hospital... and make sure to use our people. No cops—no reports—no hassles."

"Yes, Pakhan," someone replies.

"Stay with him until he regains consciousness. Make sure he understands that, if he ever comes back to any of our establishments, it will go worse for him next time." I look around and spot Dima. "Take Valentin upstairs to the conference room on the seventh floor. Wait there until I come."

"Yes, Pakhan." Dima nudges Valentin and Valentin shoots me a glance, before immediately looking away. I hope to hell he realizes how close he came to getting us all in a world of shit.

I stay outside while Dima takes Valentin inside. That leaves me with the rest of the guys. "You boys get back to work. The show is over. You—Alexei—and you—Viktor— take over downstairs and make sure none of the other patrons have any problems. Keep an eye on things and...."

They all stare at me waiting to hear what I say next. Usually, I'd tell them to report to me if anything goes wrong, but that's the last thing I want right now. I don't want anyone disturbing me while I spend the rest of my night with Natalya.

Tonight will be about fun. Tomorrow, I will start to plan for her preparation. Because I've already decided. She will be my challenge.

And if she can survive that, then maybe I will make her my wife too.

"Pakhan?" Viktor asks, snapping me from my thoughts. "What should we do if anything goes wrong?"

"Call me on my phone," I grunt. "I'll deal with it myself. You heard me. Get back to work."

The group breaks up and Vadi opens the door for me. I stride straight past everyone. There's only one thing on my mind. Her. I can't stop thinking about her. But I know I can't go back to Natalya until I put Valentin in his place.

He needs to fucking learn already.

In the past, I've found a challenge in taming his brutish ways; grooming him for a real leadership role. But for obvious reasons, I'm in no mood for that tonight.

I run up to the conference to find Valentin sitting in a chair and Dima standing guard over him. When I enter, Valentin looks up at me, then immediately goes back to staring at the floor. "I'm...."

I must be the only person in the world who can turn this fearsome beast meek. It's a responsibility I don't take lightly.

"Don't even say it," I snap. "Don't tell me you're sorry. Tell me you'll do better. When are you gonna grow up, huh? It isn't like you're my rowdy kid brother or something. You're thirty-five years old and this is how you act?"

Shit. He's barely a year younger than me. This shouldn't be happening.

"Yes, Pakhan," he mutters.

"How much longer were you gonna rock his skull in for? Why? He wasn't going to learn anything more while he was unconscious. What would you have done if you killed him out there? Right on our fucking doorstep! Do you have any idea how many problems that could have created for us?"

"Yes, Pakhan," he rasps.

"We have enough trouble in this town as it is. The police are already looking for any reason to bring us down. Same with the feds and the politicians. We might have half of them on our payroll, but that doesn't mean much if the other half is still out for our blood. If you can't control yourself, maybe you shouldn't be my second-in-command..."

Valentin stiffens and starts to raise his head, but he quickly catches himself and lowers his gaze back to the carpet. No one challenges me.

No one but Natalya, apparently.

"Yes, Pakhan," Valentin quietly nods. "You do what you think is best. If you demote me, I'll be grateful for your mercy."

I glance over at Dima and take a deep breath. I'm not telling Valentin anything he doesn't already know. There's no way I can demote him. He might be a loose cannon, but he's the closest thing I have to a brother and everyone knows it.

If there's one thing I've learned from coming up in this dark and brutal world, it's that when you find someone you can trust, you hold on to them, no matter how much trouble they are.

With a frustrated sigh, I clamp Valentin's shoulder in a tight grip. "Go get yourself cleaned up and get downstairs. Tell Viktor and Alexei to report to you instead of me if they have any problems."

"Yes, Pakhan. I'm..." He stops himself from saying he's sorry again. I don't want to hear that, not now or ever again.

With a curt nod I turn and leave. The door hardly shut behind me before I'm beating it back to my office.

My cock pulls me forward. My heart pounds. My vision narrows.

I need to taste her again. I need to fuck her.

My shoulder flies into the office door and it bursts open.

My pounding heart freezes.

The chair I left Natalya on is turned back to face me, but she's not on it. In fact, she's nowhere to be seen.

"Fuck," I growl, storming over to my desk just to make sure she isn't hiding underneath it.

She isn't. My stomach turns.

Why would she leave?

Damn it. It doesn't matter. I should have done with her what I do with all my property.

Locked it up.

With a frustrated huff, I head for the door. If I'm not too late, I might be able to intercept Natalya before she leaves the building. But the second I turn back around, Valentin pushes into the office, eyes glued down at his phone.

"Hey, I just got a call from Luigi Corao," he says, looking up. "He's the Santarelli family's consigliere. I—"

I blow past him, pushing into the corridor. "I know who the hell Luigi Corao is. You don't have to tell me. I thought I told you to leave me alone. Why are you here?"

It takes Valentin a second to realize I'm not standing around waiting to hear whatever it is he's trying to tell me. He hurries after me and catches me on the stairs. "He wants a meeting."

"Tell him I'm busy."

"You can't tell him that!" Valentin waves his phone in agitation. "He's..."

I burst out onto the mezzanine and cross to the spot where I first noticed Natalya. With a racing pulse, I search the dance floor, but something in my gut already knows she won't be there.

"Where did you run off to, you little minx..."

Valentin pulls up next to me. "Seriously. What do you want me to tell him?"

I point down to the bar. "Get down there. I want you to find four girls—one of them is wearing a little black dress. She has blonde hair and blue eyes. If you can't find her, then find one of her friends. Find out what happened to them. I want names, phone numbers, and home addresses on my desk in an hour."

Valentin raises his eyebrows at me. "You want girls—now? What about..."

"Did you hear me? They were just down there by the bar. Find out who they are and where they went."

Valentin crams his phone into his pocket. He's always better when he follows orders. That will bring him back out from the doghouse quicker than anything else. And right now, he's my best shot at tracking down Natalya.

Without another word, he takes off downstairs and I go back outside to find Vadi. The big bouncer straightens up immediately. "Can I help you with anything, Pakhan?"

"Yeah, Vadi. You let a group of four girls into the club a little while ago. One of them was wearing a tight black dress. Another was in some kind of sequined monstrosity. Both were blonde. I can't remember what the others looked like. Do you know who I'm talking about?"

He thinks on it for a moment before nodding. "Yeah. I let them in."

"Did they use IDs? Did you catch any of their names?"

I can see him desperately trying to remember.

"No," he finally says, shaking his head. "They didn't use IDs. The fancy one showed me one of those passes we handed out last month. It was expired, but I let them in anyway because they were a nice-looking group of girls. Valentin told me to take it easy on the ladies, especially the ones that looked high-class."

I punch my fist into my palm. "Shit!"

"Did I do something wrong, Pakhan? I was just following orders."

"No, Vadi. You did fine. I'm mad at myself, not you."

He relaxes and I drag my enraged ass back inside. Fuck. I should have never let Natalya out of my sight. At the very least, I should have found out everything about her before I left to deal with Valentin and that waste of flesh Mike.

I have to find her.

I'm already committed. Obsessed. Starving for more.

My fingers fold into fists.

I *will* find her.

No matter the cost.

Valentin catches up with me on the stairs. "Sorry, man. The girls are gone."

"I know that. Who are they?"

"I don't know. They didn't pay with a credit card."

"How did they pay?"

"They didn't. The girl in the sequins told the bartender she was friends with Elina and the bartender didn't ask any questions."

Damn it. Fate better not be fucking with me on this one. Just when I find a girl I can stand, she vanishes without a trace.

"Do you want me to keep looking for her?" Valentin waits a second longer before he summons the courage to ask. He's still jumpy from earlier. "Don't you at least want to hear what Luigi had to say?"

"Fuck it," I nod. Together, we head for my office, but my heart isn't in it. All I can think about is her. Those lips. That pussy. My challenge. I know I won't be satisfied until she's back under my desk, sucking my cock.

Next time, I'll just have to remember to chain her down. That way she won't ever be able to escape.

Natalya doesn't know it yet, but she's mine.

And I don't ever give up what's mine.

6

NATALYA

I stumble trying to run in my cracked high heels but I can't slow down. It doesn't matter how weak my knees are, or how hard my heart pounds, I skid around a corner and race for my apartment building.

The dried blood staining my thighs feels so thick and heavy. My mind is a jumbled mess. My fingers fumble getting my keys out of my handbag to unlock the door. I keep glancing behind me all the way inside the building.

Every labored breath I take is joined by the same surreal thought.

Holy shit. I just lost my virginity to a mob boss. And he was *not* planning on letting me go.

My pulse flutters while I dash up the stairs. The elevator has been broken since I moved in, and usually, I don't give it much thought, but the lights in the stairwell have been smashed out and I can't help but wince away from every shadow and pocket of darkness.

Andrei could be waiting around any corner to grab me. I left. I disobeyed him. A man like that can't be happy about such insolence. But I am worth chasing?

God, I hope not.

I keep my hand on the railing to check where I am between landings. My nerves unravel behind me. Every other step seems to be coated in some kind of sticky or slick liquid. The air is dusty and filled with the scent of mold.

I cough.

This place will be the death of me long before Andrei can find it. But I'm used to decrepit apartment complexes. What I'm not used to is men like him.

Powerful men.

A shudder runs up my spine as I remember what he felt like.

Terrifying. Painful.

Incredible. Intoxicating.

The handrail gives out under my weight and I stumble forward, desperate to keep going. That's when the rickety heel on my left shoe finally decides to give out. It snaps and I fall. I've hardly hit the ground before I'm back on my lopsided feet, scrambling to the dirty safety of my apartment.

"Fuck, fuck fuck..."

My curses echo through the damp darkness.

This building isn't the Ritz Hotel, but it's the closest thing I have to a sanctuary. If I could afford a fortified castle, then that's where I'd be running to. But I can barely keep up with my monthly payments here—so it will have to do.

This is what you deserve.

Torturous squirms of adrenaline jitter through my stomach as I race up through the dark stairwell. I can't stop thinking about Andrei. About what we did. About what *I* did. God, what a slut I turned out to be. Not only did I let him fuck me, but I sucked his cock under the desk too. What was I thinking?

That he's the hottest guy you've ever laid eyes on. That you would never get another chance to really let it all go like that. That it was only polite to return the favor after he rocked your world.

I might as well have been high. Now I'm coming back to Earth real quick and the thought of what I did makes me want to disappear. I sucked a gorgeous Bratva boss's massive cock and I loved it. I felt so fucking hot and wicked hiding under his desk and licking him while he talked to one of his men. I would have gone on forever if he'd let me. But powerful men are busy, and he didn't have time for it or me.

... I wonder if he could tell I was a virgin?

It feels like the last thing I should be worried about, but once the thought appears in my mind, it won't leave.

Shit. He definitely didn't make me feel like it was my first time. Sure, I'm still burning from head to toe, and so sore I could fall back to the ground at any second, but the ache is a good one, like a searing afterglow.

He didn't baby me, and I'm strangely thankful for that. Something about the way he handled me was so... generous. Almost like he was leading the way, even when he made it seem like I was in control.

If only I'd known sex could be that wonderful then maybe I'd have given in and done it sooner. Maybe I could have found some small pockets of happiness in my sad life. Maybe I could have made Andrei cum again before he had to leave...

The thought is dirty enough to shock me out of my own daydream. I remember where I am and why I'm sweating.

A sharp tingle washes across my body and I shiver. I ran from him. There's no going back now. I can never do anything like that again—no matter how good he felt.

Bursting out of the stairwell, I limp straight for my apartment. It only takes a second to unlock the door then relock it behind me. Taking a shaky breath, I toss my keys aside, kick off my broken shoes, and lean against the peeled wall. I'm home. Thank God.

I should feel relief. Instead, something makes me pause. I'm just about to take the handbag off my shoulder when a cold breeze rushes over my skin—it's accompanied by the faintest smell of gasoline.

Shit, did I leave the stove on?

I look over to the kitchen, but the light isn't on. In fact, none of the lights are. Except for the small red square pouring in through the window from the Coca-Cola sign next door, the apartment is bathed in impenetrable darkness.

Slowly, I sniff the air.

The stench of gasoline remains. I'm not imagining it.

"Where is that coming from?" I mutter, looking over my tiny apartment.

I call this my apartment, but it's really just a studio room. The kitchen sink, counter, fridge, and a few shitty cupboards cover one corner and part of the wall. The other three walls are relatively barren, save the door behind me and the window ahead.

My single bed sits in the other corner. It isn't much, but at least I'm not sleeping on the floor anymore. My eyes squint through the darkness. Something feels off.

My stomach drops when I see the open window. The one that leads to the fire escape.

I didn't open that window. I never do. Because once it's open, it's nearly impossible to shut again.

My heart starts to pound, slower and heavier than before.

I glance around the room again, but I can't tell if anything is out of place. Holding my breath, I cautiously make my way over to the window and stick my head out, looking out at the street beyond the fire escape. I don't see anything, but the hair on my nape stands on edge. It feels like someone is watching me.

I sniff the air. But there's no stench of gasoline out here.

Shit.

Pulling my head back inside, I grab the window to shut it.

"You look so nice when you bend over like that. You'll have to make a habit of it."

The deep rumbling voice comes from behind me.

I whip around, a violent gasp ripping from my throat. But I don't see anything. The apartment is still dark... except for that square of faint red neon light coming from the flashing Coca-Cola sign across the street.

"Who... Who's there..." I somehow manage to squeak.

I can't move. My heart stands still and I don't dare to breathe.

The feeling that someone is watching me intensifies.

A cold sweat breaks out over my damp skin. Then, I see something separate from the shadows by the fridge. The dark figure glides across the room until the red neon light reveals a huge giant of a man.

He's at least a foot taller than Andrei and way more muscular. He turns toward me, his misshapen face lit by the crimson light from outside. Dozens of scars crisscross his cheeks, forehead, and neck. They make him look grotesque and monstrous. Scraggly hair dangles from his scalp; it sways when he breathes.

Without saying a word, he raises a cigarette to his twisted mouth and drags on it. Thick smoke billows in front of his hideous countenance. "Don't look so shocked now, girl," he rumbles. "I might take offense to it."

I struggle to get my voice working again.

"Who... Who are you?"

The monster takes a deep breath. "The name is Nikolai," he says, slow and purposefully—like a predator getting ready to pounce. "But you can call me Nicky. How does that sound?"

My lips open to respond, but my mouth is too dry. There's something deeply terrifying and unsettling about this man. He isn't like Andrei. There's no charm to him. Only horror.

Yet they must be connected. This can't be a coincidence.

... Did Andrei send him here to collect me?

Terror skips across my skin as I feel for the windowsill

behind me. I need to get out of here, but he's blocking the only path to the door. The open window is my only shot—not that I trust myself to get out through it before he can catch me. He's too big and I'm so broken.

"I... I..."

I can't talk. There's no way out. I'm trapped.

The monster seems amused by my fear.

"How wonderful. A mute," he taunts. "Don't worry. That works for me. I hate chatty girls. But that doesn't mean you're allowed to keep completely quiet, girl. A man like me might hate to hear a girl talk, but I love to hear her scream."

He steps forward and something in me snaps.

With all my remaining strength, I deliberately try to push my fear into anger. "Who the fuck are you?" I yell, my voice cracking with every word. "What the hell are you doing in my apartment? Get out before I call the police."

He only chuckles. "You won't call the police. In fact, you won't be doing anything without my approval ever again. You belong to me now. I own you. Accept it. That will make this so much easier..."

"What are you talking about?" I gulp, desperately trying to slink further away. But there's nowhere to go. "I don't belong to anyone, let alone you."

He takes another pull on his cigarette. "Wrong. You belong to me. That was the deal. And I am *so* looking forward to finding out if you live up to my wildest fantasies... and my darkest desires."

Another shiver runs up my spine. This guy is crazy. He must have broken in here to—

No.

I shake that disturbing thought from my head. I can't think about what he wants with me. I have to figure out how to get out of here. But one wrong move and I'm done for.

I can already tell that this man won't hesitate to hurt me. A glint of sadistic fire flashes in his eyes when he smirks. He probably hurts people just for fun.

The monster takes another step forward and my body reacts. Before I can give myself time to think, I dart around him and lunge for the door. I'm only halfway there before I remember that I locked it behind me.

I dive for the knob anyway, but he catches me with mind-numbing speed.

A cry tears from my throat as he rips me around to face him. A deep laugh scatters from his mangled lips, echoing through my dark apartment.

I try to scream, but he takes me by the throat and twists my head around hard, forcing me to look right up into his twisted face. Deep scars cut through his hardened skin. One of them is so sharp and black that it almost looks like a tattoo...

"Where ya going, little girl?" he snarls. "You should know better. No one runs away from Nikolai. No. One. Escapes." He strokes the fingers of his other hand down my cheek and the sensation makes my skin crawl. "I gave up good money for you and now you're gonna make it all worth it..."

The sight of his gruesome face up close is so terrifying that I lose my mind. Somehow, I manage to struggle out of his grasp just enough to tuck my chin and sink my teeth into his hand.

I bite down with all my strength.

He bellows in rage. His fingers loosen. I fall to the floor. Without thinking, I scramble in the only direction left. The window.

I dive through the opening, out onto the fire escape. My ears perk up with fear, expecting to hear his heavy footsteps pounding after me.

But incredibly, he doesn't follow.

I look over my shoulder. My stomach drops.

The monster stands in the center of my apartment, just grinning. I'm momentarily frozen in fear again. All I can do is watch as he brings his cigarette to his lips for one last deep draw. Then, without losing that evil grin, he flicks the burning bud onto the carpet.

Flames immediately leap up from the floor. Insanely, my first reaction is to lunge back towards my apartment, but sanity stops me just short of the window. Everything I own flickers behind a growing fire, including the laptop I just went into debt to get fixed—that hunk of junk was my only chance to get into architecture school. Now it's already starting to melt before my very eyes.

There's nothing I can do but stare. It feels like I've been engulfed by a suffocating nightmare. What the hell is going on?

There's no time to stand around and figure that out, a voice screams from the back of my racing mind. *Run!*

Tearing my eyes off the flames, I search for Nikolai. To my horror, he still hasn't moved, but when he finally does, it's not toward me. Instead, he goes over to the stove and picks up a bottle of olive oil. Without so much as stopping to think about it, he smashes off the neck and spills the insides over the burgeoning fire.

Oil sprays across the floor and the whole carpet erupts in flames. He laughs again and my heart leaps into my throat.

He's going to burn my entire apartment to the ground. But it's too late to save anything except for myself. I can't stay here.

With a jagged gulp, I force myself to turn from the hellish scene. The last thing I see is that twisted monster standing in the center of the burning room, flames licking and rising all around him. His deep, ominous laughter haunts me as I scramble down the ladder.

By the time I reach the bottom of the fire escape, hot tears are pouring down my cheeks. My lungs are thrashing. But fear won't let me stop. Dropping to the street below, I take off running, stumbling on my bare feet over the alley trash.

I don't know where to go, but anywhere is better than here.

7

ANDREI

Valentin bumps my shoulder. "Did you hear me?"

"Huh? Sorry."

"I said Luigi Corao wants a meeting. What's wrong with you today? This is important."

"I know." I rub my temples. "Sorry."

My gaze drifts over to the window and I float back into a daydream about last night. I can't stop thinking about Natalya.

"Well?" Valentin demands. "What do you want me to tell him—and don't give me that shit about you being busy. You have to give him something. Hell, just give *me* something to work with."

I drag my attention back into the room. I'm sitting on the couch in my sunken living room atop the highest residential building in Chicago. The penthouse gives me a sweeping view across Chicago, all the way to the lake in the distance. It's a view that usually relaxes me, but right now, its beauty only makes me think about something even more beautiful and alluring.

Her.

Valentin sits across from me with one ankle crossed over his knee. He scrolls through his phone while we talk. He's already forgotten all about last night. That's both good and bad. I hate having to discipline him, but it's my job to keep things under control, and that means keeping him on a leash. We aren't equals and he doesn't want to be, but sometimes, he needs to be reminded of that fact.

"Luigi says Antonio Santarelli wants to offer you his daughter Giovanna's hand in marriage to seal the alliance."

"What alliance?" I mutter.

Valentin cracks a huge grin and pretends to fight it back. Why do I even bother? "The alliance you're going to seal with him and his family by marrying his daughter. None of these Italians can fall over themselves fast enough to make a pact with you. They don't see the consequences or understand that they're just helping you solidify your power. It's so short-sighted. On our end, though? It's a no-brainer."

"Just what I want to hear..."

He laughs and gets to his feet, paces around the living room, squints at the view, and then returns. "This is big. None of the other crime families have ever wanted to come under a Russian banner before. You could unite everyone under your rule. It's a historic opportunity."

I roll my eyes. "Don't you see? They're only brown-nosing because all the Bratvas came under my network last night. They're scared of becoming irrelevant, and rightfully so."

Valentin doesn't even pretend to hear me. "The only question is which of the Italian families you're going to marry into. This is the third offer you've had this year. First it was Tizziana La Plata...."

"I am NOT marrying anyone named Tizziana!"

Valentin explodes in laughter. "Oh, come on! Do me a big favor and give me something to joke about for the next forty years. My life is boring enough as it is."

"Nina Cuozzo is better looking," I carelessly note, just to appease him.

"But older," he points out. "She's our age. And that might not be so good as far as... you know... breeding goes."

I wipe a hand down my face. "Jesus..."

"So... which of their offers are you going to accept?"

"None of them yet. Maybe I'll listen to their propositions, maybe I won't. But I'm not making any decisions until I know what the payoff will be."

"The payoff can be whatever you want it to be. If you marry one of their daughters, you'll be allies. You'll all be playing in the same sandbox."

I clench my teeth. "I don't want any Italians playing in my sandbox."

"You want Tizziana playing in your sandbox, though, don't you?"

I shoot him a murderous glare, but he only sticks his tongue in his cheek and grins even wider. Son of a bitch. Does he want me to kick his ass?

Without wiping that shit-eating grin from his face, Valentin pulls out his phone and holds it up. "So what do you want me to tell Luigi? Seriously. I can't keep putting it off."

"Tell him we'll meet. Get the time and place. That's all. No promises."

He taps on his phone. "This is gonna be great. The Italians are finally going to be our little bitches—not that they aren't already."

I ignore him and turn my attention back to the windows. I don't want to think about all that right now. I want to think about Natalya. I can't get her out of my head.

But it's not just her body that intrigues me. Not just her mouth or her tongue or her pussy.

It's her spirit.

She's different.

The way she stood up for herself last night made me short-circuit. The cleverness and quick thinking saved her ass, both from Mike and from me—shit, if she hadn't run off who knows if I would have ever let her leave.

For someone who isn't from this world, she sure does operate like a woman who could succeed in it... at least, with a little guidance.

I could provide that guidance to her, one delicious lesson at a time.

Licking my lips, I think of turning her flat belly round. Filling her up with my heir would be the ultimate reward.

She's exactly what I need.

I just have to find her first.

"Holy fucking shit!" Valentin whispers.

"What is it now?"

"Luigi is offering to make me consigliere of a united Italian crime syndicate under your rule."

I snap alert. "What?"

He nods and sits down, still gaping at his phone. "I'm telling you this is big."

"It could be a trap."

"It couldn't be a trap, not if they want you to marry the godfather's daughter. That's practically like handing you a personal hostage. You'd be family. We would all be family."

"Swell," I grumble. "... Or they could be hoping to kill you to weaken me."

His eyes shoot up. "They wouldn't do that. We're blood brothers."

"They don't know that, do they? We don't know if they even know about blood brothers, much less what it means."

He shrugs and reclines back on the cushions. "Either way, we'll find out at the meeting. He's sending the info now."

"Don't get comfortable. I want you to go find that girl."

He looks up again, still holding his phone. "Seriously?"

"Of course. Did you think I was just talking to hear my own voice?"

"I... shit. You've asked me to track down a lot of people before, but never a random girl you met at the club. What are you planning? Is she that important?"

I don't even hesitate.

"Yes."

Valentin raises his eyebrows, but his surprise only lasts for a split-second before he melts back into line. With an accepting huff, he gets up. "Okay. I'm on it."

We bump forearms and he finally leaves. I sink into my chair, gazing out onto the beautiful Chicago skyline.

Natalya's sexy silhouette would look perfect at the center of it all. I'll have to make her strip for me. Right here.

Running a hand through my hair, I let my mind drift back to last night again. My pants tighten at the memory of her silken tongue. The way it teased me so wickedly. And don't get me started on that tight little pussy...

Fucking hell.

I need to feel it all again. And again, and again...

I'll have her. It's only a matter of time.

The only question is: will she be able to handle more of me?

8

NATALYA

With a heavy sigh, I sit up and put my feet on the cold, hard ground.

The noise in this homeless shelter is nearly impossible to sleep through. Now I feel like I've been run over by a train.

Last night, I tried to make it to a friend's place, but with no money to my name, it was hopeless. Everyone I know lived too far to reach. I had to settle for this place. It was the best I could hope for.

At least it's better than the street. Barely. I managed to take a cold shower and wipe the blood from my thigh before collapsing into this cot. What happened after that is a blur.

I rest my head in my hands and struggle not to fall deeper into despair. This is definitely the lowest I've ever been. Sure, I've spent nights in homeless shelters before, but it's never hit me as hard as this.

I shudder at the memory of what happened... and the mystery of why...

But it's impossible to make sense of—not that it matters if I do. The results are the same.

I lost everything I own when that monster set my apartment

on fire. But it's not the mattress or the clothes that has me sniffing back tears. It's that god-forsaken laptop. I sunk everything I had into fixing that finicky machine—actually, that's not true; I spent *more* than I had.

I took out a loan with far too many zeroes. All because the opportunity that specialized computer promised was supposed to be my way out of this constant cycle of hellish poverty.

My ticket into architecture school.

But now my ticket has turned to ashes, and all that's left is the debt I took out when I initially tried to tape it back together. I should have known there was another catastrophe lurking just around the corner. In my life, there always is.

I gulp down rising anguish thinking about it all. Last night bubbles to the surface. I can hardly make sense of what happened.

First, I lost my virginity to some gorgeous stranger on his office desk, then I paid a devastating price. Would any of that other stuff have happened if I'd stayed in?

Deep down, I know the answer. Still, I feel dirty and tainted.

I wish I could go back and do it all over again. Really, that's the story of my life; always wanting a do-over—if only that's how any of this worked, then I never would have accepted Yelena's invitation to the club.

I knew it was a mistake. I should have listened to my gut. I would have spent the night studying and I would still be looking forward to architecture school now instead of listening to a bunch of other homeless people crying and yelling and coughing up their rotten smoke-riddled lungs.

Well, that, or I'd be tied up in that monster's basement, pleading for mercy.

A horrific chill skates up my spine.

Are Nikolai and Andrei connected? I can't make sense of it. It somehow feels like they both are and aren't. They must be... but how?

Stop thinking about it, I try to order myself. *You can't change anything now. So look forward. Keep moving.*

But that thought hardly helps. My future is just as bleak as my past, if not infinitely worse.

Shit. I have a shift today and I don't have anything to wear. My work uniform would be back at my apartment, and there's no way I'm taking the chance to see if anything survived the fire.

What if that maniac Nikolai is still there?

My stomach drops.

Some of his brutal words come racing back.

I own you.

What the hell did that mean? I swear he said he'd paid for me, but that doesn't make any sense. I've never laid eyes on him in my life. And I haven't seen a dime of any payment.

He must have just been some random maniac...

Shaking my head, I try to tear my thoughts from that disaster.

I can't afford to think about that stuff. If there's ever been a time when I can't miss work, it's today. I'm worse than broke, but the one bright spot in my broken life is that at the end of my shift, I will be handed a fat juicy check.

Well, I'll be handed *a* check. After some expenses, it should be enough for a meal or two.

My stomach grumbles as I try to stand up, but a searing headache sends me back onto my ass. I rub my temples, but the pain doesn't subside. My skull pounds with all the problems I have to solve. First and foremost being my work uniform.

Fuck everything else. I can't miss that shift.

With one last jittery breath, I wipe my eyes and rummage through my handbag, searching for my phone. A jolt of panic flashes through me when I don't find it.

I'm on the verge of another breakdown when I remember. I

left it in Yelena's purse to charge. The same Yelena who's probably already on her flight to Milan.

I'm fucked. I don't have any phone numbers memorized. I can't call for help. I can't even check my messages to find out where I'm working tonight.

But even if I do, by some miracle, find out where we're working tonight, it will be useless without a uniform. My boss Saul has literally sent servers home for having a stain on their company shirt before. Showing up with no uniform at all might get me fired.

I can't afford to get fired.

There's only one option.

Without any other option left, I decide to go to the catering company kitchen across town. I can check the bulletin board for the time and location of tonight's shift. Maybe I'll find a way to scrounge a uniform while I'm there.

The workers at the shelter are generous enough to spot me a few bus tickets, and my mind races the entire trip. The day shift is coming off duty from a brunch party and I watch from down the block until I see a young man go inside.

I slip through the kitchen to the staffroom, desperately trying to hold onto even the faintest bits of hope. That's when I spot Tom. He's standing alone at the end of the hallway with a backpack slung over his shoulder, twiddling with his phone. Usually, I'd never approach him without witnesses—he's been hitting on me non-stop since I first started working here—but it's not like I have a choice.

He enters the staffroom and I follow him inside.

Sure, enough we're all alone. I force a smile and walk up to him. "Hi, Tom."

He frowns, immediately on the defensive. "Why are you being so friendly? I thought I was a creep..."

I stifle my disgust. He's right. He is a creep, and I finally said it to his face just last week. More bad timing on my part.

"I was wondering if you would do me a favor," I swallow.

"Give me one reason I should."

"I need to borrow your uniform... you... you won't regret it."

He doesn't seem to notice me I flinch as I force the words out... or he just doesn't care.

"What do you have in mind?" he asks, raising an eyebrow.

"What do you want?" I already know the answer.

He breaks into a big grin. My heart lurches. Maybe I really am turning into a slut...

"I'll let you borrow it if you let me watch you change into it."

This time, my smile for him is genuine—not because I want him to see me naked but because he agreed to give me the uniform, and he probably could have asked for a lot worse.

I can weasel my way out of this one. He's simple enough to trick.

"I'll make you a deal," I tell him, in the huskiest voice I can muster. The black smoke settled in my lungs probably helps. "I'll come to see you at your place tonight after work. You know, so I can thank you in person."

His eyes pop and his cheeks flush. "Really?"

I saunter closer to him. "Sure. You deserve that much, don't you?"

His color gets even brighter and he fumbles to undress. "You got a deal."

Idiot. Stupid horny idiot.

If only I could feel superior to him in any way. But I'm only in this situation because I was a stupid horny idiot too.

With a childlike giggle, Tom throws his backpack on the floor and starts ripping his clothes off. He doesn't stop until he's down to his boxers. Then he hands over the smelly uniform. I pretend not to notice him already getting hard thinking about me coming over tonight.

Fat fucking chance.

"What will you wear?" I ask, as he scribbles something onto a piece of paper and hands it to me.

"Here's my address," he says. "And I have my street clothes in the backpack."

"Great." I smile one last time. "Thanks."

Before he can get another creepy word in, I hurry out of the staff room and throw the paper in the trash. I have no plans to remember that address. I only care about getting paid tonight. Call it ruthless or cruel, I don't care. At least I'm punching up, because no one could possibly be below me.

Thankfully, the notice on the board tells me the location of today's job. It's a fancy dinner at a five-star hotel back across town. I have to be there at six o'clock tonight.

It's a long, stressful trip, but I manage to make it to the hotel just in time. Somehow, I'm even able to evade detection as I slip into the lobby bathroom and wedge myself into Tom's uniform. It doesn't fit as well as it could and I have to roll up the pant legs and sleeves, but it should do the job.

Gathering myself, I head back outside to find Saul up to his neck in the food deliveries. Usually, I'd leave him alone, but I'm too desperate to wait. "Hey, Saul!" I call out, pushing myself in his direction. "Can I talk to you?"

"What?" he immediately sneers.

That's not a good sign. But after dealing with that monster last night, Saul doesn't seem so bad.

"Could... could you maybe advance me my pay for tonight?"

"I never give advances," he barks over his shoulder. "It's bad discipline and encourages sloppiness. So, if you aren't *too* busy, I suggest you go inside and start rolling those napkins."

Without another word, he races off. I hopelessly tag after him. "Can't you make an exception just this once? I'm desperate and I've never asked before."

"I said no. Don't ask again."

He walks away and I have no choice but to give it up. His

reaction was expected, but it still hurts. At least I'm still getting paid. I'll just have to suffer for another few hours. I can do that... I hope.

Calling on my last bits of strength, I make my way back into the kitchen, but just as I find the napkins that Saul wanted me to roll, a bunch of servers come in carrying leftovers from an earlier event.

Cracked lobster tails spill their juicy meat all over the plates. The sight and the smell combine to make my mouth water and my stomach rumble. I haven't eaten since last night.

It's too tempting to resist. First, I check both ways to make sure no one is watching. Then I grab one of the lobster tails, hide in the closet, and stuff my face as fast as I can.

I steal two more batches of leftovers before I get back to work.

The first thing I'll do with my paycheck is buy some groceries, I decide. But my stomach tightens when I realize I don't have a stove anymore.

Shit.

Putting my head down, I start rolling napkins, all while descending into another black depression.

This must be rock bottom.

No. Don't jinx it, I tell myself. *Things can always get worse. And if your life is any indication, things will get worse.*

As if on cue, Saul storms into the kitchen and starts yelling at everyone. The servers assemble to receive their instructions, but I barely hear. I don't care about anything but getting paid later.

When Saul finally tells us to get off our asses and start serving, I grab a tray of champagne flutes, quietly grateful for the task. I don't know what this stupid party is for and I don't care. With this job, I'll barely have to deal with anyone. I just have to walk around serving champagne. That's it.

With a small sigh, I lift my chin. Up ahead, I spot Tom

among the other servers. He spots me back. The creep has somehow managed to get his hands on another uniform. He smirks at me, his thin lips filled with suggestion. But when I try to smile back at him, it comes out more as a grimace. I already know I'm going to have to avoid him all night. Hopefully, I can slip away after our shift without giving him the chance to collect his payment.

I think about my escape plan as I wait for the other servers to get inside the dining room. When the way is clear, I start forward.

I'm hardly out of the door before I almost drop my tray in shock.

Barely thirty feet ahead, standing in the middle of a group of powerful-looking men, is one of the demons I ran from last night. But it's not the scarred monster who burned down my apartment.

It's the gorgeous devil who seared away my innocence.

Andrei.

My body goes numb. My instincts take over. I have to get away from him, but when I try to back out of the room, I run into a bunch of other servers.

I stumble, twisting and twirling as I struggle to hold my tray straight. Eventually, my back hits the wall and I steady out. But when I look up, I see him again.

The commotion has captured his attention. Those brilliant emerald-green eyes lock right onto mine.

My stomach drops. The nightmare I went through last night blazes across my mind. Fear grips me.

Without hesitation, I drop my tray and bolt for the kitchen. But I know there's no use in running. He'll catch me.

I need to hide.

9

No. Fucking. Way.

Those wide blue eyes cut through the crowd like a dream. My heart skips a beat. The incessant chatter surrounding me fades into silence.

It's her.

Before I can even blink, though, Natalya turns and runs, dropping her metal tray in the process. It clangs loudly on the floor, but no one notices.

Everyone's attention is on me.

Luigi Corao cluelessly presses my hand between both of his. "It's so wonderful to finally meet you in person, Pakhan. I know our families will form a strong alliance. Together, we can rule this city for all our benefit."

For a moment, I can't respond. I'm still shocked by what I just saw.

She's here.

Slowly, a smirk washes over my face.

Good.

"Introduce me to your Godfather," I tell Luigi, turning back to the circle. "Then we'll see where this relationship goes."

Blood rushes below my waist and I clench my fist to keep from getting a very public hard-on. Even in that baggy uniform, Natalya looked hot as fuck.

I know what hides beneath those ratty clothes.

Heaven.

All I want to do is tell this slimy Italian to fuck off so I can go chasing after her. But I promised Valentin and myself that I would at least try to be diplomatic tonight. And if Natalya is working this event, she's not going anywhere.

There's nowhere to run this time, little deer. I'll have you.

Fixing my tie, I let Luigi usher me over to an old man with grey hair and a pronounced stoop to his back. The geezer can barely stand up straight enough to look me in the eye.

"This is our Godfather, Antonio Santarelli," Luigi begins. "Godfather, this is Andrei Zherdev."

The old man shakes my hand and I feel his arm trembling. His weakness is a stark contrast to the Russian Pakhans I'm used to. No one in the Bratva world can afford to get this decrepit—the second they did, someone like me would swoop in and violently take their crown.

Hell, that's almost exactly how I got this job. The last guy showed weakness, and I pounced.

"It's an honor to make your acquaintance, my boy," the old man quavers, before turning to Luigi. "Have you introduced him to Giovanna yet?"

I stiffen when he calls me, *my boy*, and I sense Valentin stepping in to correct the old man, but I stick my arm out to stop him. This dinosaur clearly doesn't understand that he's dealing with an equal—and he definitely doesn't get that I'm about to become his superior.

"I have not met Giovanna yet," I humor him.

Luigi laughs. "Let's change that."

Seemingly out of nowhere, the young Italian pulls a beautiful girl from the crowd. She shoots me a seductive smile.

I'm unmoved.

"Pakhan, this is Giovanna Santarelli," Luigi announces.

The thin young model holds out her hand. Her smile widens. I hesitate to return the gesture. Part of me doesn't even want to look at another girl, let alone touch one.

Natalya is the only woman I'm interested in.

But before I can hesitate for too long, I remember my promise. *Be diplomatic.* I try to hide my indifference as I take her hand and kiss her knuckles. "Delightful to meet you."

Giovanna blushes, but I recognize the spark of knowing in her eyes. She's been around mobsters all her life. She understands power. She wants power.

She wants me.

A familiar flash of annoyance causes me to drop her fingers. She's no better than the others. What a pale imitation of my true challenge.

Just like that, my mind switches back to Natalya. Valentin has been searching for her for twenty-four hours straight, but he couldn't find a single trace. It was almost impressive. But now, by some stroke of corrupted luck, she's here.

I won't let her get away from me a second time.

I've been diplomatic for long enough.

But Luigi is already motioning another man toward me. It's Marcello La Plata, Tizziana's father. I've met him before. Leaving before he can say hello would be a blatant insult. But I'm quickly losing my patience. I need to see Natalya again.

"Would you excuse me for a second?" I say, touching Luigi's elbow.

He doesn't get a chance to answer. I just turn away.

Valentin follows after me. "Where are you going? You can't leave now."

I point towards the doors. "Cover for me. I'll be right back."

I break away, but only manage to make it halfway across the dining room before those same doors burst wide open.

Suddenly, Ilya Rykov and his crew are streaming in. When he spots me, he spreads his arms and comes barreling forward. "Pakhan! Thank you for the gracious invitation. You are making this Russian feel right at home."

All I can do is grin back and clap him in a hug. "Welcome, brother. Come over and meet your new best friends."

He laughs loudly as I point toward the Italians.

"I'm not sure I could ever be friends with an Italian."

"And that's why you're right at home with me," I nod. "But that doesn't mean we can't humor them. Go introduce yourself. Ask for Luigi. Tell him you're one of my closest associates. He'll make sure you're taken care of. I'll be back soon."

Ilya doesn't hesitate to follow my instructions, and I'm finally left alone.

Pushing my way through the crowd, I stride out into the lobby and look both ways. Servers pass back and forth ferrying food and drink from the kitchen into the dining room, but Natalya isn't with them.

Where did she disappear to?

Quickening my pace, I make my way into the kitchen and search it from top to bottom. But once again, Natalya is nowhere to be found. A sneer curls onto my lips as I turn and walk all the way back to the dining room just to make sure I didn't miss her.

But there isn't a trace of my little deer.

Are you really playing hide and seek with me, princess? I won't let you win.

When a server walks by, I reach out and grab him. "I'm looking for one of your coworkers," I bark, ignoring all decorum. "Can you help me?"

"Yes, sir," the guy eagerly replies, a familiar tint of fear yellowing his eyes. "Which server are you looking for?"

"She's a short, thin girl. Blonde hair. Her name is Natalya..."

A huge grin explodes all over the server's face. "Ah, yes, I know Natalya. What do you need her for?"

"That's none of your business."

"I see... well, don't keep her long. She has somewhere to be after work."

I scowl at him. "What the hell is that supposed to mean?"

"That's between me and her," He winks. But when my fingers dig deeper into his arm, that ignorant twinkle in his eye is smothered. "Hey, what are you—"

I shove him against the wall so hard it shakes.

"Where is she?"

The fucker's eyes glaze over with fear.

"She... she went back into the kitchen... even though she's supposed to be working the floor..."

That's all I wanted to hear.

How did I miss her the first time?

Turning my back on the asshole, I storm away. But when I get to the kitchen, there's still no sign of Natalya. Instead, I'm greeted by a chaotic scene. Servers and cooks rush about as the boss barks orders at everyone.

That piece of shit lied to me.

My fists clench.

If I see him again, he's getting a black eye—maybe something worse, depending on how he explains his rude-ass comments.

That's between me and her.

A pang of jealousy lashes through my chest. I'll have to find out who that fucker is to Natalya—and then I'll have to destroy whatever's going on between them.

Because if anyone so much as talks about her like that again, there's going to be hell to pay.

I search the kitchen again, increasingly obsessed with finding my little ghost. But she's disappeared. I'm just about to give up and go back to the dining room when I spot a closet near the stairs. The door is closed, but something draws me to it.

I sniff the air. Even through the smell of all the food, I can detect a familiar fragrance. My pants tighten.

I squint my eyes and head for the closet. When I pull the door open, Natalya leaps away with a scream.

"Shit!"

She tries to retreat, but she's already jammed herself so far back against the wall that there's nowhere left to go. All that's left for her to do is to look around wildly as she hopelessly searches for some way out.

But I block off the only exit. There's no escape.

"What are you doing in here, little deer?" I ask, lifting an eyebrow in feigned ignorance.

"None of your business," Natalya shivers back. "So leave me alone, okay?"

She tries to shut the door in my face.

I reach out and stop it with a single hand.

"I just want to talk."

"No. I can't talk to you. I... I won't."

"And why is that?" I demand to know, my calm façade breaking. "I've been looking for you all night. I can't stop thinking about you..."

The confession just slips out of me. But Natalya doesn't seem to hear it.

"You ruined my life," she croaks. "Isn't that enough for you? Go. Please... find some other girl to bother."

I scowl into the closet. Ruined her life? What the hell is she talking about?

Before I can ask, Natalya lunges at the door and tries to yank it shut. I'm not having it. Stepping into the closet, I slam the door shut behind me.

She winces away, retreating back to her wall.

"No..." she whimpers.

It just makes me want her more.

"Talk to me," I bark, increasingly displeased. "I'm not going to hurt you. I promise."

"You criminals and your empty promises..." she murmurs, shaking her head. "No. Take your promises with you. Leave me alone. I... I have to work."

I make a fist and slam it against the wall. The entire closet rattles.

"You're hiding in a fucking closet," I snarl. "If they needed you to work, they'd be out looking for you. But I was the only one doing that. Well, now I've found you. So start talking. That's an order."

Those big blue eyes suddenly freeze over... before melting into a swell of tears.

"You don't get to order me around," she rasps, far more emotional than I expected. "You've already hurt me enough. I've lost everything. I need this job. I need the money. I... I have to go back out there before someone comes looking for me..."

A single tear drops down her cheek and my fists uncurl.

"I don't hurt women," I tell her, trying to soften my harsh voice. "And I would never hurt you. Now tell me what's going on? What do you mean when you say you've lost everything? What happened?"

A curious calm has come over me. It's like a dam holding back a flood of raging rapids. I'm not mad at her, but I'm ready to erupt at whoever's made her cry.

"You know," she hisses, a sudden rage scrunching her button nose. "You must know. How else..." Her eyes drop to the ground and she momentarily drifts off. When she comes to, it's with a shake of her head and a whole new flurry of fear.

"Natalya," I take a step forward and she flinches.

"Please... leave me alone!" With one final cry, she turns to the wall and starts shivering. "Stay away from me. I'm in enough trouble..."

"I'm not going anywhere." I ease over to her and try to touch her shoulders to calm her down. "Let me help..."

But the second my fingers touch her clammy skin, she turns and slaps them away.

"Stop it!" she begs. A panicked anger trembles over her sharp features. "I don't need your help. I just need to get back to work. Why won't you let me do that? Why... why are you even here?"

I open my mouth to respond, then stop myself. Something doesn't add up.

"It doesn't matter why I'm here," I tell her. "But neither of us need to stick around. Listen, you don't have to work anymore. I don't think you quite grasp the reality of who I am. If you need something, anything, I'll take care of it. I'll take care of *you*."

She pauses for a second at that idea, before grumbling, "I don't want your dirty money. And I definitely don't want your hands on me again. I may have acted like a whore the other night, but—"

"What did you just say?" I interrupt, rage momentarily blinding me. No one's allowed to talk about Natalya like that—not even her.

"I am not your whore," she snaps.

The strength of the declaration hits me like a sledgehammer. This pale, petite, little doll was just about to start convulsing with panic. Now, she's baring her teeth at me like a caged animal.

It's exhilarating.

My chest deepens with every new breath. Any ounce of sympathy I'd had leaks away. Only one thing remains.

"You're no whore," I tell her. Staring deep into her shimmering blue eyes, I let myself tower over her. "But if you'd like, I can fuck you like one."

She takes the bait even quicker than anticipated.

"You son of a bitch!"

Making a fist, Natalya swings for my chest. I grab her wrist. Any excuse to touch her. To handle her. To take her again.

With a rough tug, I pull her into my body. I can practically smell the spice on her warm breath. This girl is a firebomb. A fucking wonder of the world.

She is mine.

But she doesn't give up just because I'm bigger and stronger than her. She doesn't give in. I remember why I was so intrigued by her. It all comes rushing back. No one fights me like this. Not anymore. I miss a good challenge. And this is the very best kind.

"No one calls my mother a bitch," I taunt. Spreading my free hand across the small of her back, I take the brunt of the impact when I push her against the closet wall.

My cock immediately swells. My heart thrashes. My lips curl.

"Let me go," Natalya breathlessly gasps.

I lean down to her ear. "Not until I make you pay for that insult."

"I'm... I'm so fucking tired," she weeps.

Just like that, all the resistance melts from her body. She sinks beneath my grip. I'm all that's holding her up.

A strange, heavy sensation joins her dead weight. It's something I haven't felt in a very long time.

Guilt.

"Easy, little deer," I whisper, rubbing my hand across her back. "Rest. I'll protect you."

My pants remain tight, but a new primal instinct slowly overtakes that arousal. This broken angel needs mending.

That's not something I'm used to doing. Hell, it's not something I'm sure I know how to do. But I feel the desperate need to try.

Natalya is too precious to let go.

"Fuck..." she sighs into my chest. I'm allowed to carry her

shattered body for just a little bit longer. Part of me hopes she never recovers. I've never seen or felt a creature so gut-wrenchingly beautiful. She needs me.

It already feels like I need her to

"It's okay, little deer," I coo.

"... Why is life so hard?"

Finally, Natalya lets out a shuddering breath and straightens up. Her hair gets caught in her eyebrows and my jacket pulls the blonde strands in front of her face.

I stroke my fingertips down her forehead and cheeks to straighten her hair back into place. That's when I catch her looking up at me.

My cold dead heart clenches.

Those eyes speak volumes, even if I don't understand all the details. I don't need to. Without thinking, I lift my fingertips back to her forehead and caress her cheeks one more time.

That's all I need, just one more time.

"I can make your life so much easier," I tell her.

Natalya doesn't move. She just stands there looking up at me with that searching gaze. Her eyes open a window to a bottomless well. I can't look away.

"Life is never easy..."

Her sigh is that of a defeated woman.

No. I won't allow for that.

Strengthening my grip, I cradle her face in both hands and kiss her. She doesn't move except to breathe... until she starts to kiss me back.

Immediately, I can tell this is different from last night. That was wild. Feral. This is so much more tender and meaningful. It feels like I'm touching her soul.

If only I had a soul for her to touch back.

I pull Natalya in closer and her mouth opens. She smells and tastes so fucking beautiful. So delicate and responsive. I feel like a beast gently smelling a field of wildflowers.

Then, her tongue meets mine and all the passion from last night explodes out again.

I circle my arm around her waist and lift her against my chest. She dissolves in my grasp and her arms slither around my neck. Her body tenses to press into me.

"You will be stronger, little deer," I rumble. "Do you understand?"

"No," she quietly rasps, her breath hot and heavy. "I'm not strong."

"You are. And I'll show you."

My tenderness flickers as a wild and familiar desire reappears.

With increasing strength, I crush her fragile body. Against the wall. Against my chest. But no matter how hard I push into her, I need more. My fingers lace into her hair. I shove my swollen bulge into her. Gradually, she begins to ride my cock through her clothes.

Fuck. I missed her warmth. It fills this tiny closet like a comforting fire. But when I drop my lips from Natalya's to kiss her throat, a stiff hesitation returns to her tiny body.

"We shouldn't..." she whispers. "I can't... I'll get fired..."

I feel no such hesitation.

"No," I heave, slamming her against the wall. "They won't be able to fire you because you're going to quit. Consider this your severance package."

A deep gasp escapes Natalya's perfect pink lips. Something clicks.

"Fuck it."

Her lips snatch at my mouth and her tongue scorches in a wicked corkscrew around mine. I can practically feel her lips on my cock again. I want to guide them back between my legs.

But Natalya is way ahead of me.

"I'm not a quitter," she sighs. Hitching up my torso, she

throws her legs around my waist. Then, in a much quieter voice, she squeaks, "That must be why I can't quit you."

I can't help but smile.

She's desperate for me.

Good. I feel the same way about her.

"Prove it then," I challenge her. "Don't quit on me. Not until I've made you fucking erupt."

I drive my hips between Natalya's legs and grind my cock against her cunt. She whimpers and trembles, but I pin her even harder against the wall, holding her in place so she can take every last inch of me. For a brief moment, I worry it might be too much for her, but she only escalates to match me.

"I can't control when I cum," she rasps, scratching her fingernails over my shoulders to my chest.

"No, you can't. But I can."

A high-pitched gasp rips from her throat. I steal it right out of her mouth. While I kiss her, Natalya starts yanking at my tie and flicking my shirt buttons open. She sneaks her small fingertips between the gaps and my whole body turns to fire when she touches my bare skin.

Where is this coming from?

It's a thought I had the other night too. There's so much wonderful filth lurking behind her pure and innocent façade. I'm desperate to find out what else she's hiding.

"How many licks will it take to figure you out, angel?" I ask out loud, before biting down on her lower lip.

"There's only one way to find out."

The minx.

I try to pull her clothes off, but this sexless uniform gets in my way. In any other circumstance, I'd rip it right off. But that would only serve to traumatize Natalya even more. And that won't do. She still has to leave this closet and come home with me.

So, instead, I ease backward and drop her legs to the floor.

But even as I do, she won't stop kissing me. The little deer has turned into a fox. She even nicks my lips with her teeth.

"Careful there, kitten," I growl. "Or I'll have to punish you."

I tear off her mouth and look down to get hold of her waistband. But she beats me to the punch again.

"You've already punished me enough," she breathes. "Now it's my turn to punish you."

Without hesitation, she rips my belt free and starts massaging my bulge. My already swollen cock somehow gets even harder. So hard it hurts.

But no matter how much I like it, I can't stand for it. Not yet. Natalya has to earn the right to take control. I'll make sure she earns every moment of it.

"No," I silently roar, grabbing her tiny wrist. "You've had a hard day. Relax. I'll take care of you."

A small smirk invades my lips as a scowl comes over hers.

"I can take care of—"

"Enough," I stop her. "I *will* take care of you, and that's the end of it."

She just barely bites her tongue. "Fine," she huffs.

"That's a good girl."

I strip her pants down to her thighs and plunge my fingers into her panties. She's already dripping wet and my fingers vanish into a warm, wet, pulsating world of heat and bubbling goodness.

My swollen cock surges.

Natalya whines and bows her head when I start fingering her. She gasps and pants through bared teeth and her precious little head falls back onto my chest.

That's where you belong, I think. *Right next to my cold dead heart. You make it warm enough that it could almost thaw. I'd welcome the pain.*

She quivers and spasms every time I glide my fingers into her soaking little hole, whimpering the whole way through.

"Quiet, angel," I whisper, placing my palm over her mouth. "Or else everyone will hear."

"I don't care anymore," she pants, and I know she's lost her mind.

"You will," I warn. "I won't stop just because someone's watching. But I will kill them afterward."

She tenses at the threat, but I calm her with a gentle kiss on the forehead.

That's the last bit of tenderness she'll receive from me today. My cock is so swollen and hard that I can't take it anymore. I *need* relief. And I *will* take it from her.

A million dirty thoughts race through my mind, each one more depraved than the last. I want to do everything with this little deer. I *will* do everything with her. But if I start too strong, she could shatter.

I'm walking a fine line. One that I'm not patient enough to toe. I need to fuck her. So, I begin with something I already know she can take.

My cock.

I pull my fingers out and she looks up. Her eyes gleam with some wild, crazy power that grips me deep in the chest.

I kiss her again, harder this time. "Turn around," I order.

Without waiting for her to listen, I steer Natalya into position. She doesn't resist.

"What are you doing?" she whispers, her back turned to me as I lift her wrists and place her hands on the wall in front of her.

"I'm doing exactly what you want me to do," I say, leaning into her ear. "Preparing you. Now, do you want me to fuck you or not, angel?"

Natalya gulps but doesn't respond.

I wrap a stern hand around her throat. "I said, do you want me to fuck you?"

"... Yes."

"That's what I thought."

Unhanding her, I push down on the small of Natalya's back, so that her spine arches and her ass sticks out in just the right position. She complies with every move. An obedient little slave.

A heavy breath of satisfaction fills my lungs. *You sure made me work for this, little deer. Now it's time for my reward.*

I bite down on my lower lip and trace down her sides.

"So you want to punish me too, huh?" I remind her. "Well, here's what you can do. When I'm inside you, squeeze those toned ass cheeks of yours. Hard. Suffocate my cock with your pussy. Strangle me. Try to make me cum so fast I regret it. Because I'm going to try and make this last forever. Understand?"

With that, I wrap one arm back around Natalya's waist.

"I understand," she rasps.

I smile. "Then let's begin."

I run my hand up her stomach to her chest and finally back around her neck. She tenses when I take hold of her, but all that tension erupts as I slip my fingers into her tight wet pussy.

"Do you think I'll fit again?" I snarl in her ear. "Or do I need to warm you up a little more?"

"I can take whatever you give me," she whines, grinding her ass back against my hand. She corkscrews her pussy onto my fingers and her little moans start winding up to full-blown screams.

I have to talk louder just to hear myself over her yells. "No, you can't, little dove. But don't worry. I'll change that."

I'm beyond caring about whether or not anyone will hear.

I can't take this anymore. I slide my fingers out of her and kick off my pants. My hard cock breaks free. I don't hesitate for a second. With a low, guttural grunt, I ram into her pulsing cunt.

Natalya screams, and when my pelvis slams against her toned ass, she collapses against the wall.

"Oh my god..." she gasps.

I grab her wrists and hold her hard in place, but she keeps arching her ass into my thrusts.

"Why would you ever run from this?" I growl into her ear. "Are you scared of how good it feels? Don't be. I won't let you shatter, little one. And even if you do, I'll be right here to pick up the pieces and put you back together."

Natalya shakes in my arms. Her cries become hoarse. She cranes her head back in my hand and comes to rest on my shoulder.

I reach around and rub her clit while I fuck her, but instead of screaming more, she goes quiet, silently shuddering and panting in ragged gasps while her body convulses in my arms. Then, she seems to remember what I told her.

Her pulsing pussy starts to contract. Her ass cheeks clench. Her pussy tightens around my cock.

My roar fills the tiny closet.

"Don't you dare make me cum," I demand, but when she lets up, I lift my hand and spank her raw.

"Sorry," she apologizes, squeezing her cheeks together again. "I forgot..."

"Don't apologize," I demand. The pleasure is starting to build. I'm going to lose control. "Just keep going. Don't you dare stop."

Her wetness drowns my cock. She feels impossibly good. I bite down on the side of her cheek and she whimpers.

"Andrei!"

Natalya stiffens in my arms. I'm just barely able to pull out of her before I explode too. My cum erupts over her perfect porcelain back, and I rub my throbbing cock through her trembling ass cheeks until I'm completely empty.

"You're mine now, angel," I pant, staring down at the proof.

10

NATALYA

I can't believe I let that happen... again.

My cheeks glow red as I shoot an uncontrollable sidelong glance at Andrei. He's pulling his pants up over those powerful thighs. Dark tattoos wrap around his sculpted muscles, slithering into his tight briefs. Even soft, his bulge is huge, and oh-so-tempting...

I gulp.

He looks up and catches me staring. "Everything alright, angel?"

I flinch at that word. *Angel.* It makes me remember his promise.

I'm going to burn those wings right off, and you're going to fall into my kingdom.

Looks like he got his wish.

No. Not yet. Shit, I may be in hell, but it's not his hell. And I won't allow myself to fall for him any further. I can't. It's too dangerous.

"I... I'm fine," I nod. It's all I can manage to squeak out. What else do you say to a guy after he fucks you in a hotel kitchen closet?

"Are you too full of regret to speak?" he asks, half-taunting me. His playful tone is too familiar. He doesn't know me well enough to act like this. We're barely more than strangers. But he's so comfortable.

I blush and try to look away, but his eyes won't let me. "I don't regret it. I'm just...I guess I'm disappointed..."

"Disappointed?" he asks, cocking his head to the side. "I've never heard that before. I guess I'll have to stop holding back with you."

"I'm not disappointed in... what we just did," I scoff, unintentionally getting in Andrei's rhythm. "Or with you. I'm disappointed in myself. For doing all that. For... shit. I should be working." I pick up my clothes and start to cover myself. "I can't afford this distraction. My boss will take any excuse not to pay me."

To my surprise, Andrei laughs. "For someone who doesn't seem interested in mine, you sure do mention money a lot."

"That's what happens when you don't have any."

That gives him pause. "I know what that's like... or at least, I did."

"Sure."

I pull the last of Tom's smelly work clothes on, but before I can make a move toward the closet door, Andrei steps in front of it.

"What did you mean earlier when you said you lost everything?"

I shrug. I can't meet his eyes. "Nothing. I just...I have my problems and I can't keep glossing them over. This is nothing more than a distraction. I really need to straighten out my life and you aren't helping."

"Only because you won't let me."

"No, you can't help me. Not really," I hold my own hand as the hellish memory of what happened at my apartment lashes up from the back of my mind. I've finally decided that Andrei and Nikolai aren't connected—even just for the sake of my own sanity—but that doesn't mean Andrei's much better. Hell, maybe he could even help me with that monster... but at what cost? "I should get back to work. I can't afford not to get paid tonight."

"I meant what I said earlier," he says, not budging. "I can help you. I *will* help you. There is a future for us, Natalya. And I won't stop this until you see it too."

"Us? There is no us," I mumble, shaking my head. "And there is no future. Not unless I make it myself. We don't even know each other."

"Then let's change that."

I make a face. "Let's not."

"I don't think you quite grasp the reality of this situation, angel. I'm not asking you questions. I'm telling you the answers. Now, here's what you're going to do. Give me your last name. Whisper it into my mouth. If you don't want me stalking you, I won't. But right now, you know my last name and I don't know yours. That gives you leverage. Do you know what I do to people who have leverage over me?"

He leans in closer and I can smell myself on his hot breath.

"I can guess," I swallow.

"I know you can, smart girl. Now fix that wrong and you will be rewarded."

I study him. Those green eyes shimmer with a rigid power that feels so at odds with the flexibility with which he fucks me. Telling Andrei my last name would be foolish; I'd essentially be signing myself over to him. But with those fire-filled eyes, he could intimidate anyone I work with into exposing everything about me. At least if I tell him myself, then I hold on to some semblance of autonomy, even if it's a farce.

"It's Datsyuk," I finally surrender. "Natalya Datsyuk."

Andrei's hard face breaks into a soft grin. Those hidden

dimples are revealed, and I get another glimpse of the mischievous boy hiding behind that big, bad, mob boss exterior.

I hate how his smile makes me want to smile back, no matter how upset I am.

"Well, it's very nice to meet you, Natalya Datsyuk," With that big grin still plastered on his stupidly handsome face, he sticks out his hand. "I'm Andrei.... Andrei Zherdev. But you already knew that."

Somehow, that manages to draw a stifled smile out of me. I hate each and every syllable of my silly little laugh, but it's uncontrollable.

"Nice to meet you too," I huff sarcastically. Reluctantly, I shake his hand. The warmth of his massive palm spreads through me like a forest fire. Why does he have to be so fucking charming? "Do you come here often?"

"Do you mean on you or to this hotel?"

A flash of embarrassment blasts through me and I try to pull my hand away, but Andrei doesn't let go.

"Easy, little deer. I'm only joking. There's no need for those cheeks to turn so red."

Releasing me, he reaches for my face, but I turn away.

"I think I've had enough banter," I mumble.

Andrei shakes his head. "I haven't. It's not every day I meet a woman who can keep up with me like this."

"I'm sure there are plenty out there. And I'm sure they'd all be happy to fall at your feet. So why don't you leave me alone and go find them?"

"Because I don't want them. I want you."

The redness in my cheeks rushes down into my chest. Below that, a flock of butterflies flash through my stomach. With every ounce of willpower in me, I keep myself turned to him.

This man is dangerous—and I'm not just talking about his

profession. It feels like he could talk me into a cage. And, right now, my biggest fear is that I'd happily let him.

So, I do the only thing that seems to trip him up. I keep my mouth shut.

The silence lasts for an uncomfortable amount of time before Andrei finally breaks it.

"Very well, angel. We can talk more about this later."

Stepping aside, he opens the closet door. Keeping my mouth shut, I drop my head and follow him outside. But he stops so fast that I run into his broad back.

"What the..." I peek around him and my heart drops to the floor.

Tom is standing right there, feet planted in the hall, glaring at both of us.

He narrows his eyes at me and then at Andrei.

It's obvious he heard what we just did.

Before anyone can say anything, though, he turns and takes off through the kitchen, dodging cooks and other servers like a runaway bull.

"No, no, no, no!" I gasp, my panic rising with every word. "I'm fucked. I'm so fucked. He's going to tell Saul. I'm finished."

With a reassuring weight, Andrei touches my shoulder. "Don't worry. I'll handle it."

"You don't understand." I cover my face and teeter on the brink of tears. "My life is in the gutter and now he's going to snitch on me to my boss. That means no paycheck. I can't fucking win."

"I will handle it," Andrei growls. "Now stay here. If you run away on me again, I might change my mind about us. Understand?"

Without waiting for an answer, he takes off through the kitchen. I quickly lose sight of him, but the stone in my gut stays put.

What the hell am I doing? Here. With Andrei. With my life. Fuck.

A deep existential crisis threatens to crush me into the floor. Beads of cold sweat trail down my forehead. I've never felt so lost before. I don't know what to do.

A light chill comes over my skin and I hug myself, but it feels so useless. My arms aren't as strong as Andrei's, or as warm, or as protective...

Stop it! I plead to myself. *He's a criminal. You're a victim. And if you don't get a hold of yourself, you'll never stop being that same old struggling orphan. You'll never stop being a victim. Find power within. Not in anyone else.*

Not in him.

Somehow, I manage to rip my feet from the ground, but the moment I turn away, I collide with someone. I bounce off them with a yell and almost lose it completely when I realize who it is.

Saul.

"Where the hell have you been?" he snaps. "It's a mad house out there and you keep disappearing."

"I... I know," I stammer. "I just...."

"Save it. You won't be earning a paycheck tonight. Maybe tomorrow... if I'm feeling generous."

My stomach drops and I feel myself nearing the end of my tether. "No! Please! I'm sorry, Saul. I...I'm trying. Just...give me another chance. It won't happen again."

"It's too late. In fact, I want you to leave. I'll pick up your slack. I always end up doing it anyway. Better to know I can't count on you than to keep expecting it. Save me the pain. Goodnight, Natalya."

"Saul... no..."

"Enough. You're finished. If you can prove yourself to me tomorrow, I might decide to keep you on, but if you don't, you can go slack off on someone else's time. Now get out of here before I fire you outright. I don't want to see you again tonight."

With that, he storms off.

I just barely manage to hold it together just until he's out of view. Then the tears well up in my eyes. My mind goes numb. I'm not even thinking as I blunder through the kitchen to the back door.

What's the point of even trying?

I stumble outside and look around. There's nowhere for me to go. I don't even have an apartment anymore. I don't have any clothes. I have no money. I can't afford to buy myself something to eat.

I should just crawl into a pit and die. It would be better than this constant stream of disappointment. I'm all ready to stumble off and find said pit when a growl stops me in my tracks.

"You tell anyone about this and I'll make sure you never work in this town again. Do you understand me?"

Andrei's voice rumbles through the night like angry thunder. The deep timbre hits me right in the gut, cracking the pit of despair lodged deep inside.

I look around, but can't see him. That voice wasn't far off, though.

Momentarily snapping out of my funk, I sneak around the corner and see Andrei nose-to-nose with Tom on the loading dock. Andrei towers over him.

"Yes, Sir. I... I understand completely," Tom stammers, nodding down at the pavement. He refuses to raise his head.

"Whatever you think you saw or heard, you didn't. Understand?" Andrei continues. "Not that it would be any of your business anyway. I mean, what would your boss think if he knew you were gossiping about the private affairs of guests at his event? He probably wouldn't be too pleased, now would he?"

"No, Sir," Tom croaks. "You're absolutely right, Sir. I'm sorry. You can rely on my utmost discretion."

"That's a good lad," Andrei sneers. "Oh, and another thing. Natalya Datsyuk. If I ever hear you say even one snarky comment about her to anyone again, I'll snap your neck. Is that clear?"

"Yes, sir," Tom stammers, eyes trembling with fear. "Perfectly clear."

Andrei steps back and glares at him, but I don't stick around long enough to hear anything else.

Watching Andrei in action only threatens to make me sick. He's not doing any of this to protect me. He's a violent man, and he's looking for any excuse to get violent. I've met plenty men just like him throughout my tattered life.

The only thing special about him is the suit.

The way he makes me feel with his tongue and his cock is just an illusion. That seems clear now. The warmth I'm engulfed by when I'm near him isn't real.

But this darkness is. The chilly wind and the dirty alley are. This is where I belong. My life is meant to be devoid of warmth. Always has been, always will be. It's about time I accept that.

Turning my back, I stumble through the alley, hopelessly lost.

There's only one thing left to do. Find that cold, dark pit to go die in.

At least that way, I'll finally feel at home.

11

That fucker is lucky I didn't want to implicate Natalya in a murder—otherwise, I would have gouged his eyes out and left him to die next to the trash, right where he belongs.

Instead, I just gave him a stern talking to. If he had any brains behind those dull, lifeless eyes, he'd already be praying at Natalya's feet, thanking her for the mercy she inspired in me. Instead, he'll never talk to her again.

That's good enough for me.

I re-enter the hotel kitchen to find the catering boss having a tantrum on a bunch of servers. "That's right. You heard what I said. I threw her out and I'll throw out anyone else who slacks off. You're here to do a job, not to fuck around and waste my time. She won't get paid tonight, and if you want to get paid, you better shape up or ship out."

The servers stare up at him with huge, unwavering eyes.

I clench my fists. My heart twitches with anger. He can only be talking about one person. I got to that jackass Tom before he could rat on Natalya, but her boss must have caught her anyway.

And that means Natalya is already gone.

She's slipped through my fingers again. But this time, it isn't her fault.

But I know whose fault it is.

At first, I just listen to the catering boss from a distance. I could bust his ass and humiliate him in front of his whole staff —that would be exactly what he deserves for treating his people like this—but I have better things to do with my evening.

So, I wait until he sends the servers away, then I watch as he goes through the kitchen, putting the fear of God into the chefs and dishwashers.

This dipshit really gets off on throwing his weight around. Fortunately, the best way to deal with a guy like this is to show him just how small of fish he really is. That shouldn't be much of a problem for me.

I tail him through the kitchen until he goes into an office. I wait a beat before following him inside. He's bent over the desk checking some paperwork when I knock on the door.

His face drains of all color when he recognizes me.

"Hello, Saul." I stroll to the other side of his desk and spread my hand out over his documents. "Do you know who I am?"

"Yes... Pakhan..." he stammers. "Can I—"

"What do you do with the money you steal from your employees?"

"I... what do you mean... I have never..."

"A girl named Natalya Datsyuk works for you. Well, she did. Word is, you sent her home... and without pay."

"Yes.... Pakhan.... I had to."

"I doubt that, but I'm not here to tell you how to run your business. I want you to give me her paycheck.... and her address."

He hesitates. "That.... isn't legal, Pakhan. I could lose my license...."

I raise my eyebrows. "You're telling *me* what's legal?"

He gulps. "No, Pakhan." He starts rifling the papers in front of him and pulls out a piece of paper. It's Natalya's paycheck with a receipt attached to it. "Here it is, Pakhan. Her address is on it."

I glance down at it. The address is an apartment number on the south side of town. Looks like she told the truth about her last name. Datsyuk.

I have to smile. Knowing she didn't lie in that closet makes the moment even more special. Maybe she's starting to trust me.

"If Natalya comes into work tomorrow, you give me a call," I tell him. "My wish is that she chooses to wipe her hands with you and this job. But controlling a woman like that is a real... challenge. You, on the other hand, are no such challenge. If you give her any trouble, I will not be happy. Am I understood?"

Sault doesn't hesitate.

"Yes, Pakhan. I understand completely. I'm sorry, Pakhan."

"Apologize to her, not to me. You can go back to work now."

I walk out of his office and push him from my mind. I don't give a shit about some pissant caterer, not when I have Natalya's address in my hand.

Still, I'm a little pissed off about how easy that was. I guess I'm finally getting used to a good challenge again.

The thought fills my chest with a light flutter.

With the faintest smile weighing down my lips, I head back over to the dining room. But I have no intention of wasting any more time with the Santarellis.

If only Valentin and I were on the same page. It doesn't take long for him to spot me.

"Where have you been?" he asks, meeting me in the lobby. "All the Santarellis are asking after you."

"Go back in there and tell them I'm leaving. That's all they need to know."

His face goes pale. "You know I can't do that."

"Tell them I'm not interested in eating their food or marrying their daughters until we have a deal on the table ready for negotiation. Once you tell them that, come back and meet me here. We have something much more important to deal with."

That piques his interest.

"What?"

I glare at him. "Did you just hear me give you a direct order? Why are you standing around? Go in there and deliver the message."

With one last suspicious glance, he beats it.

While I'm waiting for him to return, Ilya shows up. He can immediately tell I'm on edge.

"Pakhan? Is anything wrong?"

I'm about to tell him to leave it, when I have a better idea.

"Actually, yes," I nod. "I need your help, Ilya."

"Anything, Pakhan. Just name it."

"Come with me and Valentin. We're going on a job."

He rubs his hands and grins. "Finally."

The sly enthusiasm nearly makes me laugh. Then Valentin returns, and I focus back on our task.

"It's done," Valentin says. "But they're all hot and bothered now."

"That's fine with me," I huff. "Let's go."

We hit the doors and Valentin calls up my car. I give my driver the address for Natalya's apartment.

You've done an impressive job so far, little deer, I think. *But you can only run from me for so long. There's nowhere left to go.*

Valentin breaks in on my thoughts. "Are you gonna tell us what's going on?"

I pause for a moment, unsure of how much I want to reveal.

"We're going to find that girl," I finally confess. "The one from the club last night."

I ignore Valentin and Ilya as they exchange a puzzled look. "Is that more important than cutting a deal with the Santarellis?" Valentin asks.

"There is no deal with the Santarellis, and until we have one on the table, this is much more important than attending their self-serving parties. If they aren't making me an offer, I'm not interested in wasting my time with them."

"Um..." Ilya fakes raising his hand and exaggerates his already thick accent. "Excuse me. I am new in town so I don't understand all these details, but... how is a girl more important than making a deal with the Italians?"

"It just is."

It's impossible to find the words to properly explain it to these hardened men. So I don't.

Instead, I just stare out the window until I find what I'm looking for.

"There it is," I grunt, glaring down at a dilapidated building. "Her apartment is number 478."

When we find the front door locked, Ilya and I turn outward to keep watch while Valentin jimmies it open. That doesn't take long, and soon enough, we walk into the shittiest excuse for an apartment complex I've ever seen.

Fucking hell. Natalya deserves better than this shit. No wonder she's so jittery all the time.

"Smells like mold," Ilya remarks. "Reminds me of home."

His dark chuckle echoes through the empty lobby as Valentin presses the button for the elevator. But nothing happens.

"Looks like it's out of service," Ilya notes.

Valentin just shrugs. "Stairs it is."

Somehow, the stairwell is even worse than the lobby. Nearly all the lights have been smashed out and there's trash and broken glass covering almost every step.

Still, we stoically climb up to the fourth floor, only flinching when we push out into the hallway. An acrid stench fills the corridor.

"Are you sure we're in the right place?" Valentin asks, pinching his nose.

"It better be," I grumble.

"What kind of girls are you into?"

"Only one kind..."

Her.

We pass several closed apartment doors, but when we reach number 478, we all stand outside the apartment and stare in shock.

The door and most of the outer wall are missing. We can see all the way to the outer window... the whole interior of the apartment has been charred black. The scorched framing studs show through and the whole place stinks of smoke, ash, and charcoal.

Valentin whistles through his teeth. "Are you dating a fucking ghost?"

I ignore him.

This isn't what I was expecting to find. A tiny seed of dread is planted deep in my gut. I try to suffocate it as I step through the missing wall into the apartment.

Nothing remains of any furniture or carpet. Most of the floorboards have been burned out and I have to tiptoe not to break through the few that are still intact.

The melted wreckage of a fridge stands next to the kitchen counter and sink, which are just about the only recognizable things in the place.

Next to them, a pile of ash shows where a bed used to be. I can't see any other signs of furniture. The window frame leads out onto the fire escape. The window is open, but most of the outer wall is totally gone.

When the fuck did this happen?

Ilya is way ahead of me. "I am searching Fire Department

records, but there is no report," he says, scrolling through his phone. "I will check the Police."

"See if you can find out when it happened."

"I can tell you when it happened without seeing the report," Valentin responds. "Fire Department records load up within three days, which means this happened less than three days ago."

I spin around to stare at him, but I can't speak. Three days. Natalya wouldn't have gone out to a high-end club with her friends if her apartment had just burned down, right?

Shit. This doesn't make any sense.

The fire must have happened that night, either while she was at Club Silo247 or just after she left. It's the only reasonable explanation.

And it explains a hell of a lot.

Shit. She really did lose everything.

Why the fuck didn't I take her more seriously?

The seed of dread in my gut grows into a thorny vine of guilt. Her running from me makes more sense now. She didn't need my trouble, she already had enough of her own.

"I'll question the neighbors on that side," Valentin, says, pointing to the corridor outside "You take this side."

He leaves and starts knocking on doors. I shake away my guilt and go the other way, rapping on the first door I come to. I need to figure out what happened here. And I need to make it right.

For Natalya's sake.

It takes a minute, but eventually, a stooped, wrinkled little old lady answers in her bathrobe and fuzzy slippers. "Yes? Can I help you?"

"I'm sorry to bother you, Ma'am," I say. "I'm trying to find Natalya Datsyuk, the girl who lived in that apartment that caught fire."

The woman's expression changes to a cheery smile. "Oh,

yes. She's a nice girl—always says hello to me. It was a real shame what happened to her apartment."

"And what exactly happened? Do you know?"

She shrugs. "You know... I shouldn't... but I couldn't help but hear the Police and Fire Chief talking after it happened. You know how it is. These walls are so thin."

"What did they say?"

"The Fire Chief said the fire started from a cigarette being dropped on the floor. They said it must have been an accident. That's all I heard."

I frown to myself. That makes no sense at all. Natalya told me herself, she doesn't smoke.

But even if she did, a cigarette wouldn't do all that damage. Only some kind of accelerant could make a fire spread and eat out the walls like this. I've seen it before in mob-style arson hits.

I clear my throat. "Would you happen to know where Natalya is staying, Ma'am?" I ask. "I... I'm worried about her."

The woman's smile falters briefly as she gives me a once-over. It makes me like her even more. Clearly, she's concerned about the well-being of her neighbor and wouldn't want to send the wrong people after her.

"I can see that, son," she soon nods. "I'm worried about her too. You might try the homeless shelter on 83rd Street. She's stayed there a few times in the last couple of years—I would have let her sleep on my couch, but she hasn't been around since the fire."

I guess I passed the test.

"Thank you, Ma'am. I appreciate your help."

"My pleasure, dear."

I head back over to the burned-out apartment to find Ilya on his phone again. "Anything?"

"Still nothing on the Police system," he sighs. "This fire definitely happened in the last two days."

"Keep looking. See if you can find anything on the girl."

"You say she was at Silo247 last night?" Ilya asks. "I can use your security camera footage to track her down. I would just need to collate your footage with other security camera footage from across the city. It might take some time, but it shouldn't be too hard to find her that way."

I clap him on the shoulder. "Do what you can. I'll see you both back at the penthouse."

I break away to the stairwell. "Where are you going?" Valentin calls after me.

"I'm going to follow up on another lead," I say, picturing Natalya's beautiful blue eyes. My pulse quickens. "Don't wait up."

I'll have her. And I'll give her the life she deserves—but only after making her work just as hard for it as she's making me work for her.

I'm not a charity, angel. I'll give you exactly what you need...
For a price.

12

NATALYA

I sit up and groan again when I realize where I am.

During most other periods of my life, waking up in a home-less shelter for the second morning in a row would be verging on nightmare territory. But I know better now. The real night-mare is out there. And it's hunting me.

Still, I allow myself to feel the disappointment deep down in my core.

So much for getting back on my feet.

I try to run through everything that's happened over the past couple of days, but it's almost impossible to concentrate here. The noise in this shelter is even louder than the last. I can't block it out, and that's part of the reason I'm so exhausted —it's hard to sleep when you're forced to keep one eye open.

I yawn and look over my shoulder. My thin nerves stretch thinner when I see the shelter administrator going from bed to bed making sure everyone gets up. I already know the drill. Without exception, every last person here has to leave by nine o'clock. No one is guaranteed a place tonight. It makes every day a constant struggle to survive.

... If only my friends were still in town, then I could at least couch surf. That would have made things so much easier. Hell, if I still had my phone, I could call one of them and ask for a spare set of keys. But I never bothered to memorize their numbers by heart. Why would I when I always had their contacts saved?

I bury my face in my hands and take a deep, shaky breath.

On top of it all, I have to work tonight too.

A pit of dread opens up in my empty belly.

Shit. I can barely see straight, but Saul is going to be looking for any excuse to fire me. At this point, the question isn't *if* I'll make a mistake, it's when. And then I'll be out of a job—add that to the list of things I don't have anymore, including an apartment, any money, a future, hope...

The administrator moves to the aisle next to mine and I know I'll have to leave soon. With a weak sigh, I get up and start making the bed. Tom's ratty clothes hang off me like a stained reminder of how far I've fallen. I could smell him on me all night long. But I could also smell Andrei...

No. Don't think about him.

Shaking my head, I try to focus on something good. There isn't much, but I do find one thing. At the very least I don't have to get dressed for work tonight, since I'm already in uniform. As long as Saul doesn't get a good sniff of me, I should be fine.

But who am I kidding? With my luck, he'll take one look at the plume of despair hanging over my head and use it as an excuse to boot me back out onto the streets.

We wouldn't want to make the guests uncomfortable now, would we?

Focus, Natalya. On anything but the bad. Please.

The desperate little voice squeaks out from the blackness of my mind.

Fine, I huff back.

Before work, I'll go to two other shelters and put my name

on the waiting list for tonight. Anything's better than sleeping on the street.

A door slams somewhere across the building and I nearly jump out of my skin. When I spin around, I fully expect to come face-to-face with one of my two monsters. Nikolai or Andrei. Clearly, they're both cut from the same cloth. And for one reason or another, they're both after me.

But when I turn, I'm not met by any towering beast. Just more struggling souls. Everyone is clearing out. Heads down, mouths shut. My tired heart twitches.

The administrator slots into my aisle. But I don't need to be told to leave. I'm over all this confrontation. So I just nod at her and pick up my stuff. But for some reason, she still stops next to me.

"You need to come to the office, honey."

My brow furrow in confusion "What? Why?"

"I'm not sure," she shrugs. "All I know is someone is there asking to talk to you."

I pass my hand across my eye. "Who?"

"That's none of my business," she says, pursing her lips. I can already sense her getting fed up with me and my questions. This is not a person I can afford to rub the wrong way. I might have to sleep here again soon.

"Okay," I sigh, too tired for suspicion. "Where's the office?"

"Just around the corner. First door on the left."

She points the way and I give her one last long look.

There's no fear on her face, only exhaustion. If Nikolai or Andrei had just invaded her office, she'd be afraid, right? Who wouldn't be?

So maybe I'm safe. Maybe it's even the police. I'm sure they want to know what happened to my apartment—that is, if they care enough about investigating a crime in such a shitty part of town.

I guess I'll find out.

I grab my handbag, make one last check of the bed to make sure I didn't leave anything behind, and then head for the office. I need to get this out of the way quickly so I can get a top spot on another shelter's waiting list.

Keeping my head down, I turn down the hall and step inside the office.

The air is immediately sucked from my lungs.

Andrei's fiery green eyes blaze back at me. My heart leaps into my mouth.

I dive for the doorway, but he moves way too fast. His thick arm crosses in front of me, blocking off my escape. "No, little deer. It's over."

"The police are here," I foolishly bluff.

"I own the police."

"Well, you don't own me," I try to push past him, but he only steps in my way. That powerful body might as well be a stone wall. There's no getting past it.

"Not yet. But we can talk about that."

"I don't want to talk to you. Get out of my way. I'm leaving."

"Not until you hear what I have to say."

"No!" I snap, a gust of fire rising from somewhere deep inside my exhausted soul. "You think because we fucked a couple of times that you can just barge into my life and start telling me what to do? Is that why you're here? You want to fuck me in a homeless shelter now too? No. Fuck that. I'm not your whore, Andrei. Clearly, that's what you want. So go and find one somewhere else."

He barely flinches, but I can see that something I've said has cut him deep. I try to take advantage by making another charge for the door, but he snaps out of it instantly and catches me. I'm held like a prisoner in his massive arms.

It's shocking, how truly powerful he is—even if I can tell he's only using a fraction of his strength.

"Enough, Natalya." He pushes me back from the door, and

when I try to struggle, he straightens me out and forces me to stand there at arm's length. "You will listen to me. And not because you're my whore." His lips curl as he leans into my ear. "It's because you're mine. *Period.*"

He holds me in place for what seems like an eternity. It's long enough that I start to feel the heat of his hands. I hate how good he feels. I fucking hate it.

But I know I'm not going anywhere. And not just because he's physically holding me in place...

"Say what you have to say," I sigh, giving in.

Andrei makes sure I'm not going to bolt for it. Then he puts his hand inside his jacket and pulls something out.

"I brought this for you," he says. "And I think you'll find Saul far more pleasant to deal with now—that is, if you ever choose to go back to work for him."

I stare at the paper in his hand. "That... that's my paycheck... How did *you* get it?"

"My new friend gave it to me," he smirks. "And I didn't come here to have sex with you, Natalya. I came to help you"

I blink down at the paper. It's really my paycheck. It isn't much—only enough for a week or two, and not nearly enough for me to get another place to live—but it's a hell of a lot better than what I thought I had.

I reach out to take it from Andrei, but he pulls it back.

And then, right in front of my eyes, he tears it in half.

My heart drops off the face of the earth. "Why..." is all I can manage to squeak out. "Why would you do that..."

"Because you don't need money anymore. From now on, I'm going to take care of you."

That's when the cruelty of it all clicks. Something inside of me ruptures.

I scream out in horror and charge him. "You son of a bitch! You bastard! You cocksucker! You piece of shit! I hate you!"

I pound Andrei's chest and shoulders with my fists. He

doesn't stop me. Not at first. When he's had enough, he grabs me in those big arms again and pins me against his body. To my surprise, though, he doesn't try to stop me from hitting him more. Instead, he just tilts his head out of range and lets me throw myself against his massive strength.

"You fucking monster!" I continue to croak. "You're just like everyone else. Just like Mikey. Just like fucking Nikolai. I don't belong to you. I fucking *hate* you! I hate you!"

Andrei doesn't say anything in response. He just lets me rage at him until I finally hit him so many times that I can't raise my arms anymore. With a frustrated cry, I slump and land a few more half-hearted thumps on his chest, but he just keeps holding me until I wilt completely.

I can't believe I almost let myself believe he was better than the other monsters I've come across. He isn't. He's just better looking... and far crueler.

I double over with a pathetic sob. Just when I thought my life couldn't get any worse, this happens.

"Why me?" I croak.

"Because you're special."

Cupping my chin, Andrei leads my eyes up to his.

"You've got the wrong girl," I plead. "I'm not special."

"You'll learn to see the lie in that," he says, pursing his lips. How can someone so savage hold me so tenderly? "I meant what I said, Natalya. I came here to help you. You don't have to spend another night in this shelter... or in any other shelter."

"Then I'll sleep on the street."

Andrei smiles, but it's a small, sad smile. "I know your apartment burned down and I also know Saul threatened to fire you if you messed up at work again. But if you do as I say, you won't have to work anymore. I'll take you somewhere nice to stay. You can finally get a good night's rest. Wouldn't that be nice?"

I snort. "And what do I have to give you in return? I bet I can guess..."

"I bet you can't," Andre quickly counters. "Listen, you don't have to have sex with me ever again if you don't want to. I can promise you that."

But his words make it sound like more of a challenge than a capitulation.

I stiffen, ready for another fight. It's a fight I don't have the energy for. "You know the old saying: if it sounds too good to be true, it is. You want something from me. Men always do. So, if it's not sex, then what is it?"

"I'll explain everything," Andrei assures me. "You just have to listen. Listen and do as I say. I know it will take some time for you to get used to that, but you'll learn. I'll make sure you learn."

"You're fucking with me. It can't be that simple."

"It is. Do what I say and you will be forever protected from the evils of this cruel world."

"You are the evil of this cruel world."

"That's right," Andrei nods. "But I am the most evil and the most cruel, and every other beast in this land knows it. No one dare's fuck with what's mine."

"And I'm supposed to be yours?"

"You're supposed to do as I say."

"And you'll tell me to have sex with you," I sneer, desperate for some honesty.

"I do not enjoy repeating myself, angel," Andrei almost growls. "We will not fuck unless you want to. That's final."

He's holding back. Something is missing. I can't trust this man, no matter how much part of me wants to.

Oh, to have somewhere safe to rest.

"I've heard enough," I sigh. "I have more important things to do than listen to your bullshit."

I spin around. Andrei is close enough to the door that he

could easily stop me from leaving again. But he doesn't move. Instead, he just stands in place. But I can feel those fire-green on my back. They burn giant holes of doubt in my already tattered resolve.

"Do you really want to go out there, Natalya?" he calls after me. That voice worms into my brain. I can't ignore it. "Do you really want to spend another night in a homeless shelter? Do you really want to take the chance that Saul will fire you tonight? You don't have to live this way. You deserve better. Let me help you. I will never do anything you don't want me to. If you don't understand that about me by now, you aren't the woman I thought you were."

I stop on the threshold. I shouldn't listen to him. He's a beast. A devil. He'll say anything to manipulate me. If I had any strength left, I would tell him to leave my sad little life alone. But his words ring in my head with terrible finality.

He's right. I can't keep doing this. I'm spent, and as hard as I've been hit, I know there's so much further I can fall. With my luck, rock bottom will come in the form of a body bag.

That monster Nikolai is still out there, after all.

The truth is, I can't make it on my own. Not at this pace. I need help. Otherwise, there's no hope. But Andrei doesn't inspire hope in me. Instead, he's a hazy distraction. A burst of heat in a cold world. A heavy weight crushing me into a box from all sides. Sure, at times, his obsession can feel nice, almost special, but I know all too well that if I get lost in his false sense of security, there will be no escape for me.

And so I have my choice: risk being killed on my own or allow myself to be trapped by him.

Either way, there is no easy road ahead.

"Shit," I quietly mumble.

Down the hall, I can see the shelter administrator dealing with an unruly couple. They don't want to leave and they're kicking up a fuss. The security guard moves in.

My heart sinks. I can't live like this anymore. My nerves are ready to snap. Closing my eyes, I force myself to find some good in Andrei.

He stands up for me. There's that. But is it because he thinks of me as his property or is it something else?

I don't have the energy to analyze it.

Fuck it. Being the Bratva boss' property can't be much harder than this. Maybe, with him watching out for me, I can finally get some rest. Then I'll be able to think straight. Then I'll be able to think of a way out of this mess. Maybe I'll even be able to study again...

My stomach churns when I remember what happened to my laptop.

I'm so fucking lost.

With a deep breath of surrender, I turn back into the office.

Andrei is waiting for me like he already knows what I'm going to say. But there's no resistance left in me. No fear either. Only emptiness. I'm ready to give myself to him.

"Fine," I whisper in defeat. "I'm yours."

To my surprise, Andrei doesn't smile or gloat. Instead, he just steps forward and takes my hand.

"I'm proud of you, angel," he says, his voice surprisingly soft. "Now come with me. Your new life awaits."

13

The drive out of town is quiet, but inside I'm celebrating louder than I have in a long time.

I won. Natalya is mine.

Well, physically she is. The first challenge is complete. Now, it's time to win over the rest of her. Mind, soul, and everything else I can grab hold of.

What a fucking thrill.

So far, she hasn't disappointed in any way. The fallen angel is even more of a challenge than I'd hoped for. And we haven't even gotten to the good stuff yet.

Oh, what I have in store for you, little deer.

Gazing into the glass of my tinted window, I watch her quiet reflection. She sits on the far side of the limo, leaning against the door and staring off into the distance. She's pale. Exhausted. Defeated.

An unexpected pang of guilt slashes through me.

Fuck. There it is again.

This is all I wanted. So why does the sight of her sulking like this threaten to dim my celebration?

Maybe it's because I didn't break her on my own. This cruel

world conspired to shatter her spirit behind my back before I could take control of it for myself.

Her apartment burned down. Her boss fucked with her livelihood. I was only a cog in the machine. But now I'll be her *everything*. And I'll protect her from all the evils of this cruel world, just like I promised.

Nothing will get between us again, I think, glaring at her through the glass. But I don't speak a word out loud. She deserves the rest. Right now, silence is the most meaningful gift I can give her.

So I keep my mouth shut as we drive out of Chicago toward my estate on the Rock River. Still, the closer we get, the more excited I become. By the time the limo wheels into my driveway, my guilt has been crushed by the carnal thoughts of what's to come.

"Home, sweet home," I mumble, my pulse quickening. This is where I'll put my plan into action.

"Holy shit..."

Those are the first words out of Natalya's mouth in hours. Her nose scrunches against the glass as she gapes up at my estate, and an audible gasp escapes her lips when we pull up to the front yard.

A new color seems to fill her pale skin.

It makes me smile.

"Not bad, huh?" I tease.

Natalya opens her mouth to respond, but then seems to stop herself. Dipping her chin, she grabs at the door handle to let herself out. "What the..."

A clear look of confusion twists her pretty face when it doesn't open.

I can't help but laugh. She's still so new and naïve to my world. But soon enough, she'll know every in and out. I'll make sure of that.

"This way," I tell her. The chauffeur opens my door and I

hold out my hand. "Come with me."

She doesn't take it. Not right away.

"This is too good to be true," she mumbles, clearly more to herself than to me.

"It's not. You've earned this. And you've earned it the hard way. You're not exhausted because we've been up all night fucking. That will come. You're tired because you've worked hard to get this far. It's time to rest. You deserve that much."

I reach my outstretched hand closer toward her, but instinct makes the little deer shrink further back into the seat. A pair of sunken, wild eyes glare up at me. She's been through so much. Part of me wants to snap my fingers and make her behave like a mindless slave.

But another, stronger part of me kind of likes that Natalya still doesn't trust me. Not only does it leave room for improvement, it's also a breath of fresh air.

I've never had a girl fight me so hard on anything, and if they did, it wasn't long before they were leaping into my arms or into my bed.

Natalya isn't like that. She's a fighter. The more she wants me, the more she holds herself back. It makes every little inch I gain on her all the more satisfying.

"Are you going to spend the night in there?" I ask, retracting my hand.

Standing up straight, I wave off the chauffeur. No one else is allowed to impede on these precious moments. This battle is between the two of us.

"It's better than where I've been sleeping," Natalya huffs.

"Wait until you see inside."

With a hesitant sneer, she finally unwedges herself from the far door. I reach my hand out again, but she completely ignores it, instead climbing out of the car herself.

I watch with amusement as she gingerly stands up and has

to grab onto the car for support. She is so uniquely stubborn. Even at her lowest, she's still fighting for autonomy.

It'd almost be admirable if it wasn't so foolish... or so familiar.

Shit, I suddenly think. *Am I attracted to Natalya because she reminds me of... me? Am I really that narcissistic?*

Possibly, I accept. *But that's not it. There's something else about her...*

I chuckle as the proud little deer turns her nose up at me and pushes herself off the car. With nothing more than a grunt, she brushes straight past my shoulder, making a beeline for the front door. I turn to watch.

She stumbles around the chauffeur and he raises his eyebrows at me. I ignore him. I can't stop grinning.

Natalya is here.

And the fun is just beginning.

"Wait for me, angel," I chuckle, following her to the door. Unlike in the car, she doesn't even reach for this handle. Instead, she stands off to the side, resting against one of the Roman columns, trying her best not to make eye contact with me.

A sigh of annoyance rushes out of her when I easily click the door open. "My front door doesn't need to be locked," I explain. "I have... other types of security."

"I can see that," Natalya eye-rolls, noting the security cameras hanging above.

"Those barely scratch the surface." I nod inside. "Follow me."

I step through the doorway and I feel her reluctantly follow. But the second she passes the threshold she stops. Another gasp lifts from her mouth. All of her stubborn resolve fades as she gets her first good look inside her new home.

"This... this is incredible," she breathlessly admits, taking in the foyer's marble floors, the statues, the fountain, and the trees rising to the glass atrium roof arching high overhead.

'What were you expecting?" I gently prod. "A dark castle?"

"Maybe... but not this. It's all so elegant."

"My suits didn't tip you off?"

"Your suits might as well be masks."

The cutting remark is mumbled so casually that I almost don't catch it.

"Watch yourself, angel. If you really know what's behind my facades, then you should understand not to test me."

But Natalya is hardly paying attention to me anymore. Her focus is directed to the well-crafted opulence surrounding her.

"Yeah... yeah..."

All I can do is shrug. "I'll let it pass... this time. Soak it in, angel."

Stuffing away my pride, I stand back and watch as she gazes around at it all. She might as well be a newborn seeing the world for the first time. We start exploring. Every room she walks into tears a gasp from her tired lungs. Hell, even the kitchen and servants' quarters behind the dining room seem to impress her.

How novel.

I follow close behind as she passes through the grand dining room. Eventually, we make our way into the library. She stops breathing altogether when she enters the winter garden. It's full of tropical trees and centered by a charming array of tables and chairs that bask in the early afternoon sunshine

"How is this place real?" she repeats, over and over again before it's all too much.

Retreating to the library, she traces her fingertips over the polished wood, the leather sofas, and the high-backed chairs. When we finally return to the foyer, those tired sunken eyes are shining once again.

"I take it you're happy," I observe.

"This is your place?"

"Yes. It's my house... well, *one* of them."

Her jaw almost hits the floor.

"You have more than one of these things?"

"They're all unique in their own way," I shrug, trying to hide how much fun it is to watch her genuine reactions.

Such sincerity is a lost art in my world. It makes me feel warm in a way I haven't felt in a long time... maybe ever.

"How many do you have?"

"Well, let's see. I also have a penthouse downtown that I use when I'm doing business there..."

Before I can continue, Natalya gets distracted again. Her pessimism melts away as she wanders back out through the front door. "You own all of this?"

She stands on the front steps and surveys the grounds on both sides. From this perspective, the property looks essentially endless.

"Yes."

She gapes for a little while longer before shaking her head. "You must have a small town's worth of staff to help you run this place."

"That's right."

She turns around to face me. The wonder on her face is gone. It's been replaced by a more serious concern.

"So what do you need me for?"

"You'll see," I tease, nodding toward the stairs. "Now come with me. I'll show you to your room.

"Tell me," she pleads, following me upstairs. "You already got me here. There's nowhere for me to go. I'm at your mercy. So why make me suffer? Why not just tell me what to expect?"

"Because that wouldn't be as much fun."

Stopping at the third floor, I turn down the long corridor that leads to the guest room.

"I'm not here for fun," Natalya insists.

"You're here to do as I say," I remind her. "And I'm telling you to let me have my fun unquestioned."

"I can't just stop asking—"

The words catch in her throat when I open the door to her room.

"Welcome home," I tease, walking in. Natalya stands frozen in the hallway as I gesture around. "What do you think?"

Those crystal blue eyes gaze forward, filling to the brim with wonder.

Ahead, curved glass doors and windows stand open to a broad concrete balcony overlooking the grounds and the surrounding countryside. It's a stunning view of the landscape, including the manicured lawns of my property, the woods beyond, and the river winding through it all.

For a second, I'm worried I might have broken her brain, but when I open the balcony door Natalya finally comes back to life. Without a word, she rushes by me, stumbling outside to face the wind. I watch carefully as she takes deep breaths of the crisp fresh air. Her cheeks glow, but she straightens her face when she comes back inside.

"I... I didn't know air could smell so... clear."

"Not even a house this big is enough to pollute all that land," I say.

"Looks like you're trying your best, though," she counters, taking a second look around her new quarters. "This room alone is like three times the size of my old apartment..."

"It's in a nicer neighborhood too."

Natalya doesn't seem to hear me. It's like she thinks she's in a dream and she's trying to remember every last detail before she's shaken awake.

But that dream comes to abrupt end when her perfect blue eyes fall on the giant king-sized bed. The looseness of her body tenses. I follow her frozen stare through the hanging drapes and over the well-tucked bedsheets to the black and gold crest carved into the center of the headboard.

"Is... is that the same crest from your office?" she swallows.

"It is."

I stare at the gold-flaked viper and skull insignia. It always makes me feel a mixture of pride and shame. The things I had to do to earn the right to display it... the things I will do with the secrets it hides...

"Is there anything locked behind it?" Natalya cautiously asks.

"No. This one is just a symbol. I have them all over this property... and all my others."

"A symbol for what?"

My heart starts to pound with excitement. But I bite down on my tongue. Now is not the time.

"Like I said, I will tell you everything... once you've earned it."

Natalya stares at the gothic crest for a while longer before something breaks her out of her daze.

"So..." she almost whispers, fingers falling on the glass coffee table. "What do I have to do in exchange for all this generosity? And please don't give me that shit about not doing anything I don't want to do. What do *you* want me to do?"

"I told you." I perch my ass on the corner of the dresser and stick my hands in my pockets. "I want you to learn to do as I say."

"How does that work if I'm free to refuse whatever I don't feel like doing? You're contradicting yourself."

"You're free to refuse whatever I ask of you. What I crave is for you to *want* what I ask of you. To *need* it. You will learn to please me, little deer. And in the process, you will discover the pleasure in doing so. Does that make sense?"

Natalya raises her eyebrows, but she doesn't let her guard down. "So you *are* talking about sex."

I glance down at her body. I would so love to fuck her right now, but getting inside her head is almost as rewarding. "Like I said, you don't have to fuck me unless you want to. But you will *want* to. That's part of the fun."

Natalya's nostrils flare and another jet of adrenaline burns my insides. She's thinking about me making her beg for it. Does thinking about that turn her on as much as it turns me on?

It will.

I push myself off the dresser and stroll over to the balcony. "I'm telling you the truth. I only want to help you. I didn't bring you here to suffer, Natalya. But nothing in this world is free. All I ask in return is that you listen."

"Why?" she demands. "Why me? I'm nothing."

I turn around to face her. Fuck, she's beautiful. Those ocean-blue eyes crash around my stone heart. I feel a speck of rock break loose.

"I see potential in you," I admit. "And I believe it's a shame you're being held back by petty things like working, money, and stupid men. I want you to flourish. I want you to reach your potential... and I want to be the one who gets you there. I'm going to shape you into the kind of woman I need, little deer. And I can only do that because you're already the woman I want."

I can tell she isn't buying it... no matter how badly she wants to.

Just accept it, angel.

"Those are pretty words," she weakly fights back.

I move toward her. "Pretty words for a pretty girl."

"You're not smooth."

I stop in my tracks and tilt my head.

"I can be rough instead... if that's what you'd prefer?"

That makes her gulp.

"No. I'm fine, thank you."

"Have it your way."

Natalya takes her own hand and those bright blue eyes try desperately to make sense of what's happening.

"I still don't understand how any of this is going to work," she mumbles. "What exactly do you want me to do—just sit around and stare at the wall?"

"We'll deal with the specifics later. For now, I want you to make yourself at home."

"I'm not sure that's possible."

"Why not?"

"This place is... it's too big. How can anyone feel at home in such a monstrosity?"

"Oh, so now this place is a monstrosity, huh?" I smirk. "You didn't seem to think so while I was showing you around."

"It is beautiful," she sighs, looking me in the eyes. "But some monsters are."

"As are some little deers," I reply, accepting the twisted compliment. "But you don't have to worry about being overwhelmed... because most of this property will be off-limits to you."

Natalya head snaps back like I've just hit her in the face.

"What?"

"There are ground rules, angel. And you must follow them. But don't worry, you will still have plenty of room. You can go anywhere on this end of the third floor—the cutoff being the stairwell—and you are free to roam around downstairs as well. Walking the grounds is also fine, but only if you stay within the limits of the lawn. You are not allowed on the other side of this floor and you cannot go to the second floor at all. But other than that, you're free."

"That doesn't sound like freedom."

"It doesn't sound like you want freedom. It sounds like you want a small haven to rest in. That's what I'm providing. That's what you get. You will obey these rules, angel. You will listen to me. Understand?"

I watch as Natalya struggles to fall in line. It's a conflict I've seen play out across countless faces over my time as Pakhan. But it's never looked so delicious.

"Fine," she huffs. "But why can't I go to those other parts of the house?"

Usually, I'd take direct offense to someone questioning my orders. But right now, I'd rather play with Natalya than crush her.

"Because they hold my darkest secrets..." I half-lie. "And besides that, the second floor is where my other guests stay. You are not allowed to mingle with my other guests."

"Other guests?"

"Don't worry," I smile, sensing a morsel of jealousy in Natalya's voice. "They aren't the same type of guests as you. These are mostly work associates. Hardened men. Ugly men. Men who do not have permission to lay eyes on you."

I watch as Natalya awkwardly tries to recover from her envious slip-up.

"Why not?" she mumbles. "Are you ashamed of me or something?"

I can only laugh. "Quite the opposite, little deer. Quite the opposite..." Letting her mull that one over, I cross the room to the door.

"Wait. Where are you going?" Natalya asks, turning to follow me.

I raise a stiff hand to stop her.

"I have to go back to work."

"You're going to leave me alone here?"

This time, I withhold my pleased grin.

"These grounds are filled with staff who will serve your every need," I tell her. "You've seen where the kitchen is, where the doors are. You know your boundaries. Get comfortable.

Shut those pretty eyes. Relax. I'll be back later tonight and we'll have dinner together... that is, unless you really want me to stay and watch over you?"

The offer hangs in the air like a guillotine. She knows I'm taunting her, and she clearly doesn't want to give the satisfaction, but this is a big, new place, and I'm the only person here she knows.

"No. You go. I'll be fine."

Her voice cracks and I almost want to stay. But I know she needs her rest and she won't be able to get it with me lording over her. This is a fragile time in our newfound arrangement. She needs to get comfortable before we can truly get started. Otherwise, she might break too soon.

"Sleep well, angel," I nod.

She doesn't respond as I turn around and walk out of the room. The second I'm in the hallway, I pull out my phone and text Valentin.

Get the chopper ready.

Natalya's warm scent lingers in my nostrils as I march down to the foyer, push through the back door, and walk around to the landing pad on the far side of the lawn. Just as expected, my private helicopter waits for me, its blades already starting to whirl.

Inside are three men. The pilot, Valentin, and Ilya. I join them.

"Men," I nod, climbing in the back. "I hope you weren't waiting too long."

I slam the door shut behind me and buckle my seatbelt next to Valentin. The engine starts to roar. Ilya is seated across from me. He briefly looks up from his phone and we share a quick nod before he goes back to his business.

"There's nothing I enjoy more than flying out here from the city just to pick you up and then immediately fly back," Valentin snorts.

"A helicopter ride would have been too much for Natalya," I remind him, before mumbling to myself, "Not that she got much rest on the car ride..."

"Ah, yes. Natalya," Valentin muses. "Your mystery girl. Are you sure she's worth all of this effort?"

My face hardens as I look him dead in the eyes. "Yes. And don't you fucking dare ask me that question again. Hell, don't even think it. Understand?'

Valentin visibly stiffens. "Yes, Pakhan."

"Good," I relax. Reaching across the aisle, I get Ilya's attention. "I want you to find out everything you can about her."

"Yes, Pakhan," he nods, accepting the order without pushback. "But there are other issues at..."

I lift my hand to stop him. "One problem at a time."

Leaning back in my seat, I pull a headset over my ears. A moment later, the chopper lifts off. I look out of the window, gazing toward Natalya's guest room.

To my surprise, she's standing on the balcony. Her golden hair swims against a distant breeze as we watch each other shrink into the distance. Then she's gone. The mansion disappears soon after, swallowed up by the surrounding forest.

Rest up, little deer, I think. *Because when I return, there will be no time for sleep.*

Shifting in my seat, I try to get rid of the bulge swelling in my pants. I can't get too distracted by thoughts of what I'll do to her. There's still an empire to run.

I'm going back to Chicago, but I'll see Natalya soon.

"Can we finally talk business now?" Valentin's voice cracks in my ear.

"Fine," I grunt, adjusting my headset. "What's up?"

He looks over to Ilya and I immediately get a bad feeling. What is it now?

"Someone hit the Utyuzhin Bratva," Ilya announces.

I jerk around so fast I almost get whiplash. "What the fuck do you mean—hit it?"

"Wiped them out," Valentin explains. There's a barely restrained rage hiding behind his eyes. How did I not notice that before? Fuck. I must have been distracted by Natalya... "As in—all gone—dead—finished—kaput. The Utyuzhin bratva is no more. It doesn't exist. It was wiped off the face of the Earth."

The news cuts through me like a scythe.

"Why the fuck am I only hearing about this now?"

"It just happened," Ilya calmly explains.

"When?"

"About an hour ago," Valentin says. "But I didn't get the message until just before you got in the chopper—that's less than fifteen minutes ago."

My head swims. "So... they're all dead."

Ilya nods. "Sounds like it. From what I'm hearing, they were ambushed at a strategy meeting in the South Side warehouse where they store their computer equipment."

"I've already ordered some men to trace the gun details from the bullet casings," Valentin adds. "But right now, we don't know who did it."

I look down at my hands. They're balled up in furious fists, each finger curled so tightly my knuckles have turned white.

"Was it the Italians?" I ask.

"No. It couldn't have been," Ilya quickly responds. "Not the Yakuza or Triad either. I've scanned the available footage. My programs would have picked them up. This is something new. This is someone unknown."

"How the fuck is that possible?" I growl. "We know everyone and everything in this city."

"I guess not," Valentin snarls. "But we will soon. And I'll make them pay."

"Not if I get to them first."

Grinding my teeth, I glare back out the helicopter window.

The Chicago skyline grows in the distance. I stare at the buildings and imagine all the rats running through the sewers below *my* streets. Who would dare fuck with one of my Bratvas?

Someone with a death wish.

That's the only answer.

But who out there wants to die an agonizing death?

My mind races through suspects and possibilities. The helicopter goes silent. The roar of the engine engulfs us as we fly into a freshly hostile city.

Still, through it all, my thoughts flicker back to Natalya.

No. She's safe. She's mine. She's not going anywhere.

Focus.

Still, I turn to Valentin. "The moment we land, you're getting in a car and heading back to Rock River."

"What? Why?" he asks, shocked.

"I need someone I trust there to look after Natalya."

"But I just flew out to—"

"That's an order, soldier."

"I..." Valentin's hardened face momentarily twists with disappointment before he swallows his pride. "Yes, Pakhan."

"Good."

With that taken care of, my obsession with Natalya is allowed to take a backseat. I concentrate on this new threat.

Who would have thought that my boring reign would take such a drastic turn?

Oddly enough, I feel my sneer twist into a small smirk.

Hell, add one more challenge to the bucket. It will be good for me. I'll deal with this one like I deal with them all.

Ruthlessly.

And when that's done, I'll return to Natalya. She'll be my reward.

Hopefully, she learns to fall in line while I'm gone. Because I might not have the patience to put up with her if she doesn't.

No more holding back.

It's time to remind everyone who I really am.

The devil.

14

I almost fall over when I step into the ensuite.

It's nearly as big as the bedroom and just as elegant. But what was I expecting? From the moment we pulled up to Andrei's mansion, my jaw has hardly left the floor.

I knew he was rich and powerful—that shit oozes off him—but this... this was impossible to predict, especially for someone like me. My life has been completely devoid of luxury, so this is like stepping into an alien world. Hell, I haven't even seen stuff this opulent in movies. It's next level.

I can still hardly believe the grounds, the house, the windows, the balcony overlooking the woods and the river, the fucking private helicopter pad that Andrei took off in—all of it.

It's not just the massive scale of the place, either. The architecture is sublime too... if a little gaudy at times. It's a palace that belongs to a king. But no king deserves all of this. If I had my way, I'd design it into something more functional and utilitarian.

A familiar knot twists in my gut at the thought of anything architecture-related because it comes with a reminder of how far off track I've gotten.

Panic starts to rise in my chest before I forcefully shove it away with a flurry of deep breaths.

Forget what you can't control, Natalya, focus on what you can. Concentrate on what's around you.

But it's hard not to look at this massive, gorgeous bathroom and not think about the thought that went into designing it.

Ahead, a large, white royal tub sits in front of gorgeous floor-to-ceiling windows that look out over the western grounds. Even from the doorway, I can see for miles in all directions. There are no apartment buildings nearby. No houses. No way for a nosy neighbor to peek into my sanctuary. All I can see are gorgeous green canopies and a relaxing river.

I'm completely isolated.

The thought is equal parts relaxing and terrifying.

No one would be able to spy on me in here.

... And no one will be able to hear me scream.

Crossing my arms, I hold myself and shuffle deeper into the bathroom.

The marble tile floor radiates with heat. Fluffy towels and bathrobes line warm rails along the wall. There's a huge wet-floor shower on the other side with a curved snail-shell of glass bricks.

A private shower...

The sight of it alone is enough to make me keenly aware of how grubby and disgusting I must be. Suddenly, I feel very sticky. I haven't had a decent shower since that first night at the shelter and I was only in there long enough to wipe the blood from my thighs. The rest of me hardly got any attention.

Yet Andrei was still interested. He is still interested. Why? What's his deal?

I can't help but feel there's some sinister undertone to all this. Well, I mean, obviously there is, but is the danger directed more at me or at everyone else?

It's hard to tell.

Shuffling out of the bathroom, I go to the bedroom door and peek out in the hallway, just to make sure no one's around.

"Hello?" I whisper.

No one answers.

I step back inside and gently click the door shut. From there, I take a closer inspection of the room. To my surprise, all the dresser drawers are filled with clothes. Women's clothes. And their all in my size, including underwear.

A suspicious chill dances over my skin.

How does Andrei know my size?

You can ask him when he gets back, I tell myself. *For now, concentrate on yourself. You need to shower. You need to rest. Otherwise, you'll never have the energy to figure your way through this.*

Rifling through the drawers, I search for a new outfit to wear after my shower. Making a choice is harder than expected. Everything is top brand and very expensive. I've never worn clothes like this. Just one pair of panties probably costs as much as a month's rent at my old apartment. I'm almost too nervous to put anything on, less it rip or stretch.

I do not have the money to replace any of this. But I don't have anything else to wear either, and I'm definitely not walking around naked or spending a second longer in these smelly rags.

So I pick out a t-shirt, a new bra, and a pair of panties. I take everything into the bathroom and lock myself in, even if I'm sure no one will come.

Andrei doesn't want anyone to see me. And he's clearly a man who gets what he wants. People listen to him. So why has he chosen to help someone who doesn't? Why has he chosen me?

I try not to think about it too deeply as I peel off Tom's disgusting uniform and dump it on the floor. For better or for worse, I'll probably never put it on again. There's no way Saul's taking me back, especially not after I miss tonight's shift.

Shit. I guess that means I need to make this work out.

That's not exactly promising. But at least I'm not back at the women's shelter, begging for a bed.

In the bathroom, I run blasting hot water into the tub. A certain peace comes over me as I watch it fill up. I might as well enjoy this. Who knows how long it will last.

Crouching down, I search beneath the sink for soap. Instead, I find a bottle of bubble bath. I pour a dollop into the tub and slip beneath the scalding water.

"Oh shit..."

It feels unbelievable. Every fiber in my body relaxes all at once.

I could get used to this...

Sinking until my chin dips beneath the water, I turn my head and lazily gaze out at the view.

It's hard to believe a mansion like this exists so close to Chicago. All my life, I've been struggling just to survive, and in the meantime, some people have been living like this... and not that far away either.

Screw living in some penthouse overlooking the city. This is real luxury.

Emptying my mind, I slip further into the bath. The heat seeps through my skin and wraps around my weary bones. I remember how cold the water was at my old apartment. How there was no bath. How if I wanted hot water, I'd have to heat up a kettle on the old gas stove...

My nose scrunches as the smell of gasoline runs through my memories. A painful ache fills my chest. I remember the last time I smelled gas.

Even the hot water of my bath isn't enough to save me from the chill that grips me at the thought of what happened to my apartment.

I remember the flames. The laugh. The monster who was waiting for me in the darkness. I've been through so much since then that I've hardly had the time to think of it all. Not that I wanted to.

But now there's nothing to distract me.

I recall Nikolai's twisted face and his haunting words. None of it makes sense to me. If my apartment hadn't burned down, I might have thought it was all some ultra-realistic nightmare. But I guess that's what my life became for a bit there. Nothing more than a real nightmare.

I dip further into the tub, hoping the hot water will rid me of this chill. But I'm not allowed to relax.

Over the past three days, two violent, brutal men have claimed me as their own. Right now, Andrei is the victor. But men like that don't give up so easily.

Even under water, the hair on my nape stands up when I think of the inevitable.

Nikolai is still out there. And I'd bet he hasn't stopped looking for me.

If he had gotten to me first, would he have brought me to a wonderful mansion and given me my own room? Probably not.

I should feel lucky. Instead, all I feel is fear.

I've seen the monster lurking beneath Andrei's tailored suits. I've felt his cruelty. Seen his savagery acted out on others. Who's to say he's any better than Nikolai?

Who's to say I'm not screwed, no matter whose hands I end up in?

The only way to stay safe is to make sure I don't end up in anyone's hands. But that's easier said than done. I can't get too comfortable here. It could be the death of me.

The thought is so harsh it's exhausting. Never in my life have I been able to let my guard down, and now is no exception. I'm not at some spa. I'm in a cage. And eventually, I'm going to have to figure out how to escape it.

But that can wait a little longer...

Closing my eyes, I let myself soak a while before I finally

drag my water-logged ass out of the tub. Every muscle and liga-
ment in my body has been turned to rubber and I feel sleepy
and stupid, but when I put on a t-shirt and sweatpants, I can't
help but look back toward my closed bedroom door.

For all the talk about getting some rest, my mind won't stop
racing. From Nikolai to Saul, to Andrei and this mansion. I
already know it's going to be impossible to sleep.

What I don't know is when Andrei is going to be back. It
could be hours. It could be days.

What does a man like him do when he leaves for work?

I don't want to think about it. But I know there will be no
rest for me. So, instead of trying and failing, I decide to do
something semi-productive.

If I'm going to be stuck here, I might as well get to know my
surroundings. Remembering the confines of Andrei's ground
rules, I head for the door and tiptoe out of the room.

But even the hallway outside is so long and wide that I start
to get overwhelmed, especially on my sore and tired legs.
Everything about this place is absolutely fucking giant. I don't
even want to think about how much Andrei paid for it.

Strangely enough, though, he doesn't seem that interested
in it.

I guess I wouldn't be either if there was no one here to share
it with. Living on your own can get lonely. No one knows that
better than I do. All the money in the world can't change that.

Gathering my bearings, I pad down the corridor in my bare
feet. The cushy carpet silences my footsteps as I peek into the
upstairs library, another beautiful sitting room overlooking
magnificent grounds, and a few more exceptional guest rooms.

Somehow, the house is even bigger than I first realized.
Hell, I could drive a car down some of these corridors without
touching the walls.

I head to the landing and look down into the foyer. It's
empty and I don't hear any voices, but I know that's deceptive.

This place is probably full of hidden servants and maids. Security too.

Looking to the ceiling, I search for more cameras. If there are any, they're well hidden.

"Hello?" I call out.

My small voice echoes down the long stairwell.

Once again, I'm met with silence. Complete and utter silence. No one's here. At least, no one who would stop me from doing what I want... or maybe that's just wishful thinking.

Either way, I glance down the corridor leading to the third floor's east wing. Andrei said it was off-limits... but he's also not here.

No. Don't stupid... not yet.

Pursing my lips, I turn away and head downstairs and continue to explore within my well-defined boundaries. That includes checking out the bigger main library, the grand dining room, the butler's pantry behind it, the winter garden, and all the parlors, offices, sitting rooms, and lounges on the main floor.

Each new space fills me with equal parts wonder and dread. The wonder comes from the architectural beauty of it all. The dread from the wealth it represents. The power ingrained in these walls is just so daunting. Each room feels like a piece of a much larger puzzle. A puzzle meant to intimidate and impress its guests.

Well, count me as intimidated and impressed. Despite my mixed feelings, I can't stop exploring. How could I? I'm a peasant in the king's palace. I feel compelled to drink every last curve in until I can't anymore.

I'm in the middle of studying a collection of oil paintings when I hear something unexpected.

A voice.

It seeps out from the butler's pantry.

Lifting back onto my tiptoes, I quietly approach the door

and listen. But I don't recognize the low timber rumbling from behind the wood. That's not Andrei. But it sounds too gruff and commanding to be coming from a butler or chauffeur.

So who could it be?

Curiosity tugs at my chest. Without a second thought, I find myself creaking open the pantry door just enough to peek inside. But the room is empty. Still, I can hear the voice better now. It seems to be coming from another door, one situated right across the room.

My newly relaxed nerves tense up. I know I shouldn't, but Andrei's orders ring through my mind like a matador's cape. I remember what he said when I asked him why I couldn't go to some parts of the mansion.

You are not allowed to mingle with my other guests

He didn't expand on why, but now I can't help but wonder if it's because it would make him jealous.

My toes curl and my shoulders unfurl. For some reason, the idea of making a man as powerful as Andrei jealous fills me with an unexpected burst of strength.

He wants to control me—but two can play at that game.

Stepping into the pantry, I carefully make my way over to the door. But the second I press my ear against the wall, the voice goes quiet. All I can hear is my own heart beating.

... Did he leave?

I'm about to crack open the door when it swings open for me. I tumble forward, falling onto a marble floor.

"Shit!" I gasp, catching myself with my hands. When I look up, I notice I'm in the kitchen.

A deep chuckle comes from behind me.

Almost instantly, I flash back to the nightmarish scene at my apartment the night it burned down. I see the monster who lit the fire and chased me out onto the streets.

Nikolai.

"No! Please!" I cry, lifting my arm to cover my face.

"Easy there, woman. I'm not here to hurt you. In fact, I've been ordered by the great Pakhan himself to protect you while he's away."

Slowly, my arm drops. The voice is nothing like Nikolai's, even if it is nearly as deep. When I blink away the fear and confusion from my eyes, I see an oddly familiar-looking man standing by the door. He leans carelessly on the wall, studying me with a casual curiosity.

"Who are you?" I ask, trying to remember where I recognize that face from.

It's a ruggedly handsome face, filled with character and experience. But there's also a youthfulness to his hard features. He couldn't be older than thirty-five, but it looks like he's fought the world multiple times over.

"The name's Valentin. And you must be Natalya."

He nods down at me and it clicks. He's one of the men who backed up Andrei at Club Silo247 when he was dealing with that bastard Mike.

"You work for Andrei?" I ask. Rubbing my stinging hands together, I gingerly sit up.

"That's right."

"Then why didn't you catch me before I fell?"

"Because I'm not touching the boss' property," he smirks. "That's a surefire way to get my hands cut off. And I'm quite fond of my hands."

"So was I," I mumble, looking down at my red palms. "Will you at least help me up?"

"Are you trying to get me in trouble?"

"You're a big strong man, you couldn't defend yourself against Andrei?"

"I wouldn't want to," Valentin says, his smile disappearing. "No one would. Pakhan is not a man to mess with."

"Well, I won't tell him. Help me up, already."

I reach out my hand, but the giant hesitates to take it. "Tell him whatever you want to tell him," he huffs. "I'm sure I won't be the only one who gets punished."

Stepping forward, he finally lends me a hand. The second I'm back on my feet, though, he lets go and brushes past me. I turn and follow him as he pulls open the huge fridge, takes out a can of some energy drink, shuts the door with his foot, and cracks the can top.

My belly rumbles. "Got any food in there?"

"A little."

"Can I see?"

Valentin stands in front of the door, unmoving. "Better not."

That confuses me.

"Why not?"

Taking a phone out of his pocket, he types in his password and seems to search for something.

"Because you should be having dinner with Pakhan in a few hours. And I'm sure he'd be upset if you lost your appetite snacking."

"Does your whole life center around making sure Andrei isn't upset?" I snap at him.

Fuck. In all of this excitement, I forgot how long it's been since I had a decent meal. But I don't want to wait for Andrei.

"That's no way to talk to your personal bodyguard," Valentin laughs. Shrugging his shoulders, he steps aside. "Go ahead. Just don't blame me for what happens if your boyfriend finds out."

"He's not my boyfriend."

I try my best to push past Valentin as I make my way to the fridge, but he effortlessly steps out of the way, avoiding all contact.

"That's not what it sounded like to me."

"What do you know anyway," I grumble, pulling open the fridge. To my disappointment, it's practically empty. The shelves are mostly lined with energy drinks, bottled water, and pop. There's hardly any food in sight.

Valentin chuckles again and I slam the door shut.

"Is this funny to you?" I snarl.

"I'm just trying to keep myself entertained. This isn't the most exciting job I've ever had, you know."

"I don't. But please enlighten me. Who the fuck are you exactly again?"

"Me? I'm Valentin—Valentin Constanov. I'm Pakhan's blood brother and his second-in-command, so if you need anything at all, you just tell me. That's what I'm here for."

He's playing with me.

So I decide to play him back.

"Second-in-command? Blood brother? Sounds like a lot of self-important titles. I have a better one. Babysitter."

To my surprise, Valentin doesn't react anything like Andrei would. He doesn't try to intimidate me or use my resistance as an excuse to get closer. Instead, he just stays put and continues to smile.

"That's a good one," he nods. "Can't say I've ever heard it before either. Keep them coming. This is so much more fascinating than what I was doing before."

"And what were you doing before? I heard you talking to someone..."

"I was just keeping up with what's going on in town," he says, gesturing down to his phone. "Then I heard you trying to sneak up on me, and I thought I'd say hello."

"Well, I'm sorry I interrupted your super important work."

Valentin shakes his head. "It's nothing that can't wait."

No matter how hard I try to poke the bear, he doesn't seem to take the bait—though, that's probably for the best. I'm not thinking straight.

This man could kill me in a heartbeat. He's even taller than Andrei, and while not quite as broad, he does have the same unmistakable air of danger spilling off him. Black tattoos curl up the back of his hands, disappearing under the sleeves of his shirt.

There's no mistaking my situation, I'm surrounded by vipers. But Valentin doesn't seem like he's interested in taking a bite. And that's enough to calm me down a bit.

"When did Andrei say dinner was supposed to be?" I ask. Looking down at my feet, I place a hand over my empty stomach. God, what I'd give for a greasy burger.

"He didn't. Just that you should be ready when he returns. And he should return in a few hours."

"That's not exactly promising."

"If you're that hungry, I can ask one of the chefs to cook you up a quick snack. But nothing too big."

My eyes wander back up from the floor. "*One* of the chefs? How many does Andrei have here?"

Valentin tilts his head like he's trying to count. "Three or four. I haven't met them all yet. But they're all very good."

"Why does he need so many chefs?"

"Depends on the mood he's in," Valentin shrugs. "An Italian chef for when he's feeling Italian. French for French. And so on. When he's not here, the staff get their choice of food too. Andrei is a demanding boss, but he treats his people well. He'll treat you well too... if you listen to him."

Valentin's words are a simple reminder of Andrei's harsh demands. I hold onto my wrist.

"I've done all he's asked so far."

Valentin looks at me like he doesn't quite believe it.

"That's good. Wouldn't want anything getting between you two lovebirds."

"This has *nothing* to do with love," I snap.

"Sure."

"Ugh, you're so annoying," I grumble. "But if you could

order me some French fries or something, then maybe you would be a little less annoying."

"Coming right up," he quickly answers. Without hesitation, he types something into his phone. It quickly buzzes with a response. "Shouldn't take more than five minutes."

"I guess I can wait that long."

Chugging the rest of his drink, Valentin turns to toss the empty can in the trash. I stiffen when I spot a gun jammed into the back of his belt. It's a stark reminder. Valentin is a killer. And he's not just here to keep me safe. He's here to make sure I don't leave.

Suddenly, I'd rather wait for my food back in my room. But I don't let that desire show. Valentin is acting friendly now, but if I try to run maybe his killer instinct will take over...

"Why do you call him Pakhan?" I ask, trying to distract myself from the simmering fear with some small talk. "I mean, if you're his blood brother—whatever that is—why don't you call him by his name?"

Valentin shrugs the question away. "It's a sign of respect."

"You respect him?"

"Everyone does. But me most of all."

"Does he respect you?"

"He does."

"That must be nice."

That makes Valentin laugh all over. "You don't think he respects you? Even after you found out that he placed his very own blood brother on watch duty? I'm far too important to his empire to be stuck watching over something he doesn't respect. So please don't imply that he doesn't respect you, because that's more of an insult to me than it is to you."

"Sounds like you're trying to justify being stuck here."

Valentin playfully slaps his face and raises his eyebrows. "Why don't you call him Pakhan?"

"Because I don't want to."

"And he lets you get away with it?"

"I'm still here."

He turns his back on me and starts pacing. "He must really like you then."

"Why do you say that.?"

"Does he let you call him by his name?"

"Yes."

"Did he tell you that? Did he specifically tell you to call him by his name instead of Pakhan?"

My cheeks flame when I flash back to our first meeting in Andrei's office.

Say my name again. Come on. Be a good girl. Do as I say. Beg.

I clear my throat. "Yes. He specifically told me to call him by his name."

"There you go." Before Valentin can expand, a knock comes at the door. "Come in."

A dignified-looking woman in a frilly apron comes shuffling into the kitchen. My heart skips when I see the steaming plate of fries being carried in her hands.

"That was faster than five minutes," I say, licking my lips.

"Time flies when you're having fun," Valentin jokes. Opening a drawer, he gestures inside. "There's some cutlery in here. You can use a fork if you want."

"Who uses a fork for French fries?"

"That was a test," he grins. "You passed. Now get eating. You have to be hungry again for your date with Pakhan."

"I'm always hungry," I quietly note, before stuffing my face with a handful of fresh, hot, greasy fries. "But... thank you."

"You bet. Help yourself to a drink from the fridge too. No one wants you to suffer here."

I shoot him a sidelong glance. Andrei said something similar earlier, so why do I find that so hard to believe? Why do I keep waiting for someone to do something terrible to me?

The answer is obvious, and it's symbolized by the gun I now know is tucked beneath Valentin's belt.

"What does being Andrei's second-in-command even mean?" I ask, careful to swallow my second helping of fries first. "What do you do, exactly?"

Valentin quickly opens his mouth to respond, then stops himself. I watch him consider how much he should tell me before he starts again. "It means I run my own crew when I'm not backing up Andrei. I'm his main point of contact with the other criminal organizations in town. So, for example, if he wants to seal an alliance with, let's say... an Italian crime family, then I'm who arranges it."

"Wow. If that's the case you must be really important to Andrei," I say, hiding my actual feelings behind sarcasm.

It sounds like Valentin is more powerful than I thought. And that makes me feel even smaller.

"Not as important as he is to me," Valentin replies, purposely ignoring the sarcasm.

"Sounds like you two are a real team," I say through another mouthful of fries.

A more serious look takes over Valentin's hardened face. "I'd take a bullet for him any day of the week."

The sincerity in his voice is almost enough to tug at my heartstrings. Instead, I take my last handful of fries and shove them into my mouth.

"Have you ever been in a situation where you had to?" I ask, only slightly curious. Really, I just like to talk when I eat. It's an old habit I picked up from growing up in foster homes.

"We've been in multiple situations where I might have taken a bullet for him, but when the lead started flying, he was the one who took a bullet for me."

Well, shit. I wasn't expecting to hear that. For obvious reasons, I took Andrei for a selfish prick. But maybe that's because every boss I've ever had has been a selfish prick.

Andrei may be a boss, but he seems to care about more than just himself.

... So, could he actually care about me?

Valentin breaks in on my thoughts. "What about you? What's your story?"

"I don't have a story," I sigh. My plate is empty but my stomach is nowhere near full. "I was living in a homeless shelter up until this morning."

"I know all about that. I'm talking about the other part."

"How do you—" I'm about to ask how he knows about the homeless shelter before I realize the obvious answer. Andrei told him. What else has Andrei told him? "What other part?"

"The part that got you living in that shithole of an apartment. I was there with Andrei when we discovered it had been burned down. No one lives in a place like that unless they have a sob story to tell. What happened to you?"

"Nothing." I look away. I don't want to talk about it... but I guess Valentin has already told me a lot about himself. "My mom died when I was young. My dad wasn't around for much longer after that. He disappeared and my life turned to shit. For a while there, though, I had a good life... I think. I mean, I was too young to know better..." a deep, confessional sigh drifts from my lips, "... But sometimes I have dreams where I lived like a princess for the first few years of my life. Those are just dreams, though. The rest of my life has been a series of increasingly devastating nightmares."

Valentin listens carefully, and when I'm done, he cocks his head to the side, just like Andrei does. "Well, I'm sorry to hear that. But that can't be all. There has to be more."

"Why does there have to be? I'm telling the truth."

"Pakhan wouldn't be so interested in you if that was all there was to it. We've all had rough upbringings. No offense, but in this world, it doesn't make you special. If anything, it just makes you another lost soul."

I shrug and try to avoid Valentin's eyes. "If you want to hear about all the crappy jobs I've had in the last few years, I can write you out a list. I thought things were going okay there for a while, but shit kind of took a turn for the worst these last few months..."

"Well, things will get better for you from now on. Pakhan doesn't take an interest in just anyone. He'll make sure you have everything you need."

His phone interrupts him, and when he answers it, his eyes snap to my face with a sharp, meaningful look. "What's up? Yeah, she's here. We're in the kitchen. Yeah, she'll be ready for dinner..." He must be talking to Andrei.

"Got it. I'll tell her. See ya." Valentin hangs up. "Pakhan says he'll be home by six and you'll meet him for dinner at seven."

"And if I don't want to meet him?" I bluff.

"You can go back to the shelter anytime you want, no questions asked. It's your choice."

There's no venom in Valentin's voice, but I can tell he's holding back. It doesn't feel like I have a choice, no matter how many times I'm told otherwise.

"Well, I guess I can make it to one dinner," I mumble, picking up my empty plate.

"Give the guy a chance."

"Does he deserve one?" Before Valentin can answer, I turn my back on him and start to wash my plate in the sink.

"The maids will take care of that," he tells me.

"It's already done." Setting aside the wet plate, I look over my shoulder. Valentin is blocking off the doorway. "I think I want to go back to my room."

He steps aside. "On your way then."

"Thanks for the company," I say, stepping around him.

To my surprise, though, Valentin doesn't stay in the kitchen. Instead, he follows me into the butler's pantry. That's where I stop and turn to confront him.

"What are you doing?"

"I'm going upstairs."

"Why?"

"To make sure you don't go where you're not supposed to."

"I said I wouldn't."

"And I believe you."

"So why are you coming?"

"Just to appease the big boss man," he grins.

Fuck. Was Valentin just putting on a show this entire time?

"Should I tell him you were hiding in the kitchen most of the day?"

"Tell him whatever you want. I just got here. Had to grab a quick drink before coming up to check on you."

I don't know how else to respond. So I just turn around again and storm off.

Valentin keeps a respectful distance, but he still follows me all the way upstairs. Each lumbering step he takes is like a warning. He said I could leave whenever I want, but I know better than that now.

I'm trapped here. And I'm being kept under close watch.

"This is unnecessary," I loudly grumble, speeding down the hallway to my room.

"If you don't like it, then take it up with Pakhan when you see him tonight. Until then, I'll be following his orders."

His heavy footsteps follow me at a relentless pace.

But I forget all about him when I walk into my room.

"What the hell..."

To my surprise, three big clothing racks have appeared beside the bed. When I approach, I find that each one is loaded with full-length trench coats, dresses, business suits, and outfits I could only dream of wearing. There's even a fourth rack hidden behind it all that's stacked to the brim with shoes.

"These weren't here before."

I flick the hangers, taking it all in. The dresses are perfect.

There's a nice mix of casual summer dresses, nicer dinner wear, and full glamour gowns.

I stop in front of a beautiful sheer black satin gown that weighs nothing at all. I shiver thinking about wearing it in front of Andrei. This is nicer than anything Yelena has for sale in her shop. It must have cost a fortune.

Suddenly, I freeze.

Yelena.

She still has my phone.

... But maybe there's another way to contact her.

I glance back toward the door just as it clicks shut. A shiver skates up my spine. Valentin is out there. And he's acting more like a prison guard than a bodyguard.

Paranoia seeps into my bones. I glare out the huge windows ahead and see nothing but endless forest. Then my gaze slowly drifts onto that intimidating crest carved into the wooden headboard above the bed.

A deadly viper slithers through a screaming skull. There's nothing reassuring about the image. It invokes only dread.

I *need* to find a way to reach the outside world, even if it's just a safety net to use in case something goes wrong. Because something will go wrong. I'm surrounded by criminals. And I can already tell they're lying to me. I'm not free to go whenever I want. Why else would Andrei's second-in-command be sent to watch me?

But what happens when something *does* go wrong? How will I call for help if I don't have any way to contact my friends? I need a phone.

Sure, I could ask Valentin to use his, but I doubt that would do me any good. And not just because I don't know anyone's phone number off the top of my head. Andrei hasn't explicitly forbidden the use of phones, but something tells me he wants to keep me as isolated as possible.

If I'm going to find a way to call for help, it's going to have to be in secret.

My gaze shifts from the view outside to the black satin gown hanging before me.

An idea forms in my head... then slowly materializes into a full-fledged plan.

I scramble through the racks searching for the perfect outfit. It doesn't take long before I find a business suit with pockets. The blazer also has an inner breast pocket, but that won't help me now. I need to make sure Yelena gets my message.

I dash over to the dresser and rip open the drawers. Somehow, I actually get lucky and find a pad of paper and a pen. I scribble down a quick note to Yelena and stick the folded paper in the hip pocket of the suit skirt.

Why didn't I think of this before? If I'd had the idea at the woman's shelter, then maybe all of this could have been avoided.

When I open the bedroom door. I find Valentin slouched against the wall. He scrolls on his phone and raises his eyebrows when I hold out the hanger with the blazer. "Can you do me a favor?"

"Sure. What's up?"

"Could you send this suit out to have the waist taken in? It's too big for me."

He glances down at the outfit and makes a face. "Tell me you don't plan to wear this to dinner with Pakhan tonight."

"I wouldn't be sending it out to be altered if I was. I need it for later... in case."

He puts his phone away and takes the hanger. "Yeah. Whatever. Okay."

"Could you do me another favor?" My heart hammers out of my chest. Could this actually work?

"What is it this time?"

"Could you please send it to Empress Collection Imports on Van Buren? It's downtown. I know the seamstress there and she knows my measurements. She might not be there, but one of her assistants should be able to help."

He chews on his tongue for what seems like an eternity before finally nodding. "I'll send someone out."

I beam at him, genuinely relieved that he isn't asking more questions. "Thank you."

I turn back into the bedroom but stop by the door to listen. My heart lifts when I hear Valentin's heavy footsteps disappear down the hallway.

I'm in way over my head, but at least there's some hope now.

Looking up at the ceiling, I say a silent prayer.

Please, let that note get to someone who can help.

I have a feeling I'm going to need it.

15

ANDREI

I climb out of the chopper and greet Valentin on the landing pad.

"Everything under control?" I ask as the engine fades behind us.

"All quiet," he tells me. "Nothing to report."

"Where is she?"

"Upstairs in her room. Been there since you called."

"Good. Come into my office. I want to talk to you."

For as badly as I want to see Natalya again, there's something I need to get out of the way first.

"Aye aye." Valentin follows me up to my office then shuts door behind him. "Anything wrong?"

"Yes. Ilya got the forensic results back on the bullet casings that wiped out the Utyuzhin Bratva."

"And?" Valentin prompts. "Who was it?"

"No one," I sneer. "At least no one that we know. The bullet casings were totally untraceable."

Valentin frowns. "That's impossible. We have insider info on every group in North America big enough to pull off a hit like this. You must be missing something. It has to be mob-related. They didn't leave a calling card?"

"Not that we've found. But if they hid their calling card that well, then what would be the point? This was a purposeful act of sabotage. Not an intimidation tactic. And the cops on our payroll are just as stumped as we are. Hell, even the guns that were left behind are untraceable. According to our sources, they were never sold on the open market, so the killer couldn't have been a civilian outfit either—and that leaves us with very few remaining options... if any."

Valentin rubs his chin and starts pacing. "That should be impossible. We've prepared for something like this. We have fail-safes in place. Anyone foolish enough to try should have been caught in our pincers."

"And yet here we are," I grunt. "Even Ilya is stumped... and that's saying something. He's been trying to trace surveillance footage all day and he still can't come up with anything useful. That means these fuckers know this city well enough to move through it unseen."

"None of this makes any sense." Valentin comes to a halt in front of me. "But what are we going to do about it? We can't retaliate against something we can't even see."

I clench my jaw and tighten my fists.

"As much as I hate to say it, there isn't much we can do right now. Our best option is to keep it quiet until we find some more evidence. Take your crew out to case the city. Look for unusual activity—anything out of the ordinary. Whoever did this wants to send me a message. But since they haven't revealed them-selves yet, it means they're not ready for a full-on confrontation. They'll strike again. This is only the beginning, old friend. Keep your eyes peeled and your guns ready. I feel a storm coming."

"Just tell me who to kill."

"I'm not holding you back anymore. Flush the rats from the sewer... with blood if you must. Just keep the violence contained to our rival groups. We'll send a message right back to these cowards. No one fucks with us or what's ours. Now go. Take the chopper. Go and do you what you do best."

He glances over his shoulder. "You don't want to come?"

I shake my head. "Sure I do. It'd be just like the old days. But I've got a new toy and a hunger I need to satisfy. My anger can be bottled for a little while longer, especially when I have a beast like you to unleash onto the world."

Valentin bursts into a grin. "You're going to make me blush."

I walk him out to the backdoor. "Did she say anything interesting today?"

"Only what we already knew. She's a nice girl. You be careful with her." He cocks his head to study me and stops himself from saying anything else.

"I never am. Now go before I get pissed at you for talking to my girl."

"Yes, Pakhan," Valentin nods.

With that, he heads back downstairs to the landing pad. I wait in my office until I hear the chopper's roar fade into the distance. All the rage I've built up during this infuriating day sinks to the bottom of my mind. I step out into the hall and look toward Natalya's bedroom.

Make it all worthwhile, angel.

Pulling off my tie, I make my way to my master bedroom. It's not far, and when I get there, the clock above my walk-in closet says it's 6:45. That gives me just enough time to change before my planned dinner with Natalya at 7.

"What will you wear for me, little deer?" I think out loud as I strip from my uncomfortable clothes and get into something that breathes a little better.

My cock springs out when I take off my pants. I'm already half-hard just thinking about what I'll do to that tight little body tonight. She's finally here. And I have a whole lot of stress to unload on her.

It's perfect.

Choosing a black silk button-up shirt and some matching pants, I slowly get dressed. I had a shower back at my office downtown, so I should be fine on that end, but I still make my way to the back of the closet for an extra special touch.

"What scent would she prefer," I wonder, typing out the password to my vault. The lock unclicks, but before I open it, I find myself staring at the familiar crest adorning the door.

My insignia.

A wailing skull, jaw pried open by an invading python. Black scales glisten beneath the soft lighting overhead. The gold flakes staining the skull glitter too. But the black wood beneath it all doesn't. No light escapes its scratched and pock-marked façade. My chest tightens.

I remember Natalya's fascination with my crest.

How prophetic of her. Though, I might never have thought to use some of the contents hidden inside my multiple vaults until she became so intrigued by them.

Now, it's all I can think about.

I'll bind her to my past and tie her to my future, all with the same chains that were once used to restrain me. Together, we'll forge a new history. Plow a dark and smoldering path filled with screams of joy and ecstasy—and a little pain, just for good measure. Maybe I can get some more blood out of her. Wouldn't that be wonderful?

I'll have to remember to taste it this time.

With a wicked grin painted on my lips, I open the vault door and ignore the items strewn over the top shelves for what I keep at the bottom. A row of priceless colognes. I rarely wear such things. But on special occasions, I enjoy the intensity that some of these fragrances add to my already beastly scent.

I want to overload Natalya's senses. Tonight there's no holding back.

"You'll do just fine," I mumble, picking up a small black

glass bottle. It's shaped like a crystalline tear and is surprisingly heavy. I bend my neck and apply the unnatural spray. Its icy fresh scent swirls into the air; spicy notes cut through it like flame-tipped arrows.

Looking over my shoulder, I check the clock. 6:50. I'll stop back at office on the way to the dining room. There's one last thing I want to check on before I forsake my empire for this girl.

I button up my shirt as I walk. When I get to my office, I sit down in front of the computer and go through the files we've accumulated on every criminal organization from here to California.

I try to let instinct take over. It's always led me in the right direction before. But my gut doesn't kick toward a single file, even as I pass over all the usual suspects—the Italians, the Yakuza, the Triad, the gangs on the South Side. It's not any of them. It can't be.

And that just makes this challenge all the more intriguing.

Men will die. Buildings will burn. Alliances will be broken. But it's been too long since I've had any fun in this brutal game. Now, all the fun has come rushing in at once.

I know I can handle it.

All I have to do is keep my priorities straight. And right now, my main priority is tasting Natalya's sweet little pussy again. Well, that's my second priority. First on the menu is seeing how she acts when I treat her like a dark princess. That's what dinner is for. An appetizer.

The main meal will come in bed. Perhaps desert as well.

My phone buzzes. It's five minutes to seven. Everything else will have to wait.

I leave my office and head downstairs. But when I reach the foyer, I stop in my tracks.

"Well, I'll be damned."

At the top of the stairs, like a seductive angel rising over a black Christmas tree, is the only thing that could possibly snap my mind from work.

Natalya.

She's wearing a sheer black satin dress that somehow shows off every last curve and still leaves everything to the imagination. It slips and slides and glides down her tight body like a wet dream as she eases down each step.

Her hair is pulled up into a messy knot. She doesn't wear any make-up... though, I'm sure that's only because I left strict orders not to provide her with any. It's not that I don't like the stuff on a woman—if done properly it can be fittingly elegant—but I don't want Natalya hiding behind *anything* when she's with me.

Long, slim gold earrings drape her neck and a simple gold chain dangles over her mouth-watering cleavage.

My chest pounds at the delectable sight. I lick my lips. Food is the last thing on my mind, but I'm absolutely starving.

Keep it together, I tell myself. *What good is any of this if you just take her all at once? That will come. And it will be worth it.*

"Hello, beautiful," I smile when she reaches the bottom step. "Don't you look ravishing."

Her cheeks flush and she looks down at her feet.

"In this old thing...?"

I'm surprised by the softness of her voice. There's no fight in it. Just acceptance. It immediately makes me suspicious. What happened to the Natalya I left this morning?

"It fits you perfectly," I say, offering her my hand. "But it will look better on the floor of your bedroom."

"How about you treat me to dinner first." She rolls her eyes but still accepts my hand. Her fingers slide into mine. A perfect fit.

"Dinner will come. Then so will you."

"Promises, promises..." she sucks at her teeth and shakes her head.

"You're in a good mood."

Natalya opens her mouth but nothing comes out. There it is. A surefire sign that she's hiding something. That secrecy won't last for long. I'll strip her naked and discover all there is to learn about her.

Her blue eyes avoid mine as she comes up with an excuse for her changed mood.

"It's not every day a girl like me gets to wear a dress like this."

"That dress should feel honored, as should the man who got it for you."

She tilts her head to the side. "Valentin?"

I tug her into my body. A small yelp leaves her lips as she falls into me.

"Valentin is my blood brother, and I trust him with both of our lives. But when you're dressed like that, you do not speak another man's name. Not in my presence or anyone else. That's your first lesson. Do you understand it?"

Natalya tries to push away from me but I don't let her. So, instead, she does the only thing she can do.

She obeys.

"... Yes," she swallows.

"That's a good girl. But know this: Valentin didn't get that dress for you. I did. I got all of the clothes you saw upstairs."

"How did you know my size?"

"I've held enough women to give it an educated guess. Looks like I was right"

Her nails dig into my palm. I welcome the sharp tinge of pain. There's the girl I'm obsessed with.

"What? So you're allowed to talk about other girls you've slept with but I can't even mention other guys?"

Her jealousy makes me light-headed. How fucking wonderful.

"No names were mentioned," I breathlessly growl. "But

you're right. That was wrong of me. Tonight, no other girl exists. It's just the two of us—for better or for worse."

Natalya huffs. "Lucky me."

"I could say the same thing about myself."

Giving her some space, I look down at those burning blue eyes. They glare up at me with such conflict. I want to end the battle raging inside of her. I want her to accept her most primal desires. I want her to give in to me.

"Are we eating dinner or what?" Natalya asks, snapping me out of it.

I grind my teeth. Even with all the leg work I've put in today, I'm barely hungry.

"If that's what you want."

"It is. Just show me the way."

"Very well. Take my hand and I'll do just that."

This time, I don't even have to offer up my hand to her. She just grabs it and squeezes me with a demanding strength.

"Go on then."

My eyes nearly roll into the back of my head from the pleasure of her bite. The spice on her breath is enough to make me hard. Her defiance is still so fresh and new that I'm not entirely sure what to do with it.

Smother it. Of course.

"This way."

Squeezing her hand back, I lead Natalya through the foyer, down another hall, and then into a small breakfast room at the back of the house. The intimate table takes up most of the room. Two chairs sit right across from each other.

She halts on the threshold and checks over her shoulder. "Aren't we going to the dining room?"

I shake my head. "You mean like... am I going to sit at one end of the dining table with you ten miles away from me on the other end? No. I wasn't planning on that."

Natalya still thinks I'm some cartoon villain. How long will it take me to convince her that I'm something far more sinister? How slowly will I have to break it to her to keep her from running away or shutting down?

"That's actually exactly what I thought it was going to be like."

I pull out her chair for her. "Well, lucky for you, I'm not the type."

"No. You are. Just for some reason, you aren't with me."

She sits and I lean down to whisper in her ear. "That's because I like you, little deer. Accept it. People would kill to be in your shoes. And I kill people I don't like. Enjoy." My words clearly leave her shaken as I take my place across from her. "Don't worry, angel. I don't hurt women or children," I assure her.

"Is that how you see me?" she asks, her blue eyes lifting from the table. "As a child?"

"You are certainly naïve... at least about certain things. But no. I see you as a fighter. A grown woman, blessed with a beauty you don't understand."

"I understand how I look just fine, thank you. It's gotten me in trouble with plenty of creeps before you."

"Is that how you see me? As a creep?"

Her gaze temporarily lands on me before extending to the ceiling. Turning her neck, she looks around the impressive room.

"You're a little more... successful than the creeps who usually bother me."

I lean forward in my chair.

"Do you mean financially... or romantically?"

She stiffens. "I thought I wasn't allowed to talk about other men around you?"

I can't help but laugh. "You are a quick learner. Very well. I'll leave it if you'd like?"

"I would," she mumbles, pursing her lips. "Let's talk about

something else."

"Anything in particular?"

"You choose."

I have to check myself. As much as I want to interrogate her, the purpose of this dinner is not to get answers. There's something far more important at stake here.

Still, I remember something Ilya told me earlier today, and I can't help myself. There's a mystery to Natalya that I'm dying to uncover.

"You told me your last name is Datsyuk," I venture.

"That's right."

"That's interesting." I put my napkin in my lap to diffuse the tension. "I did some research on my way here and I couldn't find any record of you with that name."

"Well, it is my name. I didn't make it up."

"I didn't say you made it up. There are a few people in town with that name, but you aren't one of them."

"That's impossible. It's on my driver's license. It's on my birth certificate."

I shrug. "It's not on any records the city has."

She opens her mouth to protest, but just then, my butler Anatoly comes in. The pantry door swings behind him as he silently places a large soup dish at the center of the table. Without a word, he serves us two bowls and ladles just the right amount of soup into each one.

"Thank you," Natalya politely smiles up at him. Her lips are tight with tension, but there's a sincerity in her voice that can't be ignored. The act is so curious that I can't help but squint.

Anatoly nods and then dutifully returns through the swinging door.

"Why is he so quiet?" she whispers after he leaves.

"Because that's how he's been trained to serve," I explain, still trying to figure her out. "Butlers don't speak unless directly ordered to. And they usually aren't thanked for their services."

"Why not?"

"Because it is expected that they do their jobs."

"That doesn't mean they shouldn't be thanked."

"Perhaps."

"I guess you've never worked in the service industry."

"Do I look like I ever served tables?" I ask, raising an eyebrow at her.

She studies me for a second before bursting out into laughter.

"Sorry," she snorts, wiping her lips. "But just imagining you in an undersized apron trying to take an order from some unruly family is hilarious."

A genuine smile comes over my face. "I'd probably just end up killing them."

"But actually, right?"

I laugh, but Natalya quickly tenses back up. I guess the thought of me actually murdering a rude family isn't quite that funny to her... even if it is to me.

"I'd probably get pretty good tips, though," I try to continue, if only because I enjoy her laugh. It's so light and melodic. I want more of it.

"Maybe," she says, her voice lowering as she remembers her circumstances. "I guess you'd at least be good at intimidating a decent tip out of your customers."

"Luckily no family will ever be at risk of finding out just how I'd react, because I don't plan on leaving my current gig."

"Of course not," Natalya nods, fixing her napkin. "Why would a rich boss want to be anything like the people he lords over?"

I look down at my bowl of soup and follow the steam as it rises over Natalya's perfect face.

"They are free to challenge my position," I tell her. "Just as I was free to challenge my predecessor. It just might not work out as well for them as it did for me."

"You killed your own boss?"

"All Pakhans must. It's how we handle succession—well, that and through marriage and heirs. But both are just as likely as the other."

Silence grips the table as Natalya considers what I've told her.

When she finally speaks, it's to say the last thing I was expecting. "So, you're saying your butler is free to try and kill you and become Pakhan?"

A big hearty laugh fills my chest.

"Absolutely he is. But Anatoly is also smart enough not to try—not that he'd want to be Pakhan anyway. The man has a specific skill set, and he is very good at it. If he tried to be something more than that, others would surely put him in his place. He wouldn't last long out there. Luckily, I provide him with a fine life in here."

"Is he not allowed to leave?"

"Of course he is. Everyone here is. But why would he? I pay him well and I respect his traditional training and his code of conduct. If I didn't, he would go and find work for someone else, and I would let him."

"Would you let me leave?"

"Haven't I said as much?"

"I suppose..."

Natalya looks down at her bowl and I lean back in my chair. She's suspicious, and she's right to be. At this point, I'm not sure I would let her out of here. There's too much I want to do with her first.

"Eat," I say, changing the subject. "You've been through a lot. I won't have you wasting away on me."

I can see the wheels continue to turn in her head as she picks up her spoon. She isn't used to this lifestyle. She's never been around it before, but she'll learn. That's why she's here.

I watch as she takes her first taste of the soup. To my

delight, she cocks her head to the side, clearly impressed with how good it is.

I knew she'd like it. Something to remind her of home—at least, that's what I assume until she asks, "What is this?"

"Huh?" I grunt, confused. "What do you mean?"

"This soup. What is it?"

"It's shchi."

She blinks at me in shock. "What did you say?"

My brows furrow. "Shchi. It's a traditional Russian soup. You've never had it before?"

"It's delicious. I just..." She frowns. "What do you call it again?"

"Shchi."

"Shchi," she repeats, her accent broken and surprisingly adorable.

"Your mother never made it for you?"

"Maybe when I was really young," Natalya sighs. "But I guess she wasn't around long enough to make it a lasting memory..." She drops her spoon and I immediately want to kick myself. How could I be so stupid?

I already know about the foster homes. Part of me wants to find out more. Her and I might not be so different after all. But I leave it. I've fucked up enough.

Plus, Ilya is probably working on it as we speak. One way or another, I'll know all her secrets.

"Well, that's okay," I say, grabbing my own spoon. "It wouldn't have been as good as Anatoly's anyway. Now finish up."

To my surprise and disappointment, Natalya doesn't try and fight back. Instead, she just weakly picks up her spoon and starts eating again. She finishes it all without saying another word.

Not long after her bowl is empty, Anatoly returns, clearing

the table and replacing our dishes with regular dinner plates. Then the main course is served.

Varreniki, golubsty, piles of sizzling shashlik, and a stacked herring shuba with beets, red onion, and sour cream.

If I wasn't hungry before, I am now. The scent fills the room with warm nostalgia and reminds me of a time and place I'd long forgotten. I wonder how much Natalya knows about her Russian roots? Despite being an orphan like her, I was at least lucky enough to be brought up around a traditional setting— even if that setting didn't include the warmth of mothers... or any women at all, for that matter.

"You've never had any of this before?" I ask, watching as she gazes over the wealthy platter.

She shakes her head. "I don't even know what it is."

"This is all traditional Russian food. I thought it might make you feel at home..."

"I have no home."

"I've always felt the same way," I sigh. "But at least I know my Russian food. And now you will too. This..." I stab into a piece of shashlik and hold it up. "This is grilled lamb."

Natalya follows my lead and shoves a shank into her mouth.

She's hardly swallowed before she's reaching out for another piece.

"It's delicious."

"It's called shashlik and this...." I spear one of the golubstys. "This is ground beef stuffed in cabbage. It's called golubsty."

She's too busy trying some golubsty to acknowledge my little lesson.

"Do you like it?" I ask sarcastically.

She furiously nods, her cheeks fat with food. The wild way she feasts makes me more interested in her than ever. Hell, I can even feel my old dead heart hurting as the ice encasing it melts some more.

This little deer is feral, just like me. I'll tame her just enough to keep that part of her intact.

"I can teach you more about your Russian heritage if you'd like?"

"Is it all this delicious?"

"Not quite," I chuckle. "In fact, most of it is quite brutal."

"Well, then I'd rather not hear it."

"How about something a little lighter instead, then?" I ask, realizing that I have an opening to dig deeper into my earlier question about her last name.

"Sure."

She looks back down at her plate and cuts off a section of the shuba with her fork. I don't care that she's hardly paying attention. I enjoy teaching her like this. The dirtier stuff will come in time, but if she's going to be mine, she'll have to know more about her heritage.

"Most Russians identify themselves by three names," I start. "They start with their first name and then move to their patronymic."

"Patronymic?"

"It's their father's name and it acts sort of like a middle name in the Russian world. For example, my full name is Andrei Mikhailovich Zherdev."

Natalya scrunches her face as if remembering something. "I did know that, actually. I guess that means I'm not totally ignorant."

"So... do you know your patronymic?"

"Yes... it's Vladimirovna."

I nod more to myself than to her. "Natalya Vladimirovna Datsyuk."

"That's me."

"Interesting. Do you remember anything about your family?"

She shrugs. "Pretty much nothing. I don't think there was ever much of a family to begin with..."

"How about your father?"

"My father vanished sometime before I turned ten."

"Really? I thought you were much younger when he left you behind."

"He was already pretty much completely out of my life by the time he disappeared. He was never around. I was alone a lot. All that changed when he left was that I had to go live in foster care. Then I was surrounded by strangers until I got old enough to leave."

"And where did you live before going into foster care?"

"Some house in Chicago. I can't remember where it was. It's hard to remember much from before I was a teenager. A state-prescribed therapist once told me it was due to the trauma I faced. Apparently, going through that much shit can make you block it all out."

"Do you remember the address?"

"No," she gently shakes her head. "And I'm not sure I knew it back then either. In fact, I don't really remember ever leaving the house. Sometimes, I feel like I wasn't allowed to leave, but that can't be true."

Now it's my turn to stare. "Very interesting..."

Natalya fiddles with her food and I notice she isn't eating anymore. "I haven't really thought about it for a while, but yeah, it was weird. I saw my father maybe every other week for an hour or two. He was nice during those times, but he was way too preoccupied with work."

"What did he do?"

"I have no idea. He wouldn't talk about his work... or to me, no matter how hard I tried to make him proud... or maybe none of that happened and I'm just misremembering dreams..."

I can see her sink at the memory. Whether it's real or not, it doesn't matter. Natalya has never had a man in her life she can trust. No one who truly cared for her.

I'll change that.

"Who took care of you when he wasn't there?"

"I... I can't remember. It wasn't my mother, though. She was long gone by then. But it wasn't any one person in particular either. Different people came and went, I think. They always changed. I guess I was already in a kind of foster system before I ever officially ended up there."

I stare down at my plate. This conversation has gone off in a direction I didn't expect. I don't feel like eating anymore either.

A small silence fills the gap between us. Then Natalya says, "So, yeah, I never really had a home... or someone to teach me about my heritage. But if it's even half as interesting as the food, then I wouldn't be opposed to learning. So, I mean, if you want to teach me... that could be alright... "

She trails off and I struggle to focus.

Her strange and unexpected history has caught my attention. I have a whole new slew of questions I want to ask. They sit on the tip of my tongue. But I decide against asking anything else. The mystery of her past can wait. It's her body that I truly want to explore tonight.

"It would be my pleasure," I say, forcing my interest away from our conversation. "We can start tomorrow. I'll teach you some of the language. How does that sound?"

"Good."

I stare down at the table. There's still plenty of food left, but I'm satisfied. I can tell that Natalya is too, because when I look up, I catch her studying me.

"Have you eaten all you want?" I ask, returning her gaze.

She lays down her fork and pushes her plate away. "Yeah. I guess I'm not as hungry as I thought I was."

"We've both eaten enough," I agree. "Now it's time for your second lesson." Standing up, I walk around the table and pull out her chair. She takes my hand when I present it to her. "Are you ready?"

"Do I have a choice?"

"Yes. You always have a choice. And don't make me or anyone else believe for a second that you don't." Releasing her hand, I step aside and gesture toward the door. "I'm going upstairs. Would you like to join me?"

Her gorgeous blue eyes skate back and forth as she considers the question. I can see the burning desire in her; the red-hot memory of what we've already done. Really, this is her first real test. It's *my* first test too.

Have I done enough to make her want me?

"Yes," Natalya nods. "I'll come upstairs."

I nearly pump my fist in victory. "It will be worth it," I smile. "I'll make sure of that. This way, little deer."

I let her brush by me and then follow her like a stalking predator. The way her hips sway drives me crazy, and by the time we reach the top of the stairs, my pants are barely being held together.

I'm not sure I can take this as slowly as I planned. And I make a final decision when Natalya reaches the top of the stairs. She instinctively goes left, toward her bedroom, but I reach out and take her hand.

"This way."

"We aren't going to my bedroom?" she asks, stumbling along as I pick up speed.

"No. We're going to mine."

She swallows. "Your bedroom?"

"That's right."

"Why?"

I think of the vault sitting in the back of my closet.

"Because there's something I want to show you."

16

The second we step through the door I pin Natalya against the wall and steal my first kiss.

She gasps as my body sinks into hers... then she kisses me back.

"You could have shown me this in my room," she breathes.

"This isn't what I wanted to show you. Go. Get on the bed."

Natalya's pale cheeks flush pink as she looks down at the floor. Still, the second I release her, she obediently shuffles over to the bed

"Wait." I stop her before she can kneel on the mattress. "Undress for me. Slowly."

"What if I don't feel like going slow?" The confidence of her words is not matched by the tone of her voice. She sounds like a girl trying to cosplay a woman.

It makes me smile. She wants to be the woman I desire. But she's not there yet.

"Then you will swallow that instinct and listen to your master," I say, wiping the grin from my face. "You will have your time, little deer. But right now, I'm in charge. Do you understand?"

"... Yes."

"Yes what?"

"Yes... Pakhan?"

That nearly makes me laugh.

"No, little deer. You don't call me that. For you, it's either Andrei or sir... daddy is also acceptable.

"Yes... sir."

"That will do. Now, undress. Slowly. If you move too fast, I will rip that pretty dress to shreds and fetch another until you get it right. Go on."

Natalya meets me with a stubborn stare as she very purposefully slips out of her dress straps. The right shoulder comes first, then the left. For a moment, the entire outfit hangs precariously on her perfectly curved hips. Then, to no fault of her own, it slides off.

A deep sigh flares my nostrils at the sight of her immaculate body. The pure aura of her pale skin makes me shiver. I haven't gotten a slow look at her like this before. Our other encounters have been far more rushed.

I want to savor every moment... even if that means messing with my captured princess.

"That was too quick," I say, shaking my head. "Do it again. Slower this time."

Natalya stares at me like I've just asked her to jump off a bridge.

"That wasn't my fault. It just slid off."

"Have you never worn a dress before? That's what they do when you remove the straps. Now, are you going to listen to me or am I going to have to punish you?"

I take a step forward, but it's obvious Natalya isn't ready for that yet. She shrinks away and I stop. Still, I nod down at the crumpled dress around her ankles.

"Alright, I'll put it back on," she mumbles.

Bending at the knee, she goes to pick it up.

"No. Kick it away. You won't be using the same dress more than once. Do you really think I'd let my girl recycle outfits?"

Natalya looks around, confused, "I... I don't have another dress..."

"You have a room full of them."

"We're not in my room."

"Clever girl." Reaching into my pocket, I pull out my phone and send a text.

"What are you doing now?" Natalya gulps. I watch her throat shiver as I start to circle her.

"You'll see."

My chest pounds at the rear view I get from the other side of the mattress. The tied curtains of my canopy bed frame the perfect silhouette standing ready for my orders. Natalya's tight little ass clenches slightly when I put my knee on the mattress. I remember how it felt when she clamped her pussy around my cock.

"I'm disappointed," I rumble toward the back of her neck. "If you had done as you were told, we'd be fucking by now."

Without any clothes on, it's impossible for Natalya to hide her body's reaction. Those toned thighs flex and her toes curl. Her shoulder blades twitch.

"I'm not stopping you," she says, clearly eager... and increasingly frustrated. I want to bottle up that frustration so that it all comes bursting out when the dam breaks.

"Patience, little deer. You'd think you'd never been made to wait for sex before."

"I waited long enough before I met you."

I'm already pushing myself off the bed when the implication of what Natalya just said finally hits me.

"What does that mean?" I ask, circling back around to face her.

Those ocean-blue eyes scatter like they've been discovered doing something they shouldn't be,

"Nothing."

"No. That wasn't nothing," I push, holding onto the hope that she means exactly what I think she means. "How many men have you fucked before me?"

"I thought I wasn't allowed to talk about men around you…"

Towering over her, I reach around Natalya's small waist and clamp my hand into her ass. She squeaks, jumping onto her tiptoes before I dig my fingers into her tender meat and ease her back down.

"You have my permission. But only this once."

The tips of my fingers spread out teasingly close to the pulsing heat hiding between her legs. My breathing deepens, as does hers. We both want to break the tension. We both want me to slip inside of her. But I won't give her what she wants until she says what I want to hear.

"Well, I don't need your permission, because… there weren't any men before you."

An uncontrolled groan rumbles from my lips as I look up at the ceiling. Who knew a single sentence could contain so much pleasure.

"You're a virgin?"

"I was… until I met you.

I gaze into Natalya's eyes and a rush of warmth spreads through my chest. I feel something that I've never felt before. A connection that wants to bring me to my knees. I let it.

"The blood… I knew there was something special about you…"

"Being a virgin isn't who I am… well, it wasn't who I was."

"That's right. You're mine."

Breathing over every inch of her bare skin, I crouch before my corrupted princess. My knees fall into the soft carpet and I stare at her flat belly with all the awe in the world. Without even knowing it, she's given me something I can't possibly repay her for.

But that doesn't mean I won't try my best.

"Try to stay on your feet," I mumble. My hands clasp around Natalya's waist and my tongue flickers out. I paint her hip bones and drink in the sound of her whimpers as she struggles to obey my command.

Her knees shake when I reach her swollen clit. Her sweet nectar coats my tongue. I hold her in place and lap her soaking nub in circles. She digs her fingers into my hair and I eat her harder and harder until...

My phone buzzes in my pocket.

I take one last teasing taste and then pull back. When my hands retreat, Natalya collapses onto the mattress, gasping for air.

"You still taste as pure as the day we met," I smile, my lips glistening with her juices.

"I don't feel pure."

"Good. That's the first step."

"First step to what?"

"Becoming my queen."

Natalya's perky tits heave as she sits and watches me turn toward the door. When I open it, I see exactly what I hoped for.

A rack of clothes from Natalya's bedroom.

"What are those doing here?" she asks, still out of breath.

I wheel them in and close the door behind us. I'm sure the maid heard Natalya's whimpers, but I don't mind. As long as no man ever hears her scream again, I'll be just fine.

"Was the head so good you forgot your task?"

"My...?" her eyes bulge wide as she remembers what we were doing just before I fell to my knees. "You're going to make me put on another dress just to strip out of it?"

"Just to *slowly* strip out of it," I remind her. "Here, try this one."

Picking a purple sundress at random, I toss it at her. She's too slow to catch it, and it wraps around her face.

I let a deep chuckle fill my chest.

"On your feet, angel."

"Yes, *sir*," she snaps.

Defiantly ripping the dress off her face, Natalya tries to stand up. But her wobbly legs almost give out. She catches the bedpost just in time.

"That's a good girl." I watch with pleasure as she ungracefully shoves the pretty little outfit on. "Now take it off. Slowly."

Holding eye contact, Natalya flicks at the shoulder straps. A blue fire blazes in her eyes, but it's not filled entirely with anger or frustration. There's something about this she likes. And that's fucking perfect.

This time, when her shoulder straps are loose, Natalya grabs the dress at the waist and tugs at it in jerky motions. The first pull reveals her clavicle. The second her tits. The third her flat stomach. And the fourth her soaking pussy.

The purple sundress falls to her knees and she sticks them out just enough to keep it from falling to the floor. She holds my gaze for one long moment before finally letting them drop.

"Happy?" she huffs.

"Very. But I just realized something. You weren't wearing panties for dinner, were you?."

"I... I..."

Natalya's pink cheeks turn red.

"Don't worry, I'm not offended. It's just not the same, you know? How could I get the full experience of you slowly stripping for me when—"

"I am NOT doing that again."

I reach for my collar and pull until the buttons pop. My silk shirt comes flying undone.

"Then I guess I'll punish you."

I toss the shirt aside and rip off my belt. It hits the floor only a moment before my pants. Natalya backs up until the edge of the bed takes out the back of her knees. She falls onto her ass and I lunge over top of her.

"Andrei!" she cries.

I plant my fists into the mattress and cage her between my forearms. Her hand flies onto my chest, outstretched fingers spreading across my skin. The warmth of her touch draws a deep, gravelly breath from my lungs.

"Do you think you're wet enough to take me?"

"If I say no, will you still do it... as punishment?"

"No. I have something else in mind for that. Something far more impressive... and severe."

I thrust my bulge into her hips and her neck snaps back. The hand that's on my chest blindly finds my wrists. Natalya squeezes as I lean down and kiss her throat.

"Are you ready, angel?"

"Wait," she breathlessly sighs. "What... what is this...?" She furrows her brow and turns her head to look at the hand she has wrapped around my wrist.

"What?" I ask, equally confused.

"Are you hurt?"

That's when I understand.

"No. Not anymore."

Resting my hand on the back of hers, I lead Natalya's fingers over the rope burns on my wrist. To the naked eye, they're nearly invisible. I've covered them in so much ink that they just look like regular tattoos. But if you get close enough, they are impossible to ignore.

"What happened?"

The concern in Natalya's voice tugs at my thawing heart in a way that almost hurts. Why does she care?

"It's a long story."

"Are we in a hurry?"

I look down between my legs. My briefs have been stretched thin. My swollen cock throbs with desire.

"I'm not, but he is."

"Who's in charge?"

"When it comes to you, he is."

"How romantic."

Leaning down into her ear, I whisper nice and low. "If you want my heart, then win it."

I feel her shiver beneath me.

"Tell me what I'd be winning. Who are you?"

I bite down on my lip. This is not where I wanted tonight to go.

"I'm a broken man," I grumble. "But I have all the pieces right here with me. I plan to put everything back together. I... I just need your help."

"So you're not just helping me... you're helping yourself?"

"That's right."

Our wild lust pauses and Natalya shifts onto her elbows. Her blue eyes don't leave my mangled wrist.

"Tell me what happened... please."

Standing up, I look toward my closet. The door is open, but the lights inside are off. Still, I can see the vault that contains the answer Natalya wants. The skull and viper crest screams to me from the shadows.

"Alright, angel," I accept. "But be warned. This history lesson will be part of your punishment."

Natalya hesitates. "Will it hurt?"

"Only as much as I allow." I lean down and plant a protective kiss on her forehead. "I'll make sure you can handle it."

"... Okay."

With a heavy nod, I go to the closet and turn on the lights. The skull and viper greet me and I stare them down for a moment before unlocking the safe. This time, I ignore what's on the bottom shelf for what's above it. A black box, clamped shut by a cherry knot at the front. I carefully untie it and pull the box out.

It's just as heavy as I remember.

"The crest..." Natalya whispers, staring into the lit closet as I walk back out into the bedroom.

"This one does have something behind it."

"That box..."

I nod. "Your lesson... and your punishment."

She gulps.

"Is that what's in the cabinet at your office too?"

"No. Something else is hidden there. Something... different, but similar. You still need to earn that. This, though... you've earned this."

Tonight at dinner, Natalya revealed some of the secrets of her past to me. Now, I'll do the same for her.

I set the box down at the foot of the bed and slide the cover off. What's inside still sends a shiver up my spine. But I'm more confident than ever that I can finally slay this demon of mine... with Natalya's help of course.

"Rope?"

I can hear the fear in her voice as I pull out the long tendrils of thick, beige rope.

"That's right."

"What are you going to use it for?"

"I'm going to tie you up, angel. And then I'm going to have my way with you."

I can see the terror and arousal mix behind Natalya's face. She gently grasps at her wrist.

"Don't worry, little deer. I'll be gentle. This will be for pleasure. Whereas these were used on me purely for pain."

Her pretty face scrunches.

"What do you mean?"

I decide to tell her.

"The previous Pakhan. He knew I was a threat. One night, he ambushed me. I was captured. These were used to restrain me. For months. They were tied so tight and I still have threads embedded in my skin. No matter how hard I tried, or what evils they did to me, I couldn't break free. I still can't quite manage it..."

"Why do you want to use it on me?"

"Because I want to erase the painful memories chained to it and replace them with pleasurable ones. Do you understand?"

"I do."

"Can you help me with that, angel?"

She bravely nods. "I can."

The last chunks of ice surrounding my once frozen heart fall into the darkness and my chest swells.

"That's my good girl."

17

He ties me up so gently that it almost feels... right. Like I belong in this mansion, in this room, in this bed, under his control.

Sure, the rope is rough, and there's a deep fear simmering beneath the excitement, but the only time I feel any tension against my skin is when he hitches a line over a support beam at the top of the canopy and starts to pull.

I'm lifted off the mattress like an angel in some school play until I dangle in the air, spinning softly in the darkness.

For a moment, Andrei's giant, menacing silhouette just stands in the shadows, watching me. I can smell the intoxicating spice he's had on him since dinner. I take a deep breath of it for courage.

"Just like an angel," Andrei whispers.

My hands are tied behind my back. One ankle is dangling above my ass, the other is outstretched, held in place by a circle of rope fastened to the bedpost. A knot engulfs my hair, forcing it back into the messy bun I started the night with. Three other knots slide up my spine, taking the majority of the pressure off the rest of my limbs.

Andrei is clearly an expert at tying people up because I

hardly feel any pain as he reaches out of the darkness and touches my ankle. I slowly spin until my bare ass faces him.

"Are you comfortable?"

"No."

"Is there anything you'd like me to change?"

"... No."

"Then let's get started."

With that, I feel a familiar flicker on the small of my back. Andrei's thick, wet tongue paints a trail over my cheeks and down the inside of my lopsided thighs. I quiver as he slips it inside my pussy and reaches around to gently pinch my swollen clit between his thick fingers.

"Holy shit..." I gasp.

"Feels good, doesn't it, little deer?"

"Yes."

"It will feel better."

His tongue slides out and his fingers fit it. At first, it's just two. He pumps me until I feel my juices drip down from my soaking lips. Andrei dips his head beneath me to catch the falling droplets. He groans with pleasure as they hit his tongue. I hear him swallow.

I do the same.

"Only two people have ever been tied up in these ropes," he reminds me. "But I'll make sure your time spent under their grip is much more pleasurable than mine."

"You've never tied anyone up before?" I gulp.

Andrei curls his two fingers deep inside my pussy, spinning me around until our eyes meet. Those green emerald jewels burst with mischief and pain.

"Oh, I've tied plenty of people up. But never for pleasure. And never with these ropes. I was saving them for someone special. You are that special person."

"Lucky me," I rasp.

"I feel the same way."

Andrei uncurls his fingers and I'm rotated back around.

His teeth dig into my ass and a sharp gasp rips from my throat.

"I can't make it too easy on you, though, angel," Andrei explains, a devilish tint corrupting his deep voice. "Otherwise, how would we connect our two experiences into a single union?"

His open palm smacks against my ass and a searing hot jolt ruptures through my body.

"What are you going to do with me?"

Andrei pauses briefly before making up his mind.

"Whatever I want."

A third finger slides knuckle deep into my pussy just as his tongue is jammed into my asshole.

The thick slimy tentacle stretches me out and lubes me up until my fingers are curling into fists.

"I... I can't take it... I'm too tight," I struggle to breathe.

"I was hoping you'd say that."

"Why?"

"Because it means I'll actually be aware that I'm taking your virginity this time—even if it's with a different hole"

"But... I..." My lips gape wide open as I realize what he means. "No... Andrei, you're too big. I can't fit you up there."

His tongue flashes out of my already aching asshole. "I believe in you, angel. Here, let's try a single finger first." His fingers retreat from my pussy and I can feel his soaking thumb tracing my tiny hole. "Look, you're already lubed up."

"I might shatter..."

Andrei wraps his giant hand around my restrained wrist and squeezes.

"I won't let you."

"... Okay..."

He kisses my ass and his thumb enters my hole.

"Fuck!" I moan, clenching around him.

"Oh, fuck is right, angel," Andrei groans. "You're going to make me cum."

"Already?"

"Just thinking about shoving my cock in your tight little hole is making me drip. I'm so hard it hurts. Take my pain away, baby girl. Fucking smother it."

Yanking on the top rope, Andrei drops me until I'm hovering just inches above the mattress. His thumb furls and unfurls inside of me. His other hand starts playing with my clit. He kisses up the exposed spots on my back, even lifting the rope line with his nose just to get an extra taste of me.

The bed creaks as he stands on top of it. I can feel the massive threat of his cock burst out from behind his briefs. Its heat washes over me.

"Let's get you in just the right spot."

Andrei pulls on the rope and I'm lifted up again until I feel the girthy warmth of his throbbing head brush against my ass.

"I'll start with something familiar," he growls. "Nice and easy now."

I'm spun and led into position by the finger in my asshole. And then, just like that, everything erupts.

Andrei's huge cock rams into my pussy and I'm cracked open. I hadn't even realized how tense I'd been before. Now, though, I might as well be water—well, steam would be more accurate.

"Andrei!" I scream, my voice warbling as he pounds me into dust.

"That's right, little deer," he huffs and puffs. "Cry my name out nice and loud. Let the whole fucking world know who you belong to."

"Andrei!"

"Again!" he demands, thrusting into me so powerfully I feel it in my bones.

"Andrei!"

Another finger spreads open my asshole. I can feel his cock and fingers rubbing against each other through the thin lining that separates them. They're both overpowering, but somehow, I don't feel like I'm going to rip open—or maybe I do, and I just don't care.

"Oh my god..." I whimper, bending my neck in an attempt to smother my face into the sheets. But I'm too far away. All I can do is hang there and take him.

"God can wait," Andrei growls. "Only the devil's allowed to cum in this room."

His thumb springs out of my ass and his hands wrap around my back, engulfing my tits with his fiery palms. He leans into my ear, his hot, spicy breath filling it with burning desire. "... Only the devil's allowed to cum in *you*."

Suddenly, that's all I want... to feel his thick, hot cum fill me up.

"Please..." I beg, no matter how insane the request is. "... Please..."

Andrei roars and then his tongue is in my ear. It feels like he's completely engulfed me. I squirm beneath him, but he doesn't let up. His thrusts become more and more powerful until my eyes flutter and the pressure in my core cracks.

An earth-shattering orgasm tears through my entire body. One of Andrei's hands moves from my tit to my mouth just in time to swallow up the scream that explodes out of me.

"I'm not done with you yet, angel. You're going to give me one final gift. And you're going to fucking love it."

His cock jerks out of my pulsing pussy and is immediately pressed against my impossibly small ass cheeks. His cock is so big that it feels like I don't even have a hole.

"Look at how you've lubed up my cock with your cum," he says, spreading my cheeks apart. "Such a good girl."

"Andrei... I..."

"Don't worry, little deer. I'm not a monster... at least, not entirely."

All I can do is heave down at the sheets as Andrei gets off the bed and retrieves something from a bedside table drawer. I don't know what it is until I feel the cold lube drip across my tender skin.

"Do you really think I can take you there?"

"I know you can."

The pressure that follows is so intense I nearly black out. It feels like I'm being shoved to the bottom of the ocean from the waist down. From the waist up, though, I'm engulfed in a light fire that burns my skin in the most pleasurable way.

The pressure in my core returns. My limbs flex. My ass clenches.

My little hole is stretched to its limit.

"Yes, Natalya," Andrei groans. "Just like that."

His fingers dig into my ass cheeks as he spreads them further and further apart.

And then, by some miracle, I feel his hard stomach slap against my upper ass.

"Holy shit," we both gasp at the same time.

His girthy cock throbs inside of me as it claims its place. For a breathless moment, neither of us move. And then, Andrei takes over.

The real pain comes when he starts to slide back out. Fortunately, he only goes halfway before thrusting back into me. A soundless gasp gets caught in my throat. Then another, and another, as Andrei stops holding back.

My hands desperately try to reach for something to grab onto, but they're too tightly bound, and all I can do is grasp at the air and claw at the rope while my soul is sucked out of my fucking ass.

"You feel too good," Andrei groans. "How can anyone feel so fucking good..."

He digs his nails into the skin just below my hips for extra grip and momentarily slows his jackhammer thrusts. But that doesn't do him any good.

I can feel another swell take over his already swollen cock. It fills me up on a whole new level.

Then Andrei bursts.

I get exactly what I wanted. Thick globs of hot cum erupt from his cock and burst deep inside of me. I whine with pleasure as a second climax engulfs me.

"Yes..." I whimper. "Yes."

"You little minx," Andrei simultaneously sighs and laughs. "How dare you make me cum so fast..."

He stays impaled inside of me as we both desperately try to catch our breath.

"Twice a virgin," he murmurs. Placing a single finger on the dimple above my ass, he pushes. I swing a few inches forward and Andrei's cock slides out just enough to let some of his cum start leaking. I feel it drip down the backside of my thighs. "You did such a good job, angel."

He allows me to swing on his cock for a little longer before he pulls himself all the way out.

"Fuck," I whisper, hating how cold I immediately feel without him engulfing me. Still, the second his cock is gone, I realize how truly exhausted I am.

Andrei works on freeing me as I fight off a sudden wave of sleepiness.

"That's right, rest, little deer," Andrei assures me from above. "You'll need to be ready for round two."

"... Round two?"

"I'm not done with you yet."

He cuts me down. But it feels like I'm asleep before I even hit the mattress.

18

*The men are tall like buildings at night, and just as dark and myste-
rious. They stand in a circle around a man I can just barely see
through their legs.*

*I don't know the man well enough to recognize his face, but I
understand that he is my father. Something unseen and impossibly
heavy crashes around the room. I'm in the hallway, stuffed toy dog
pressed up against my face.*

I'm chewing on his ear when the man sees me.

*With squinted silver eyes he points and yells. My heart stops.
Someone picks me up beneath the shoulders and I'm carried away.
The tall men disappear. My father too.*

*I'm carried up an impossibly high staircase. It winds in dizzying
circles. The further we climb, the darker it gets.*

Then, the hands carrying me vanish and I start falling.

*Falling through the darkness. Through the flickering flames of
ruin and an icy-cold laugh. Through endless pain and sadness.*

Forever falling.

And then, I'm not falling anymore.

A strong pair of hands appear beneath my arms. They are strong yet gentle. Firm yet soft. I'm heavier now, but I feel light in their grasp.

When I look up, I see green eyes.

Green eyes so powerful they snap me awake.

"Shit..."

The word spills out of my mouth like water as my eyes flutter open.

It takes me a second to realize where I am, but when I do, it's not with a burst of fear, but rather with a smidgen of comfort.

I'm in Andrei's mansion, back in my bed.

Wait. How'd I get here from his room?

He must have carried me...

Stuffing my face in the pillow, I forget about my dream and remember what happened last night. My thighs clench and my toes curl. I close my eyes and drift back to sleep, sore but satisfied. *This is so much better than the woman's shelter...*

From then on, time passes on like a hazy dream. A day goes by, then another. Those days roll into a week. From the moment I open my eyes every morning to before I fall asleep at night, I think about him, no matter how much I struggle not to.

Before long, I'm settled into a strange, lazy, lovesick routine. I sleep as late as I want. I wake up and get myself breakfast whenever I feel like it. Same with lunch. In between that, I wander the grounds.

Valentin isn't around as much as I thought he would be. For the most part, no one keeps track of me—at least, not in person. Still, some doors remained locked, and guards occasionally stand ominously at lines I'm not allowed to cross. My awareness of the cameras lifts and dips depending on my mood, but even that becomes ordinary. Sometimes, I even forget about the lifeline I sent out to Yelena's shop. If it hasn't come back by now, it might never, and I'm starting not to care—especially not when Andrei is around... even if that's becoming more of a rarity every day.

The busy Bratva boss is just that. Busy. He has dinner with me some nights, but mostly not. Other nights, he comes in and does what he wants with my body. I let him. After what he's done to me, how could I not?

If only he stuck around...

It's an odd feeling, wanting him to stay by my side. In the beginning, I just wanted him to leave me alone. But then he followed me to hell and back. Now, he's the one keeping me at arm's length.

It's like he's purposely playing with my heart.

Still, when Andrei's around, the way he touches me makes me feel like I'm the only girl who's ever existed. The way he smiles and charms and spoils me sends bouquets of butterflies rushing through my stomach.

And then he leaves for work, and a coldness comes over his memory and this house. All I can do is justify every traitorous feeling I had for him while he was here. He's provided a roof over my head, comfort, food. All I could ever ask for. But without him, it just feels empty.

I don't think about school or architecture for days on end, and when I do, it's accompanied by anxiety and an empty feeling. Who am I becoming? Where is this going?

Nowhere.

At least, that's what I tell myself until Andrei returns. Then he's back, and I want him desperately again. Every time he walks through my bedroom door, my chest perks up. At this point, the sight of him alone is enough to make me wet.

Then he leaves again.

Sometimes I touch my face and feel a tear. But never when Andrei is around. Once in a while, I commit to never giving him what he wants again. Then he returns and I have to fight against myself... and him.

Maybe that's what he wants. A fight. A challenge. Maybe this is all on purpose. Maybe I'm never meant to be his equal, just his plaything.

The thought keeps me up at night. But what's even worse is the ideas I get when I wake up in the morning—that I can see myself getting used to this life...

A knock on my door startles me from my daydreams. Immediately, I know it's not Andrei. He never knocks. He just walks in like he owns the place—which he obviously does.

"Who is it?" I call out.

"Valentin," the familiar voice replies. "I have your suit. It's back from the seamstress."

Oh shit.

I hop out of bed in my flannel pajamas. I'm not wearing a bra and my hair is a mess, but I don't worry about that. Not with Valentin.

It's been a few days since we last ran into each other. But when we do, it's always with a calm, friendly exchange. For some reason, I feel like I can trust the big lug—well, to an extent. For all his brotherly charm, it's obvious where his loyalty lies, and it's not with me.

"I thought you'd forgotten..." I murmur, opening the door. *I know I nearly did.*

"I never forget a job, no matter how small or insignificant."

"Well, it's nice to know I'm small and insignificant."

"Only to me," he teases. "To Andrei, you're a lot more than that. He won't shut up about you."

"Then why isn't he around more?"

Valentin shrugs. "That's classified information."

A sudden rush of jealousy sweeps through me. It must be written all over my face because Valentin quickly tries to recover.

"It's work stuff," he says. "The man runs an empire. He focuses on that and you. Nothing else. Promise."

"Yeah. Okay."

I swipe the large white box from his hands and turn back into my room.

"Shit," Valentin grumbles, as I shut the door. "That wasn't good."

Grinding my teeth, I set the box down on the floor and try to gather my unexpected emotions. What the hell just happened? I shouldn't care what Andrei is doing out there, but for some reason, it never crossed my mind that he might have other women.

Yet something in Valentin's voice seemed to imply just that... or maybe I'm just losing my mind. I don't know what to believe as I sit down on the carpet and stare at the box.

At this point, what would I even do with a phone?

... There's only one way to find out.

With shaking hands, I open the box and pull out the suit. I'm not sure what to expect as I pat the pockets down. There's nothing in the hip pocket. That would be too obvious. But I keep searching.

Then, I find it.

The phone is in the blazer's breast pocket.

I hold the piece of plastic like it's a cursed artifact. I still have no idea if I'm allowed to have it, and part of me doesn't want to find out. For the most part, I've done all that Andrei has asked, now it's time to have something of my own. Something secret. Something possibly forbidden.

But if I ask him and he says it's fine, then there goes the one last bit of control I have over my life.

You have your whores, I have my phone, I think, surprised at the vitriol in my own mind. Where the hell is this coming from?

Andrei hasn't been home in almost two days, I remind myself. When he's home, we fuck almost constantly. A man like him needs to fuck constantly. But if he's not here, then he's not doing it with me.

With a girl scout-like defiance running through my veins, I sit down on the bed and switch on the phone. It takes a second, but when it turns on, I let out a deep sigh.

"Thank god..." The battery is full. So is my inbox.

I open up my emails. My heart races. This is the first connection I've had to the outside world since I got here. I glance back at the battery icon.

Suddenly, I realize I don't have a charger cable. I search the white box Valentin brought and pat down the suit one more time. There isn't one. I should have asked...

But it's too late for that now. And I don't know if I can risk sending another note. I'll just have to be careful about how often I use it. Still, I go through my mailbox. It's mostly filled with junk mail, reminders about overdue bills, and some messages from Saul. I delete them all without reading a single line.

Whatever is happening in this mansion, it's made me almost violently upset with my past life. I don't want to worry about bills ever again, or about Saul and work or anything.

But then what am I going to do if I ever want to leave?

That terrifying thought sits like a heavy stone in the center of my gut as I check my texts. The older ones are from my friends, texting our group chat as they take off and land in their far away destinations. I see a photo of Julia in Times Square. She has a big, carefree smile on her face.

I feel a tinge of resentment.

They don't know what I've been through since they left...

But how could they?

Swiping out of the group chat, I delete some more texts from Saul and check out the newest batch of messages at the top. They're all from Yelena.

Clearly, her assistant updated her on the contents of my hidden note.

She asks if I'm alright, what happened to my apartment,

who I'm with. She also tells me where to find a spare key to her apartment so I can stay there if I need to.

"Shit," I mumble, pinching my nose. That would have come in handy before all this shit went down.

But do I really regret being here?

My aching, racing heart won't sit still long enough to answer that troubling question. So, instead, I draft a text to Yelena.

I tell her I'm alright and that I'm being looked after while everyone is away. I also tell her that I might just crash at her apartment if I need to, but that's all I say. How would I even begin to explain this to her? I can hardly wrap my own head around it.

Still, a small sense of relief washes over me as I hit send. Now, at least, I have someplace to run to if I need to get out of here. Someplace Andrei wouldn't know about it.

I switch back to the home screen and pause.

Part of me feels like I should call the police, but what would I even say? Technically, I came here out of my own free will, and in theory, I'm allowed to leave whenever I want.

Sure, I know that last part isn't true—I'm a prisoner—but how would I even explain that to anyone outside of these walls?

My head slumps. No. The truth is, I want to be here—at least, I want to be near Andrei. But he isn't here, and that makes this mansion feel like a gilded cage.

Swiping across my screen, I mindlessly go to check on my social media accounts when a text comes through.

My heart perks up, expecting a response from Yelena. Instead, I see something that makes my head tilt.

Unknown.

That's odd.

I open the message.

I know where you are. I know what happened. I know everything. I'm sorry. I'll save you. Keep this phone hidden. When the time comes, I'll help you escape. Just be patient. I love you, my dear sweet Natalya.

My heart stops beating. My mind swims. I look around the room, half-expecting someone to come barreling at me. But no one else is here. It's just me.

I look back down at the phone.

I love you, my dear sweet Natalya.

A shiver skates up my spine. No one loves me. So who the hell could this be from?

Suddenly, a horrifying thought enters my mind. I remember the raging flames from my dream. The bone-chilling laugh. My burning apartment.

Nikolai.

He knows where I am.

19

I groan and rest my face in my hands. "Don't tell me."

"The Karandashov Bratva this time," Valentin grumbles. "Tied up and burned alive in a house in Michigan City. No calling card. No tags. Nothing."

"That makes four in less than two weeks," Ilya notes. "You must respond, Pakhan. We need to send a message."

"To who?" I growl. "We still don't know who or what we're dealing with."

"To the city," Valentin gnashes. "To anyone who will listen. This cannot be tolerated."

"No," I stand up and shake my head, desperately trying to keep my cool. "Whoever is fucking with us wants us to lash out. They want us to make a mistake. That's the only way they can win. We need to wait until we know who the enemy is."

"I'm sick of waiting!" Valentin shouts, his anger bursting at the seams. "And I'm sick of being a glorified babysitter. Don't get me wrong, I like Natalya. But I wasn't born to look after your pet project. I was born to fight. To kill."

A flash of rage nearly blinds me. All my barely-constrained frustration comes bubbling up to the surface.

"Don't you ever fucking speak about her like that again," I roar, slamming my fist into the desk. "You have no idea what she means to me... or to this empire."

Fuck. I want to see her again. But how can I justify going home and enjoying myself when all I've worked for is in such peril?

It's just another challenge, I try to assure myself. *Isn't this what you wanted?*

... No. I didn't expect to actually fall for her.

"I... I apologize, Pakhan," Valentin catches himself. "It was not my place to—"

"Enough." I raise my hand. "There's no point in fighting between ourselves. The enemy's out there."

"If only the cowards would fucking show themselves already, then we could handle this like men," Valentin barks. "If it were me, I would have left my calling card from the very first attack."

"But they aren't you," I say. Turning to the penthouse windows, I squint across town toward the lake. "And there's only one reason they wouldn't leave a calling card."

"What reason is that?" Ilya asks.

"Because they're cowards," Valentin repeats.

"Smart cowards." I clench my jaw. "Someone is trying to weaken us before they strike. They're trying to weaken *me*. But they won't succeed. I'll stay strong. *We'll* stand strong. Won't we, Valentin?"

"Yes, Pakhan."

"Ilya?"

"Yes, Pakhan."

"Good."

Silence swirls around the room as I try to spot my mansion in the distance. It's an impossible task, but still, I try.

I'm sorry, Natalya. I didn't mean for it to go like this.

Valentin breaks the silence first. "So what do we do now?"

"Bring the rest of the Bratva under my protection. We'll assign additional security to every group under my banner. No more operating independently."

Valentin's shock is palpable.

"No one will agree to that. Independence is everything to them."

"Just ask them if they'd rather be independent or dead. Their safety is my responsibility. I *will* protect them, whether they like it or not."

"And if they resist?" Ilya asks.

"Then tell them it's temporary. As soon as we deal with this threat, I'll lift all security measures and they can go back to business as usual."

Ilya and Valentin both shift their weight from one foot to the other. They aren't convinced. I turn back around to face them. "I'm not giving anyone a choice in this matter."

That's all it takes.

"You're the boss," Valentin finally accepts.

"I'm glad that's clear. You can go."

Ilya leaves, but I stop Valentin before he can go. Still, he won't look at me. Instead, he walks over to the bar and messes with the glasses, but he doesn't pour himself a drink.

"What's your problem?" I demand. "If you have something to say, you better spit it out. Do you have any notes? Suggestions? I'm all ears, brother."

"I don't have any notes," he replies, glancing over his shoulder. "Bringing the Bratva under your protection sounds like the best course."

"Then what's bothering you? Cough it up."

He shrugs and turns around, but he still avoids looking at me. "It's the Italians."

"Which ones?"

"All of them—the Santarellis, the La Platas, and the Cuozzos."

"What do they want now?"

"They keep hammering me for an answer about their marriage proposals."

I stiffen. For a moment, I'm ready to shatter the window with my fist. Instead, I burst out laughing. The fucking fools. Don't they understand what's at stake?

"Those fucking Italians. Have they met the rest of my demands yet?"

"No."

"That's what I thought. So why are they so concerned with marriage proposals?"

"I guess that's just the way they work. They want to know you're going to marry one of their daughters before they talk business."

"Well, that's not the way I work. Tell them we're doing it my way or not at all." Valentin winces and starts to turn away, but I stop him again. "Hey, what's your problem, man? Talk to me."

His jaw flexes and he shakes his head. "It's the fucking Italians man. Their messages are starting to get... well, insulting. I don't know if I can keep myself in check much longer. I want to fucking murder the lot of them."

"Excuse me?"

He pulls out his phone. "Listen. 'Good morning, Consigliere...'"

"At least they got that part right."

"Just listen. 'We are still awaiting your Pakhan's answer regarding our proposal of marriage to Tizziana La Plata....'"

"Not Tizziana again."

I clench my fists and think of Natalya all dressed in white. Then I think of tearing that gown off her body. She'd look good either way.

Fuck, I miss the taste of her. I need to get back to the mansion and clear my mind. With all that's been going on, I've been purposefully trying to keep my distance from her. But that's not going as planned. It's not clearing my mind. It's just driving me mad.

"'We have been waiting over a month for a definite answer on this matter and Tizziana has other suitors who are nearly as prosperous as your Pakhan. If we don't have a response from you by the end of the month, we will have no choice but to rescind our offer and resort to third-party remediation to resolve our differences.'"

"Are they fucking threatening us with lawyers?" I laugh. "Christ. How the mighty have fallen. I'd have more respect for them if they came out gunning for us. But this? Fucking pathetic."

Valentin puts his phone back in his pocket. "This is just the latest one. They're all like this and they keep getting worse with every passing week."

"I don't give a shit if they got their precious little feelings hurt about Tizziana or whatever the hell her name is. They can wait. Everyone can wait."

I'm even making Natalya wait. Hell, I'm making myself wait too.

"You should teach them a lesson for talking to you like this," Valentin suggests, barely containing his anger. "We should take away their use of the ports. That would show them who's boss."

"Not yet. We don't want to sour the alliance before it even starts."

"There is no alliance. You're making sure of that."

"As long as I have them hanging on my line, I have to treat them with a certain amount of grace. I can't just haul off and slap them around every time they mouth off a little."

"Don't you think you should maybe come to a decision instead of playing around with...?" He cuts himself off, but it's too late.

"Easy, brother," I warn him. "That girl means more to me

than just some pet project, okay? I need you to understand that... even if I don't completely understand it myself yet."

"Sounds like you're falling for her," he courageously notes.

"I don't have time to fall for anyone right now."

"You can't afford it either. If the Italians find out about..." He breaks off again.

"You should be happy for me," I only half-joke. "She makes me happy."

Valentin snorts. "That's the problem. Guys like us aren't supposed to be happy."

I raise an eyebrow at him. "I'm not? Since when?"

"Oh, come on, man! You know as well as I do that you're only doing this because you need a challenge. You have it all. You're king of the fucking castle. You're a cat in need of a mouse. Look, like I said, I like the girl, but she isn't from our world. It's not like you could ever marry her, and as long as you keep letting her distract you, there's always going to be an obstacle between you and a marriage that could actually get you where you want to go."

"Maybe I don't want to go down that path anymore..."

"Or maybe you do, and you're just too stubborn to admit that you're in over your head."

Valentin greets my glare as I stare him down. No one on this earth would ever dare speak to me like this... and it's exactly why I keep him around.

"Maybe you're right..." I grunt, turning back around to look out the window. "But I'm not giving her up."

"What if she asks to leave, huh? She's free to go anytime she wants..."

"No. She isn't. And I think everyone involves understands that by now."

"Do you think she does?"

"Yes. But I don't think she wants to leave."

"And if she did?"

"I'd hunt her down again."

"Fuck." I watch Valentin's reflection as he washes a hand down his face. "Why'd you have to put me in charge of this Italian shit? If it were Ilya in my shoes, I'd be right there by your side, defending your relationship with Natalya. But you gave me a job. And I never forget a job."

"I know."

"So what am I supposed to do? Keep fighting you on it? You have to marry someone to keep your grip on power. This alliance is the best way to do that, and if you have an heir with the Italians, your legacy will be incontestable. You need that now more than ever, especially with all this other shit going on. You picked the wrong time to fall in love, brother."

"Who said anything about love?"

"You said you were falling for her."

"*You* said that."

"You didn't deny it."

"I don't have time for these games," I grumble.

"What exactly are you hoping to accomplish with her, anyway?" Valentin goes on. "What's the endgame?"

I fidget in my jacket. "I see potential in her... I want Natalya to be the best she can be."

"The best what? The best mistress? The best arm candy? The best fucktoy?"

I glare at him and grit my teeth. "Watch it."

"What? You're the one who said she was your toy. You say you don't have time for games, but isn't that what you took her for? A game? A challenge?"

If this wasn't Valentin, I'd put a bullet in his skull right now. But it is Valentin. My blood brother.

I look away. I don't want to talk about Natalya, especially when I hear my own words coming out of Valentin's mouth. What the hell *am* I doing with Natalya, anyway?

What will happen to her if I'm forced to marry one of the

Italians to protect my empire? Will I just send Natalya on her merry way with my blessing and a nice fat check? Will I keep her on the side?

I couldn't have predicted that my empire would be threatened so severely the moment I took her in. If everything was running as smoothly as it was when we first met, my end goal would be obvious.

I'd marry Natalya.

But everything has been thrown into chaos. If it weren't for her, I'd be in my element right now, fighting for what's mine.

But she's changed me.

She's mine.

My fingers curl and my heart clenches.

If I don't figure this shit out on my own, then I might have to form an alliance with the Italians. I might have to marry one of their daughters. For the sake of my empire, I wouldn't be able to marry Natalya, even if that's all I wanted to do.

She's been such a good girl—she deserves it. But I have my responsibilities.

Valentin puts his glass down and sits down on the couch. "Look, you do you, okay? I'm just calling it like I see it."

"I know," I grumble. "It's why I keep you around."

"Well, that and because I'm good at killing, right."

"Yes, you're very good at killing."

That seems to make him happy.

"Look. You've been on top for ten years and you're the best this city has ever seen—a thousand times more successful than Comrade Vadim ever was. You did us all a huge favor killing that guy... even if you had to use a bomb to do it... but I will not let you end up like him."

That last line is supposed to be a good-natured insult. In our line of work, it can be frowned upon to kill your predecessor in any way other than direct combat. But Comrade

Vadim was a menace. He had to be put down. So I did what I had to do, no matter how little honor was found in the act.

"Whose idea was it to use the bomb again?" I ask Valentin, calming down a bit. It helps to remember how far we've truly come.

"I'll gladly take credit for that," Valentin nods. "Vadim was a psychopath. You remember what it was like when we worked for him. He killed randomly and not just to enforce his authority. He kept everyone living in constant fear and none of his decisions made any sense. He was a liability to all of us. We have you to thank for all this peace and prosperity."

I only huff. "You call this peace? Four of my Bratva just got wiped out in less than two weeks."

"So someone is challenging you," Valentin shrugs. "It's a miracle no one stepped up before now, and that's thanks to you. You're steady and reliable and everyone knows it. The Italians wouldn't be so anxious to align with us if you weren't. No one else could do that. Only you. You're the king, brother. And no one doubts it."

"*Someone* doubts it," I remind. "Whoever is causing all this trouble sure is acting like the old guard. They're trying to destabilize everything we've worked for."

"Well, it won't work." Valentin gets to his feet. "Listen, I better get out of here. I have work to do and so do you. I'll see you around."

He bumps my arm and leaves me alone, but I can't stop thinking about everything he said.

I haven't thought about Comrade Vadim's reign in a long time.

That freak never told anyone why he did anything. There was no rhyme or reason to his methods. No one was safe.

Sometimes I used to think it was all on purpose. An act to throw his allies and enemies off balance. But even if that was the case, it was a foolish approach. He might have thought he was keeping everyone on their toes, but, really, it only stopped people from doing their jobs. They were too busy watching him. Too busy making sure they avoided his unpredictable wrath and explosive outburst. It sapped the drive and motivation from this city.

Then I came along.

And the city rejoiced.

Valentin wasn't the only one who helped me overthrow Vadim. Practically every single one of the old Pakhan's Bratva were sick and tired of his bullshit by the time I set off that bomb. Then they practically begged to come under my banner. I didn't have to conquer or convince anyone. We were all happy to see Vadim go.

Without him around, we thrived. And we will continue to thrive. I owe that much to the people who helped me get here.

I won't let this unknown challenger shake my empire.

But Valentin was right. There's a matter I've been putting off. The Italians. An arranged marriage. Neither seemed so important before. Now, though, they could be the difference between victory and ruin.

Maybe that's why I've been keeping Natalya at arm's length lately, to avoid making a choice I know I have to make. It should be simple. The best way to secure my power for the future is to get married and have an heir. The best way to increase my odds in this coming storm is to ally with the Italians. The only way to do both is to accept one of their proposals.

So why can't I just do what I know needs to be done?

I know exactly why.

Looking back over the lake, I try to spot my mansion. An impossible task. I have too much work to do in the city. I won't make it back tonight.

But that doesn't mean I can't get what I want. What I *need*. I've always found a way before. Always.

I won't let this time be any different.

Taking out my phone, I send a single message.

Bring her to me.

Andrei's chauffeur steps into the winter garden and smiles at me. "Good afternoon, Miss Datsyuk. I'm here to take you into town."

I blink out of my daydreams. How long have I been staring across the lake?

"Really? Why?"

"Pakhan has sent for you."

I touch my forehead and turn from the window.

"Are you sure?"

"Positive."

"I... I didn't know I was allowed to leave."

"We do as Pakhan says, Miss. And he has requested your presence."

"For what reason?"

My gut twists into a knot as I involuntarily look up at the ceiling. Does Andrei know about the phone?

"He didn't say."

My paranoia grows as I consider the possibility that Andrei sent me that confusing text as a sort of test. Will he be waiting for me to tell him the truth?

... Or was the message really from that monster Nikolai?

I'm not sure which option I dread more.

"Should I change?" I ask, trying not to expose the turmoil bubbling inside of me.

I'm wearing a t-shirt and sweatpants. The chauffeur avoids looking directly at me as he responds. "He didn't say."

"I'll change," I decide. But it's less for Andrei and more for my own sake. I haven't been outside this property in weeks now. I should make an effort.

"I'll wait right here, Miss," the chauffeur nods.

He performs a subtle bow and I race past him, lost in my own thoughts. I beat it upstairs and rifle through my clothes. But I stop when I see the shut lingerie drawer where I've hidden my phone.

I still haven't responded to that mystery text—in fact, I've been trying not to think about it all. The possibilities are too uncomfortable to consider. But now I have no choice.

If this is all a test, then I'll need to come up with an excuse. I'll also need to tilt the odds in my favor. And I've found that there are only two ways to distract Andrei. With good banter and bare skin.

But the thought of dressing like a slut in front of anyone but him makes me shiver with anxiety. He owns more than just my body now. It's my mind he's invaded too.

So, how do I handle this next challenge?

I have no fucking idea.

Somehow, I end up in a simple, casual but classy beige dress and matching pumps. I fix my hair and clean my face, then hustle back downstairs. Whether this is a test or not, the last thing I want to do is keep Andrei waiting.

The chauffeur greets me back in the winter garden and leads me out front to a waiting limo. He opens the door and I slip inside. When I catch my reflection in the polished interior, my hearts start to race.

Despite my best effort, I still look like a mess. God, I wish Andrei would let me have some makeup.

The entire drive into town is spent quietly fretting over what's to come. So much so that I'm already exhausted by the time the limo finally pulls up to a massive skyscraper in the center of Chicago.

I stare up at the slick behemoth while someone approaches the chauffeur. Armed security guards pace up and down the sidewalks and talk into their earpieces. When we start driving again, it's to pull into an underground parking garage.

A dozen of the security guards follow us inside. They stand watch as the limo parks. I take a deep breath and prepare myself. But nothing can prepare me for what comes next.

The chauffeur doesn't come open my door. Instead, the entire limo starts vibrating. When I look out the window, I see the parking garage disappearing below us. Then, suddenly, were above ground, rising through the streets of downtown Chicago.

I grab onto the door handle and hold on for dear life. Logically, I know this is just a car elevator, but the glass walls are so clear that it looks like we're floating through the sky.

The cars and people below shrink into dots. When we finally stop at the top floor, the entire city is so far beneath us that it looks like a toy model. The view is absolutely magnetic and I get lost in it until the sound of the chauffeur clicking the door open makes me flinch.

"This way, Miss."

"Thank you..." I whisper, barely able to tear my gaze off the gorgeous skyline view outside. I'm finally up on one of those top floors...

The chauffeur opens another door for me and I walk into a gigantic penthouse almost as big as the mansion's ground floor. A sunken living room overlooks the lake and most of Chicago.

Couches, chairs, tables, and different sitting areas fill the apartment. An impressive open-plan kitchen covers one side of the large main room. Beyond that, sliding glass doors open onto a sunny rooftop full of trees, raised shrubbery planters, and picnic tables.

Shit. This looks like something out of a magazine.

But what else was I expecting? I should be used to this by now...

"What now?" I ask the chauffeur. "Where's Andrei?"

He taps on his phone. "He's been notified of your arrival. Make yourself comfortable, Miss. I'm sure he'll be here soon."

He goes back out to the garage, and a second later, the car elevator purrs downstairs and out of earshot.

The six security guards that rode up with us don't leave, though. Three of them stay in the elevator area, standing watch by the door. The other three head off into the penthouse, carefully and quietly inspecting every last inch.

I don't bother trying to talk to them. The men at the mansion never even look at me, let alone respond to my questions, so why would these guys be any different?

I sigh and take a cautious step forward. My nerves are still stretched thin, and the fact that I'm back in the city after all that's happened isn't helping. But the view is impossible to ignore. I want to go out onto the balcony and breath the cold, thin air.

An inviting breeze blows in from the rooftop patio, I take another step toward it. I'm just about to take the plunge and walk out there when a massive figure strides around the corner ahead.

Andrei.

"There you are," he says, a warm smile filling his ruggedly handsome face. "How was the drive into town?" He genuinely looks happy to see me, but that only causes more inner turmoil.

If he doesn't know about the phone, then that means the

message could actually be from Nikolai. If that's the case, I would have to tell Andrei about it just for my own safety.

Shit. I really can't win.

"It... it was fine," I stumble.

"You look worried."

Andrei studies me with those captivating green eyes. I try to return his intense gaze, but my paranoia spikes as he approaches.

I just stand there as he takes my face in his big warm hands and kisses me. For a split second, I feel better. Then he goes into the sunken living room and drops on the couch with a groan, and I feel isolated and alone again.

He leans back on the cushions and runs his fingers through his hair.

"You wouldn't believe how crazy it's been these last few days. I'm sorry I didn't make it home, but I've been working non-stop. That's the only reason I asked you to come here. I don't know if I'll be able to leave anytime soon."

I stay rooted in my spot.

"I... it's okay..."

He looks up and narrows his eyes at me. "What are you doing over there?"

"I... I'm standing. What do you mean?'"

"Come over here and sit next to me."

He pats the couch and I follow his casual order without a second thought, but I don't get far before he lifts his hand and stops me.

"What is it?" I ask, trying to gather myself.

"Something's wrong."

"Nothing's wrong."

"You're not happy to see me? It's been days."

"Maybe I'm not happy to see you *because* it's been days."

The confession just slips out of me. But there's no going back now.

For a moment, my words seem to catch Andrei off guard. He stares at me, but those green eyes are somewhere else. Then, just like that, they snap back to reality.

"Everyone out!" he booms.

A second later, the three guards who had been sweeping the penthouse come jogging out. The men in the car elevator leave too. Together, they disappear behind a corner. I hear a door slam shut.

It's just the two of us now.

"I've been busy," Andrei says, standing up.

"And I've been the complete opposite of busy. Do you know how mind-numbing it is to be stuck somewhere with nothing to do but think?"

He dips his head. "Yes. But I've been very clear, you're free to—"

"Enough of that bullshit!" I cry out, all the pent-up frustration and confusion coming out at once. "Let's be real with each other, okay? One way or another, I'm your prisoner."

Suddenly, Andrei is in front of me. His big hands fall on my shoulder and he holds me in place as those emerald green eyes search my soul.

"You're so much more than that."

"No..."

This time, when he kisses me, it's not as a gentle hello. His lips are like crashing waves, pushing me back while his hands pull me forward. I sink below the warmth and strength... then my eyes pop open and I push at his chest.

"Go kiss your other girls," I spit, remembering the poisonous envy I'd felt when first talking to Valentin.

Andrei grabs my wrist and twists me around. He holds my arm behind my back like a cop would a criminal. His hot breath breaks over my neck as he leans in very close.

"What the fuck are you talking about?"

"I know what you've been busy with. Other girls."

"Where the hell did you get that idea?"

Even in the heat of my anger, I don't dare mention Valentin's name. This isn't his fault, he barely said anything. I just took a hint and ran with it.

"What else would a man like you be doing?" I rasp. "When you're home, all we do is fuck. You're insatiable. Then what? When you leave for two days, you just keep it in your pants?"

He presses my wrist into my back and grabs my throat.

"I'm insatiable for *you*," he growls. "And when I can't have you, I masturbate to the thought of being with you again."

"Lies. You could have any girl you want, so why would you ever bother jerking off?"

"I don't want any other girls."

"Why? Because you're too busy jerking off all day?" I choke, unable to help myself. Andrei's grip around my neck tightens. I can feel the bulge growing in his pants. It's big and hot and it creates a pressure in my core that can't be ignored.

"Is that what you think I'm doing all day?"

"What else would you be doing?"

"I don't think you can handle that reality, little deer."

"Try me."

Andrei shoves his pelvis into my ass, then without warning, I'm thrown over his shoulder.

I scream. "What are you—"

He interrupts me with a hard spank to the ass.

"Let's see what you can really handle."

"Let go of—"

Whap! A hot sting erupts from my cheek. My tender skin throbs and I can feel his giant handprint pulsing beneath my dress. I want to kick and scream, but I can't take Andrei spanking me again. It feels too good, and I'm far too pissed off for that.

Andrei pulls out his phone and roars into the speaker. "We're coming downstairs. Don't start without me."

We get into an elevator and I catch another glimpse of myself in the mirror. If I thought I looked rough before, that was nothing. My hair is a tangled mess, my cheeks are bright-red, and my eyes are bloodshot.

"Where are you taking me?" I manage to squeak out before Andrei can spank me again.

"I have a gift for you. A gift I was going to give you anyway. But now I'm also going to show you how the meat is made. Just so you know what I do when I'm not jerking off to the thought of fucking you."

"What does that mean?"

"You'll see soon enough."

The elevator door dings open and I'm carried out into a hallway. We stop in front of a door and Andrei finally puts me down.

"You're beet-red," he says.

"No shit. I'm hot as hell."

"Agreed."

Knocking on the door, he yells a single command before someone opens it for him.

"Eyes to the wall!"

I hear feet shuffling. Andrei steps inside.

I don't follow him in right away, and when he notices that, he grabs a chair and places it against the door, propping it open so I can see inside.

A vast boardroom stretches out before us. On either side of a long, black table, stand half-a-dozen armed men. Everyone has turned their backs to stare at the walls.

... Well, everyone except two men who stand at the opposite end of the table. They stare out of a ceiling-high window.

"Come with me," Andrei grunts, so forcefully that I don't have any other choice. I cautiously follow him as he storms down the table to the men staring out the window. They don't turn around until we're within a few feet of them.

When they do turn, though, I stop dead in my tracks.

The taller of the two, an old man with wispy grey hair and hard, mean eyes, stares at me with a greedy look. But his greedy look isn't the reason I'm so shocked. No. Instead, it's the younger man next to him. A pig-faced bastard who I immediately recognize, but who's name it takes me a minute to remember.

"You..." I breathlessly gasp.

"I believe you've met Mike Spolanski before," Andrei says, looking back at me. "You two had a run-in at my club the night we first met. If I remember correctly, he's the one who asked you out for me... in a way."

I remember how Andrei held a shard of glass to the drunkard's throat and made him apologize. Then how he made Mikey say that I should go upstairs with the mysterious man holding him hostage.

Why the hell did I ever think it was a good idea to listen?

"Hey, look, I've stayed away from your clubs," Mikey protests, staring at me like a man who can't be bothered to remember all the girls he's drunkenly harassed. "There's no need to dig up old trouble."

"What's this about?" The old man speaks.

"Ah, and this is Mike's father, Federick Spolanski. He owns the building across the street from us. The one that's nearly as big as mine."

"When the renovations are done, it will be bigger," the old man smugly notes.

"There will be no renovations," Andrei states. "You picked the wrong time to try and renegotiate with me, Frederick. I know you thought it was clever, attempting to take back some of your property while my empire is under attack. But no matter how weak or vulnerable I become, you will never be on my level."

The old man takes a moment to process what Andrei is

saying. While he does, Mike's gluttonous eyes stay glued on me. I can practically hear him drooling. It makes my skin crawl.

"I see," the old man grumbles. "So, what now? Are you going to try and muscle another building out of me? Even after my son has finally learned to behave himself? Is that why you brought this whore for me? To smooth things over before—"

Andrei doesn't waste a single movement. In response to the old man's insult, he reaches behind his back, pulls out a gun, points it at the man's head, and shoots.

Frederick's head snaps back. I gasp in horror. No one else even flinches—well, no one except for ol' Mikey.

"What... What the fuck did you just do? He was cooperating. He..."

Andrei points the gun at Mikey and the blubbering mess trails off.

"You touched my girl," Andrei says, tossing aside his gun. It hits the table and slides before coming to a stop.

"I... I don't remember."

"I do."

One long step is all it takes for Andrei to grab Mikey by the throat. The drunkard's eyes go wide with fear as he wrestles against Andrei's vice grip. It's a futile struggle.

"Andrei..."

I try to gasp, but nothing comes out. The skin around Mikey's throat tears beneath Andrei's tensed fingers. Something snaps. Mikey gargles. Blood spills. Andrei shoves his foot against Mikey's stomach and kicks.

The dying man smacks against the window, his own blood smearing a crimson silhouette against the clear glass. Andrei doesn't let him go.

"I've had enough of you." With one violent tug, he pulls and Mikey's insides come spilling out. A pale body slumps to the floor, leaving only a bloody angel spread out against the Chicago skyline.

"Towel," Andrei orders.

One of the guards turns from the wall and races to a cabinet. He hands Andrei a towel and a bottle of water then returns to his spot. Andrei uses them to wipe the blood from his hands.

"I'm not holding back anymore," he announces to everyone. "My enemies will receive no mercy. And you..." he finally looks back toward me.

I gulp.

"Me?"

"You are mine. I'm sorry you didn't realize it before. There is no one else, Natalya. I want you. But you were right, when a man like me wants something, he gets it. And he keeps it. You are not free to leave."

My stomach drops.

"I... I..."

"Come here."

Andrei gestures at me with his freshly cleaned hand. Blood still stains his cufflinks. When I don't immediately respond, his motions become slower and more menacing.

I have no choice. I step over the old man's corpse and join Andrei at the bloody window.

"I lied," he says, taking my hand with his.

"... About what?"

"About there being no renovations on the building across the street. The entire place is my gift to you. Do with it what you please. Renovations or no renovations. That's one of the reasons I called you down here today."

I don't understand.

"You're giving me a building?"

"I'm giving you the world. *My* world. I've made up my mind. I'm not just preparing you for the sake of it, Natalya. I'm preparing you to be my wife. To be my queen."

My heart thumps violently against the inside of my chest. A

limb twitches somewhere on the floor. Nothing he says is registering.

"Why are you giving me a building?" I ask, if only because it's the one thing my horrified mind can latch onto.

"So that you'll have one right next to mine. Now come, little deer," he curls his fingers around my palm and presses my hand to his chest. "Let me show you the other reason I brought you here today."

21

ANDREI

We stand side-by-side before the black vault tucked away in the back of my penthouse office.

This is the third one Natalya has seen, and that puts her in rare company. Still, she stares at the skull and viper crest like a little girl lost in a nightmare.

... Or maybe that's because of what I just did back in the boardroom.

Squeezing her hand, I silently apologize for how volatile it all got. My original plan didn't involve killing Frederick and Mike in front of her, but the second that old man called her a whore, I went blind with rage.

Sure, those two were going to die anyway, but in a more discreet manner. The idea was to dispose of them quietly and then present Natalya with her gift. But she wasn't in the type of mood I was expecting, and when things got heated between us, I needed to show her the truth of who I really am.

I only hope that she doesn't shatter against the harsh reality.

"Open your palm for me," I say, as gently as possible.

Natalya doesn't resist. Her fingers unfurl and I lift her shaking hand up.

"It's going to be alright. You're going to be alright," I say, hating to see her like this. I know it's necessary, but it's far from pleasant.

"Sure..."

"Look at me."

This time, she doesn't seem able to follow through with my request, so I carefully pinch her chin and lead her face up to mine. Still, her blue eyes stay downcast.

"Natalya..."

"That... that was so awful."

"It's what I do," I tell her. "I wanted to show you where I was when I'm not around."

"I... I think I'd almost rather you be out there with other women." Her little laugh is so weak and broken I can't help but hug her.

"That's never going to happen," I say. "Sorry to break it to you."

She sinks into my chest.

"I'm not made for your world."

"That's what I'm here for. I'm going to protect you. I'm going to teach you. I'm going to make you—"

"... Your wife?" she finishes for me.

I squeeze her extra tight before finally letting go.

"Here's what else I wanted to show you."

Typing in the code for the vault, I open the door. Inside is a small black box. I pull it out just enough so that Natalya can see the strange lock protecting its contents.

"What is that?" she asks.

"Something very important."

Beside the box, deeper down the shelf, is a dagger. I pull it out and flip the gold lock cover open on the black box. Two small bowl-like indents take up most of the space. A tiny hole fills the center of both.

I prick my ring finger with the blade and let a drop of blood fall into one of the tiny bowls. The crimson liquid trickles down through the hole, leaving a faint trail along the old gold plating.

"Why did you do that?" Natalya asks.

"You'll see. Give me your hand."

She does as I say and I prick her ring finger.

"Ouch!" she winces, trying to pull away. But I hold her steady.

"Now watch."

Placing her bleeding finger over the second bowl, I let a drop of blood fall into the small hole. Then I lift Natalya's hand and suck the wound clean.

"That sound..." she whispers, quivering against the touch of my lips.

We listen as the ancient lock works its magic. A moment later, a clicking sound indicates that the process was successful.

"Pretty cool, huh?" I smile, opening the box.

"How... how did that work?"

I just shrug. "No idea. This thing came from the last Pakhan. He never explained it to anyone—not that I think he knew. But I believe it's some old, ritualistic Bratva technology."

"Ritualistic?"

"Yep," I nod.

"What kind of ritual?"

"This kind."

I slide the covering aside and reveal what I already knew was inside the little black box. A sparkling diamond ring. It sits atop a carved golden band, shining like a raging fire.

Natalya gasps.

"Is that what I think it is?"

"I wasn't bluffing in the board room."

"You want me to marry you?"

"When you're ready."

"Do... do you mean when I'm ready to accept, or when you think I'm ready to accept?"

"A little bit of both."

"... Please don't lie to me."

I rub my thumb against the back of her hand.

"What exactly do you think I'm lying about?"

"That I'd have any choice. That I have any choice right now. You... you said it yourself earlier. I'm not free to leave."

"Do you want to leave?"

Her blue eyes finally meet mine. She searches for an answer she doesn't want to find.

"That's not the point."

"To me it is."

Natalya sighs and her gaze drifts back to the shining diamond ring.

"It's beautiful."

"Fitting for a girl like you."

"Why would you marry me?"

"Because I want to."

"It can't be that simple."

"It is."

Flipping the cover back over the ring, I close the box and push it away. The vault clicks shut.

"Be honest with me," Natalya says, her limp hand finally gaining some life again as she squeezes me back. "Why are you doing this? Why me?"

"You want the honest answer?" I ask. She nods. "The truth is: I don't know. I'm only doing what my heart tells me to do. And the only person it ever talks about is you."

"Your heart?"

"Hard to believe I even have one, huh?" I chuckle. "Well, I do. And it was buried beneath frozen ground for decades. Then

I saw you at the club, and something inside of me knew that you were the only chance my dead heart hard."

Tears well up in Natalya's eyes. I brush the first one from her cheek, but more follow.

"I'm so fucking confused," she rasps. "I don't know what's going on. I don't know what I want."

"I do. I want you. And I know, deep down, you want me too. That's why I'm so tough on you—because I need you to see it. Because if you don't, then what happens to my heart?"

"You can bury it again..."

"No. You shocked it alive. And if I bury it, it will be buried alive. That's too painful."

"Do you actually care for me? I thought this was some game..."

"It was... at least, I thought it was. But I know better now. This is bigger than any game. This is the future. My future. Your future. *Our* future. I missed you, little deer. I don't want to miss you again."

"I missed you too," she sputters, sobs mixing in with laughter as she collapses into my chest.

"So let's see this through. What do you say?"

"I guess I can try."

I wipe more tears from her soft cheeks.

"That's my good girl."

"... What now?"

"Now we go to bed."

This time, her sobbing laugh is more laughter than it is sobbing.

"Is that the other reason you brought me out here today?"

"The third and final."

"I don't know if I can," she sighs. "I'm so... exhausted."

"Then let's sleep in each other's arms."

22

I snap wake up when I hear a door slam open somewhere nearby.

My hand is immediately under my pillow, searching for the gun that's usually tucked beneath the mattress, but before I can find it, I spot the source of the sound.

Natalya stands across the room, legs crossed and hand spread out over her crotch.

"What the hell is going on?" I grumble, wiping the sleep from my eyes.

"Where's the bathroom? I can't find it anywhere..."

I jerk my thumb down the hall. "Last door on the left. There's no ensuite here. You scared the shit out of me."

"Sorry."

She shuffles away and I collapse back on my pillows. For a second, I thought I was going to have to fend off an assassin. After all that's happened in the past week, I wouldn't be surprised if one eventually showed up. But they better not do it while Natalya is around. Because if they do, there will be hell to pay.

The Spolanskis got a taste of that hell last night.

Shit. So did Natalya.

I stare up at the ceiling and remember how scared she got after seeing the real me. For a second there, I thought I might lose her, so I had to do something drastic. Showing her the ring seemed to calm her down a bit. It also appeared to draw her closer to me.

We fell asleep in each other's arms and for a little while I felt at peace.

I sigh. There's no going back now, not after what I told her. She believed what I said. I could feel it by the way she snuggled into my arms. If I went back on my word, it could break her heart... and mine.

I reach over to the bedside table and grab my phone. But I don't use it. Instead, I just stare at the screen. There's a missed call from Valentin. Fuck. He'd be horrified to know I essentially promised to marry someone who isn't an Italian heiress.

I'll get no alliances from my union with Natalya, but that doesn't matter anymore, because she's already given me something so much more than that.

The bedroom door creaks open and Natalya stumbles back in. "I'm sorry, I just couldn't hold it anymore..."

"Why didn't you go earlier?" I ask, patting the mattress beside me.

"Because you were holding me so tightly."

"Shit. You should have woken me up."

"No. It's alright. I... I kind of liked it."

"Does that mean I didn't scare you off last night?"

Natalya crawls onto the bed and I push the covers aside. Her silken form caresses my side.

"I think I'm still processing what happened," she whispers, resting her head on my shoulder. Her finger starts to trace my chest. I hold her tight.

"It was a lot to put on you all at once. But you handled it beautifully. I'm proud of you, little deer."

I take her hand and gently kiss the small cut on the tip of her ring finger. She brushes the back of that hand along my palm, stopping at my wrist. Her warm touch soothes my old rope burns.

"I'm sure you've been through worse," she says.

I shake my head. "Maybe, but I've never been this worried about keeping someone alive... and happy."

"You want me to be happy?"

"I want you to be satisfied. Are you satisfied, angel?"

Natalya thinks about it for a moment.

"No," she answers honestly.

"I'll change that."

I rear off the bed and roll on top of her. She giggles awkwardly and latches onto my wrist. "Wait. What's this?" she asks, her fingers falling onto another scar of mine.

This one runs along the inside of my arm, from my elbow to my wrist. Tattoos crisscross the shallow wound, disguising it to everything but touch. Not many people notice there's even a scar there. Then again, not many people have seen me with my shirt off since I got it... or felt me this thoroughly.

"That's Valentin's scar."

Natalya scrunches her nose. "Valentin's scar? What does that mean? Did you two get into a fight?"

"No. He cut that line into my arm when we became blood brothers. He has the same scar on his arm. One that I gave him. The tats over top are kind of like hieroglyphs. They tell the story of how we were bonded in a mob war. This scar means we share the same blood. It also means that either of us can claim the other's life if we need it."

Her blue eyes widen. "You would let him kill you?"

"If it was necessary. And he would let me kill him right back."

"I... why?"

"Everybody needs someone to fight for, to kill for, to die for," I explain. "For a long time, I didn't have anyone like that. Then Valentin came along and we fought together like real brothers. That's when I knew what it was like to have family, even if it's a ragtag sort."

"You were an orphan too?"

"That's right."

"But you're not alone anymore. You have Valentin ..."

"And you. And you have me. I'll fight for you, Natalya. Kill for you."

"Die for me?"

I don't even need to think about it. In a way, I've already taken that risk, just by telling her about my intentions.

"Our marriage might be the death of me," I say with a vague laugh. "But I'll make sure it's just the start for you."

"What is that supposed to mean?" she says, dropping her hand from my arm.

I don't expand further. Natalya doesn't need to know about the Italians or how badly we might end up needing their help. Valentin can deal with the fallout. I've made up my mind. Our alliance will have to come through a means other than marriage. If that means my ruin, then so be it. I won't go without a fight.

"Look," I say, avoiding all of that. Natalya follows my eyes as I nod down to the tattoos on my chest, arms, stomach, and thighs. "All of my tattoos have their own meanings. I got most of these when I was a foot soldier for the old Pakhan. A Bratva boss marks his men after both their successes and their failures. That way, no one can question their loyalty, their history, or their skills, because each man carries a written record of everything he's done, good and bad. There's no hiding. The rest of these tattoos are from my time as Pakhan. So far, they're all victory marks."

Natalya seems surprisingly intrigued.

"I had no idea your world was so complicated."

"Complicated? No. To me, it's simple—even if those before me liked to dress it all up in ritual and tradition. I'll take the tattoos. They're enough. With these, a man like me can go anywhere in the world and get the respect he deserves. It also means it only takes one look at a stranger to know who he is."

"Wouldn't he have to take all his clothes off first?"

Natalya is half-joking, but I nod. "Yes, exactly."

Her jaw drops. "They'd do that?"

"Yes. As I have. Each man carries his resume with him. You can't hide it."

"So... what does this tattoo mean?" she asks, pointing to a bloody lion on my chest. "Wait, there's another scar behind it."

"Yep. That one is Victor's and this one is Luca's. All four of us became blood brothers when we overthrew the old Pakhan. We would never have succeeded if it weren't for each other."

"You have other blood brothers? Where are they?"

The second the words leave her mouth, Natalya tenses up. I can read her mind, she thinks they're dead.

"Victor went to New York to make his own way and Luca went back to Russia," I assure her. "I haven't heard from Luca since he left. But Victor seems to be doing pretty well. He's a boss under the New York Pakhan."

"I didn't know you could be blood brothers with more than one person."

"It was the only way. We fought together because we had to. The old Pakhan was powerful, and if we didn't win, we'd have all been put to death... or worse."

Natalya gulps. "Worse?"

I shake my head. "Enough of that. You got your fill of ugliness yesterday. Today, you're going to be spoiled." I throw back the covers and sit up. "Come on. We're going out breakfast, or brunch, or lunch... or whatever the fuck time it is."

I don't bother looking at my phone. The time doesn't matter. I just want to reward Natalya for surviving last night. It's given me a new hope.

Still, she stares at me as I head to the closet to pick out some clothes.

"You're taking me outside?"

"Don't act so shocked," I smile back at her. "It's about time I show you off."

"Do I have to?" She stretches out naked on the mattress and extends her arms above her head. "I think I'd rather spend the whole day in bed. I'm still so tired..."

"That's a tempting offer. But I'm not giving you a choice. You're getting spoiled today, angel. Deal with it."

"Okay, fine." She sits up and I admire her while putting on a shirt. Fuck, we haven't had sex in way too long. I'm so horny it hurts. But after last night, I'm going to need to show some self-control. She can't shatter on me.

"Wait. I don't even have any clothes here," Natalya realizes.

"You have that dress from yesterday."

"You want me to wear that thing again?"

I pull on my pants and march over to the bed. "Honey, if it were up to me, you'd never wear clothes again. But then I'd have to keep you locked away, because no man gets to see that body and live. Understand?"

She gulps. The threat is all too real for her now. Good. It's better she knows I'm not fucking around.

"I understand."

"Good. So those are your choices. Get ready and come with me, or stay naked and be locked inside forever."

As if on cue, her belly rumbles.

"I choose the option with food."

"Smart girl."

I yank her out of bed and spank her ass in the direction of

the bathroom. She stumbles down the hall and I finish getting ready. Then I grab her dress and wait outside the door.

She comes out with a towel around her head and that's it.

"Here you are," I nod, handing her the dress. "Put it on before I change my mind."

Natalya hesitates and the bulge in my pants grows.

"I wouldn't want that."

My foot taps impatiently as she dresses. *Tonight,* I tell myself. *You'll have her again tonight. But if she's going to be more than just a project, then you better learn to keep it in your fucking pants.*

"Ready?"

Natalya tugs at her dress and looks up at the ceiling. "My hair is still wet."

"It will dry on the way."

I grab her hand and pull her to the elevator. The towel falls from her head in the living room and her wet hair springs free. She smells so fresh I can't help myself anymore.

"Come here."

I pin her against the wall and steal a long, violent kiss. She sighs as I bite into her lip.

The elevator doors ding open. I just barely manage to push myself off her in time.

"Saved by the bell," she gulps.

"Good to see your wit is still intact."

The limo is already waiting for us. I text the driver the first location that comes to mind. Then I throw Natalya in the back seat and pounce on her again.

"We have five minutes tops."

"Andrei... I..."

"What?"

Those ocean-blue eyes sparkle up at me.

"Nothing."

She grabs my collar and we start kissing. At first, her lips are soft, but the harder I thrust into her, the more desperately she kisses me back. By the time I've unbuckled my belt, she's biting onto my tongue.

I can feel the change in her. She's starting to understand. The fear is falling away. When that's gone, all that remains is the lust and the power. I know it well.

"Hush now, angel," I growl, hiking up her skirt. "This car isn't soundproof. And no one else is allowed to hear you scream."

"What—"

I place my hand over her mouth and shove my cock into her wet pussy. She lurches, and a loud cry crashes into my palm.

"You feel so fucking good, little deer."

Natalya's eye flutter as I pound her on the stretched-out leather seats. The harder I thrust, the louder her muffled cries become. But I hold her down.

"Bite into my palm, angel. Draw blood. Anything to keep you quiet. You can start screaming again tonight."

Her sharp teeth dig into my palm and I let out a deep groan.

"Just like that, little deer. Don't stop."

I feel the limo turn a corner and I know we can't be far. My desperation to finish drives me forward, faster and harder until...

"Open that pretty mouth for me," I roar.

My hand slides off Natalya's lips and I pull my cock out of her pussy. She starts to cry out, but when I shove my dick down her throat, there's no room for anything else.

"Take it all," I pant, exploding into her. "Every last drop."

She does just as I ask, and when there's nothing left in me, I carefully pull out. Her lips drip with saliva and cum. But I place my finger on the bottom of her chin and lead her mouth shut.

"Swallow, angel."

That's exactly what she does. And then only one thought fills my satisfied mind.

Fucking hell.
I think I might be in love.

23

NATALYA

I can still taste his cum on my tongue. But that's not what occupies my mind as we sit on the patio of a beautiful downtown restaurant.

Instead, I keep thinking the same thing over and over again. He's buying it.

But I don't know how much longer I can keep this up.

Wiping the back of my hand across my cheek, I feel the leftover heat from what we did in the car. But it's not as strong as the fear. Fuck. No matter how good the sex is, no man is worth what Andrei put me through last night.

I need to get back to the mansion and get my hands on that phone. I need to make sure I have a way out—if it comes to that. And something tells me it will.

"Full already?" Andrei asks. He sits across from me on the streetside patio. Dozens of armed men stand watch around us, some more discreetly than others.

I remember the way he brutally murdered those two people yesterday. It takes every last ounce of strength in me to keep from shaking.

I look down at my plate. The salmon is only half eaten. It

was delicious, but I'm not in the mood anymore. I keep flashing back and forth between the violence of yesterday and the way Andrei handled me afterward.

He was oddly sweet. Hell, he gifted me a fucking building and then practically proposed. But all that only made the magnitude of my situation that much more damning.

Part of me is falling for this man, but every other instinct in my body is yelling the same thing.

Run!

"Sorry, it's really good. I'm... I think I'm just still tired."

He studies me with those fiery green eyes and I can feel my heart begging to be with him. The conflict makes me want to cry. But I've made up my mind. The rational side of me is too strong.

He killed two men in front of me. I need to get out. And the phone back at the mansion is my only way to do that.

"It's alright. I'll take you back up north this afternoon and let you sleep it off," he says, almost reading my mind. "But don't worry, I won't leave you again. The work I need to do can be done from my office there."

I hide my gulp with a sip of water.

Shit.

"I'm... I'm sorry for how I reacted yesterday," I meekly mutter. "I mean, before all that stuff in the boardroom happened. About how you weren't around enough. I know you're a busy man, but I guess I was just kind of losing my mind from boredom."

"I understand. I'll find a way to fix that. I guess the books in the library aren't exactly up your alley?"

"I haven't read a good book in years," I admit. "All I do these days is study."

These days. It's wild to think that the last time I studied for the biggest test of my life was almost a week and a half ago.

Guilt joins the fear and confusion raging inside of me. At

this point, I don't even know how far away my entrance exam is. I've lost track of time.

"Study?" That peaks Andrei's interest. "For what?"

I'm almost taken aback by the question. It really hits home how little we actually know each other—or, rather, how little Andrei knows me... because I now know plenty about him.

"Architecture school," I say. "I was supposed to take an entrance exam this summer, but I don't think that's going to happen anymore."

"Why not?"

I gesture at the armed guards surrounding us. Acknowledging them makes me even more self-conscious about the scene we're causing. There are other people eating here. How could they not notice?

"My life has kind of gone to shit in the past two weeks," I remind him.

"It's been difficult," he agrees, before cracking a smile. "But now you have your very own downtown property to design. Shit. An architect. I knew you were smart."

"I'm not an architect yet," I say. "And I won't ever be one, even with your gift..." I trail off thinking about the opulence of it all. I still can't believe I supposedly own a building in downtown Chicago now. How does that even work?

"Don't say that. I'll get whatever textbooks you need at the mansion."

"Textbooks aren't enough these days," I explain. My gut twists as I remember what happened to my laptop. Suddenly, flames fill my vision. My skin crawls. I realize Andrei still doesn't know about Nikolai... "Everything I needed was on my computer, but it was lost when my apartment burned down. My application essay. My portfolio. CAD drawings, sketches, and diagrams..."

"You didn't back any of that stuff up online?"

I shake my head. "It costs money to have access to that much storage space, and that was money I didn't have."

"Well, I have plenty of money. I'll get you a new computer and whatever else you need. You have a dream, Natalya. That's a special gift. Most people don't know what they want to do. You do. I admire that."

I stare at him, hardly believing that this guy could be the same person who brutally murdered two people yesterday.

"Why would you help me like that?" I ask, confused. "Just to keep me busy? I heard you yesterday, Andrei. It doesn't sound like you want me to be anything but your wife."

"Then you weren't listening very carefully," he says, leaning forward. "Because I've been saying the same thing since we first met. I want you to reach your fullest potential. I want you to be satisfied. And that's not just in bed."

I raise a brow at him.

"You'd support my dreams?"

"In every way I can."

The conflict inside of me spikes as I sit back in my chair. Why can't Andrei just be the asshole he's supposed to be? Why does he have to have this sweet and caring side? Even if it's rough around the edges, he can still find a way to make me feel so special. So wanted.

I've never felt like I matter this much before.

Why the hell did my first time have to be with a murderous psychopath?

"What kind of buildings do you want to design?" he asks, leaning forward.

I hesitate. "I... well, everyone wants to build skyscrapers and palaces..."

"You don't?"

"No. I do. But I also want to build shelters and orphanages and affordable housing. But not in a stereotypical way..."

"What do you mean?"

"Well... usually, places that are used to shelter the less fortunate are rundown and simply re-purposed to help the only people who can't refuse them anymore. I... I'm sick of that. I want to make something from scratch. Something beautiful for people who are struggling. Something that proves to them that they are worthy of the effort. Something built for *them*. I don't know... it sounds stupid, but..."

"No, it doesn't sound stupid," Andrei nods, more invested than I expected him to be. "It sounds beautiful. I can't wait to see what you come up with."

I shake my head.

"I don't know if I'll be able to focus at the mansion," I say, already coming up with excuses.

"If you found a way to study at that old dingy apartment of yours, then I'm sure you'll find a way at the mansion. I believe in you."

All of a sudden, the hairs on the back of my neck stand up.

But it's not just because I'm flooded with fiery images of what happened to my apartment. It feels like someone's watching me. Someone sinister.

I look over my shoulder. Am I imagining this?

"What's wrong?" Andrei asks. The fear must be written all over my face.

"I... nothing..." I mumble. But the feeling won't leave me alone. I hold myself and try not to shiver.

"Talk to me, Natalya."

My eyes race around the patio, but I don't see anything out of the ordinary. Just other patrons and a whole bunch of Andrei's guards. They aren't looking at me, though. No one seems to be.

"I'm just a little uncomfortable," I try to play it off. "You know, with all the security. I guess it feels like people are staring."

Andrei nods. "I understand."

Lifting his hand, he gestures for a waiter.

"Yes, sir?"

"I'm picking up everyone's tab, please clear out the restaurant."

The waiter is just as shell-shocked by the request as I am.

"Andrei, you don't—"

"It's alright, little deer. I own the place."

The waiter stands up straight and gives Andrei a hard look over. "I'm sorry, sir, but I know the owner and you are not him. Though, if you'd like, I can introduce you later? He's in a meeting, but they're just in the back office..."

"Bring him out to me, tell him Andrei Zherdev requests his presence."

"Sir, as I said, he's currently in a—"

"Tell him my name and I'm sure he'll come out." Andrei interrupts. Then, he reaches into his pocket and pulls out a wad of cash. He doesn't even count the money, he just splits the wad in half and hands it to the shocked waiter. "The other half is for when you bring me the manager."

"I... yes, sir... I... I'll be right back."

The waiter clumsily stuffs the money into his apron then wanders away, almost in a daze.

My jaw must be on the floor, because Andrei just smiles at me. "Violence isn't always the answer. Sometimes, I like to use honey to catch my bees."

It only takes a minute before the waiter returns with a portly bald man. That must be the owner. He already looks nervous.

"I'm sorry, Mr. Zherdev. I... I appreciate your request. But we simply cannot tell everyone to leave. They would never come back. I'm trying to run a business here. Please understand. I don't mean any disrespect."

The man wipes a fountain of sweat from his forehead.

Andrei nods. "I do. I understand. But it's not your business anymore. I've decided to buy it."

"You... you want to buy this restaurant?"

"I *am* buying it. And I think you'll gladly agree to the price. Here, write down your email."

Andrei takes out his phone and hands it to the man. He looks confused and suspicious and absolutely terrified all at once, but he must know who Andrei is, because he reluctantly starts typing on Andrei's phone.

He understands that he has no choice.

"Mr. Zherdev this is—"

"Here's my offer," Andrei stops him, taking the phone when he's done. "It will take the form of a direct deposit to your email. Don't worry about it not going through because it's too big. I have friends at the bank. All of my transfers are accepted."

Andrei types a number down and shows it to the owner.

He nearly collapses. Thankfully, his waiter is there to prop him up.

"It's a very generous—"

"Just tell me what I want to hear," Andrei says, reaching out his hand.

The owner just laughs. "The place is yours."

They shake hands and Andrei stands up. "There, the money is in your account. Now," he points at the other guests on the patio. "Everyone out!"

Immediately, Andrei's guards get to work. But they don't immediately use violence on the guests unwilling to leave their unfinished meals. Instead, they start handing out cash. Wads just as big as the one Andrei gave to the waiter.

"And this is for you," Andrei says, handing the second half of his wad to the stunned waiter. "Finish up here with us then take the rest of the day off."

At first, I watch everyone being herded off in complete astonishment. But as they start to understand what's happening, their eyes creep in our direction, and I start to sink from embarrassment.

Fortunately, it doesn't take long for Andrei's men to clear out the last of them.

Just like that, we're all alone.

"Feeling more comfortable now?" Andrei asks, sitting back down in his seat.

"No," I mumble. "Everyone was staring."

"No one is staring anymore. Now, what were we talking about?" He takes a sip of water and then nods. "Ah yes, your study arrangements, and how much better they'll be than your old place. Oh, that reminds me. Things have been so chaotic recently that I keep forgetting to ask. How the hell did your apartment burn down?"

I'm still stuck in a daze over what just happened. Sure, I knew that Andrei was rich, powerful, and oh-so dangerous, but actually seeing all these parts of him in action is something else.

"I... I'm not sure," I say, trying to gather myself. In my mind, the last thing I should do is bring up Nikolai to Andrei, especially now. I've seen how he gets when someone threatens me.

On the other hand, that monster Nikolai isn't like Mike or his father. He's still out there, and if I'm right, he not only knows about the mansion, but he also knows about my phone too.

"You just showed up and it was gone?" Andrei prods.

"The place was old," I shrug. "Probably faulty wiring."

I don't know what else to say. I'm slowly sinking into a mess of tangled lies and emotions. Andrei turns me upside down and shakes. All my senses are jumbled. I don't know who to trust or what to do.

"Perhaps," Andrei says, pursing his lips. Clearly, he's not convinced. "Are you really full?"

He nods to my plate and I look back down at the half-finished salmon. My appetite is gone, and so is my ability to think rationally.

"Yes. I... I think I'd like to go back to the mansion."

Through all the madness, only one thing seems to stand out clearly to me now. My phone. For some reason, it feels like the answer to a question I haven't thought of yet.

... Or maybe I just need to have it nearby because it's the only thing keeping me from falling completely under Andrei's influence.

He owns me. My body. My mind. My soul. If it wasn't obvious before, it is now. It's also finally clear to me that he really does own everything else in this town too.

That means there's no escape—not unless I'm smart about it. And I'm definitely not feeling smart.

I don't know what I'm going to do next. But one thing is clear, I need the option to choose for myself. Otherwise, I'll lose myself to him completely.

And there's no coming back from that.

24

It's been two days since our lunch on the patio—three since Andrei murdered two people in front of me—and I still haven't found the courage to do what needs to be done.

My phone trembles lightly in my hand. I keep glancing toward the battery. It's just under half gone. *That's enough. I've got plenty of time,* I tell myself. *Well, the phone does. I'm the one who's starting to lose it.*

"Shit." I nearly jump out of my skin when a door slams outside. Footsteps grow in the distance. Andrei is coming. I stuff the phone under the mattress and try to act normal.

My mind races. Everything is a jumbled mess.

I still haven't thought up a response to the mystery text, and I definitely haven't figured out how to use my phone to get myself out of this jam. Calling the police seems useless— Andrei's already said he owns half the force—and I don't want to put Yelena or any of my friends in danger by roping them any further into this.

But it feels like I need to do something. Anything.

You are doing something, I think. *You're studying. You're recreating the files that were lost in the fire. You're recapturing your life.*

It's true. Andrei got me a powerful desktop that I've been using for the past two days. But it's only making me feel worse.

I'm remembering my dreams. My ambitions. All the hard work I've put in. It's making me feel more trapped than ever. It's so depressing that I'm almost ready to take my chances with the mystery texter. Hell, I've been hard at work trying to convince myself that it's not Nikolai. But that's easier said than done.

I look down at my hands. They're still shaking. Andrei's footsteps are getting louder. I race into the bathroom and shut the door.

"Get a hold of yourself, Natalya," I whisper, turning on the sink. Water splashes around the bowl. I take a deep breath.

"Everything alright in there?" Andrei asks, knocking at the bathroom door.

"Yep! Be out in a second!"

I pretend to wash my hands and do my best to smile at him when I walk out. "Can I help you with anything?"

He flops on the couch. "Funny you should ask. I've been having a shit day."

"And you want me to make it better?"

He smiles. "You already have."

My heart twitches. This is what I'm talking about. When Andrei acts like this, it's almost impossible to ignore my feelings for him. Strip away the power, the danger, and the violence, and what remains is a man I can see myself with.

But without all of that baggage, Andrei isn't Andrei. So what am I actually attracted to?

He undoes the top few buttons of his dress shirt, revealing his powerful, tattooed chest.

Oh, yeah. That.

His smile deepens at my obvious reaction. The dimples come out.

That too, I guess.

"If I didn't know any better, I'd say you liked me," he teases, dragging his belt from his waist.

"You're not giving me much of a choice," I blush.

It's the truth. There's no denying I've fallen for this man, and that's the most frustrating part. Do I give into his demands and throw away my life, or do I reject him and try to find a way out of this?

Reject him. Fuck, that's so funny it almost makes me laugh. No one rejects Andrei.

But if I play my cards right, maybe I can escape him.

"If it's any consolation, I like you right back," he grins.

"I'd hope so, with a proposal like the one you gave me."

"Not a proposal, little deer. A promise. You keep on this path, and I'll give you more than just that ring. I'll give you the world."

"I'm happy with the computer."

"And the building?"

Fuck. I still can't believe that.

I nod. "And the building."

"Good. Now make me happy."

"My presence isn't enough?"

He laughs. "It always is, but I think I need something extra special right now."

A deep breath fills my core.

"What did you have in mind?"

He strokes his chin.

"Remember when I made you strip over and over again until you got it right?"

I gulp. "Yes."

"Well, you never got it right, did you?"

"You want me to strip for you again?"

"That would help."

A pang of panic jitters through me.

In the back of my mind, I'm still thinking about what to do

next. Escape. Give in. Text that stranger. Throw away my phone. I don't know.

When Andrei takes me, I can empty those thoughts and enjoy his lust. But to stand here and try to ignore all that's happening inside of me would just be too uncomfortable.

"I... I don't think I'm in the mood."

He stands up.

"Well, I am."

Spurning Andrei's advances rarely works out, but ever since he showed me that ring, I have been getting more confident with him—if only because I now know this isn't just some twisted game. He actually respects me. Why else would he want to make me his wife?

"Andrei, I—"

"Would it make you more comfortable if I started?"

The question catches me off guard.

"You're going to strip too?"

"Someone has to show you how it's done."

Andrei pulls off his shirt and throws it aside. It flutters onto the bed. I have to stop myself from wincing at the thought of what hides beneath the mattress. He can't know about the phone.

"Your turn."

I stare at his mouth-watering body before looking down at my own. All I have on is a long t-shirt and some sweatpants.

"I'm not exactly wearing stripper clothes," I note.

"So go change."

Andrei nods toward the closet and I feel the same little thrill I always get when he tells me to do something I would never have thought of before.

"Fine," I huff, trying to hide my excitement.

Why does he always have such an easy time winning me over?

I go to the closet and pick out the sluttiest dress I can find. An O-ring cut-out tie. Backless. Shit, it's practically a bikini.

Andrei visibly stiffens when I return in my new outfit.

"That's more like it."

"Are you sure?" I ask, looking over my choice. "There isn't much to take off."

"Then I'll take another turn first."

Picking his belt up from the couch, he slings it over his shoulder and thrusts out his hips.

I burst out laughing.

"Oh my god..." I cover my mouth.

Andrei laughs too.

"What? Was that too much to handle for you, angel?"

"I didn't think you could move like that."

"You should know better than that by now."

He grins, his six-pack flexing as he prowls forward in a seductive rhythm. My back unfurls and a tight smile stays painted on my lips.

What the hell is going on? Who is this man?

Fuck. It doesn't matter.

"Work it, baby," I yip.

In response, Andrei lashes his belt around my neck and pulls himself in close. His shirtless body grinds against mine. My next breath is jittery.

"I only listen to tips, baby girl. If you want to tell me what to do, you better make it worth my while."

I gulp. "Yes, sir."

With a deliberate stare, I 'seductively' slip my index finger beneath one of my shoulder straps and slide it down my arm.

"That's right, little deer. Nice and slow."

"Like this?"

"Perfect."

Before I can reach for the other one, Andrei does it for me.

"I thought I was supposed to strip for you?"

"Oops," he smirks. "I've still got my pants on. Strip me."

He holds the belt around my neck with one hand as his other disrobes my shoulder strap. The dress tumbles down my tits. Andrei starts kissing my neck.

My eyes flutter as I look up to the ceiling and clumsily unbutton his pants. When that's done, I immediately set to work on removing his briefs.

He stops me.

"Not with your hands. With your teeth. Like this."

Keeping the belt strapped around the back of my neck, Andrei descends down my body. When he gets to the spot where my dress stopped, he takes it in his teeth and brings it the rest of the way down with him.

"Your turn," he says.

I kick the dress aside. He stands back up, towering over top of me.

My leash tightens as I drop to his stretched briefs. The bulge is so big I hit my chin on it. It twitches. Andrei groans.

I take his band in my mouth and pull at it with my teeth. As a thank you for freeing it, Andrei's cock slaps me in the face.

"Ouch," I fake cry.

"Make it pay for that."

The second his briefs hit the floor he pulls me back up with his belt. When I reach his cock, the belt drops and his hand spreads out across the back of my skull.

I open up just in time to fit him down my throat.

"You're fucking perfect," Andrei groans. "Even better than you were the first time. I knew you would come this far, little deer. I fucking knew it."

I take his praise with joy as he uses my face for his pleasure. He swells in my mouth and I reach down to touch myself. But before I can get there, he pulls me off his cock.

"No. I'm the only one who's allowed to touch you down there."

He yanks me back onto my feet and tosses me onto the bed. I hardly even think about the phone hiding beneath the mattress. I'm having too much fun.

"Holy shit," I cry.

Andrei is on me like a ravenous beast. His thick tongue swirls around my swollen clit, sucking the life out of me by force. I grab onto his hair and thrust into his face.

It doesn't take long for me to shatter. The first orgasm has me breaking like glass, but the moment I start convulsing, Andrei removes his tongue from my pussy and replaces it with his cock.

I don't know how long he fucks me for and I don't care. It's just the right amount of time. I cum twice more. Then he cums once. After that, he holds me tight until he's hard again. Then we start round two, rinse and repeat until I'm so exhausted I could pass out.

"Let's sleep here tonight," Andrei pants, finally collapsing beside me.

I look toward the window. The sun was still out when we started. It's dark now.

"You don't want to go to your room?" I ask, rolling over to face the ceiling.

I don't want to let him see the concerned look on my face. Usually, we sleep in his bed. That's the only reason I felt comfortable hiding the phone beneath this mattress.

"Not tonight."

Andrei takes my hand and places it on his chest. His heart is still pounding like crazy, but slowly, it eases back into a steady pace. I beg for him not to feel my pulse. It's absolutely racing.

What if I get a message and the phone buzzes? Will I be able to hear it? Will he?

What then?

My first thought is how it will ruin the fun we had tonight;

how it will pierce this light bubble that's appeared around us. My second thought is how crazy that first thought is.

My real concern shouldn't be that my secret might ruin this fun little night we've had, it should be that it might turn this satisfied and happy Andrei into the murderous and vile Andrei. But somehow, that worry doesn't stick—not completely. Something inside of me is certain he wouldn't hurt me, not unless it would cause me pleasure.

Still, I can't calm myself down.

I've deceived him, and the evidence of that is lying half a foot beneath our panting bodies. But all I can do is lie there, staring at the ceiling until Andrei's breaths deepen to a sleepy cadence. Only then do I dare look over at him. His eyes are shut. His thick lips are slightly open.

He's asleep.

Now is my only chance.

As carefully as possible, I slip my hand from his chest and crawl out of bed. That's the easy part. The hard part comes as I crouch down and slide my arm beneath the mattress, blindly feeling for the phone as I keep my eyes peeled on the sleeping giant.

Somehow, I manage to find it without much of a fuss. But no matter how badly I want to, I can't just run. Instead, I carefully tiptoe to the bathroom and click the door shut behind me.

I sigh in relief. But my job isn't done yet, not until I find the perfect hiding place beneath the sink, right behind a dozen rolls of toilet paper. Hopefully, they will help muffle any sound. I'm about to stuff the phone away when the screen turns on. No message appears, but the light makes me pause. I pull it back to my chest.

What am I doing?

Glancing toward the door, I half expect Andrei to come barging in. Part of me hopes he does. After tonight, I don't want to keep secrets from him. And not just because it's too stressful.

Tonight was the first time he actually felt like my boyfriend. The first time we felt like a couple. Like we had something special.

We made each other laugh and cum. We fell asleep side by side, satisfied.

I could get used to that.

I look down at my phone screen and sigh again.

Part of me wants to text Yelena, just like she sometimes texts me about boys. But Andrei is no boy. He's all man. And getting Yelena involved in this mess doesn't seem like a good idea.

Still, I want to vent to her. I want to tell her what's happening and how I feel, even if it's just to try and make sense of it for myself. From the moment I came here, all of my thoughts have been bottled up inside. Now, they want to spill out, especially as I realize what I'd actually say to Yelena.

I don't want to leave.

Whatever I have with Andrei, it's the first time I've felt cared for. Respected. Prized.

We actually had fun today. He was oddly vulnerable. I doubt anyone else has ever seen him act so goofy before. And I'm positive no one's ever seen him do a strip dance.

He may be a monster. But he's my monster.

My heart thumps.

I scroll to my texts, but before I can reach Yelena's thread, I see that ominous message.

Unknown.

Fuck you, I think. *Try to come after me, see where that gets you with Andrei.*

I press on the contact and finally know what to say.

Leave me alone!

I click send.

Adrenaline bursts through my veins and I shove the phone under the sink, but before I can drop it behind the toilet paper, it buzzes loudly in my hand. Far too loudly.

"Shit," I mumble, yanking it back to my chest.

I stare down at the screen and my stomach drops.

I've already gotten a reply to my text.

This is not who you think it is.

I stare at the message for what seems like an eternity before coming to my senses.

How would you know who I think you are? I reply.

I just do. Trust me.

Why the hell should I trust you?

The next text takes a second to come through, but when it does, my entire world comes crashing down.

Because I'm your father.

25

ANDREI

I lie awake thinking things over, but I make sure to keep my eyes closed so Natalya thinks I'm still asleep when she returns to bed.

I knew something was up the second she reached under the mattress. But I wasn't sure what she was hiding until just a few minutes ago.

A phone.

I heard the unmistakable buzz of an incoming text as I stood outside the bathroom door and quietly listened.

Part of me is proud of her for being so brave and stealthy—there was no way she was going to sneak out of bed without waking me up—but to have somehow smuggled a phone up here?

Impressive.

Still, that pride is accompanied by a simmering rage. The night we shared was so whimsical it almost felt like it belonged to someone else. I'd never felt so comfortable around someone before.

I should have been expecting the other foot to drop. Natalya waited until I fell asleep and then she betrayed me.

But for what?

For who?

I simmer in silence as she falls asleep next to me. Hours pass and all I do is stare up at the ceiling. I want to shake her awake and demand answers, but I don't. No matter what she's done, she's still earned enough of my respect not to be treated like that.

But that doesn't mean she's getting off scot-free.

I wait until the sun rises and Natalya wakes up. I even let her take a shower. Then, when she's sitting on the edge of the bed getting dressed, I pull the trigger.

"You look tired," I start. "Didn't sleep well last night?"

"First off, rude," Natalya jokes. Her laughter wraps around my heart and squeezes. "Second off, yeah, I didn't sleep well."

She subtly glances toward the bathroom door.

"Why not?"

Those ocean-blue eyes look over at me like they're trying to figure out what I already know. It's disappointing that she would try to trick me. Still, I can't help but play along.

"It's... nothing. Sometimes... at night... I have terrors about the fire. I couldn't sleep much. I know I'm safe here, but I can't..." she trails off. The lightness in her face fades. Something clicks. "Can... can I tell you something?"

I try to disguise my relief as I prepare to hear her confess. *That's a good girl. Come clean to me, then I can forgive you... after a little punishment.*

"Of course."

Natalya looks down at the floor.

"It wasn't faulty wiring that caused the fire. It was a guy. A guy who broke into my apartment. He was waiting for me when I got home from the club. When I didn't leave with him, he lit a match and burned the place down."

My relief evaporates.

"Why didn't you tell me this before?" I growl, fists clenching.

I'm not sure who I'm angrier at, Natalya or the guy she's talking about.

No. The answer is obvious. The fucker almost killed my girl. He's going to pay.

But so is my girl.

Natalya winces at my reaction. "I was scared to... especially after I saw what you did to Mike and—"

"Who was it?" I interrupt.

"I don't know. Some scumbag. He could have just been mentally ill. He kept raving about how he owned me. But I'd never seen him before in my life."

How the fuck did I not get this out of her before? What the hell is wrong with me?

My fury turns inward. I can't stop scowling. This is my fault. She hasn't trusted me enough to tell me about this until now.

... Or maybe it's just a distraction from the phone.

Well, if it is, it's worked, because I don't give a shit about that fucking phone right now.

"Did you get a name?"

She hesitates. "I... I think he said his name was Nikolai."

"He's a dead man."

I turn around and pull my phone out, but before I can make the call, I feel Natalya's hand on my back.

"Andrei!" she softly cries.

I turn back around. Her blue eyes are open wide, her bottom lip is shivering.

"What?"

"Kill him."

I'm shocked. So shocked that her words don't quite click right away. But when they do, a swell of pride returns to my hollow chest.

I lean down and clamp her face between my palms. Then I smash my lips into hers.

She kisses me back just as hard. But the second her hand brushes across my face, I pull away.

"That's exactly what I'm going to do," I tell her, still seething. "But first, you've got some more questions to answer."

I grab my phone. Natalya stares up at me as I make a call.

"I'll tell you everything..."

I shake my head. "I won't be asking the questions."

"Then who will?"

I pinch her chin and listen as my phone rings.

"Someone you can't lie to."

26

Andrei barely talks to me until we hear the roar of the approaching helicopter. Then, he takes my hand and leads me down to the kitchen.

We aren't there long before a man carrying a laptop bag walks in.

"Natalya, this is Ilya Rykov. Ilya, this is Natalya. You two are going to figure out who this Nikolai fucker is."

"Nice to meet you," Ilya nods.

I'm immediately struck by his Russian accent.

"I, uh... nice to meet you too."

I look over at Andrei but he's hardly paying attention anymore, something on his phone causes him to sneer.

"Did you hear about this?" he barks over to Ilya.

"Yes, Pakhan. I can deal with—"

"No. You stay here and question her. I'll be back."

"You're leaving?" I ask, shocked.

Andrei takes my hand and looks me in the eyes. "Don't try any funny stuff with Ilya. He can't be deceived, it's why he's the best. He's also the best at figuring impossible shit out. So answer his questions honestly and help us track down this fucker who's giving you nightmares. I'm the only man allowed in your dreams, little deer."

He kisses me on the forehead and turns away.

"Wait!"

He stops at the door.

"What is it?"

My heart is still racing from what happened this morning... and what I learned last night.

"I... I'm sorry."

He knows about the phone, I can just tell.

"Don't be sorry, be good."

Andrei glares over at Ilya. "Take it easy on her... but make sure you get everything you need."

"Yes, Pakhan."

"See you both soon."

Before he leaves, Andrei gives me one last long look, like he wants to say something, but can't bring himself to.

So, instead, he just nods. The door swings shut behind him.

Suddenly, it's just Ilya and me. I turn around, a jumbled mess of nerves.

Still, I have enough sense to be shocked that Andrei would leave me alone with another man, especially one as clearly handsome as Ilya.

But I guess he trusts us both... even if he shouldn't trust me.

I'm feeling strangely guilty over keeping this from him. The phone too. A pit opens up in my stomach.

The phone. Fucking hell.

I still can't believe that he knows about the phone. I mean, he must, right? That's what he was about to bring up before I tried to save myself by telling him about Nikolai.

I want to bury my face in my hands. But it's not just the fact that Andrei must know about the phone. It's about what I know because of that phone.

I'm your father.

The message blares through my mind like a train horn.

How is that possible?

I try to swallow my fear and confusion, but my throat is too dry, so I go to pour myself a glass of water. Ilya sets up his laptop, paying little attention to me as I chug it all down. But even that is harder than it should be. My hands are still shaking.

I don't believe you.

That's what I'd finally managed to text back.

I can prove it.

How?

That's when I'd heard the noise at the door... or thought I had. Was Andrei listening? Somehow, I know he was.

If that's the case, what is he going to do about it?

What am *I* going to do about it?

In the distance, I hear the private helicopter taking off. Andrei must be going into the city. He won't be there forever. My little attempt at distraction isn't going to last long.

Sure, I bought some time by finally telling Andrei about Nikolai, but as soon as that dust settles, he'll remember my phone.

He looked so betrayed when he brought it up. It makes my heart hurt.

"I'm all ready," Ilya says. "How about you?"

I gulp down another sip of water and nod. "I'm ready too."

He lets me take a seat at the island before he starts.

"The man who burned down your apartment, did he give you a last name?"

"No. He just called himself Nikolai."

"A very common name," Ilya remarks. "There are millions of Nikolais in the world."

"I'm just telling you what I know."

"What did he look like?"

"He was big—tall and broad."

"Like Pakhan?"

"Bigger. He was noticeably taller and much bulkier."

Ilya frowns. "Interesting."

"Why is it interesting?"

"I was being sarcastic." The dry humor coming out of a Russian accent takes me by surprise. I didn't expect this. "I need more."

I shake my head. "Sorry. He had a very heavily scarred face, crooked teeth... he looked like he just crawled out of the sewer. His hair was even wet... I think."

"Must have been a big sewer."

I throw up my hands. "I don't know what else I can tell you."

"Anything that will help me identify him—tattoos, scars...."

"I just told you his face was covered in scars."

"Any tattoos? Nikolai is a Russian name and the Russian Bratva uses tattoos to mark and identify its members."

"I didn't see any tattoos. He was fully clothed."

"His hands? His neck? His face? Any tattoos there?"

I strain to picture the monster, but I've been trying to block him out for so long that it's harder than I thought.

"I can't remember... wait... one of the scars on his face... I remember it almost looking like it could be a tattoo."

"Now *that* is interesting," Ilya notes, typing something into his laptop. "Did he mention anyone else?"

"No. I don't think so."

"Did he say what he wanted from you?"

"Not really... at least, I don't think so. Just something about him owning me. I can't remember the exact words."

"Owning you how?"

"It sounded like he'd paid for me or something. I don't know. That doesn't make any sense, though, does it?"

"Not yet it doesn't."

"Is it helpful at least?"

"It could be. I'll let you know."

We sit in silence for a bit as Ilya leans into his laptop and starts typing away. At one point, I cough and he looks up, almost surprised that I'm still here.

"We're done, thank you," he says.

"That's it?"

"That's it. I will let you know if I need any more information. Don't go far."

That draws an uncomfortable laugh from me.

"As if I have anywhere to go."

Ilya doesn't pretend to be amused. He's already lost in his work again as I awkwardly leave the kitchen.

That wasn't so bad. From how Andrei talked about Ilya before he arrived, I was half-expecting some type of monstrous bad-cop interrogation. This was nothing like that. Ilya wasn't so bad, even if he was surprisingly sarcastic.

Still, my nerves are a mess as I head back to my room. I know what I have to do. Andrei is gone. Ilya is distracted. Valentin is nowhere to be found.

If I'm ever going to figure out who the hell has really been texting me, now might be my last chance to do it.

Locking myself in the bathroom, I shimmy the phone out of its hiding spot. A text is already waiting for me.

When it's safe, go into the master bedroom. Near the back of the walk-in closet, there should be a vault. The password is your birthday. Month/Day/Year. Open it. Look inside. It will prove to you that I am who I say I am.

My pounding heart clenches. He's talking about the vault where Andrei keeps that rope. What else is in there? Why the hell is the password my birthday? How does this guy know about it?

My head starts to swim. But I only care about getting the answer to one question. One that might calm the dread growing deep inside me.

What will I find in there?

I hold my breath and wait for a response. It doesn't take long.

Me.

The dread explodes.

What does that mean? I start to type, but my fingers go limp as a million thoughts and questions swirl through my mind.

What the hell is going on?

Turning around, I splash some water on my face. It doesn't help. The world sways in dizzying confusion. I look down at my phone and see my unfinished message still waiting in the text box.

I hit send.

Go, my sweet girl, while you still have the chance. Trust me, please. I need you to trust that I know what I'm doing.

I pinch the bridge of my nose and try to focus.

Until now, I thought my father was dead. Hell, I hoped he was dead. That at least would have been a good excuse for abandoning me.

Now, though, I don't know what to think.

So, I latch onto the one thing raging inside of me that isn't fear, dread, or confusion.

Curiosity.

"What the hell am I doing..." I mumble, stuffing the phone under my waistband.

Unlocking the bathroom door, I grab onto the walls for support and carefully make my way in the direction of Andrei's bedroom. I know the location well enough by now, and I'm sure the path will be clear of prying eyes. It always is.

Still, I hardly breathe until I'm standing in front of the closet. Only then does a shallow breath tremble from my lips.

Andrei's crest glares at me from the darkness. The skull's mouth opens wide in a scream that will never be heard. The black viper curls through its sockets. I step toward it.

"Month, day, year..." I whisper to myself, typing my date of birth into the security pad.

A green light flashes on the screen. The lock clicks open. My emotions start to swell. Could it really be true?

I stare down at my phone and gulp.

Papa?

Yes. Do as I say, my darling daughter. There should be a flat wooden box. Look in there.

The vault door creaks open.

In the middle shelf is a black box I recognize all too well. I know Andrei's rope is in there. Below that sits a row of artisan glass bottles, almost like small decanters. I stand on my tiptoes and glance at the top shelf.

Sure enough, a dark wooden box is tucked against the corner. I take it.

It's light and unassuming, and it pops open easily enough. Inside is a folded, pockmarked piece of paper, white enough that I can see that there's an image printed on the inside.

I take a deep, shaky breath and unfold it.

"No..."

The box falls from my hand. But the image stays gripped between my fingers.

The paper has been gouged, slashed, ripped, burned, and punctured. Black and dark red stains litter the page. Hate seethes off every crumpled inch.

I can't look away.

I'm forced to stare at the torn and tortured photograph of a man I only barely recognize, but who is absolutely unmistakable.

My father.

What the hell is he doing here?

27

NATALYA

I slam the bathroom door shut behind me and sink to the floor.

Tears fill my eyes. My chest feels like a hollow cavern. Not even my racing heart registers as I press my hands into my face and sob.

That was the first picture I've seen of my father in over a decade, and it was so mangled that I felt every ounce of pain that I've been bottling up since he left. It became so overwhelming that I had to fold it back up and lock it away again.

I made sure the vault was properly shut, then I raced back to my room.

"What the hell is going on?" I cry, whimpering into my hand as the last tears empty from my sockets.

I look up at the ceiling and sigh. My eyes burn. I feel empty.

Then my phone buzzes against the bathroom tiles and my attention is snapped toward it. An odd sense of relief washes over me when I see that it's not a new message. But that relief doesn't last long.

"Shit."

Picking up the phone, I inspect the battery icon on the

screen. It's in the red. I'm not going to be able to use it much longer.

Kicking myself, I remember how I forgot to turn it off last night after I was spooked by the sound at the door. So much for being careful. Everything is falling apart and I'm still completely lost.

My phone's almost dead, I text the man who's supposedly my father. *I'm not sure how much longer—*

Before I can finish writing that second text, I'm interrupted by a response to the first.

Are you alone?

Yes.

Can you go outside?

I think so.

Gathering myself, I stand up and wobble into the bedroom and head for the balcony.

There's a shed on the southwest edge of the property. If you can't wait until dark, go there now. It's behind the marble busts and around the other side of the hedges. I have something there for you.

I blink down at the instructions. Every inch of me screams to stay put. None of this sounds right. But this man was right about what I'd find in Andrei's vault. What else will he be right about?

Ok.

Stuffing my phone away, I turn on my shaky heels and make my way downstairs, through the back doors, and out onto the long lawn. I try to act as casually as possible. Out of the corner of my eyes, I can see patrolling guards. But I've wandered the grounds before. I'm allowed to be out here. I just need to act like I belong.

To my surprise, no one stops me—not that they ever have before. I guess I'm just expecting something to go wrong. Things always do.

That heavy dread stays with me as I find the marble busts and slip around the tall, manicured hedges.

Just like he promised, there's a ramshackle shed hiding beneath some overgrown shrubbery. I take one last look over my shoulder before pushing inside.

It stinks of dust and mold. There are spiderwebs in every corner. The floorboards creak beneath my weight.

I ignore that all for my phone.

I made it.

The phone instantly starts ringing with a call.

It's from the unknown number.

My dread grows. My vision tunnels into the little screen. My heart pounds.

But I know I have to answer it.

"... Hello?"

"It's so nice to hear your voice again, Natalya."

The voice on the other end is huskier than I remember, but even after all these years, it's somehow unmistakable.

"Papa," I croak, new tears welling.

"Don't cry, darling. There will be time for a teary reunion later, but now is not that time. Can you hold it together for me? For your papa?"

My entire body shakes as I swallow biles of grief.

"Where have you been?" I ask, surprised at the sudden anger shaking my voice. I've thought about this moment for years—or something like it. Even when I thought he was dead, I'd always imagined how I'd spit in his face. But now, all I want is my papa.

Still, the anger doesn't go away. It just joins the sadness and desperation.

He's been alive this entire time... and he's kept away while I've suffered.

"I've been trying to reclaim the life that was taken from me," he explains, a familiar fury undercutting his voice. "I've been trying to reclaim you."

"Then come for me," I blurt out. "I'll go with you."

The abandoned little girl inside of me screams out for her papa. Everything else fades into the background, even Andrei... until...

"I can't," Papa says. "Not yet. The man who's holding you is too powerful."

"Andrei..."

I hear my father spit. "Curse that name. Andrei Zherdev. He thinks he's invincible... but every king must meet his ruin. I have a plan, my dear sweet daughter. A plan that will destroy him and save you."

I blink in confusion.

"A plan?"

My gut starts to churn. Something feels off, but I can't put my finger on it.

"That's right. I've hired a guardian angel to protect you. And he will do whatever it takes to pry you from that devil's cold, dead hands."

I shiver at the hate in my father's voice, it reminds me of the hate I felt on that mangled photograph of him in Andrei's vault.

"That picture in the vault..." I start.

Papa cuts me off. "Not now. I'll explain everything when you're safe. But you are not safe there. I will help you escape. You need to escape."

"Why?"

"Why?!" my father explodes. "Andrei Zherdev is a ruthless murderer, my dear, that's why. I would never let you associate with a monster like that. I will remove you from his influence as soon as possible. Make no mistake about that."

"How do you know who he is?" I ask, more shocked than I am surprised.

"Now is not the time, Natalya. How much battery do you have left on your phone?"

With increasing suspicion, I take a look. "Less than five percent."

"That's fine. When we hang up, smash that phone. Destroy it. Hide the pieces. Do not let Andrei Zherdev know that we spoke. He will make us both pay."

"How will I contact you if my phone is gone?"

"Look behind you. There should be a workbench. Open the seat and tell me what's inside."

I can still hardly believe who I'm talking to, but it doesn't matter. I do as I'm told.

Dust fills the room as I push aside the slab. Inside is the last thing I'm expecting to see.

"A cell phone?"

"There should be a charger in there too. Take them both. I know the number. Destroy your old phone. Hide this new one. I will get you out of there, Natalya."

"How... how did you do that?" I whisper, picking up the shiny new phone.

"It's best you don't know. That way, your captor will never know either. Just do as I say, and I promise everything will work out. Do you trust me?"

Yes. No. I don't know. My mouth opens but nothing comes out.

This man abandoned me. He left me to fend for myself when I was only a child. Now, he's crawled back into my life, and for what? To save me? From what?

He doesn't know what I've been through. He doesn't know what Andrei is really like.

I do. It took a while, but I when I look at Andrei Zherdev, I see the man behind the emerald eyes.

I see someone who sees me.

My father hasn't seen me since I was a child. And that must have been by choice... right?

Part of me wants to believe it wasn't. But I don't push the matter. Especially not when I hear a dread-inducing sound.

"I've got to go," I scramble.

Somewhere in the distance, I hear the roar of an approaching helicopter. Andrei is returning.

"Take the new phone. Destroy the old one. Be safe and don't worry, dear. The nightmare is almost over."

No, it's not, I think.

"I'll be in touch," I mutter coldly.

He hangs up and I look around the dusty shed. Taking a hammer down from the wall, I place my old phone on the workbench and smash it to pieces.

I shove those pieces into my pocket. A gift for Andrei. Something to prove my loyalty. Because even if I'm not currently sure where that loyalty lies, I need him to believe it's with him.

Wrapping the charging chord around the new phone, I place it back beneath the work bench. Andrei can't find this. For as upset as I am about my father, I do believe that he can get me out of here.

Now, it's up to me to decide whether or not I'll take him up on that offer.

Until then, I can't let Andrei find out about this new phone. If things go wrong, it will be my one escape route. At the very least, I need that.

Taking a deep breath, I try to steady myself before pushing out of the shed. At a brisk pace, I walk back around the hedges, past the marble busts, and across the lawn. I'm back in my bedroom just in time to see the helicopter land from the balcony.

But Andrei doesn't come out. In fact, it doesn't look like he's even in it.

Instead, I watch as Ilya strides across the landing pad,

laptop in hand. He gets in the back and it takes off again.

The roar disappears in the distance.

My heart drops.

I'm already alone again.

And now there's nothing to distract me from my awful decision.

28

ANDREI

Valentin and I sit in silence as we wait for the third member of our party to arrive.

"Fuck," I grumble, wiping a hand down my face.

I can't stop thinking about Natalya and what she was hiding from me.

The phone thing is impressive and almost understandable —I'm sure she was just trying to stay in contact with her friends —but not telling me about the guy who burned down her apartment?

I clench my fists until the knuckles turn white.

"Anything wrong?" Valentin asks. He's standing behind me, admiring the skull and viper crest that centers the bookshelf.

"Everything."

"Good to know we're still on the same page," he chuckles. I watch as he starts to pace, but he keeps coming back to the crest. "You've never told me what's behind this one before," he notes.

"It's personal."

"More personal than the one at the mansion?"

"I don't know what you're talking about."

"I'll never forget all that cologne," he jokes.

I don't smile back. All I can think about is how I used those ropes on Natalya. That already feels like a simpler time.

"If you help figure out who keeps attacking us, then I'll give you the keys to that vault," I snort. "You can keep what's inside too. I think you'd like it."

"We have ourselves a deal."

Just then, the office door opens up and Ilya walks in.

I can't help but wonder how far he got with Natalya. But right now, there are more pressing matters at hand. I already know he spent the entire helicopter ride going over the corrupted footage Valentin sent him.

"Did you get it working?" I ask.

Ilya sits down across from my desk and takes out his laptop. "Yes. We finally have the security camera footage from the jewelry store," he says. "It took the whole ride, but I managed to recover it all."

"And?"

Ilya opens his laptop and turns it around. Valentin and I approach, squinting down at the screen. Ilya clicks on something and the video starts.

"Fucking hell," Valentin barks, angered by the footage. "This is the third business they've hit this week. Then they had the fucking gall to assassinate the jewelry store manager outside his home too. The bastards are bleeding this conflict into civilian life. It will be the end of us all."

"Not if I can help it," I growl, leaning in closer. "Ilya, have you already watched the video?"

He nods.

"So what am I looking for?"

"You won't be able to miss it."

I watch carefully as the grainy security video rolls through the attack. Then, Ilya pauses it, just in time to freeze on a huge figure blasting the jewelry store from up close.

My rage spikes.

"Son of a bitch!" Valentin hisses. "That's Nikolai Fist."

Ilya raises his eyebrows. "You know this man?"

"We both do," I reply. "He's the most notorious assassin on the continent. But I haven't heard of him doing a job for years. The man doesn't come cheap. Most can't afford him."

"He also doesn't do single, isolated hits like this," Valentin points out. "Our mysterious challengers must have hired him to carry out these attacks against us. It explains why they've been so brutal. Nikolai doesn't know how to work any other way."

Ilya suddenly jerks the laptop back around to face him.

"Hey, what the fuck are you doing?" Valentin shouts.

"Nikolai Fist... No, they couldn't be connected... Yes, they have to be."

He starts typing furiously. Valentin and I share glance.

"Talk to me," I demand.

"This is Nikolai Fist, yes?" he asks, turning the laptop back around.

An old mugshot fills the screen.

"Yes," I sneer.

"Then it's the same man who burned down Natalya's apartment."

My rage erupts.

"What?"

Ilya chews on his tongue. "Natalya told me that the man who burned down her apartment was named Nikolai. She said he was big—bigger than you even—and that his face was heavily scarred like this man's. Look, he even has a tattoo of a black scar across his cheek, just like she said. It must be him."

I see red. But Valentin just frowns at the screen. "He looks different in the video than he does in the mugshot. A lot rougher around the edges."

"This mugshot was taken over a decade ago, it could just be aging."

Valentin shakes his head. "No. It's something else. On the video, it looks like he just crawled out of the gutter. A man like that usually takes pride in his personal appearance, even if it's just to strike fear into his enemy. This is not the same man who was so feared all those years ago."

"You're right," I say leaning in closer. "This isn't that same invincible assassin we knew. This man is vulnerable, and he's trying to make us just as weak as he's become. I won't allow it."

"He's just a symptom," Ilya reminds me. "Whoever hired him is the real problem."

No, the real problem is that he tried to take my girl, I want to shout, but I restrain myself.

Why the hell did Nikolai Fist go after Natalya? And the night I first met her too? Was he watching? Could he tell I was obsessed? Did he want a hostage?

Or is this all just one big coincidence?

These questions race through my mind like speeding bullets. I slam my fist against the wall.

"This has to have something to do with the Italians," Valentin growls. "They must be trying to strong-arm you into sealing this alliance. That's the only explanation."

"It is not the only explanation," Ilya stops him. "In fact, it is no explanation at all. Hitting our businesses and killing our people is no way to seal an alliance. Not even the Italians could be so stupid. They would not want to weaken Pakhan when they are hoping to come under his protection. Use your head, my friend."

Valentin huffs and rubs his chin. "Okay. You might be right about that."

"I am right." Ilya turns to me. "Well, Pakhan? How should we deal with this fucker Nikolai Fist?"

I crank my neck.

"Ten years ago, I would have said we should save ourselves the trouble and just outbid his current employer. But not anymore. Valentin is right. The man in that video looks less refined... less dangerous..."

"But still dangerous," Ilya points out.

"Yes, he's still dangerous. But so am I."

Especially when he's fucked with what's mine, I think. *My businesses. My empire. My girl.*

Most fucking importantly my girl.

"Let's fucking get him," Valentin roars.

But Ilya has more sense than the both of us. "If he's as dangerous as you say, then no matter how far he's fallen, we still need to be careful. He's taken out half of our front businesses and massacred countless people. Chasing after a man like that is asking for trouble."

"I'm done asking for trouble," Valentin says, pounding a fist into his hand. "It's about time we start handing it out again."

"Why must I be the voice of reason?" Ilya sighs, looking at me for backup.

I grind my teeth, calculating every angle.

"Maybe we don't go after him," I say. "Maybe we find a way to bring him to us."

"Bring him to us?" Valentin blares. "All he's been doing is going after us. I say we go to him."

"We don't know where he is," Ilya points out.

I nod. "Precisely. But he knows where we are."

"So why hasn't he come?"

"Because he's waiting."

"... For?"

"The right bait."

My mind splinters with possibilities. I try to peer through my anger and reach the cunning that has always served me so well. But it gets harder with every passing second.

He scared Natalya.

He needs to pay.

I storm to the office door.

"Where are you going?" Valentin calls after me.

"The armory."

The door slams shut behind me. I want to punch the wall, but I know my hands will be better served around some high-caliber weapons. Nikolai Fist doesn't come to a fight empty-handed, if I'm going to try and trap him, I'll need to be ready.

But I can't kill him right away either, I need to find out who he's working for. And he *is* working for someone. A man like that doesn't have his own ambitions. He just loves to kill. So why not get paid for it? That's all there is to him.

How do I trap a man like that?

I'm still working through the possibilities when I reach the cellar downstairs. It leads directly to the armory. I can see the armored door ahead. But I don't move toward it.

Something feels off.

I reach for my gun, only to realize I've left it upstairs. Usually, I don't have to be armed in my own establishments.

Usually.

Suddenly, the lights switch off and the basement is plunged into darkness. I tear out my switchblade and move backward toward the steps.

"Andrei Zherdev..."

The voice comes in a low rumbling growl from somewhere in the darkness ahead. I stop at the foot of the stairwell and get ready for a fight.

Something tells me I already know who it is.

"Come out and face me like a man... Nikolai."

A deep booming laugh echoes around me.

I sneer.

Then, a single light switches on in the middle of the room. The darkness shifts and an imposing figure lumbers into the dim beam.

"How'd you know it was me?" Nikolai asks, his crooked smile twisting his scarred face.

"Wishful thinking."

He shakes his head and I have to tilt mine up just to get a good look at him. This fucker is even bigger than I remembered. Shit, even if I manage to kill him in a knife fight, there's a good chance he does enough damage to take me with him.

I'm fine with that, I've always wanted to die in battle.

No. Think about what you have to live for now, an inner voice calls to me.

Natalya.

Shit. I can't die. Not here. Not now.

"You're scared," he grins. "But don't be afraid, little boy. I'm not here to hurt you. I only carry a message."

"From who?" I think fast. I have Nikolai alone. I can't fight him, but maybe I can buy him off. Fuck what I said earlier. This doesn't look like a beaten man. This is a hungry beast. "I'll give you five million dollars to tell me who you're working for."

He only laughs.

"Not enough. I've been promised so much more."

Fuck.

My grip tightens around the blade of my knife.

"What's the message?" I growl.

The smirk he gives me sends a chill down my spine. I grimace. It's been decades since someone has had that effect on me.

What the hell is wrong with me?

"I'm the message," Nikolai booms.

Without another word, he steps back into the darkness. The single light switches off. The darkness shifts, and when the lights click on again, the cellar is empty.

Nikolai is gone.

"Fuck!" I roar.

Fury and frustration flash through me as I rip out my phone and call Valentin.

He answers right away.

"Nikolai Fist is here," I bark. "The fucker is somewhere in the building. He was just in the basement. Shut this place down. Find him. Use everyone. This ends tonight."

29

NATALYA

We've been on lockdown for a week, so why has Andrei finally decided to take me out now?

I look up at him, trying to piece it all together, but he just glares straight ahead, his big hand clamped around mine. Bright sunlight glimmers off his dark sunglasses. I squint.

If I didn't know better, I'd say he was still angry over the phone. But that can't be right. I remember the way he smiled when I meekly presented him with the broken shards. The way he hugged and kissed me. The way he asked what I used the phone for, and the way he believed me when I said it was to contact my friends. That was the half-truth. I wasn't lying. And neither was he when he said we were going back into the city. He didn't want to be that far from me ever again.

What he didn't say, however, was why he really wanted to bring me into the city.

A strike of fear passes through me and I let my gaze fall from him. Looking over my shoulder, I catch a glimpse of our entourage in the passing storefront windows. We cast a strange and intimidating reflection. Six men in black suits and dark shades encircle Andrei and me. Valentin leads the group.

Everyone stares. But I'm used to it by now.

What I'm not used to is being outside again. In public. Surrounded by people. It reminds me that there's a big wide world outside the dark drama that's invaded my life.

Andrei squeezes my hand as we turn a corner. I still don't know where we're going, but I trust him.

Does he trust me?

Shit. Should he?

I feel like I gained back his trust when I showed him the pieces of my smashed phone, but that just makes me feel even more guilty about the secret of my new phone.

Two days ago, when Ilya left the mansion and I knew I was alone, I tried to turn it on but the battery was dead. So I spent the rest of the day finding a useful hiding spot. Right now, that phone is plugged into a power adapter under the back porch.

I haven't been able to use it yet. Later that night, Andrei returned. We talked, and he told me he knew about the phone. I showed him what I did to it, we kissed, he carried me to the helicopter and he flew me into the city.

I've been confined to his penthouse since then—well, until today. For some reason, Andrei decided that this morning was the perfect time to interrupt my sentence.

"Are we almost there?" I ask, feeling the sweat drip down my forehead. It's a hot day and I've gotten used to a sheltered, air-conditioned lifestyle.

"Just a little bit longer."

"Will you at least tell me where we're going?"

Dipping his head, Andrei looks at me over his shades. Those emerald green eyes sparkle in the sunlight.

"Nowhere."

"Nowhere?"

"We're just going for a walk."

"Why?"

"Because we can."

"Then why is this the first time we've done it all week?"

Andrei stops. So do his guards.

"I already told you. We're under attack. Someone is after you. It was safer in the penthouse."

"It's not safer there anymore?"

"It still is. I'm just tired of hiding you. This is a show of force, Natalya. We are being watched. I'm sure of it. Our enemies need to know that they can't keep us in the shadows forever."

"Why didn't we do it sooner?"

Andrei's grip around my hand tightens.

"Because I thought we'd have caught the fuckers by now. But they ran and hid in the same shadows they want us to drown in. So, I'm making the first move. If they want a fight, they can come and confront us in broad daylight."

Despite the heat, a chill washes over my skin.

"Wait... Are we supposed to be bait right now?"

Andrei laughs. "No, little deer. I would never put you in that kind of danger. What we're doing is purely to send a message."

"But if they come, you'll fight. Right?"

Andrei pinches my chin. "That's right. You're starting to get it." A smile lingers on his lips as he looks at me. "You sound like a Bratva queen."

I blush. "What does that mean?"

"It means you're starting to understand the strategy of leading an empire. My empire." He leans into my ear. "*Our* empire."

The cold chill I felt is replaced by a warm wave. I remember the ring in Andrei's vault.

I also remember the torn and tattered photograph he had of my father. The thought still makes my head spin. What's the connection? Did my father plant it there? How?

I desperately want to ask Andrei about it, but I know that

would be foolish. He can't know that I broke into his vault, and he definitely can't know how I knew the password.

"Our empire," I quietly echo, thinking about my betrayal and all the confusion it's led to. "If it's our empire, then why haven't you married me yet?"

"Because you do not deserve to inherit an empire at war. First, I will destroy whoever challenges us. Then I will give you what you deserve."

"That's a pretty promise."

"No. It's a violent one. Now, let's move on. We've come outside to enjoy a nice, sunny day together. Tell me, how has your application process been going?"

With that, Andrei tugs at my hand and we start walking again.

"I... I haven't been able to work on it since I've been at the penthouse."

"Is the laptop I got you not good enough?"

"No. it's amazing. It's just... I'm at a roadblock and I don't know where to go from here."

"You can't find a solution online?"

"I've been trying, but my mind always works better with physical books. I used to love going to the library and getting lost in the architecture section."

Andrei nods. "I see..." He seems to think on that for a moment. "Valentin," he calls out ahead. "Where is the nearest library?"

Valentin peaks over the wall of guards surrounding us.

"How the fuck should I know?"

"You don't read?"

"I read braille," he grins, raising his fists.

Andrei chuckles and looks down at me, shaking his head.

"I don't get it," I admit.

"He's saying his knuckles are the braille. So when he punches people, it's like they're reading his message."

"That message is: fuck you!" Valentin boasts.

I think on it for a second. "That doesn't really make any sense, though. You should have said you *write* in braille. If you read it, then that means you're the one getting punched in the face."

Andrei laughs so hard his hand falls on his stomach. "She's right!"

"Well, I mean... I have been punched in the face plenty of times before. So I guess it still works."

I can't help but laugh along as the two blood brothers share a moment.

"Natalya?!"

That laughter breaks when I suddenly hear a familiar voice call out.

"Woah, little lady, where are you going? Can't you see we're walking here?"

Up ahead, I watch as Valentin catches a woman by the arm.

I stop in my tracks. Andrei does too.

"This is a public sidewalk, thank you," the woman charges. "And that is my friend, so please and kindly let me go."

Valentin looks over the wall of bodyguards toward Andrei. Andrei glances down at me. I can't quite see the woman through our entourage, but I'd recognize that voice anywhere.

"Yelena?"

I slip from Andrei's hand and race forward. "It's alright, Valentin," he says.

I reach Yelena just as Valentin lets her go.

We collide in a hug,

"Holy shit!" she cries. "What are the chances? I've been trying to reach you forever, but my calls have been going straight to—"

I slap her on the back before she can continue on about the phone. That's still a sore spot. She seems to get the hint.

"I'm sorry," I blush. "It's been a crazy month. You wouldn't believe what I've been through."

Yelena peeks over my shoulder at the intimidating posse I've just emerged from. "Looks like you got yourself quite the man caravan. Whatever you're doing, keep at it. And also, where can I sign up?"

"If only you knew..." I giggle weakly, not wanting to get into the details. "How was Milan?"

"Wonderful," she smiles. "Everything is going as planned. Soon enough, I'll have my own little fashion empire all set up. You know what that means, right? Free dresses for my girl until the day she dies."

Yelena giggles but all I can think about is how much has changed since we last met. If I never get a free dress again, it will still be too soon. Andrei has gifted me more outfits than I could wear in a single lifetime.

"Natalya, aren't you going to introduce me to your friend?" Andrei's low voice rumbles up from behind me as his warm shadow blocks out the sun.

Yelena looks up at him like she's staring at a god. "And who do we have here?"

"Andrei Zherdev," Andrei says, nodding. "And you are?"

"Yelena Laskin."

"I recognize you from my club," he calmly notes.

"Which club is that?" Yelena jokes, whipping back her hair. "I'm sorry, I frequent many such establishments."

"Club Silo247."

Yelena's jaw drops as she gapes at me. "Say no more. It all makes sense now. So that's where you scurried off too. And here I was, worried. How foolish of me. I should have known better. You always know how to take care of yourself."

She gives me a knowing wink. My gut churns a little.

Andrei never asked how I got the phone, but one wrong

word and Yelena could be implicated. She doesn't deserve the drama—although, she might enjoy it more than I do.

"I think it's time we get moving," Valentin butts in. "We need to stay on schedule."

"We're just out on a walk," Andrei reminds him. "There's no hurry."

"Yeah," Yelena teases, looking over her shoulder at Valentin. "There's no hurry, right? Unless you're trying to get rid of me."

My jaw nearly hits the floor. Is she flirting with Valentin?? I want to grab Yelena's shoulders and shake some sense into her, but I know that would only make her want him more.

"Now why would I want to get rid of such a pretty bird?" Valentin taunts back. "Unless you're trouble?"

"I'm the furthest thing from trouble," Yelena replies, turning around to face him. "But if I hear you call me a bird again, that might just change."

The sass hits Valentin like a head of steam. For a moment, he just stands there with his lips parted. Then, he looks over at Andrei and me and grins.

"I like this one."

"I'm right here," Yelena says. "You can talk to me."

Valentin bites his bottom lip. "I think we've done enough talking."

Yelena gasps. Valentin steps forward, covering her in his own shadow. Keeping his eyes locked on hers, he reaches into her purse and pulls out her phone. Then he takes Yelena's hand and presses her finger on the screen to unlock it.

All she can do is look on in astonishment as he types something into the phone then slips it back inside her purse.

I can tell she was not expecting that—hell, neither was I.

Sure, Yelena is used to dealing with powerful men, but I can't imagine she has any experience with someone like Valentin. I'm nervous for her. But she doesn't seem nearly as afraid as she should be. In fact, I recognize the little shock of thrill in her eyes. It's the same feeling I get when Andrei surprise me with something unexpected.

"Now fly home, little bird," Valentin smiles. "We're walking here." Lifting his hand in the air, he motions our entourage forward. "Let's go."

Andrei takes my hand. "You heard the man."

He tugs me forward and I stumble after him, but I keep my eyes locked on Yelena. She's still dazed from her encounter with Valentin.

"I'll be in touch," I assure her.

That seems to snap her out of it.

"How?" she calls after us. "Did you change your phone number? Can I email you?"

"I... uh... no... I'll find a way to get a hold of you." Valentin has her number, I tell myself. If I need it, I'll get it from him. But something tells me he only wants it for himself.

All I can do is wave as Yelena disappears in the distance—a suffocating reminder of how little control I have over my life.

I can't even contact my friend without asking for permission.

A cloud rolls through the sky, temporarily blocking out the sun. I look up Andrei. He's staring ahead again.

I need that phone.

"I think I'd like to go back to the mansion," I mumble, making my disappointment clear.

He looks at me and clenches his jaw.

"I'll think about it."

30

ANDREI

I drop Natalya back off at the penthouse and we hang out for a bit before having dinner. But the whole time, my mind is a million miles away.

Everything is still fucked to hell. Yet, when we're together my life somehow feels slightly better. And that's too bad, because I can't afford to feel better right now. That will have to wait until I've wiped my invisible enemies from the face of the earth

Today wasn't just supposed to be a show of force, it was supposed to clear my mind. I desperately need a fresh outlook on everything. It feels like I keep hitting dead ends. It's turning into a nightmare.

Somehow, Nikolai escaped from the club last week. But his message was enough to snap me awake. This is a man who's more dangerous than any I've ever faced before, and he's specifically targeting me and my empire. Natalya too.

That left me with no choice. I had to bring her into the city. I own nearly every building on this block, and I can have men guarding the street 24/7. She's safest here. But I already know

I'm going to have to send her back to the mansion soon—and not just because she wants to return.

I can feel the storm coming. She can't be here when the violence erupts. I won't put her in that much danger.

After dinner, I leave Natalya with her studies and head to my office at Club Silo247. Valentin is waiting for me when I arrive. I drop into my chair. He stays standing.

"There's still no sign of Nikolai," he updates me. "But we have all our people working on it. We'll find him. We have to. That fucker can't hide forever."

"I swear I felt him watching us today on our walk," I grumble. "Did you?"

Valentin nods. "I was hoping he'd try something."

"No. Not with Natalya there."

"Ah, Natalya," he sighs, stroking his chin. "She attracts quite the company, doesn't she?"

I tilt my head at him. "Are you talking about Nikolai or Yelena?"

He opens his mouth to say something but thinks better of it. Instead, a sly grin takes over his face.

"Enough about our riveting social lives," he shrugs, shaking away the grin. "I think you should send Natalya back to the mansion. It would be for her own safety."

"I was already planning on it."

"Good. You know how dangerous Nikolai is."

"I do. You don't have to keep reminding me."

I feel a burst of rage as I remember our encounter in the cellar. He made a fool of me.

Valentin keeps pushing. "Apparently, I do. He's the only real threat to us right now. The Italians are nothing compared to him, even if they're the ones who hired him."

"Are you still harping on that? The Italians didn't hire him."

"Then who did?"

"You tell me," I return. "You're the one who's supposed to be tracking him down. He has to sleep somewhere. He has to eat somewhere. He has to spend money. He can't just disappear."

"I. Will. Find. Him," Valentin barks. "Just give me a little more time. Then I'll kill him in front of everyone. I promise."

"Not everyone," I tell him. "Keep it away from the cops. And make sure we get some useful information out of him first. His corpse is useless to us if it doesn't spill its guts first."

"I'll try my best," Valentin grumbles. "But we have to make an example of him. The entire underworld needs to see what happens to those who challenge us. You know what will happen if you don't. Every two-bit hustler on the street will be out for your throne."

I sneer. "I'm well aware."

Valentin goes silent for a moment and I start to drift into my own thoughts. "What's on your mind?" he asks, slowly calming back down. "You've been quiet today."

"Nothing. I'm just thinking about Nikolai," I half-lie. Sure, Nikolai fills up most of my mind, but Natalya occupies the other half. She always does. I don't want to send her away again, but I know I'll have to.

"Anything specific?"

"I offered him five million in the basement to rat out his employer, but he just laughed and said that wasn't nearly enough to buy him."

Valentin furrows his brow. "That's odd. He never charged that much before."

"He doesn't charge that much now. No one does, which means he's working for some other price."

"What do you think it is?"

"I don't know. But he must want something... something he can't get with money."

"The Italians definitely wouldn't be able to afford anything like that."

"I'm telling you the Italians aren't behind this," I sneer. "It has to be someone else."

"Well, you do have a long list of enemies..."

"None of my enemies operate like this. They'd want me to know this was their doing. They'd leave breadcrumbs, calling cards, something..."

Valentin stands up. "Do me a favor, will you? Don't rule out the Italians so easily. Sure, they're negotiating an alliance and throwing their daughters at you, but I don't trust them. Even if this isn't their doing, I don't fucking trust them."

"Neither do I," I agree. "I'll keep my eye on them."

Suddenly, both our phones buzz at the same time.

"Fuck," I curse, reading the message. "Not again."

<hr>

Ilya points to his computer screen. "They broke in here—through the backdoor. Then they shot four clerks and wounded three others before going to work on the safe."

He rolls through footage from one of my money-laundering outfits on the other side of town. A gang of men in black ski masks kneel down by the safe. They lay explosives by the hinges and blow the door off.

"This wasn't Nikolai," Valentin snarls in my ear. "He always works alone. It must have been—"

"It wasn't the Italians," Ilya cuts him off. "They share a fifty-percent stake in this operation. They would never risk such a loss simply to make a point."

"Well, they think the same thing about us so we better start putting that option on the table." Valentin turns back to me. "I've fielded forty messages from all three families demanding to know why *we* hit their money-laundering office. They think we did it because you won't seal the alliance. They think you're fucking with them... and if you ask me, I'm starting to think the same thing."

I sneer at my blood brother. "Watch yourself." He's getting dangerously close to bringing Natalya up by name. I won't allow it.

Valentin bites his tongue but doesn't back down.

"I ran facial recognition on the footage," Ilya interrupts. "It managed to pick up enough to identify more than half the attackers, even through their masks. These men are from a mercenary group based out of Albania. They have no connection to the Italians or to Nikolai Fist. They're independent..."

"Don't give me that shit," Valentin explodes. "The Albanians don't give a fuck about some Bratva in Chicago. They have to be working for someone else."

"Actually, I agree," Ilya snips. "They were definitely hired by someone else, but whoever hired Nikolai Fist would not need this group. It must be another challenger."

I pound my fist on the desk. "You've got to be fucking kidding me."

"That's it," Valentin barks, turning his ire toward me. "I may hate the Italians with a burning passion, but if you and Ilya are so sure they're not in on this, then you can't just keep ignoring them. An alliance is critical."

He holds his ground, but I can tell he's scared.

I glare back at him, hating how right he is. But he's getting too personal. He's one step away from saying I need to dump Natalya.

I won't have this conversation in front of Ilya. This is between blood brothers.

"Thank you for your work," I nod to Ilya. "You can go."

"Of course, Pakhan." He snaps his laptop closed and leaves without another word. Then it's just me and Valentin.

I can just feel him chomping at the bit to tell me off about Natalya. I won't argue with anything he says. The threat our empire is facing would immediately lessen if I married one of the Italians' daughters. But I can't go through with that. The thought of letting Natalya go makes me sick. Cutting her off isn't an option.

She started out as a fun project, a toy to play with. Now I don't want anything to take her away from me. But would I sacrifice my empire for her?

"Listen, man," Valentin begins. "You wanted me to become consigliere to the Italians, so it's my job to advise you on how to handle them."

"I know."

"Well? Which one is it going to be—Tizziana La Plata, Giovanna Santarelli, or Nina Cuozzo?"

I shake my head. "Give me a second to think." I go sit down on the couch and rub my temples as I stare off into space. There has to be a solution to all my problems. I just need to find it.

Think, Andrei. This is the challenge you've been waiting for. Natalya was meant for you. She prepared you for this. Find a way to win. You always do.

Valentin and I sit in silence as we consider our options.

"You know what this is?" I ask finally say.

Valentin's head snaps around. "What?"

"This." I wave my hand at nothing. "All this bullshit. Someone is trying to recreate the exact same circumstances as when I took over."

He blinks at me and then frowns. "I... guess so."

"They're creating chaos and probing for weakness so they can overthrow me and become the new Pakhan. They're doing exactly the same thing that I did to Comrade Vadim. That *we* did."

"But why?" Valentin asks. "Nikolai doesn't have a following. He's a lone wolf with no gang. How would he even rule?"

"I'm not talking about Nikolai. I'm talking about whoever

hired him. Nikolai could have brought in those Albanian mercenaries, but mercenaries aren't going to be eternally loyal to him. Unless he plans to wipe out every last Bratva and mafia family, he would never be able to hold onto power once he got it."

"And neither would whoever's hired him."

I nod and we both fall silent again. This isn't getting us anywhere. Still, we both hold out hope, desperately trying to think up solutions as we pace around the office. So many conflicting thoughts crowd my brain that I can't hold them all together.

I start to get restless. I think about Natalya. About how I'll send her back to the mansion tonight. There's no point in waiting until morning. Something drastic needs to happen soon.

Still, I hate the tug and pull that I'm putting her through. Sending her back and forth between cages of various sizes. It must be exhausting for her.

Just a little longer, angel, I think. *Once all this is done, I'll loosen your leash and replace that collar with a ring.*

My fingers curl into fists. The Italians won't like that. But by then, I won't need them anymore...

Suddenly, I have an idea.

"You really think the Italians are the ones behind this?" I ask Valentin.

"I don't know. But I can't think of anyone else. It has to be them, no matter what Ilya says. He's smart, but sometimes you can't think so much. You just need to act."

"Then let's act," I tell him. "Set up a meeting with the Italians. Tonight. Tell them to bring their daughters. I'll make a choice, and we'll have our alliance."

I can practically hear Valentin's jaw hitting the floor.

"You're actually going to marry one of them?"

"No," I grunt. "But I need them to think I am. I need the

entire underworld to think that their Pakhan is ready to seal an alliance. That's the bait. That will draw out the truth. If our mysterious challenger isn't part of the Italian mob, then he will have to attack before the alliance is sealed, and we will have drawn him out of the shadows. If it's been the Italians this entire time, then the attacks should stop, right? Let's call that bluff. If Nikolai stops after this news spreads, then we know the Italians were involved. Then we get our retribution and you will have my permission to slaughter the lot of them."

A mischievous grin fills Valentin's face.

"Sounds good to me.'

"Perfect. You set the trap. I'll be the bait. Text me the details. I'll meet you at the event."

I head for the door, already feeling bad about doing this to Natalya. Not that she'll ever know about it. She'll get her wish. I'll send her back to the mansion tonight, far away from all this shit. And when the dust has settled, I'll set her free. Then we can live wherever she wants.

But first, I need to get us there.

"Wait. Where are you going?" Valentin calls after me.

"To the girl I'm actually going to marry," I shout back at him.

I should bring her something to make up for all this, I think, before getting an idea.

I know just the thing.

I've been staring at the same 3D model on my computer for what seems like hours when I hear Andre return.

Shit, I think, looking down at my body. It's still wrapped in the same short towel I used to dry off with after my shower earlier. I haven't been able to bring myself to change. I'm too distracted to get anything done.

I'm stuck in a rut and I don't know how to get out of it. Maybe architecture school isn't for me. Maybe I should just give up and be a dutiful housewife...

"Natalya?"

I sigh. "In here."

I sink into my chair and lazily swivel around just in time to see Andrei lumber through the doorway.

My jaw drops.

"What are all those?" I gasp.

He's carrying a stack of books so high that I can't even see his face.

"These are called books," he jokes, crouching down to place the pile on the floor.

"You don't say." I spring out of my chair and kneel beside

him. My heart starts to thump. "These are architecture text-books. Where did you get them?"

"The University of Illinois bookstore," Andrei pants. He runs a hand through his sweaty hair. I can't imagine how heavy all these books are, and he carried them all the way here for me? "I cleaned the place out."

"You... you remembered what I said."

"That you prefer to study with real textbooks. I listen, little deer. Believe me, I do."

My fingers race through the pages of the thick book at the top of the pile. It's filled with blueprints and full-color images. I'm already half-lost in a bit of text when I snap myself out of it.

"Thank you," I say. Lunging forward, I let the towel slide off my body as I wrap Andrei up in my arms.

He hugs me back.

"Happy birthday, little deer."

I scrunch my nose. "It's not my birthday."

"Then why are you in your birthday suit?"

He leans back and takes a long gander down at my naked body. I blush—as if he's never seen me naked before.

"I... I just got out of the shower," I lie.

Andrei takes a strand of my hair in his hand.

"Your hair is dry."

"Well, that shower was a few hours ago."

He cups my face. Those emerald green eyes dig deep into my soul.

"Are you alright?"

I sink into his touch. The warmth of his palm melts away my stress. I try not to think of the difficult decision I still have to face. That can wait. This is much easier.

"I'm fine. Just a little stressed."

"Well, I've got another gift for you."

I cock my head to the side. "Another one?"

"I'm sending you back to the mansion, just like you wanted. The helicopter should be here any minute."

"Are you coming with me?"

Andrei smiles, but there's something sad about the look in his eyes. "No, angel. I'm needed here. But I will come visit every single day. It won't be like last time. I promise."

The stress returns.

Without Andrei at the mansion, I'll be free to use that cursed phone. But after his thoughtful gift, I'm having even more doubts.

"Are you happy with the books?" he asks.

"Yes."

"You can take them with you... if there's room on the helicopter."

We share a little laugh. Andrei keeps his gaze locked on me.

"Thank you," I whisper.

"It's what you deserve."

"... I'm not sure I do."

My chin drops and Andrei brushes my cheek with his fingers. Then he takes my hand and lifts it to my face.

"You deserve the world, little deer," he says, kissing the back of my hand. "I love you."

My thumping heart stops dead. The world goes silent.

Did I hear him right?

Did Andrei Zherdev just say he loves me?

"Really?" I hear myself ask, but it's like watching a movie. I've been detached from my body.

"Really," Andrei nods. Those emerald eyes burn stronger than ever. "Do you love me?"

His thumb presses into my palm as he holds my hand up between us. My mind starts to race. I say the only thing I can say. The truth.

"I... I don't know."

His grip around my hand remains steady, but the fire in his

eyes flickers. I can tell he's hurt, and it makes my heart ache. But I also know I couldn't lie to him.

I don't know what the hell is going on. And he's not making it any easier.

"Understood."

In the distance, a low rumble grows to a full roar.

"The helicopter is here," Andrei says. After lifting me up, he finally lets go of my hand. "Go get dressed. I'll deal with the books."

"Andrei, I—"

He lifts his hand, stopping me.

"Do as I say, angel. It's time to go. I'll see you soon."

Tears well up in my eyes as I turn and walk away.

What have I done?

It's been two days since Andrei's confession, and I still wince at my reaction every time I think about it. But that doesn't mean I'd change anything.

He kept his promise, visiting the mansion twice a day since I got back. But we've only had dinner and shared small talk. He kisses me, but we don't fuck. He listens, but I feel like he isn't there.

My heart is so heavy my chest hurts. I haven't even been able to bring myself to go anywhere near my hidden phone. But it's not like I can study either. Not even Andrei's wonderful gifts can keep me focused. Whenever I flick open the pages of one of the textbooks, all I can think about is him.

Do I love him or is this just some sort of deranged Stock-holm syndrome?

I don't have the energy to understand it, let alone dissect it. Mostly, I've been staying in bed. When I get hungry, I wander to the kitchen. There are more guards stationed here now, but they always leave a clear path to and from my bedroom. I'm thankful for that. I don't want anyone to see me like this.

I turn over in bed and check the clock. It's 2am. Usually, I'd be fast asleep by now, but my body is becoming restless from lack of use. I stare up at the ceiling and try to think clearly, but all my thoughts are a jumbled mess.

Andrei and I had dinner tonight, but I could barely eat. We mostly just sat there in silence, occasionally trying to start a conversation. They never took. Finally, Andrei got a call and left. I heard the helicopter fly away, then I went to bed.

I've been tossing and turning ever since.

Why does this have to be so difficult?

I stare at the ceiling for a little while longer. Then my belly starts to rumble. I haven't had a full meal in almost two days now, but I don't feel like I deserve to either.

I try to suffer through the hunger pains until they become too much.

"Fuck it," I mumble, throwing aside the sheets. Like a sleepwalker, I slowly march through the dark halls toward the kitchen, but I stop just outside the door.

I hear voices.

Someone's in there.

"Pavel stop!" a girl giggles.

"Only if you beg."

My pulse starts to quicken as I lean against the wall and listen. I recognize the girl's voice—it belongs to one of Andrei's cooks... Anya, I think her name is—but the man's is unfamiliar to me.

Shit.

I'm starving, but there's no way I'm walking into that kitchen when there are other people in it. Maybe if I wait here for a little bit, they'll leave...

"Pavel. I'm begging you to stop," Anaya continues. "We'll get in trouble."

"Pakhan isn't here. I'm the only one who's going to punish you."

"Natalya is here. She could catch us and tell him."

"That's not going to happen. She keeps to that bedroom of hers."

"... Unless she's hungry, then she comes to the kitchen."

"It's too late for her to be up. Stop worrying."

"No. I'm serious."

I press my cheek against the wall and peek through a crack in the door just in time to see Anya slap Pavel's shoulder and shove him away. He doesn't take the hint, and before I can blink, he's back on her.

This time, Anya slaps his face. Pavel's head snaps to the side and she slips around him.

"I told you to stop!" Anya shouts in a hushed breath.

"Whatever," Pavel grumbles, nursing his damaged ego. "I just thought you'd want to enjoy this mansion while you still can, but I guess that's too much to ask..."

"What do you mean, *while I still can*?"

Pavel huffs. "Haven't you heard? Pakhan's getting married. When that happens, he won't need you around anymore. You'll never get this close to fucking in a mansion like this again. I just thought I'd help you take advantage of that while it lasts..."

I lean in closer. What is he talking about?

"Oh, shut up," Anya fires back. "His wife will have to eat too. I'm not going anywhere."

"Wishful thinking," Pavel taunts. Leaning against the counter he looks down at his feet. "Words out. He's marrying an Italian girl from one of those mafia families. They like different food than we do... you know, like Italian food. Your specialty is Russian food. There won't be any need for that. She'll probably bring in her own cooking staff. Then we'll all get fat off of fettuccine and cannoli... well, everyone except you..."

"You're such an asshole," Anya huffs.

They keep talking but I don't hear them. A cold sweat has broken out over my entire body. What the hell is Pavel talking about? Since when is Andrei marrying an Italian?

A pit of dread fills my throat as I slowly tune back into Pavel and Anya's conversation.

"It's true," Pavel shrugs. "Pakhan is meeting with the Italian families as we speak to seal an alliance. We all got the announcement yesterday. They'll be married soon enough. It's got to be quick with all the shit that's going down."

"No way..." Anya gasps mirroring my disbelief.

Goosebumps race over my skin. Is this the real reason Andrei sent me back to the mansion, to keep me away while he married someone else?

My heart shatters into a million pieces.

Why would he do that? Is it because I didn't say I loved him back?

Dread claws at my stomach. I want to kneel over and puke my guts out, but I'm paralyzed against the wall. It feels like the sky might fall any second now.

"They've been talking about this for ages," Anya continues. "I'll believe it when I see it. Pakhan is way too attached to his food. Maybe his wife will eat Italian and he'll eat Russian."

"Pakhan only cares about power," Pavel reminds her. "He'll do anything if it solidifies his reign over this city. And from what I've heard, Italian girls don't make forgiving wives—especially not if they're from mob families. He'll do whatever he has to do to keep her happy."

"He's marrying her. That's enough to make any girl happy," Anya returns. "Once he seals the alliance, he doesn't have to be nice anymore. He'll treat her like any other girl..."

Pavel breaks into a grin. "And how does he treat every other girl? He seems to be pretty nice to Natalya."

"Yeah, well—"

"What do you think will happen to our little house guest?" Pavel interrupts.

"Who knows... You're right, though. He clearly likes her. Maybe she'll be moved to one of his other properties so he can keep her hidden away."

"I doubt it. The Italians wouldn't be happy if they find out."

"You're kidding right?" Anya snorts. "Every don in this city has at least one mistress. It's practically a requirement for the Italians. I don't know why..."

Their voices fade away as I start to hyperventilate. Tears fill my eyes. My cheeks burn.

This can't be real.

No, I tell myself. *It is. It all makes sense.*

I've been wrong about Andrei this entire time. I'm nothing but a dirty little secret to him. Did he ever really care about me?

Fucking hell. He said he loved me... and now I learn this? The manipulative bastard.

I spin away and run for the stairs. I don't want to hear anymore, but I can't get their words out of my head. Andrei... getting married... to an Italian...

He said he would take care of me, but in the end, he just turned me into a prisoner. I can't let him trap me forever. I won't let him make me his permanent captive.

I make a u-turn at the stairs and head for the back porch.

I need that phone.

32

ANDREI

"That was a pain in the ass," I grumble, ripping off my tie.

"But worth it," Ilya notes. "The Italians seemed convinced you were being genuine... not that you had me fooled."

"So you figured it out, huh?" I huff, looking out the limo's tinted window. "Or did Valentin tell you?"

"I'm no snitch," Valentin mumbles, rocking in his seat. He's still a little tipsy from the meeting. It was the only way he was going to get through an event with that many Italians without getting into a fight.

"You're playing a dangerous game, Pakhan," Ilya warns.

"I always am."

"What happens when they find out you're playing them?"

"I'll deal with that when it comes. Now, have a drink and say a toast to my fake marriage and a real alliance... or you can stay sober and be Valentin's designated driver for the night. I'm sure he's going to get absolutely wasted."

"You want to party?" Valentin grins at me.

I shake my head. "No. I'm going back to the mansion. The helicopter is already waiting."

"Spoken like a true married man."

"If only you were returning to your actual fiancée," Ilya remarks.

"I am. Natalya will be my wife... eventually..." I stroke my chin and think about how foolish I was for telling Natalya I loved her. Fuck. What's wrong with me? I've always had more control than that. But she just fucking does something to me...

It's not that it wasn't true, either, but rather that I'd never even thought of using that word until it slipped out. Still, I'm glad she knows the truth. Someday, I know she'll reciprocate the feelings. I just have to work a little harder. And that will start when I get back tonight. No more awkward dinners. No more small talk. I'll tell her everything. She won't like this whole mess with the Italians, but she needs to know. No more secrets.

"What the hell is that?" Valentin pounces off his seat and shoves his face against the window as the limo turns a corner.

I follow his gaze.

"Is that a fire?" I ask, leaning forward.

In the distance, a wide orange glow covers the skyline. Black smoke billows up into the dark night sky.

"That's a *big* fire," Ilya clarifies.

"Where's it coming from?"

Suddenly, all of our phones start wildly ringing.

"It's one of ours," Valentin roars.

Ilya starts furiously taping on his screen. "The attackers are still on location," he snarls. "We can catch them in the act."

"Finally," Valentin growls, sobering up.

I slam my fist against the partition and the driver rolls it down.

"Change of plans," I tell him. But I pause before giving him our new destination. Part of me still wants to go back to the mansion and patch things up with Natalya.

No. I can't. I have my responsibilities.

She'll have to wait.

"I guess it wasn't the Italians, after all," Ilya smirks as the limo screeches into action.

"No need to rub it in," Valentin chuckles, checking to make sure his guns are loaded. "But I'll forgive you... if you manage to kill more of these fuckers than me."

"That's a game I'm more than happy to play."

I cock my own gun.

"This is no game," I snarl. "This is war."

33

NATALYA

My right foot taps incessantly against the dusty shed floor as I nervously wait for a response to my latest text.

I want out. Now!

My cheeks are raw from crying, but I've wiped the last tears away. All that's left is a furious determination.

Andrei used me. He betrayed me. But he also gave me the excuse I needed to finally break free from him.

So why am I not happy? Why am I so miserable?

Because you love him back, I scream at myself. *Because he just broke your heart.*

The phone shaking in my hands buzzes and I snap my attention to it.

Everything is ready for your escape, my dear. Are you ready?

My heart twists but I don't hesitate.

Yes.

Where are you right now?

In the shed.

Good. I have a vehicle waiting for you. All you need to do is get to it. Leave the shed and cross the grounds toward the woods. Follow my instructions exactly. Walk. Slowly. Don't bring attention to yourself and don't start running until you hear the first shot.

My thumping heart skips a beat at that last word. Who is this man?

What shot?

Just do as I say. I am your father. Trust me. Now is your chance to escape. I'll save you from that monster and I'll make sure he never hurts you again. Now leave and don't look back. Go!

My pulse races. There's no time to ask questions. I'll have my answers soon enough.

This is it.

With one final deep, shaky breath, I push my way out of the rickety cabin. To get to the forest, I'll have to make it back to the lawn and go north.

I start walking.

It's not cold out, but my legs feel numb. I hardly even notice my feet hitting the ground.

The phone buzzes again.

When you reach the trees, stop. Wait for that first shot. When you hear it run to your right. Toward the driveway. No one will follow you. I'll meet you there. Good luck, my dear sweet daughter. I know you can do this.

Looking over my shoulder, I glance back at the mansion. It gleams with a hundred lights. The warm glow emanating from my bedroom still shines off the balcony. My computer screen blinks against the wall. My application project is on that hard drive. All my books are in there.

I'm not just walking away from Andrei, I'm walking away from all that too. He tried to give me the chance I never had. I tried to take it. Now it all seems so distant. So cold.

I swallow a shaky breath.

What will Andrei do when he finds out I'm gone? Will he treat me like an enemy? Or worse, a stranger?

Will he try to kill me for betraying him?

I don't know. What I do know, though, is that he'll never willingly let me go. No matter what, he'll keep hunting for me, just like he did after we first met. He's too determined to give up what he wants.

And he wants me.

At least, that's what I thought...

I'm ripped out of my thoughts when a gunshot explodes through the quiet night air. It echoes across the landscape.

Then the night erupts.

My phone buzzes, but I don't check it. The roars of growing gunfire rocket me forward. I break into a run.

I don't have time to think where I'm going. I dash the rest of the way across the field to the trees, veer hard to my right, and keep on running for the driveway.

Booming gunshots fill the air in a suffocating cacophony. It feels like my eardrums are going to burst. I can't think straight. I just keep running as fast as I can.

I hit the driveway and skid to the left, making for the road. But when I get there, I don't see a car. Am I even in the right place?

What happens if I miss my mark? I'm miles from Chicago. There's no chance I get there before Andrei—

All of a sudden, the crackling air is overcome by the squeal of screeching tires. I scream out loud when a white van blares up from behind me, coming to a stop just feet away.

The passenger door slams open and I stare inside.

I instantly recognize the man in the driver's seat. It's the man from my dreams. From my nightmares. The man in that hate-filled photo in Andrei's vault.

"... Papa?"

He jumps out of the car and folds me in his arms.

"It's okay, darling," he says. "You're safe now."

34

ANDREI

I stare up at the shattered windows that lead to Natalya's bedroom. Bullet holes mark the balcony. Dead bodies litter the lawn.

I clench my fist and punch a marble bust, smashing it into rubble.

Natalya is gone. And I'm ready to burn the world down.

This is all my fault.

"What. The. Fuck. Happened?"

Even Valentin flinches against my wild fury.

"It was a set up," he snarls, pointing to the woods behind the grounds. "The shooter was positioned over there. But they must have been moving pretty damn fast to hit so many targets before the alarm went off. It sounds like he took out our whole security detail with headshots from more than five hundred yards. Then he went around the other side of the house and finished off the rest of the staff. The whole attack took less than fifteen minutes."

"Nikolai." I snarl.

Valentin nods. "Must have been. No one else could have pulled this off. The fire downtown was a distraction. He's working with the Albanians. That's pretty much confirmed now. The survivors we captured earlier are still being interrogated, but I'm sure they'll let it slip eventually—especially when they learn that Nikolai set them up to fail."

"That fucker. Where did he go? Where the fuck did he take Natalya?"

"We're still tracing the tire tracks from the driveway, but it's pretty clear the van never entered the grounds..." Valentin swallows, dreading what he has to say next. "It looks like she went out to meet the driver."

I round on him, hissing through gritted teeth. "What the fuck does that mean?"

He looks at his feet. "It means she wanted to leave."

I hate to admit it, but that's the most logical explanation. This was a coordinated attack and Natalya must have been in on it.

Fuck. Fuck. FUCK.

Why? How?

... *The phone...*

"Pakhan, you need to see this." Ilya stands in the doorway, gesturing us forward.

"What?" I snap.

"I'm not sure, but I feel like you'll know."

Flexing my jaw, I follow him to the driveway. The black tire tracks taunt me. The thought of Natalya voluntarily leaving with a stranger makes my blood boil.

"Over here."

Ilya crouches down by the side of the pavement and points to something in the darkness. I can't make out what it is until I crouch down beside him.

"What the fuck..."

I reach down and pick up a familiar crest. My crest. The screaming skull is stained with dark blood. The black viper hisses up at me.

"This is your crest, is it not?" Ilya asks. "Why would someone leave it here for us to find?"

Valentin joins us and I can feel him tense up when he sees the calling card. "What the hell is that doing here?" he asks, puzzled.

It takes a second for the pieces to click together, but when they do, my blood runs cold.

"It wasn't always my crest," I rumble, standing up. My head is pounding. My heart twists in fury. "I stole it from the last Pakhan when I overthrew him. I made it my own. But before it was mine, it belonged to him."

Ilya tilts his head. "He's dead, isn't he?"

"He's supposed to be."

Valentin takes the crest and examines it. "Look at the marks on it. The gashes. The blood. No... this couldn't be..."

"Speak," I order.

"The explosion we set... the one that killed the last Pakhan... it was at his office. We'd been there plenty of times before. Doesn't this crest look familiar? I mean, they all look the same, but the size of this one?"

"You think this is the crest from his office?"

Ilya inspects it. "It sure looks like it survived an explosion."

"That makes me wonder what else survived the explosion..."

A cold wind howls between us.

"No," I sneer. "He's dead. He's been dead for over twelve years."

Valentin grimaces. "We could never identify his body."

"That's because every corpse in the ruins of that building was burned to a crisp. No one could have survived that shit."

"Then who left this calling card?"

I take the crest and twist it at the edges until the metal is bent and misshapen. Then I launch it across the driveway. It clangs away, echoing through the night air.

328 SASHA LEONE & JADE ROWE

"It must be from someone who's still loyal to him."

"Impossible," Valentin reminds me. "No one was loyal to him. That's part of the reason we won."

"Well, it's either that or he's still alive."

"I mean—"

"He's *not* alive."

"Then who took Natalya?"

I go blind with rage. The next thing I know, I have Valentin by the collar.

"Pakhan..."

The look on his face snaps me out of it. This is my blood brother. He's on my side. Everyone here is.

For the first time in years, the burn marks on my wrist start to throb. I remember the rope. I remember the vow I took when that man locked me away and tied me up like an animal. I remember the cold, lonely shack I had to hide in after I finally escaped. For months, I lived like a coward because I wasn't strong enough to take him on. All I could do was hang his picture on the wall and take out my infinite rage and hate on it. I burned it. Shot it. Gouged it. Stabbed it. But it didn't make anything better.

Nothing got better until he died. I killed him.

He can't be alive. I won't allow it.

I look over my shoulder. "Ilya. Do your thing. Figure this shit out. We're taking the chopper back into town. I want answers by the time we land."

He nods dutifully. "I'll do my best."

Valentin stays silent, but I know he has my back. He follows me as I turn and lead the way.

"This ends tonight."

———

"No fucking way..."

We've been sitting in the back of the limo for ten minutes now, silently seething as we head toward my office downtown when Ilya suddenly looks up from his laptop.

I look at him. "You have my answers?"

"I... I don't know. This sounds too insane to be true."

"Explain. Now."

He turns the laptop to face me. "This. It's about Natalya. I was at a dead end so I followed a hunch. It felt like she was connected to all this. I... I think I was right."

My entire body tenses.

"How?"

"It's... well, you know I've been looking for more information on her—as per your orders. But all this time I've been searching for background on the Datsyuk family. More specifically, I've been looking for Natalya's father, Vladimir Datsyuk. He didn't seem to exist. To an extent, neither did she. I didn't think she was lying, but something wasn't adding up..."

"We know this already."

He holds up his forefinger. "Ah, but that's the problem, you see?"

"No. I don't."

He laughs nervously, like he can't quite believe what he's about to say. "It turns out Datsyuk was not her family name, after all. At first, I assumed someone had deleted her family records. But just now... shit... I've discovered that Datsyuk was her mother's name, which means that her father Vladimir had a different family name. Her mother's name was..." He does something to his computer and brings up a picture of a beautiful woman—a woman who looks exactly like Natalya. "Vera Datsyuk."

I stare at the picture. This has to be Natalya's mother. They look like sisters.

"She died twenty years ago when Natalya was two years old. It looks like Natalya was then briefly raised by her father who gave his daughter Vera's last name, but her true name remained on her original birth certificate. That's why we couldn't find anything on her. She went into foster care when she was around eight and she told the foster care workers that her last name was Datsyuk. They created a new identity for her—a new birth certificate and everything—but that name was... what do you call it—an alias."

"So who is she?" Valentin interrupts. "What's her real last name?"

Ilya does something else to his computer. "Vera Datsyuk was married... to Vladimir. Vladimir Anatolievich Dimitrov... or, as you call him, Comrade Vadim—the Pakhan you deposed."

My stomach drops.

Natalya... is my most hated enemy's daughter?

"That can't be right," Valentin gapes at me. "I never heard about Vadim having a daughter."

I suddenly remember the first dinner I had with Natalya at the mansion. How she told me about the faint memories she had of her childhood. She mentioned how she was rarely allowed to leave her father's house growing up, if at all.

"No..." I grumble, shoving my hands into my face.

Valentin barks over at Ilya. "You're wrong. That can't be right."

"No. It's correct. The evidence is right here. I can hardly believe it myself, but it must be true. Natalya is the daughter of the man you killed... well, *supposedly* killed."

I rip my face from my hands.

"You think *he* took her?"

"It would make sense, wouldn't it?"

Valentin snorts. "That would mean Vadim was working with Nikolai. But that's impossible."

"Why?"

"Because if Vadim was somehow still alive, then he'd be

broke and powerless. We seized all of his assets when we took over. Tell him, Pakhan."

My mind races as I try to make sense of it all—if this is true, then have I been setup from the start or is this just a wild coincidence?

My heart shivers when I think about the way Natalya has screamed my name. The way she's hugged me. Smiled at me. Laughed with me. Fell asleep in my arms.

"She said her father disappeared when she was a girl," I murmur more to myself than to them. All the agonizing pieces fall into place. It makes me sick.

"It must have been when she was around eight," Ilya sighs. "And Vadim's death certificate states that he died twelve years ago. She's almost twenty, right? The timeline adds up..."

"Twelve years, fuck," Valentin curses under his breath. "If he had any sense, that would be plenty of time to come up with some cash. Plus, he stole a literal fortune when he was hitting up our money-laundering operations."

"Nikolai did that," I remind him, dragging myself back to attention. "And that means Vadim wouldn't have had that money to pay him to do it yet."

Ilya shrugs. "Maybe he promised him a cut of the profits?"

Valentin doesn't agree. "No. That doesn't make any sense. You have to pay a man like Nikolai in advance. Otherwise, he'd just take all of the money he steals, then kill you. It's happened before. For all of Vadim's insanity, he'd understand that much."

"So then how did he get Nikolai to work for him? How'd he get him to massacre our men and rob our businesses? How'd he get him to burn down Natalya's apartment? Why did he?" Ilya is clearly just thinking out loud, but it helps me put it all together.

The limo stops outside Club Silo247 and I kick the back door open.

"Fucking hell!" I shoot to my feet and point at Valentin. "Get every man we have out on the streets. If we weren't at war before, we definitely are now."

"Yes, Pakhan."

He's already on his phone commanding the troops when we get to the armory downstairs.

"We need to get Nikolai first," Ilya strategizes. "If he's dead, it won't just give us one less threat to worry about, but it might destroy the morale of the remaining Albanians and whoever else Vadim has managed to hire."

Valentin sets his phone aside. "We've been looking for Nikolai this entire time. What makes you think we can find him now?"

I smash in the code and push open the armored door, but before I step inside, I turn to Valentin and Ilya.

"Find Natalya," I explain, trying not to get lost in my growing rage... and increasing concern. "We find her and we'll find him."

"Wouldn't she be with Vadim?" Valentin asks. "He's her father, after all."

I grunt and grab the biggest fucking gun I can find.

"No. She won't be with Vadim." My gut churns.

"Why not?"

I snarl. "Because I know how Vadim paid Nikolai. It wasn't with money... it was with his daughter."

I cock the gun and imagine shooting two bullets through each of their skulls. Those fucking animals. That's how Vadim got Natalya to leave the mansion with him. He's her father. He's supposed to protect her. She believed he would. Now, he's going to feed her to the wolves.

No.

I won't let him.

Valentin and Ilya both halt in their tracks. "He paid Niko-lai... with his own daughter?"

"Don't you remember what Vadim was like?" I grunt. "He'd

use intermediaries to strike his enemies while keeping his own involvement secret. He'd make his enemies doubt their allies until they turned against each other. He's doing the same thing to me. He made me doubt the Italians and delay making an alliance with them. I don't doubt it anymore. He's alive... but he won't be for much longer."

I sling the rifle over my shoulder and take a Glock down from the wall. It goes under my belt. As do two more pistols.

"But how do we find Natalya if she's with Nikolai?" Valentin asks. "We haven't had any luck tracking him down this far..."

Ilya perks up.

"I have access to the security cameras at the mansion..." he thinks out loud. "If the van was caught on camera, then I might be able to track it down. All I'd have to do is combine the satellite feed with a new algorithm I've been working on..."

"Do it," I order. "And as soon as you have the location, transmit it to all our people and prepare to attack."

"What about calling in the Italians?" Valentin asks. "They're supposed to be our allies now, remember?"

"No," I growl. "This is my fight."

And my girl, I think.

You are officially forgiven, little deer.

But only if you stay alive long enough for me to save

Something feels off.

It's an uneasiness that's followed me all the way from the mansion. And it's only grown heavier the further we drive.

"Where are we?" I ask, peering through the van window.

"Somewhere safe," Father says. "Somewhere far away from Andrei Zherdev. Don't worry, dear. It's over. He'll never find you..."

We slow down next to a warehouse in an industrial neighborhood.

"He will... eventually," I sigh, almost without thinking.

"No. He won't," Father snarls in response. "That's why we're here. It's the last place he'll look. And that bastard *will* be out looking for you. Fortunately, I've set off a number of other distractions to better occupy his time."

"Distractions?" I ask, confused.

My mind has been swirling since Father picked me up outside of the mansion. I've wanted to ask him so many questions, but he seems too on edge to answer.

I don't want to ruin this reunion. But I desperately want to know what's going on. It feels like there's way more to this than meets the eye. Clearly, Father isn't working alone. Someone powerful has helped him. It sounded like an entire army showed up back at the mansion, but where the hell did my dad find an army?

"We're here." He turns off the motor and rotates in his seat to face me. "You forget about Andrei Zherdev. Do you understand me? He's dead to you. And soon, he'll be dead to the world too." He opens the door and steps out of the van. "Now come with me."

I hesitate. My heart has turned so heavy I'm not sure I could even lift it.

"You're going to kill him?" I ask, before the absurdity of that plan dawns on me. "... How is someone like you going to kill a man like that?"

That makes my father snap. He rushes around the van and rips the passenger door open.

"You will never speak to me about Andrei Zherdev again!" he shouts, unhinged. "You will never even think about him. Is that clear?"

He grabs my arm and yanks me into the warehouse.

"Stop! Papa, you're hurting me."

He tugs me forward and I stumble through an open doorway.

"No. You're hurting *me*," he snips. "You have no idea what's going on. I worked my whole life to keep the Bratva away from you and then that bastard shows up at exactly the wrong time and drags you into the middle of it all. He doesn't even know you're my daughter, and he's still rubbing my face in it." A horrific sneer twists his face and he stares off into the distance.

"I ruled this city once... until he tried to kill me. Did you know that? That Andrei Zherdev tried to kill your own father? He stole everything I ever worked for—everything! And now my own daughter doesn't even believe I can kill him? I'll show you, Natalya. I'll show everyone."

Blood rushes into my ears.

"What did you just say?" I mumble trying to make sense of it all. "You ruled this city? What are you talking about?"

"Silly girl. I thought you might have figured it out by now, but I guess not. Before Andrei Zherdev, I was Pakhan. He overthrew me. And he nearly killed me in the process."

I gasp when Papa lifts his shirt, revealing a mangled torso covered in burn marks and deep scars. "I escaped that explosion by the skin of my teeth. But my nightmare was only beginning. For twelve years I've had to hide and live like common filth. But finally, it's my time to rise again. And you are my key."

He steps toward me but I flinch away.

"You were Pakhan?" I gape, hardly believing my ears.

"That's right. And I will be again. Soon."

"Why... why didn't you tell me?"

"Because you were a child. A precious little girl who wasn't made for this world. I had to keep you pure. I had to keep you safe. I —"

"Safe?" I interrupt. "You abandoned me! For the past twelve years, I've struggled to survive. I've been on my own, Papa. Alone. So alone... where were you?"

"Preparing."

"Preparing for what?"

"Preparing for this. For my revenge. For my return. For you..."

I shake my head. Any happiness I felt at finally seeing him again evaporates. All that remains is the resentment. "You never gave a shit about me."

"I did what I had to do!" he roars. "And now it's your time to return the favor. My only wish was that I could have kept you locked away up until now. That I could have saved your purity. Then, you would have fetched me a much higher price. But it's fine. I forgive you. It will still all work out as planned."

I swallow. "What... what are you talking about?"

Father rolls his eyes. "Taking down an empire is expensive work, darling. You are my payment. For that, I thank you."

Suddenly, a nightmarish laugh fills the barren warehouse. I shiver in fear and start to stumble backward, but I quickly hit a rusty wall.

That laugh. I know that laugh.

"What a nice speech that was, Comrade Vadim."

Nikolai steps out of the shadows and joins my father at his side.

My knees give out on me and I sink to the dirty floor.

"You... you sent him to my apartment..." I realize.

Father just shakes his head. "No. You aren't mine to deal with anymore, darling. Nikolai and I made a deal. You belong to him now. He went to fetch what was his. I wasn't involved."

The sky comes crashing down as Nikolai pats my father on the shoulder and starts moving toward me. I want to crawl into a ball and disappear. I want to wake up from this nightmare. But I know there's no escape.

I ran from the only man in this world who truly cares about me and now I'm going to pay for it.

How could I be so stupid?

Remember what you overheard in the kitchen, I try to tell myself. But the words fall flat. Anything is better than this.

"Andrei..." I quietly rasp, my aching heart ripping through my chest.

"What was that?" Nikolai taunts. "Speak up, girl. Daddy can't hear you."

Something in me snaps. I whip around and bolt for the warehouse entrance. But Nikolai moves so fast I don't even see him until I collide face-first into his massive chest. He grabs my arms and pins them behind my back.

I try to fight him, but it's no use. He laughs that horrible, maniacal laugh and I go cold.

"Let me go!" I sob.

"Now why would I do that?" Nikolai continues to laugh. "It's a dangerous world out there. But you're safe in here with me."

"Andrei will find you," I hear myself shout. "He'll kill you."

"I doubt that."

Nikolai grabs a fistful of my hair and drags me kicking and screaming across the dusty warehouse floor. My father calmly steps aside to let him pass.

"Help me," I beg.

He barely even shrugs.

"Why don't you take a seat," Nikolai grunts.

He flings me into a metal chair so hard that I lose my breath. I gasp for air as he pulls a length of rope from the ground and starts binding me down.

"He'll find you," I gasp again. "He'll kill you."

"He wouldn't dare. Not with you by my side. For all of his power, Andrei Zherdev is soft. He wouldn't risk hurting you. I, on the other hand, have no such restrictions."

Nikolai flicks my chin when he's done tying me up. I try to struggle free, but the rope just digs deeper into my skin. Tears fill my eyes, but I don't want to cry. These men don't deserve the satisfaction.

Papa just stands there and watches with a grotesque smile on his twisted lips. Nikolai turns his back on me and dusts his hands off.

I hang my head.

Sadness outweighs the dread as tears start to drip down my cheeks. I remember how Andrei said he loved me. It was so genuine. So tender. I believed him. But I didn't want to believe my own heart. I love him too. I was just too afraid to admit it to myself.

And then when I heard he was marrying someone else, it felt like vindication. I was right not to open my heart to him— at least, that's what I thought. Now, I regret it. Oh, how I regret it.

If I'd been honest with myself, then I would at least have some hope left.

But now all hope is lost. Andrei isn't coming to save me. He's found someone else and I pushed him to do it.

"This isn't going to be easy on you, girl," Nikolai bellows. He grabs my scalp and rips my head back. "You ran from me when you were already mine. You let that traitor defile you when he had no right to. You will make up for it. And not gently. I'll use you how I please, then I'll use you to draw that fucker into a trap. He'll pay for taking you from me, just as you'll pay for letting him."

"Just remember our agreement," Papa interjects. "I'm the one who has to kill Andrei Zherdev. I've waited over a decade for my revenge."

"You get your prize and I get mine." Nikolai runs his fingers down my face. "You'll kill the man who betrayed you. And I'll make your dear, sweet daughter wish she was dead. It's the only way to make things right."

He grabs my throat and squeezes.

"Now leave us, Vadim. Your daughter and I have some lost time to make up for."

I squint up at the warehouse. "Are you sure this is the right place?"

Valentin checks his phone. "These are the coordinates Ilya transmitted. If someone made a mistake, it was him—and we both know he doesn't make mistakes... no matter how much I hate to admit it sometimes."

"It looks deserted." I peer through the open garage door on the ground floor. "The van isn't here."

"They could have moved it... or hidden it."

"Maybe." I scrutinize every empty window on the walls above. "This isn't like Vadim at all. There are no guards, no watch-outs, nothing."

"The only explanation is that he doesn't have anyone but Nikolai left. Those Albanians who started the fire must have been all he could afford right now—and we either killed or captured the lot of them."

"If that's the case, then he's lost his mind," I grumble. "He struck too soon. We could easily storm the place." I pass my hand across my eyes. "I don't like this."

"Well... it could also be a trap."

"That's what I'm thinking. But I'm not willing to wait around and find out. If Natalya is in there, we need to get moving."

"Ilya seems convinced that she is." Valentin holds up his phone to show me an enhanced satellite image of a white van pulling into this warehouse. "Wait. He's sending something else."

He swipes left and a video replaces the image. I watch as another vehicle pulls into the warehouse. An embedded image pops up in the corner. It shows a view of the driver's wing mirror.

"Fuck," we both curse at the same time.

It's Nikolai.

I clench my jaw and turn back to the building. He's in there. He's got my girl. He's going to fucking die.

"Fuck!" Valentin hisses again. "There's another one coming in. Look."

He lifts his phone again. This time, the white van is leaving the warehouse. The embedded image pops up and we both see Vadim at the wheel.

I might as well be staring at a ghost.

So, he is alive.

I'll fucking change that.

"Where the hell are you going?" I growl down at the image. Every instinct in me is screaming to chase after him. But if he's leaving, that can only mean one thing.

Nikolai is in there alone with Natalya.

At that very moment, a piercing scream tears out of the building. I instantly recognize the voice.

Natalya.

"Fuck this," I roar, jumping out into the street.

But Valentin shoots out a hand and grabs me. "You are NOT going in there alone. We don't have any backup yet and this smells like a trap."

"I don't fucking care."

"At least wait for the boys to get here. You're the one who ordered the assault."

"No. If this is a trap, Nikolai is expecting a siege. I'll go in alone. It might be foolish enough to take him by surprise."

Valentin pulls me back even harder.

"You've lost your fucking mind. I know how tough you are, brother. But you can't go against Nikolai Fist alone. It's suicide. At least let me help."

"No. I need to do this alone. You and Ilya track down Vadim. Capture the fucker. Alive. I want to make sure he's really dead this time. So hold him until I can do it myself."

I try to break away again but Valentin uses all of his strength to whip me around.

"Andrei..."

Hearing him say my name almost snaps me out of it. Valentin never calls me Andrei. Not unless it's serious.

Then I hear Natalya scream again and I make up my mind.

"Listen," I tell him, grabbing his shoulders. "If anything happens to me, you take over. I trust you. You'll make a good Pakhan."

His face twists, but he finally seems to get what I'm saying. I need to go in there. And I need to do it now.

He nods and lowers his eyes. "All right. Go. Rescue your girl. I've got your back."

Valentin turns his forearm outward to me and I bump mine against his. Then we both throw our arms around each other and I break away.

I don't look back as I race across the street. I trust my blood brother. Valentin will do what needs to be done. So will I.

Keeping a low profile, I enter through the garage. The whole ground floor is deserted, but that scream came from the upper stories. I head for the stairs, storming up the steps until I reach the seventh floor. Then another scream shreds through the walls and I know I'm in the right place.

She's here.

"I'm coming, little deer," I growl under my breath.

I pull my silenced sidearm out of my shoulder holster and squeak the door open just a crack. Sure enough, Nikolai stands across the open floor, his taunting laugh echoing through the darkness. The sight of him alone is enough to make me rage, but then I spot Natalya and my stomach drops.

She's tied to a chair. Her cheeks are red and raw from crying. Her sobs are hoarse.

"Just kill me," she defiantly begs. "I will never be yours."

Nikolai's laugh only grows louder. "No. You aren't of any use to me dead... yet."

My grip tightens around my gun when I see the knife. Nikolai drags the dull edge down her cheek, over her neck, and onto her cleavage. I get ready to pounce.

Before I can storm inside, though, I catch a glimmer coming from the upper corner of the room. My attention snaps to it. A fishing line is hooked to the ceiling. It runs the length of the room, straight towards the door.

Fuck, I think. *There's the trap.*

Something must be dangling just above the doorway. If I push inside now, it's going to drop directly onto my head. If I know Nikolai, that'll be a grenade or another type of explosive. I'll be ripped to shreds.

I won't let Natalya witnesses that. I need to find another way in.

"Fuck you," Natalya croaks as I quietly rush across the stairwell. There's a cracked window in the corner. I carefully push it open and look down.

"Shit..."

Staring back at me is a hundred-plus foot drop. One wrong move and I'm dead. But I don't give a shit. Natalya needs me.

Re-holstering my gun, I climb onto the ledge and slowly shimmy toward another set of broken windows.

"Before you are allowed to die, you must make me king of the underworld," I hear Nikolai say. I get into position. "Do you know how you're going to do that?"

I peek through the stained glass just in time to see Natalya spit directly in Nikolai's face. He immediately slaps her across the face. Her head snaps to the side.

I grab the window frame and tear out my gun. Fury spots my visions... then Natalya's eyes flutter back open. I can see the flash of surprise spread across her face when she spots me. Her mouth opens to call out, but I lift a finger to my lips and plead for her to stay quiet. She understands. Those ocean-blue eyes sparkle. A bruised smile fills her cracked lips.

I smile back.

Then Nikolai grabs a fistful of her hair and yanks her back into position. "Are you listening to me, girl?"

"No," Natalya says. An insane little laugh trickles from her throat.

That's my fucking girl.

"Well, you better start. Because I'm going to tell you exactly what's going to happen, and I will not repeat myself. First, you're going to get on your knees and worship me. Then, you're going to cry tears of happiness when I shove a ring on your finger. You'll smile at our wedding. You'll let the underworld know that I'm the new king. Then, you'll watch as I slaughter your father in front of everyone. The bastard isn't powerful enough to rule anymore. Not smart enough either. He was so desperate to regain his legitimacy that he couldn't see how he was handing it all over to me. I have the former Pakhan's daughter. I'm his rightful successor. I will be king and you will be—"

"You won't be king," Natalya interrupts.

Easy there, little deer, I want to tell her. *Give me a second before you push him any further.*

My eyes race across the walls and over every corner of the room as I desperately search for signs of another trap. More fishing lines crisscross the first, but as far as I can tell, none of them lead toward my window. I just have to make sure. I won't risk Natalya's life.

"I am the greatest killer this world's ever seen," Nikolai roars. "But that's not enough anymore. I've grown bored. So now I will subjugate every last Russian, Italian, and criminal syndicate in this city. They will kneel at my feet—because if they don't, I will personally end their existence. That's what a proper Pakhan does. Not like your father, who hires men greater than him to do his bidding."

"You. Will. Never. Be. Pakhan," Natalya swallows, a new maniacal smile stretching her lips.

"Why the fuck not?"

"Because there's only room for one. And Andrei Zherdev's going to kick your ass."

"You bitch." Nikolai lets go of Natalya's hair and raises his knife. "I'll show the world what happens to those who defy me. It will be carved all over your face."

That's enough.

"Like fuck you will," I roar, kicking through the window. The glass shatters around me as I take aim at Nikolai. He looks up, his yellow eyes narrowing.

I pull the trigger.

"Take that," I cry as Nikolai stumbles backward.

The knife drops from his hand. The echo of Andrei's gunshot fades. I look over to my brutal savior. He winks at me and my heart springs back to life.

"Are you alright?" he asks, rushing forward.

"I am now..."

I strain against the rope to get closer to him, but before he can reach me, a furious groan replaces the faded gunshot.

Andrei stops in his tracks and lifts his weapon again. Out of the corner of my eye, I see Nikolai's massive body jolt from the floor. Before I can blink, he's up on his feet.

Andrei fires at him. The bullet hits Nikolai square in the shoulder, but it hardly slows him down. The murderous beast still somehow manages to pick up his knife and lunge at me.

Another bullet blasts over our heads, but Nikolai dodges it and Andrei is forced to hold his fire when Nikolai presses the blade of his knife against my throat.

"You've gotten sloppy," he growls at Andrei, heaving like a wild animal. Blood trickles from his shoulder, but he doesn't look hurt. Just pissed off. "The Andrei Zherdev I'd heard of would have put that first bullet in my head. The second one too."

"There's still time," Andrei barks, straightening his gun.

But Nikolai just shakes his head. "No. This girl distracts you. It will be your downfall. You had your chance. This is over... unless you want me to cut her throat..."

He presses the blade deeper into my skin.

"No!" Andrei shouts.

There's a vulnerability in his voice that I've never heard before. At first, it fills me with hope—he actually cares about me; he actually *loves* me—but that hope is quickly overcome by fear.

He's scared.

For the first time since we met, Andrei isn't in control.

Nikolai is.

"You should have gone after Vadim instead of coming here," Nikolai hisses. "But I understand why you did. You want to watch me make your little fucktoy scream. Don't you? She's good at that..."

"Back. The. Fuck. Off."

"What are you going to do if I don't?" Nikolai sticks his giant hand inside his jacket and pulls out a gun. In response, Andrei fires his.

With lightning reflexes, Nikolai ducks, once again avoiding the bullet that would have pierced his skull. For a moment, the knife drops from my throat. But before it can even hit the ground, Nikolai shoves the barrel of his gun into my temple.

"Try that again and I won't hesitate," he snarls. "She goes first. Then I make you suffer."

"You wouldn't fucking dare," Andrei says, stepping forward.

Nikolai presses the gun deeper into me. "Try me, boy."

"I heard what you said. About your plans to take my place. You need her."

"No. I don't need her. She would just make things easier. If this girl dies, I'll buy another and massacre whoever gets in my way. Just like you did, *Pakhan*."

"You are not him," I hear myself swallow.

"That's right," Nikolai smirks, glaring down at me. "I'm better."

Andrei takes advantage of Nikolai's wandering eyes. Three thunderous shots fill the room, erupting into Nikolai's chest. Nikolai's gun goes off too, but not before he's pushed backward by the force. His bullet just grazes the tip of my ear.

"Get away from my fucking girl," Andrei roars.

Nikolai swings his gun around, but Andrei charges him too fast. He crosses the floor in half a second and tackles Nikolai backward. They slam into the wall and Nikolai's gun goes off again.

I scream and tumble backward to get away from the chaos. But all that does is tip my chair. I fall onto my side. The two men quickly join me, grappling, wrestling, and hitting each other as they roll violently across the floor.

More gunshots blast through the warehouse. I can't tell which gun the noise is coming from. I try to struggle free from my restraints so I can help Andrei, but the rope is too tight. It digs into my skin like a painful fire. I start to bleed.

... Then, slowly, the rope loosens, lubed by my own blood.

Grunts and roars threaten to tear the room apart as I somehow manage to slip my right wrist out. The rest is easy. Before I can scramble to my feet, though, a flurry of bullets rips over my head. I hit the floor again.

"Run, Natalya!" Andrei yells.

He's quickly interrupted by a sickening crunch as the bigger Nikolai lands a direct punch to his face. Andrei's head snaps away.

I watch in horror as Nikolai hunches his massive frame over Andrei and grabs his head with two giant bloody hands. He squeezes and another stomach-turning crack makes me freeze in place.

"Run, Natalya!" Andrei screams, his cries becoming more muffled. "I love you. Now fucking run! Please!"

My heart catches in my throat. But my fear is less for my own safety and more for his. I need to help.

Without thinking, I start to scramble toward the fallen knife at the foot of my tipped chair. Nikolai's fiery gaze rips onto me.

"You're next!" he rumbles.

Andrei grabs at Nikolai's wrists and he manages to flip them both over just enough so that he can look at me again. Those emerald-green eyes plead for me to listen. "Run..." he chokes. Nikolai's giant hands close in around his throat.

I can hear the desperation in his voice. It tugs at my heart like a final order.

I don't want to leave. But I know I need to listen, even if it breaks me.

"I love you," I mouth, unable to get the words out.

Andrei's eyes shimmer with understanding. His face is turning red.

"I'll be okay," he rasps.

With a stifled roar, he flings Nikolai onto his side. The two men roll into the wall so hard the entire building seems to shake.

I snap to.

I need to listen.

With tears filling my eyes, I shoot to my feet and dive for the door. Nikolai doesn't look up. He's too busy dealing with Andrei.

Someone yells. At this point, I can't tell who. But the blood-curdling screams follow me as I hurdle down the dark stairwell.

I bite back tears. I can't break down now. I have to get help... but how? I don't know who Andrei came with. I don't know where we are. I'm useless.

I kick myself when I remember how I left my phone in Papa's van. The bastard handed me over to Nikolai and then just drove off. I can't believe I ever trusted him.

I charge out of the stairwell, across the ground floor, skid onto the sidewalk... and scream when I run full tilt into Valentin.

He grabs my arms and wrestles me still. "Hey! Hey! Easy there, Natalya. What's going on? Where's—"

"Andrei!" I choke, pointing a shaky finger back the way I came. "He... he's in trouble. He needs help..."

I want to cry. Valentin will save Andrei. He has to.

Andrei's blood brother stares up at the building, but he doesn't rush in to save his life-long friend. Instead, he grabs my hand and starts pulling me away.

"Come on!"

"What about—"

"Come on!" he shouts. "Don't argue now! I need to get you to safety. That's what Andrei would want."

He tows me across the street and down several blocks. A black van sits parked out of sight and the side door slides open as we approach.

I halt in my tracks when I see a dozen men tightly packed inside. They all carry rifles and are covered in tactical gear, bulletproof vests, earpieces, and flack helmets.

Valentin jerks his thumb behind him. "Let's go!"

The men stream out of the van. Then more armed men flood into view from around the corner.

Valentin shoves me into the van. "Get in there and stay put!" he orders. "Do NOT get out of this van, no matter what. Do you understand me?"

I nod fast.

"Thank you," he says, his tone softening briefly.

I climb inside and he slams the door shut. When I turn around,

I find Ilya in the front passenger seat. He types furiously on his laptop, hardly even looking up to acknowledge my presence.

"Fuck!" he yells. "It's too late... Nikolai has already taken Pakhan out of the building."

"What?" I gasp. "Where are they going?"

"I can't tell, but I'm tracking them. They won't make it far... not if we have anything to say about it."

I gulp down panic. "Is he... is he still alive?"

Ilya smacks his lips. "Nikolai wouldn't take Pakhan to another location if he was dead. There would be no point."

I don't respond. I can't. A lump has appeared in my throat. The tears I was holding back earlier start to come out.

"I... uh... what are you doing?" Ilya shifts uncomfortably. "Oh, no... please... please don't cry... I'm... everything will be alright... I think."

I try to wipe the tears away, but they just keep coming. "I'm sorry."

"It's... it's alright."

I feel an awkward tap on my shoulder. When I look up, I see that it's Ilya. He's trying his best to comfort me, but he clearly has no idea how.

"Thank you," I whisper.

He nods. "We'll find him."

He's being kind, but we both know this is all my fault. Andrei wouldn't be in so much danger if he hadn't come to rescue me, and he would never have had to rescue me if I hadn't run off.

If you survive, I'll never run off again, I think. *Please, just survive.*

Suddenly, the van door slides open and Valentin appears again. "He's gone. Nikolai took Pakhan."

"We know," Ilya replies.

"Can you track him?"

"Yes. I'm just trying to figure out... shit... I think I know where he's going."

"Where?" Valentin and I both shout at the same time.

"It looks like they're heading towards Vadim's current location."

I gasp, remembering how Nikolai promised that my father could kill Andrei.

"Then that's where we're going." Valentin pulls me out of the van and all the armed men start loading back up. "Send the coordinates to my phone."

Ilya nods. "Aye aye."

"What are you going to do?" I quaver as Valentin leads me away.

"What do you think? I'm going to get Pakhan."

"Let me come with you."

"No way in hell," he fires back. "Your safety is my top priority."

"Even over saving Andrei's life?"

He pauses, then nods. "That's what he would want."

"No! Listen to me, Valentin—"

"No. You listen to me," he snaps. "Andrei is my Pakhan. He's my blood brother. He is my leader. I do what he wants. I *know* what he wants. And he wants you. We'll save him. But you need to be waiting when we get back—otherwise, he'll wish he was dead."

"I can't just do nothing."

"You will do nothing, and that's an order. Someday, you may be the queen I serve, but until then, I will do what's best for Andrei and Andrei alone. Right now, that means doing what's best for you."

My mind races as I remember how Nikolai nearly crushed Andrei's skull in. He's a monster... but he's not the one who will be killing Andrei. My father will be.

"I can help," I squeak.

"Listen, I appreciate the effort, but we don't need help. We just need to get moving."

"No, you don't understand. You'll go after Nikolai, but that will leave my father free to kill Andrei. He's the one who's going to do it."

"So we'll kill him before he can."

I start to argue before it hits me that Valentin doesn't seem surprised to learn who my father is.

I don't push it. There are more important things to worry about right now.

"My father is a snake," I warn him. "A coward. He won't let you just waltz up and kill him. No matter how many men you have. He'll use Andrei as a shield. You need someone to distract him."

"I can do that."

I shake my head. "You can't. He doesn't care about you. But I believe, deep down, he still cares about me. I can talk to him. I can distract him while you and Ilya and everyone else get into position. It might save Andrei's life..."

"... While putting yours at risk."

"I don't care."

"I do. He does."

"He won't care about anything if he's dead."

Valentin thinks on it as the van holding his men screeches off into the night.

Finally, he shakes his head. "Fine. I'll take you with me."

"Thank you, Valentin!"

"I'm just doing my job. Now let's go."

I race to keep up with him as he leads me further down the street. More black vans peel out of the area until we're all alone.

"Here we are." Valentin opens the driver's door on a black sedan with heavily tinted windows. "Get in."

"What?" I ask, shocked. "I... I can't drive."

"You have a license, don't you?"

I nod.

"Then you can drive. I would, but it's safer if I can hold a very big gun. Now get in and help me save Andrei."

That's all he needs to say. I square my shoulders and slide behind the wheel. The keys are in the ignition. I turn the motor while Valentin climbs into the passenger seat.

"Where do you want me to go?" I ask, putting the car into gear.

He checks his phone. "Get on Highway 294 and head north."

I peel out and follow Valentin's instructions, speeding toward the highway.

While I drive, he leans into the back seat and pulls forward a long, square case. I watch from the corner of my eye as he unclips the lock and draws out a massive sniper rifle.

"Turn off here," he tells me.

"Where are they?"

He puts the case away, rests the gun in his lap, and checks his phone again. "Nikolai was heading north, but he's turning off now. Looks like he's on his way east, toward South Side."

I spin around to stare at him. "That's my old neighborhood."

We drive further into the night before Valentin frowns down at his phone again. "He's stopping... right outside your old apartment building."

"Why??"

"I don't know," Valentin shrugs. Sticking his phone into his pocket, he picks up his rifle, and squints through the window at the city passing outside. "But it doesn't matter. He'll die just the same."

38

I cough and taste blood.

"Fucking hell..."

A blistering headache rips through my skull, threatening to tear it apart. I blink and try to get my eyes to focus, but I can't move. Hard ropes dig into the skin around my wrists, ankles, and arms.

"Glad to see you're awake again," Nikolai taunts. The car engine revs and we hit a bump. Pain erupts through my body. "Thought I'd killed you by accident. We can't have that—I mean unless you want to do the job yourself..."

He laughs and I feel the grenade wedged against my shoulder. Slowly, I remember how he tucked it under my chest when he loaded me into the trunk. Then, with the safety lever compressed against the floor, he pulled the pin. If I move even an inch too much, it will all be over.

Fuck. After that, I blacked out. How am I still alive?

"If I let this thing go off, it'll take you with me," I groan.

"You must have been unconscious when I explained that part," Nikolai chuckles. "I've got armored sheets covering the inside of that trunk. The glass partition between us is 4-inches thick. I won't even get your blood on my hands."

My mind faulters as he talks and I come dangerously close to passing out again. There's no way I get that lucky twice. If my eyes close, I'm dead.

... But at least Natalya will live. She escaped. That's all that matters.

"You're bringing me to Vadim," I cough, willing myself to stay conscious.

"Look like I didn't knock all the brains out of you... yet"

"You don't think I'll tell him about your plan to take the throne for yourself?"

Nikolai huffs. "You underestimate me, boy. I'll make sure to tape that loud mouth shut before Vadim can hear a peep out of you... but even if you manage to squeak it out, that will just give me an excuse to kill him sooner."

"You're scared of him."

That makes him laugh so violently that he nearly loses control of car. We hit another bump and I grimace, desperate to keep the grenade from rolling out of place.

"That fear you're smelling... it's yours, boy."

"I've never been afraid to die."

"... Until now. Until her."

I want to yell. I want to break out of my restraints and gouge Nikolai's yellow eyes out. But I can't move. If I do, it will all be over. And he's right.

I've never been afraid to die... until I fell in love with Natalya.

"I'm happy to die knowing she's safe. My men will protect her with their lives."

"Then they'll die screaming. And hopefully, so will she." Nikolai sighs as he purposefully hits another bump. A jolt of agonizing pain threatens to send me into permanent darkness. "Oh, how I reveled in those few moments at the warehouse when she finally screamed for me instead of you. Do you know how long I listened to those recordings and wished it was me doing those things to my prize?"

"... Recordings?" I ask, confused.

Nikolai ignores me. "You may have ruined her purity. But I ruined you. And, in the end, that might just make up for it—as long as Vadim plays his part properly..."

We take a hard right and my aching shoulder is smashed against the inside of the trunk. I grunt loudly.

Nikolai takes great joy in swerving across the road as we pull up to an unknown destination. I must black out for a moment because when I come too, the trunk is cracked open.

Nikolai's blurry figure bends down and examines me. "Still alive. Too bad."

He sticks the pin back in the grenade and puts it in his pocket. I blink, and all of a sudden I'm on a dusty floor. I try to roll onto my knees, but someone kicks me in the spleen and I collapse again.

"Do you recognize the ropes?" A taunting voice asks. *Vadim.* "I had Nikolai bring them from your mansion. Along with this."

My eyes flutter as a piece of paper flutters to the floor next to me. It only takes a moment for me to recognize it.

"How did you get this?" I grumble, fighting to breathe.

Vadim crouches down and shoves his fat finger onto the mangled photograph of him that I keep in my vault. A reminder of what I overcame to get where I am.

"She had to see me like this," he says, replacing his finger with the barrel of a gun. "My own daughter. Now I'm going to make sure she finds you in the same state."

"How the fuck did you get into my vault?" I roar, biting through the pain. "Answer me!"

"You're in no position to make demands," Vadim sneers. The butt of his rifle comes down against my jaw and my cheek cracks against the floor. "But I'll tell you anyway..." he grabs me under the chin and forces me to look at him. That's when I notice the smell... smoke and charcoal... it's distant but unmistakable. Where are we? "You never changed the password, you fucking moron. And we both know who that vault belonged to before you stole it from me."

"Why would I change the password? You were dead..."

"You *thought* I was dead. You *hoped* I was dead. But you were wrong. Dead fucking wrong. Luckily, your complacency worked in my favor. You never swept for bugs, for internal cameras or listening devices..." Vadim's dirty fingernails dig deep into my skin. "You made me listen as you defiled my innocent daughter... and with these very ropes..."

"You were listening to us?"

"The entire time."

Fuck. Those must have been the recordings Nikolai was talking about in the car earlier. A shiver runs over my skin, but it's not for my sake. It's for Natalya.

Her own father listened as she begged me to take her, as she pleaded for more, as she fell for his greatest enemy...

"You fucking pig," I spit.

"I'm a fucking genius," Vadim barks back. "I'm a survivor. I saw what you kept in that vault and I used it to my advantage. I'm still using it to my advantage..." he looks down at my bound body. "Now answer me: do they feel familiar?"

I roar in his face and he shoves my head into the ground.

I hear him click off the safety on his gun as the world spins around me. Before he can shoot me, though, my vision refocuses and I finally realize where we are.

Natalya's burned-down apartment.

I strain my neck to get a better view—there has to be a way out of this, there always is—but the place is barren and black...

And then I see it.

In the window, a flash of perfectly circular red light. It comes from a building across the street. Instantly, I know what it is: the lens of a sniper rifle's scope reflecting off the buzzing Coca-Cola sign that hangs just outside.

Someone is watching. Someone is waiting.

But is it a friend or foe?

There's only one way to find out.

"The Bratva will never follow you," I try to stall. "Not again. Not after the travesty of your reign."

"They'll have no choice. Killing you means I'm the new Pakhan. And I'll do it without dragging the underworld into a long war. The Italians will love that. They'll welcome me home and everyone will be forced to follow."

"Is that a chance you're willing to take?"

"Who's going to stop me?"

The longer we talk, the clearer it becomes that whoever's behind that sniper is waiting for something. If they're on my side, then I need to provide an opportunity for them to shoot. Maybe their angle is off, I don't know. All I know for sure is that I need to do something. Otherwise, I'm dead.

I groan and roll onto my knees.

"Ah, execution style," Vadim notes. "Excellent choice."

"Natalya and I are married."

The lie cuts through the room like a sharp blade.

"You fucking... what the hell does that have to do with anything?"

"It's everything. She's still out there. If we're married and I die, that means she's the de facto leader of the Bratva. And if you want to kill her and take over, you'll have to go through my men. That will start a war. That's a war you won't win. But even if you do, the Italians won't be happy about the carnage. You'll have to make concessions to align with them—and even then, you'll be outnumbered. There will be no Russians left to stand with you, because you'll have to kill them all..."

"I don't think you understand what you're arguing for," Vadim growls. I feel the cold steel of his gun press into the back of my skull. "I don't care if you married her. I don't care if you *ruined* her. There won't be a war. I'll find my daughter and I'll drag her back here to see your corpse and the ashes of her old life.... and then I'll kill the disobedient little bitch."

"She's not yours to kill anymore," Nikolai speaks up. The burnt floorboards creek and moan as he steps forward. "I've done my job. She's mine now."

I sense Vadim turn to confront Nikolai and I know this is my only chance.

Filling my lungs with air, I jump to my feet and charge past Vadim toward the biggest threat in the room.

My shoulder slam into Nikolai's stomach before he can draw his attention away from Vadim. We both slam onto the ground. Vadim roars, and from the corner of my eye, I see him swing his gun in our direction.

I roll onto my feet, but with my hands tied behind my back, there's nothing I can do except duck for cover. And there's only one object here that's big enough to hide behind.

Nikolai.

He lifts himself off the ground just in time for me to rush his back. Vadim's gun goes off and the shot hits Nikolai right between the shoulder blades. The force tears his shirt enough for me to see the thick bulletproof vest covering his body.

"You fucking bastard," Nikolai yells.

"Get the fuck out of the way!" Vadim snaps back.

"I'll fucking kill you."

Nikolai charges Vadim and I drop to the floor, slipping my bound hands under my feet so my arms are finally in front of me. But I'm still tied up and useless.

"He's going to get away," Vadim screeches.

Nikolai stops in his tracks and glares over his shoulder. I meet his furious gaze.

"You're doing this on purpose," he sneers.

I look to the window and think, *now would be a good time to shoot, whoever the fuck you are.* But no shot comes and the sniper scope's reflection has disappeared.

I'm on my own.

I look back at Nikolai just in time to see him yank out his gun and aim it at me. I hit the floor again and the bullet whizzes over my head.

"He's mine to kill!" Vadim insists, pulling at Nikolai's shoulder.

I use the distraction to rush at the two men.

With all my remaining strength, I fling myself into Nikolai's body. He grunts and stumbles backward, knocking over Vadim in the process. Both of their guns hit the floor... as does the grenade Nikolai was keeping in his pocket. It spins across the floor and bumps into the wall.

Nikolai struggles to catch his breath. Vadim is out of sight. Their guns are too far for me to reach but the grenade isn't. I make a split-second decision and lunge for the wall.

I land in a pile of broken glass and try to reach for the explosive. But with the ropes restraining me, I can't open my hands wide enough to grab it, let alone throw it.

Then, just like that, I feel a giant force pick me up by the collar. I just barely manage to grab onto a shard of glass before I'm ripped from the ground. My feet kick out, colliding with the grenade. It slides across the apartment.

Nikolai doesn't seem to notice it. Instead, he bellows with rage and tosses me against the wall. The broken glass cuts into my hands... as well as the ropes. They loosen. I concentrate everything I have on cutting them the rest of the way.

The fibers separate just as he hurls me across the room. I slam into the far wall and everything goes black.

When I blink back to consciousness, I see blood. It trickles from my head to the blackened floor, pooling around the forgotten grenade.

I reach for it and the ropes fall from my wrists. My fingers close in around the cylinder and I roll over just in time to see Nikolai pointing his gun at me.

"It's over," he pants, looking from me to Vadim. "Fuck our deal. He's mine to kill now. And I'm going to enjoy it."

A wicked grin twists his face as he clicks down on his safety.

"Fuck you," I snarl.

Pulling the pin, I throw the grenade at him.

His smirk evaporates as the trinket rattles to a stop directly between his feet.

"Sh—"

I cover my head with my arms and the grenade detonates. A shattering cloud of blood, gore, and broken bone erupts across the apartment. The viscera splatters above me with a sickening sound.

And then there's silence.

I grunt and groan on the floor, trying to fight through the overwhelming pain.

Think of Natalya, I tell myself. *Survive for her.*

So that's exactly what I do.

I think of my little deer. My fallen angel. I think of all that we still have to do together. I think of her smile and her spunk and her passion. I think of how I need to survive just long enough to fulfill my promise to marry her. How I need to see her graduate from school and become the architect she's always dreamed of becoming. How I need to see her grow old with me. How I need to see her rule with me.

"I'm coming home," I rasp.

Pushing myself onto my knees, I lift my head...

Only to be met by the barrel of Vadim's gun.

"I thought you would have learned your lesson by now," he snarls, the side of his shirt burnt off so I can see his grizzly torso. "Explosions don't kill me."

"Fuck you."

His finger tightens around the trigger.

"Go to hell, you traitorous—"

"Papa!"

Natalya's distant voice is so unexpected we both spring to attention. I straighten my neck. Vadim looks over his shoulder.

That seals his fate.

I roar and rush into him, hitting his stomach with all my weight. His gun goes off and I feel the bullet tear through my abdomen, but I don't slow down. I keep pushing him back until we topple through the shattered window and onto the fire escape.

"Stop!" he cries as I jam my legs into the rattling cage and slam him hard against the railing. The gun flies out of his hand.

"No. You fucking stop," I growl. "She's mine."

Fear fills his eyes. I smash my forehead into his and throw him over the side.

He screams the whole way down.

Then, everything goes quiet.

Through the steam rising from my wounds, I look over the railing, just to make sure he's dead this time. There's no doubt about it—his body is flattened; a bloody Rorschach test painted across the pavement.

"Natalya," I whisper. Was that really her voice I heard or am I just imagining things?

No. Vadim heard her too...

Leaning back, I fall to my knees.

The world flickers in and out of focus. I hear footsteps bounding up the fire escape. Valentin gets to me first, sniper rifle in his hand.

"I couldn't get a good shot because of the fire escape," he desperately explains. "It kept getting in the way. I'm sorry... I'm..."

"Andrei!"

Natalya's voice springs me back to life just enough to feel her throw herself against me.

"Are you okay?" she sobs, hugging me so tightly it hurts.

"I am now," I cough, sinking into her warmth.

She grabs my cheeks and looks me in the eyes. "I'm so sorry... this is all my fault..."

"It's alright... Everything's going to be alright..."

Her ocean-blue eyes shimmer and I sigh with satisfaction. If I'm going to die, this is the way to go. I couldn't ask for a better last view.

"I love you," Natalya cries. Her lips smash into mine for a final kiss. I think back to the warehouse, and how I swore I saw her mouth that very same thing when I told her to run.

Finally, I think. My heart filling to the brim. *Finally...*

"Did you hear me?" Natalya panics. "I need you to hear me. I love you."

My eyes close and a bloody laugh trickles from my lips.

"I know," I grin, drifting off. "I heard you the first time..."

39

NATALYA

A light rain falls from the grey sky as I hurry along an empty street, hunched over in an attempt to protect my textbooks.

"Come on," I mutter to myself. "Just a little luck... for once just let me have a little luck... please..."

Somewhere in the distance, a clap of thunder breaks through the dark clouds. I feel a lonely chill run over my skin. The rain starts to come down harder.

I look around for shelter. But there's nothing. The shops are closed. The windows are dark. The awnings are all pulled up.

The streets are empty. No one had the good sense to go out with this weather forecast.

No one except me.

But I have somewhere to be. It may be a lonely journey getting there, but what else can I do?

I allow one little sigh to escape my lips before I shut them tight and start moving again.

My feet splash through the growing water. The rain becomes thick with fog. In my mind, I know where I want to end up, but I'm losing sight of how to get there.

Just keep moving forward, I tell myself. One step at a time.

The rain gets so heavy I have to dip my head. Still, I stare at my blurring feet and trudge forward.

Just one more block, then everything will be alright. Happiness is always just one block away.

I hear a car horn blare and I look up just in time to run headfirst into a solid chest.

The contact stuns me, but when I look up, everything instantly becomes better, and I know everything will be alright.

It's him.

I wake up with a textbook splayed across my face.

"Not again," I mumble, pushing it aside.

A lingering loneliness holds me hostage as I stare up at the ceiling. Then, I feel something move in bed next to me and I turn to look.

Andrei groans. His eyes are closed. His body is wrapped up like an Egyptian mummy in casts and bandages. I remember my dream and a pool of warmth fills me to the core. He was who I ran into on that lonely, grey street. He shielded me from the rain and sheltered me from the storm.

I've been looking after him ever since.

"Can I come in?"

A knock at the door creaks it half-open. I see Valentin standing in the hall.

I quietly nod him inside. "He's still sleeping."

"Looks like you just had a good nap too," he chuckles, pointing at my face. "I bet I can guess what you were reading."

"Why? Because it's the same thing I'm always reading?" I look down to the floor. The bedroom is practically overflowing with textbooks. Beautiful musky textbooks.

Valentin shakes his head.

"Because it's literally written all over your face... or maybe 'imprinted' is a better word."

"Oh yeah," I laugh, wiping the sleep from my eyes.

"How's he doing?"

"He'll be alright," I say, remembering what the doctor told us.

Andrei suffered several broken ribs, a cracked skull, and bruising to his internal organs. But fortunately, the bullet they found lodged inside his gut didn't hit anything vital. He'll make a full recovery... eventually.

Valentin squeezes my shoulder. "You really need to get some real sleep. Stop studying for a bit. You've been up here for days. You'll make yourself sick if you don't rest."

"I'm okay." I take the cap off my highlighter and pick up my book. "I don't want to sleep too much. He might need me."

"I'll keep watch. You aren't the only one who cares about him, you know."

I look up and smile. "I know. I just don't want to be anywhere else."

"I understand. At least let me bring you something from the kitchen. When was the last time you ate?"

I rub my eyes again. "I can't really remember."

"My point exactly." He cocks his head to study me. "Don't go anywhere, okay? I'll be right back."

"You know I won't."

Valentin stops in the doorway and pauses. "Oh, by the way, before I forget... I didn't just come up here to play butler... I needed to tell you something."

"What?"

"Your friend Yelena is here."

That news nearly knocks me off the bed.

"She is? Why?"

A mischievous grin crosses Valentin's handsome face.

"I invited her. Figured you might need a touch of femininity to help you through this rough time... Plus, I hired her to make matching suits for Pakhan and me. It's a thing we do after a

SASHA LEONE & JADE ROWE

winning war... kind of like our matching tattoos. Just a little gift to ourselves."

I grin at him. "Is that really a tradition or did you just make that up so you could invite her here?"

Valentin places a hand across his heart like I just offended his very soul. "What are you trying to say?" he playfully gasps.

"That's a pretty convenient tradition, isn't it?"

"In the Bratva, we make our own conveniences," he smirks. "Anyway, I'll keep her busy until you want to come down. If you don't make it in the next twenty minutes, I'll send your food up. No rush..."

"I'm sure there isn't," I laugh.

Valentin just shrugs and disappears into the hallway, gently shutting the door behind him.

"Yelena's going to get that boy in trouble..." I think out loud.

Then Andrei stirs and I turn my attention to him.

"Hey, sleepy-face. How are you feeling?" I ask as his eyes flutter open.

He groans and tries to sit up, but he can't quite make it yet.

"I feel like shit," he says with a painful chuckle. "But I've got the best medicine in the world."

"Morphine?"

"You."

Somehow, he manages to roll onto his side and take me in his non-casted arm. I giggle, but I don't even playfully resist. He's too fragile for that right now.

"You're such a charmer," I roll my eyes.

"Only for you," he jokes, running his fingers down my arm. He stops when he gets to the rope burns on my wrists.

"They aren't going away," I sigh.

"They won't ever go away. Not fully." His hands wrap around the wounds in a warming balm. "But we can cover them up in tattoos."

"Like yours?"

"Exactly like mine. No one will know they're there. No one but us. They'll be our little secret."

He rests his chin against my arm and before I know it, he's fallen back asleep. I don't dare move, not until Valentin comes back with some food and Andrei wakes up again.

"What's happening out there?" Andrei yawns. "Is everything under control?"

"Don't you trust me?" Valentin teases.

"With my life. I'm just bored out of my mind. Give me an update."

"Well, we've finally recovered all the money from the money-laundering outfit, and—"

"Give it to the Italians," Andrei interrupts.

"I've already given them their half," Valentin replies. "The other half is being deposited in—"

"No. Brother. Give them every last cent. It will help make up for what we have to do next..."

"What do we have to do next?"

"Set up a meeting with the Italians, preferably today."

Valentin looks shocked. "You're in no shape to—"

"Today, brother."

Valentin and I exchange glances. Andrei shouldn't be straining himself now, much less holding high-powered meetings from his sick bed.

"And what will I tell them this meeting is about?" Valentin asks.

"It will be a confession. I'll tell them that I have no need for their daughters and that our alliance will never be sealed with a marriage."

Valentin's face drains of all color. "You're joking, right? You can't just drag them in here while you're covered in bandages and tell them you lied before."

Andrei takes my hand.

"That's exactly what I'm going to do," he tells Valentin.

Then those emerald green eyes land on me "I have other plans, but I'm ready to talk about new terms for our alliance. I'll make concessions if I have to. No amount of power is worth giving up on the woman I love. I won't even pretend to do it. Not anymore."

My heart swells and I feel like I could cry.

"Andrei—I..." I don't know what to say. Since he's been in recovery, he's already explained what really happened with the Italians and how I misunderstood what I overhead in the kitchen. But this... it sounds like he's going to make a formal announcement.

I remember the beautiful ring he showed me in his penthouse vault. It feels like a lifetime ago.

Butterflies flutter through my stomach.

But Valentin just gulps. "They won't like it."

"I don't care. I'm their Pakhan and they will accept my generous terms... or else those terms will become far less generous."

Tension fills the air. And then, an idea pops into my head.

"What about bringing them in on the skyscraper project?" I suggest.

"What?" both Andrei and Valentin ask at the same time.

I look at Valentin, since Andrei already knows this first part. "Andrei wants me to come up with a design to join our two skyscrapers downtown into a massive headquarters. If we ask for their help on such an important project, they might not feel as slighted. In fact, they might even feel honored to be involved in the empire in such a personal way. We can even design a section just for them. A symbol of our unity."

Now it's time for Andrei and Valentin to share looks.

"I told you she'd make the perfect queen," Andrei beams.

"Yeah, yeah," Valentin laughs. "I guess you struck gold. Lucky accident..."

"No," Andrei says, taking my hand. "I worked hard for this girl."

He places a gentle kiss on my lips and I sink into him.

"Now get out of here," he grins at Valentin. "I've got some even more important work to do."

"I'm way ahead of you," Valentin says from the doorway. "Don't forget to eat, Natalya."

"Me first," Andrei growls.

His bruised hand slips between my legs, but before we can do anything spicy, another knock comes at the door.

"What is it?" Andrei booms.

"Hi, Pakhan... sir... this is Dr. Molginy. We are scheduled to check up on you."

"Come back later. I'm—"

"No. He's ready to see you," I interrupt, springing from the bed. Andrei looks bewildered. I smile and shake my head down at him. "You need to rest and recover... I'll be back later to see how you've progressed."

"And if it's to a satisfactory level?"

"Then you can eat to your heart's content."

Andrei licks his lips and I lean down to give him a peck. He grabs my cheeks and holds me tight. "I fucking love you."

"I know" I smile. "I heard you the first time..."

He lets go and I grab the plate Valentin brought in. "He's all yours, boys," I giggle, slipping past the medical team. They rush in and I make my way downstairs.

I wander down the hall away from our master bedroom, taking in just how much the place has changed since I first arrived a lifetime ago. It feels strange seeing the place filled with so many people. Each guest room seems to be filled. Every hallway is constantly being cleaned and maintained. I never thought these grounds could feel so alive.

I walk past the library and hear a dozen high-powered computers loudly whirling. When I peek inside, I see Ilya and his crew. They talk rapidly in Russian, both to each other and into their phones.

Ilya sees me and we exchange a nod before I move on.

Eventually, I stop by the kitchen and grab a soda from the fridge. When I push into the breakfast room, though, I nearly drop my plate.

Yelena hunches over the table, hard at work sizing sheets of blue-black cloth—with all that's going on, I'd nearly forgotten that Valentin told me she was here.

"Yelena!"

She whips around and screams when she sees me. I scream back.

We collide in an excited hug.

"Look. At. You," she grins from ear to ear before leaning into mine. "Valentin's updated me on everything. You're a real mafia princess now, huh? That's amazing..."

I turn bright red and hide behind my soda can. "Not exactly."

"Don't be so modest! You look the part. Beautiful. Powerful. *Fabulous.*"

"Do I still have textbook print stamped into my face?"

Yelena laughs. "It's part of the charm."

"You're too kind."

"No. You are. Letting me come to your amazing house to work on this project."

"Oh, it's not my house..."

"Valentin sees it differently. He says I was only allowed because he knew you'd like it if I showed up."

"Well, he was right about that."

"... How often is he right about things?" Yelena questions, curiously twirling her hair around her finger.

"Enough that I'd trust him with my life."

"He's interesting, isn't he?"

"If you like the Bratva type."

Yelena purses her lips. "That's where I keep getting stuck. He doesn't seem like the Bratva type."

"That's what I thought at first too. Then I saw him in action."

"Are you telling me to run?"

"I'm telling you that if you do, he'll catch you."

I spot a familiar jolt straighten Yelena's spine and I recognize the conflict playing out behind her beautiful eyes.

Careful, girl, I want to warn her. But I know that telling someone like Yelena not to do something is a surefire way to get her to do it.

"Well, I'm certainly not running in these heels," Yelena laughs. "But enough about me. How are you feeling? You've been through so much lately."

"I'm alright. Honestly, I'm just relieved that Andrei's going to be okay."

"He makes you happy, doesn't he?"

I smile. "Yeah, I guess he does."

"You deserve it. Everything." She waves at the mansion around us. "And this is... well, it's pretty fucking amazing, isn't it?"

"It's like a dream."

"It suits you."

I have to laugh. "You look more at home here than I do."

"Nonsense. You look like you own the place. And, well, it sounds like you do."

"I don't know about that..."

"Always so modest. Here, give me some of that modesty, tell me what you think about this material. I'm planning on using it for Andrei's and Valentin's suits."

I join her at the table and feel the cloth. "It's so soft."

"And very sturdy. You could do a backflip in it... or whatever men like Valentin do..."

"I'm sure you'll find out soon enough."

"Let's not get ahead of ourselves," Yelena resists, a sudden somberness coming over her playful tone. "I'm a working girl and he's... well, he's a criminal. I can't get involved with someone like that."

"He might not give you the choice."

"You're making me nervous," she chuckles awkwardly.

"I'm sorry. Let's forget about Valentin. Tell me about your project."

Yelena stares down the table and shrugs. "Oh, it's not that interesting. Suits never are. But I'll tell you what I'm really looking forward to working on."

"What?"

"A certain someone's wedding dress."

My heart stops beating. Andrei hasn't mentioned anything about marriage since that night...

"I wouldn't hold your breath," I mumble. "I don't know if that's ever going to happen..."

"That's not what I heard."

Before Yelena can expand, the door swings open and Valentin walks in. His piercing gaze switches back and forth between the two of us before reluctantly falling on me.

"You can go back upstairs," he gestures. "The medical team is finished and Pakhan has requested for you join him for his meal."

My cheeks turn red, but Valentin doesn't seem to get the implication... or maybe he does and it's just turned his interest elsewhere.

"You be careful with her," I whisper in his ear on my way out.

"I'll try my best, ma'am."

The door shuts behind me and Yelena's words echo through my ears. Andrei's given me everything I could have ever dreamed of and more. It feels selfish to ask for anything else.

Still, when I look down at my hand, it seems so empty. I

can't help but imagine that beautiful ring wrapped around my finger.

I hear myself sigh.

A girl can dream.

40

"Look at you," I hear Valentin say. "Finally up and limping about. I haven't seen you this nimble in months."

I smile and turn from the crest in my Club Silo247 office, careful to hide the keys that I subtly stuff back into my pant pocket.

"Bet I can still outrun you."

Valentin shuts the office door behind him and stops there, daring me to limp all the way over to him.

"How much?"

I pretend to think on it for a moment before gesturing around. "If you win, I'll give you this office."

That draws a belly laugh from my blood brother. "As if you'd ever give this place up—if I remember correctly, this is the first space you had custom-built after becoming Pakhan. It's a symbol of your success."

"It's a symbol of *our* success," I remind him, walking around my desk to sit on the edge. "And now it's yours."

I'd wanted to make some big speech about how much Valentin means to me and this empire, but I think this fits him better. Short, sweet and straight to the point.

Pulling the keys from my pocket, I toss them at his chest.

He catches them without blinking. But a confused look quickly takes over his face.

"What are you talking about?"

I push myself off the desk and place my hand on his shoulder. "You're being promoted. From now on, this will be your home base."

He stares at me like I've lost my mind.

"How can I be promoted? I'm second-in-command to the Pakhan, there's nowhere to go. Unless..." His eyes go wide as he comes to the wrong conclusion. "Pakhan, I..."

"No. I'm not retiring," I quickly correct. "But I am shifting gears."

Valentin's relief is palpable. "Shifting gears how?"

"All these years, I've been trying to build my empire. Now it's time to start growing my family."

He tilts his head. "Natalya?"

I nod and smile. "Natalya... and you. These past few months have made me appreciate those I care about more than ever. It's also made me realize that this empire won't matter if all we worry about is building new relationships. What's truly important is fostering the ones we already have. Strengthening them. Supporting them. And that means supporting you and your dreams."

Valentin looks touched but still confused.

"I understand... I think... but I still don't get how it ties into a promotion. There's nowhere to go for me but down. I'm consigliere to the most powerful Pakhan in this city's history and I'm not replacing you. So what comes next?"

My grin grows wider as I take one last look at him before his life changes forever.

"The Bratvas that were wiped out by Nikolai and Vadim," I start, turning my back on him to limp back to the crest carved into the wall behind my desk. "They will need rebuilding, and then, when they are rebuilt, they will need a leader—someone they can look up to directly."

"They will look up to you."

"And I will look down on them. No matter how personal I want to make this empire, it is still a vast organization. I can't be there for our men all the time. But you can be. I'm giving you the Bratvas, Valentin. All of them. You still answer to me, but otherwise, you will be in complete control. It will be your job to build them back up from the devastation Vadim and Nikolai put them through. I can't think of anyone better for the job."

"Pakhan... I... I don't know what to say."

"There's no need to say anything. I've made up my mind. Hell, you already have the keys to your office. Everything in here belongs to you."

He steps up behind me and glares over my shoulder. "Including the vault?"

"That's right."

The respectful air in the room starts to spark with excitement. He seems to forget all about the weight I just placed on his shoulder. Typical Valentin "Does that mean I finally get to see what's inside?"

I step aside. "Be my guest."

"Shit," he mumbles, opening up the cabinet. "Have you ever shown anyone what's inside before?"

He pauses when he sees the keypad.

"The password is the date we officially won the war," I hint.

"Which one?"

"The first one."

He types it in and the lock clicks open.

"And to answer your question: no. No one but me has ever seen what's inside—well, me and the last Pakhan. But I've added some things that he never saw. Now they're for your eyes only. Take whatever you want. Leave whatever you need. And add whatever your heart desires."

Valentin's jaw drops when he pulls aside the black door. Its black wood sheltering is covered in scratch marks, shallow bullet holes, and dried blood.

"Holy shit," Valentin gasps, leaning in to get a closer look before taking a step back. "Are these..."

"Yep. And look on the top shelf."

My heart clenches a little at Valentin's reaction.

Awe and fear, disgust and intrigue, surprise and understanding all flash across his face—and I can't help but wish I got to see Natalya's response as well.

She had asked about the secrets behind this particular crest all the way back when we'd first met. I couldn't show her the contents back then, she would have short-circuited. But I bet I could reveal it all today and she'd have a similar reaction to my blood brother—though, maybe not entirely the same...

"You really are the devil," Valentin says, shaking his head in mischievous disbelief.

"And now you are too."

A swell of pride puffs out his chest and I know I made the right call. I would have liked to share some of this with Natalya, but she already got to experience the contents of my other vaults. The rope. The history lesson. The cologne.

And now...

"What's this?" Valentin asks, interrupting my train of thought. He reaches around something heavy and pulls out an ornate metal box from the back of the vault.

"Shit," I grunt. "I'd forgotten about that..."

"What's inside?"

He hands it to me and I lift it to my ear and shake. Something shifts.

"I don't know."

"What do you mean, you don't know? It's yours, isn't it?"

I let him take it back. "It belonged to the last Pakhan," I explain. "But I never figured out how to open it."

"There's a latch right here..." Valentin pulls down on a silver clasp but it doesn't budge, so he smacks the side. Suddenly, a section of the box swings open like a rigid door. Two small silver bowls pop out. Each has a small hole in the middle.

Valentin notes the shocked look on my face.

"Never thought about smacking it before, huh?"

I laugh. "I always thought it was a puzzle..."

"Sometimes you just need to *make* the pieces fit by force."

"Sometimes," I grin, staring down at the two small silver bowls. How fitting. I know exactly what those do... I think. "And sometimes it takes a combination of both. Looks like you're going to have to figure that out the hard way."

I feel my phone buzz and I look toward the office clock.

It's time.

"What does that mean?" Valentin asks, looking down at the two silver bowls. "What are these?"

"That's for you to figure out." I pat him on the shoulder and turn around. "Think of it as a rite of passage. Good luck."

"Where are you going?" he calls after me.

I don't even stop in the doorway.

"You aren't the only family I'm promoting tonight," I shout back.

"Don't you dare peek," I warn, squeezing Natalya's hand.

"How could I possibly peek?" she says, turning her head from side to side. "I'm blindfolded."

"Is it turning you on?"

With an exaggerated gasp, she blindly reaches out to slap my shoulder but whiffs completely.

We both laugh.

"Come here so I can hit you."

"That kinky stuff can wait," I tease. "We're almost there."

"Where?"

"You'll see in a second. Keep climbing."

"You're lucky I trust you."

My heart swells.

"The luckiest." We climb a few more flights of stairs before finally reaching the door. "Here we are." Holding on tight, I lead her out onto the roof. A gust of wind blows her hair back.

"Thank god." She reaches up to remove the blindfold.

I grab her hand. "Not yet."

"Aw, come on! I want to see your handsome face."

"You'll see it plenty. Just a little further."

"You said that fifteen minutes ago."

I laugh again. "It will be worth it. Trust me."

She groans, but I can tell by the smirk on her lips that she's enjoying this just as much as I am.

I pull her to a stop. "We're here." I take off the blindfold. "You can look now."

Those gorgeous ocean-blue eyes spark as she blinks away the darkness. "Where... where are we?"

"We're on a roof."

She giggles and shakes her head. "I got that. Which roof?"

"This is the roof of the City Hall building."

Her smile twists in confusion. "Why are we on top of City Hall?"

I walk over to a tarp by the parapet and rip it off. Natalya gasps at the table hidden beneath it. A bright bouquet rises up from the center. I pull a bottle of champagne out from the ice bucket next to it.

"We're here to celebrate your acceptance to architecture school."

The smile returns to her face... before quickly submitting to confusion again.

"Yeah, but...." She searches the surrounding blocks. Cars

whizz back and forth on the street below. It isn't the most romantic spot in town... or so she thinks. "Why here?"

I pop the cork and pour two flutes full of champagne. I hand her one, take the other for myself, and raise my glass. "Here's to you, my love—the smartest, most talented, most brilliant architect that ever lived."

She laughs. "I haven't even started school yet!"

"Doesn't matter. I believe in you."

"I appreciate it... but I don't think I'll get the same respect from other architects. Not until I've done something to prove myself."

"Well, what a coincidence. Because that's exactly why we're here."

Her pretty face scrunches with even more confusion. "We're here so I can prove myself?"

I nod and wave my glass across the street. "Precisely."

She follows my gaze to the shopping center in the near distance. "I don't understand."

"There's been a change of plans," I explain. "We aren't demolishing the two buildings downtown anymore. They won't be our new headquarters. There isn't enough room there for your creativity to really shine. Instead, we'll turn them into affordable housing, properly run foster homes, and shelters. Everything you've wanted to build will come pre-made. That way, we can start helping people immediately."

"That's amazing!" she gasps, her blue eyes sparkle with happiness. "They will be perfect. I... I don't think I was ready for a project like that anyway..."

I put down my glass and take her by the shoulders. "No. You are. I'm still hiring you to design our headquarters. But I propose we start with something even bigger. Something isolated enough to hone your skills with while you go to school and learn how to construct your perfect building. A playground of sorts."

"What could possibly be bigger than two skyscrapers in downtown Chicago?"

I shrug. "I don't know. Maybe something like a giant shopping center..."

Her jaw drops.

"Andrei..."

I place a finger on her lips and turn her around to face the sprawling property. "It's perfect, isn't it?"

"It... it would be huge..."

"A perfect symbol of our empire."

"It would be *too* big."

"You can add some more of your passion projects to the area," I promise. "Keep part of the mall. Fill it up with grocery stores and other essential businesses. Build some more high-end, yet affordable housing nearby. A community center or two. Then, on the plot of land closest to the street, you leave room for our headquarters."

"That would be wonderful...." I watch as her mind turns in a thousand directions. "But I..." She looks down at the roof under her feet and shakes her head clear. "Do you really want me to design your new Bratva headquarters right across the street from City Hall?"

I beam at her. "Yep. I can't let all those city officials forget who really runs Chicago." I slip my arm around her. "It will take years, but I know as well as anyone that the best education is practical. There's no hurry. Start when you're ready. You'll be able to tweak everything to your heart's desire. I'm sure you'll learn a billion new techniques at school, use this site as your sandbox. I'll make sure you have an entire construction company at your fingertips... and a demolition team too."

"I don't know what to say."

"Say you'll do it."

"... I'll try my best."

"That's my girl."

I kiss her on the forehead and let her gape at the massive lot across the street as I quietly step behind her.

She doesn't notice when I pull a tiny black box out of my pocket and get on one knee.

"Oh, and there's one more thing I need to ask you tonight," I say.

"What's—"

She turns around and freezes.

"Will you marry me?"

Those big blue eyes stare at me in disbelief as the ring from my penthouse vault glimmers beneath the night stars. For what feels like an eternity, she's too stunned to speak.

"The ring..."

"That's right. A family heirloom. Your family heirloom... before it belonged to me, it belonged to your mother. But your father locked it away when she died. I took it back, and now I'm giving it to you. On one condition..."

Natalya just stares at the glittering diamonds.

"Don't know what to say?" I smile.

She furiously shakes her head, snapping out of the shock. "No. I know exactly what to say."

"Then let me hear it, little deer. Will you marry me?"

"Yes!"

I stand up just in time for her to jump into my arms. My body still aches from my injuries, but the pain quickly melts away as the woman I love wraps herself around me.

"I want to spend the rest of my life with you, Natalya Vladimirovna Dimitrov."

Her tears fall against my cheeks as we hug. "Never call me that again," she whispers. "From now on, I'm Natalya Zherdev. Understand?"

"Loud and clear, my queen."

She pulls her head back and I kiss her harder than I ever have before.

"I love you so fucking much," I say, feeling every inch of her.

"I love you," she rasps back.

I slip the ring on her finger. It fits perfectly.

"Let's rule this world."

"Only if we can do it together."

I hold her tight.

"You've got yourself a deal."

EPILOGUE
NATALYA

1 year later...

The hard hat tips over my eyes again, and for the hundredth time today, I have to push it back up over my noggin'.

"You'd think with all the money we've put into this project, I'd be able to afford a properly fitting helmet," I playfully mumble, unable to feel even the least bit of real annoyance. I'm living a dream, and no matter how much hard work my days are filled with, it finally feels like I'm getting somewhere.

"They don't make hard hats that small," laughs my construction site manager, Evgeni. "These things are built to fit around thick-skulled Neanderthal heads like mine."

He taps on his forehead and I join in on the fun.

"Give me your best skull-growing tips. I'll start working out tonight."

Evgeni shifts on his feet, his gaze subtly flashing down to my stomach. "I'm no doctor but—"

"Boss!"

A worker appears around the corner, a wild look filling their eyes.

"What is it?" Evgeni and I both respond.

We share a look and break out laughing.

"Oh, I'm sorry Mrs. Zerdhev. Evgeni is needed in the hole, there's a problem with one of the excavators."

Evgeni tips his hard hat at me. "Ma'am."

I nod back. "You go help the boys. I'll keep looking over the blueprints."

He rushes away and I turn back to the table at the center of the makeshift office I've claimed at the center of the torn-down mall. In the distance, construction equipment screeches and groans. It sounds like heaven. Everyone here is committed to working on my vision—even if I'm not entirely sure what that vision is yet.

"If we just put the affordable housing units here, then we can add the grocery stores and subsidized restaurants over there and fit it all together like a big puzzle," I think out loud, looking down at the blueprints. "Then we can move on to the headquarter sections..."

I sigh with delight at the idea of how much this project has grown since Andrei first proposed it. But I don't mark anything off yet. In the end, I'm still just a student. I'll wait until Evgeni returns before I settle any plans.

Leaning on my forearms, I take some weight off my feet. The two bands on my ring finger shimmer under the filtered light above. I stare at them lovingly before letting my eyes fall onto my wrists. Fresh tattoos wrap up my arms, covering the scars. My heart flutters. I can't wait to get home and see Andrei...

"Natalya? Oh thank god..."

A familiar voice turns me from the table. I'm shocked to find Yelena standing against a cement pillar, looking like she's just seen a ghost.

I take off my hard hat and go to greet her. "Yelena! It's been forever. How... wait, are you okay?"

Beads of sweat fill her forehead. She's paler than I've ever seen her. It looks like she could faint at any moment.

"I... I'm fine," she swallows, her gorgeous eyes darting around before falling to her feet. "No... that's not true. I'm not fine."

I take her hand. "Here come take a seat..."

"No. I can't stay for long," she says bolting upright again. "I... I'm sorry."

I furrow my brow at her, concern filling my stomach. Something's clearly very off.

"What's wrong?"

"It's... well, I..." she pauses when I mindlessly place a hand on my belly. For a moment, those big eyes forget what she came here for. "Are... are you pregnant?"

"Second trimester," I smile. "I've been trying to get a hold of you since we decided to start telling our—"

"I'm so sorry." Yelena's face drops. It looks like she might cry. "I've been the worse friend."

"No! Stop it! We've both been so busy. Me with school and this project. You with building up your business. We haven't had the time to catch up. That's just as much my fault..."

"You're such a good person," Yelena sighs, hugging me. "You deserve all this. I'm so happy for you."

"Thank you," I say, patting her on the back. She lingers, holding onto me for longer than expected—it makes me even more concerned. "Now, tell me what's up."

She pulls back and the jitteriness returns to her eyes. My stomach churns. I've never seen my friend like this before. Usually, it seems like nothing in the world can bother her. But clearly, something has.

"I need your help," she whispers. "But you can't tell anyone. Not Andrei, not Ilya... and definitely not Valentin."

I tilt my head. "What's happened?"

Yelena opens her mouth but stops herself when she looks down at my bump again.

"I don't know if I should—"

"Tell me," I insist. "I can help."

She takes a deep breath. Her bottom lip begins to tremble. Those big eyes lift back up to mine.

"I'm in serious trouble."

Printed in Great Britain
by Amazon

39669426R00223